South Pass

by
Bob Crawford

PublishAmerica
Baltimore

ISBN: 1-4137-6939-X
PUBLISHED BY PUBLISHAMERICA, LLLP
www.publishamerica.com
Baltimore

Printed in the United States of America

Dedicated to Esther, Jay and Cathy.
This story would have never been told without their help.

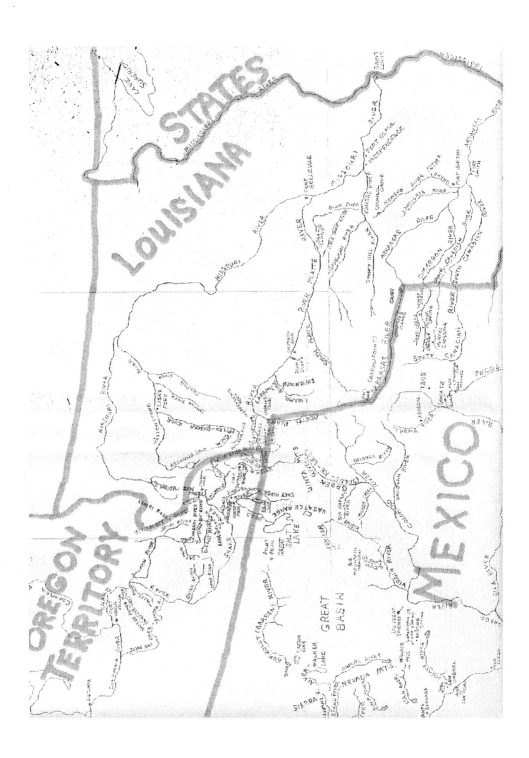

Part One:
Coming Together

Chapter One

As they moved along through the Missouri countryside, Joe Walker was well aware of the potential explosion that was under him. His horse felt full of himself, and a gusty midmorning breeze carried the brisk taste of fall. Walker knew that the big chestnut colored stallion would eagerly test his rider if he sensed even the slightest amount of inattention.

The ground was dry, and the seventy-four head of better-than-average saddle horses kicked up small clouds of dust. They were headed southwest for Fort Gibson, the westernmost Army post along the Arkansas River in 1830. Captain Walker was convinced that the soldiers stationed at Gibson would want the best horses they could find, and they'd have payroll money in their pockets. Walker watched, listened and took notice of everything around him. He turned to check his men's location.

Billy B. Alexander and Swit Boone rode together when they could. Billy B. was a good talker, or at least a prolific one, and Swit was the champion of all listeners. They could travel together mile after mile doing what they both liked best, providing the horses cooperated by trailing along in a manner that Billy labeled as "pleasurable as eatin' sweet potato pie."

"Ya take Cap'n Joe there," Billy was saying. "Now you'd think to look at him, he's just a dude playin' the mountain man part. I'll tell you what, don't be fooled one dab by that freshly tanned and trimmed buckskin garb, or that feather in his hat. Cap'n Walker knows zackly where we are now, and where we'll camp tonight. He'll know if there's any Injuns around before they can figure we're out here trailin' all these nags. He ain't called cap'n for nothin'.

Whatever you do, don't mess with that horse he's ridin'. He sure is some looker, ain't he? Don't let that fool ya. He skinned up so many of the boys around Independence that they started callin' him 'Scab.' Do you remember old Dan Tuck?"

This was one of those times that Swit thought he probably should pick up his end of the conversation. A "Sure do" or "Yeah" would work nicely, but today a glance over at Billy and a nod was the best he could offer. Swit could tell when Billy B. was about to launch a new tale. He'd shift himself kind of sideways in the saddle and finger his mustache in a fancy way. Swit sure wished that he could grow a mustache like Billy's.

"Well now, old Tuck," Billy didn't require answers to his questions, just a capacity to listen, "he told me he first met Joe Walker in the spring of '19. It was before I knew him. They was both ridin' on a steamer up the Missouri. Said he took to Joe Walker right off. The cap'n tells Tuck that he's a lookin' for land to settle his family on, so Tuck, he tells Walker about the country around Fort Osage, and how he could leave the river at Franklin and follow the old Osage Indian Trace to the fort. Weren't much for roads out there in them days."

As Billy B. talked, Swit watched the smooth, coordinated connection between Joe Walker and his horse. He'd heard many men comment about the captain's superb horsemanship, and now watching him handle a rank horse, he knew it was true.

"Walker wouldn't talk much, but as near as Tuck could scope it out, the cap'n was born in Tennessee, and old Tuck, he figured that Joe Walker was raised a frontiersman. As a pup he prob'ly knew more about livin' in the wild than most so-called mountain men."

Swit liked hearing about places, but with people it was hard to get a feel for who they where unless you ask a lot of questions. Billy B. always seemed to make friends real easy. That mustache probably helped.

"Tuck says that when the cap'n was only fifteen Joel and him fought with Old Hickory when they whopp't the Creek Injuns at Horseshoe Bend. Joel's the cap'n's older brother. I think he's…"

"Look at him now," Swit interrupted. "I'll bet at fifteen he was bigger than most men."

This new introduction of thought caught Billy somewhat off-guard, but it was true. Joseph Rutherford Walker, at six feet four inches tall and two hundred and forty pounds, was a huge man. Billy could think of only one other man he had known that was bigger, and that was the captain's younger brother John—everyone called him Big John. The captain's full beard and his long hair, worn in the Indian style, only added to his presence.

If Joe Walker had been given to oral expression, which he wasn't, it would have been hard for him to phrase his present feelings. It felt so good to be aboard a fine animal, trailing off across the country. The territory west of the Missouri frontier wasn't all completely wild or mostly unexplored by white men like it had been when McKinney, Tuck and Choquette had showed him the old Indian traces headed west. That was back when just a few would dare to chance a visit to the beaver-rich streams of the upper Rio Grande River, where a young Joe Walker sharpened his exploring and trapping skills— always aware that one slip could land him behind bars down in Chihuahua.

After the Mexicans gained their independence from Spain, the trade restrictions lifted, and Joe Walker had, more by accident than purpose, evolved from trapper to a leader of men. Lord, how good it was to again be dressed in comfort and have his rifle resting easily across the saddle as he showed the way.

"Anyhow, by year's end, the whole Walker family is settled in along a creek just west of the post." A slight interruption was not about to turn Billy from his tale. "Old Dan said it was the damnedest thing you ever seen. The winter weren't no easy one. Tuck's a fightin' snow, workin' his way back to the States, when he rides into their encampment. The cap'n is there with his two brothers, a sister, her husband and kids, a widowed cousin and her younguns, just carving out a settlement slick as you please. Hell, they even had a slave, named Hardy. 'Cept they didn't act like he was a slave, more like he's family. Tuck said they was as busy as ants buildin' a hill. Gave no matter-you-mind to the weather or anything else. Just spread out and went about their business of settlin' in like it was old hat. The old folks was still back in Tennessee. Seems like the pap had died a few years back, and the mamma, she'd elected to stay put with an older daughter's family—at least till things got squared away."

Swit wished he could get to know some of these people that Billy kept talking about. The next time they hit town he was going to partner up with Billy B. and make acquaintances. Cleaning up was Billy's first thing when he made town, and it seemed that the girls just could not stay away.

"The cap'n sees that the stranger ridin' in ain't no stranger at all, but the very same man that he'd met on the steamer." Billy noticed that Swit had that faraway look he got whenever his mind was drifting off and needed pulling back to the story. "Anyhow, they welcomed him like he's some kind of a lost kin out of Tennessee. According to Tuck you wouldn't have been better treated or cared for if you'd stopped in St. Louis—maybe some fancier, but not…"

"They got some real fancy ladies in St. Louis." Swit was still thinking about Billy's girls.

"Hell's fire, Swit." Billy jumped back from being cut off in mid-sentence, "we ain't discussin' St. Louis women. We're talkin' about what we're doin' out here, trailin' these beasts and followin' the man towards Injun country."

"Well, now, as I recall there was a few Indians in St. Louis. They was some of 'em women, though I can't remember 'em being very fancy." Swit felt qualified to comment—he'd been to St. Louis.

Billy realized that Swit's attention span was used up, and spurred his horse forward. It surprised Swit when Billy's horse lunged ahead. He'd noticed the bay mare slowly leading a few other horses off toward the trees, but he thought that in time she'd probably work her way back to the bunch. Swit wondered if he should catch up and lend a hand. He really liked Billy, but right then he didn't mind him riding off. Usually Swit could listen to Billy talk day and night, but sometimes he felt as if he needed a shield he could hang over his ears to keep the words out. Swit decided he'd stay put. Captain Walker had told him, "Stay back, keep the stragglers up with the herd, don't push hard, keep a sharp eye on me and Billy B.—all will go well." He thought how the captain didn't talk much. But when he did, he said more than most.

Captain Walker had been watching Billy and Swit riding along together. It could cause men to get careless. The horses were fairly gentle and had taken to trailing in just a few days, but he knew that the flat-footed bay mare was just waiting for a chance to cause trouble. Billy was a good hand, but Walker was beginning to regret letting him and Swit trail together when he saw Billy take action. He watched to see which way Swit would jump. It pleased him that Swit Boone stayed steady. Before Billy could return the mare and her bunch to the herd, Joe Walker had turned his thoughts to the change that his life had taken three years ago.

Walker had agreed to accept the Missouri governor's appointment to be the first sheriff for the newly created Jackson County. That put an end to his trailing off into the unknown. He missed traveling through and living in country settled only by Indians, and the newfound freedom that so attracted him to their way of life.

For the most part, Joe Walker felt satisfied about the way he had handled his job as sheriff. He marveled at how the little settlement of Independence boomed. The community was now the primary staging area for the transportation of goods down the Santa Fe Trail—or, for that matter, any movement out onto the prairies and beyond. In the summer of '28, the citizens had showed their approval of his appointment by giving him an overwhelming majority in the first local election.

Joe Walker understood why he had agreed to be sheriff. Joel and sister Jane's husband, Abraham McClellan, were very much involved in the development of the county. Duty to his family was important, but he gradually discovered that he didn't care much for peace officer work. You got a heavy dose of the worst human traits. It seemed he couldn't get use to the evil one man could, and would, inflict upon another. One of the toughest tasks he had been asked to perform was to see to Hanna's punishment.

Hanna was a slave that had been accused of trying to kill her master. It was Joe Walker's belief that she had justification for her actions, and if ever a man needed killing, it was Asa Say. It seemed to Walker that the jury and judge were more interested in whipping slaves than finding justice. When the judge said, "It's the sheriff's duty to see that Hanna receives thirty-nine lashes across her bare black ass," he knew it was time for him to move on. Joe Walker decided right there and then that next summer there would be no reelection for him. He turned over almost all of his sheriff chores to his deputy, and spent the rest of his term in the outlying regions of the county.

The days were becoming shorter and cooler. It was the time of year that Walker enjoyed, and he felt at home to be trailing through the countryside. It didn't matter that the trail was already established, and he was only in charge of two young men and a herd of horses. Fort Gibson might just mean more to him than a place to sell horses.

Chapter Two

Captain Benjamin Louis Eulaile De Bonneville was standing in his quarters at Fort Gibson, watching the morning sun shine through the window and offer it's warming touch. The leaves from the big oak trees that covered the hills around the Fort had changed into their fall colors and were dropping to the ground—another season would soon be gone.

Captain Bonneville was spending most of his time leading patrols. Duty away from the post was what he liked best. He didn't much care about hanging around inside the stockade; too many of the personnel stationed here sickened and died. More than a few thought it had to do with the green logs they'd used when they built the fort, while others blamed it on a disease carried in by the breeze from the swampy canebrakes. Whatever the cause, it made most of the men assigned to Fort Gibson wish they were elsewhere.

As Captain Bonneville looked to the west, out across the Grand River, he thought how peculiar it was that just about everyone he knew wanted to move back East. Yet, he had this compelling desire to head West. Not just anywhere, he wanted to see the country that the trappers talked about, and there was money to be made in the fur business. Bonneville didn't have a frontiersman's background. He'd been raised in New York and educated at the West Point Military Academy. For the last ten years he'd served in the frontier forts of the Southwest, and was confident leading men into the wilderness, but he realized he didn't have the proficiency of an experienced trailblazer. He longed for the opportunity to develop those skills. Now, at thirty-four years of age, it looked as if luck may have come his way.

There was no knock, just a slight rattle before the door was flung open. In walked a man dressed to look part Indian and part Eastern merchant. Behind him was a sergeant in the U. S. Army.

"I'm sorry, sir," the sergeant was saying, "Mister Houston asked me to show him to your quarters. I had no idea he…"

"Frenchy, you got any good Tennessee sippin' whiskey cubbyholed anywhere around this here death fort?" Houston cut the sergeant off. "I'll not hang around here long without some fortification." Ben felt that he was as American as most, even though his place of birth was Paris, France.

"It's all right, Sergeant Willis," Bonneville said. "Sam and I are old friends."

The sergeant nodded and backed out slowly, shaking his head and mumbling to himself. "I don't know what the hell Captain Ben sees in that half-ass Indian go-between."

Both Houston and Bonneville could hear the sergeant's comments, but Sam didn't give it any more mind than a bear would a honeybee.

"I heard from the general," Houston said. "Walker's headed this way with a string of horses—should be here in a few days. I'll tell you right now it's just pure sweet luck he's available for your expedition. I've known him since he was fifteen. You couldn't have better if you had the pick of any mountain man alive."

"I've met Mister Walker, but it was hardly more than a hello. I doubt he will remember the meeting." Bonneville was relieved that Sam Houston hadn't taken offense from the sergeant's departing remark. Sergeant Willis evidently wasn't aware that Sam had once been an officer in the Army, and several times had distinguished himself in battle. His leaving the military had been a matter of honor.

The Army had appointed Sam subagent for the Cherokees, probably because he had lived with the Indians when he was a young boy. As a courtesy to his Indian friends he dressed himself more like an Indian than an Army officer when he appeared before the secretary of war in their behalf. His cause was just, but the secretary was infuriated with Sam's disregard for his Army uniform. Several days later Houston was called into the War Department and accused of smuggling slaves. In the investigation that followed, Sam Houston was found completely innocent, but the secretary would not even offer the young Army officer an apology. Houston resigned his commission.

"He'll remember. He don't forget anything," Sam said. "It's not my job to advise you. I'm just supposed to bring you this message about Walker and help you two get together so that the general's grand plan can be realized. If you don't mind some advice where Walker's concerned, I'd pay more than a little attention to anything he might care to tell you. He don't talk much, but he don't miss much either. He has that knack of being right in his decisions, especially during a crisis, and his ability to lead men just comes natural."

It seemed strange to Bonneville that Sam Houston still referred to Andrew Jackson as general instead of president. He knew that their friendship went back to their early days in Tennessee. Sam had returned to Tennessee after he left the Army and rode a political rocket from lawyer to attorney general to United States congressman before landing in the governor's chair in Nashville. Jackson had helped open some of those doors for his friend, and Sam had worked untiringly for him in his run for the White House.

Sam Houston's fall from grace had been as dramatic as his climb. It began with his failed marriage. Eliza Allen had been married to Sam for only three months when she suddenly went back to her parents. Houston went into seclusion. It was whispered around that her ambitious family had pushed Eliza into the marriage, and when Sam found her crying over the old love letters of a young lawyer named Will Tyree, he exploded into a rage. Eliza would not explain her leaving, and Sam Houston would never say a word about the problem, not to the president, not to anyone.

Rumor and gossip took over, and the vultures circled. Sam resigned as governor and moved in with his Cherokee friends in the territory close to Fort Gibson. He was helping represent his Indian family in their dealings with the government agencies, but Sam spent a good deal of his time drinking whiskey and playing poker. Captain Bonneville thought how circumstances had surely changed for Sam Houston, and yet here he was apparently acting as an emissary for the president of the United States.

"Just how much does Walker know about the president's plan?" Captain Bonneville asked.

"He shouldn't know much, just that you'll be leading a fur trapping and trading venture into the mountains on the western slope, and need someone with his experience," Houston answered. "It'll be a good opportunity for you to see if any information has leaked out about the real reason for your trip over the divide. I'll guarantee you one thing, if anyone on the frontier has any idea about what's going on, Walker will know."

"Sam, this meeting is real important to me." Captain Bonneville had first heard about the fur trapping expedition from Alfred Seton. Seton was a member of a well-established mercantile family in New York City. He indicated that arrangements might be made for the captain to lead a fur company up into the Oregon territory. An exploration of California may also be possible. There had been no mention of President Jackson. "I've had this desire to explore the territory of the trappers for some time, but I never thought I would get the chance. The Army has been my life, and you know how that works—mostly you get to do what the Army desires."

Captain Bonneville wanted Alfred Seton's proposal to move forward, but wasn't exactly sure what all and who was involved. Now Sam Houston was telling him that it was President Jackson's grand plan. One thing he did know, Alfred Seton didn't seem to have care one about him getting a leave of absence from the Army.

Houston watched Bonneville as he moved around the room. He was a friendly and easy person to be around. He looked to be about the same age as Walker, maybe a couple of years older. His face had a leathery tan that told you he spent most of his time outside. It was hard to find a distinguishing physical characteristic until he removed his hat. His high forehead and balding head immediately grabbed your attention. There was a distinct line of color contrast just above his eyes where his hat rested. A tanned face below the line, and the white, almost polished, stonelike head above accentuated the baldness. He seemed older, and was really two different physical specimens. With his hat on you had trouble remembering what he looked like—hat off, you never forgot him.

"I don't know why I was selected," Ben confessed, "but I have the feeling that someone thinks it's very important that Walker make this trip with me. So important that if I can't get him to accompany me, I suspect my leave of absence from the Army will probably not be granted, and my financing from the East will dry up."

"Hell, Frenchy, you don't have much to worry about," Houston said. "Joe Walker will be more excited to get going on this new adventure than you. I don't know what you've got in mind for him, but if he thinks he'll get a chance at breaking the crust into California, you'll have a hard time leaving without him."

Captain Ben has got this thing figured about right, Sam thought. There was no way Old Hickory was going to send Bonneville out into that unknown without someone like Walker along to supply a steady hand.

"You want to know something true, Frenchy," Houston continued. "I don't claim to be privy to all goin'-ons, but I know Andy Jackson about as well as anyone, and what I don't know, I'll bet I can guess at and be pretty close. Fact is, if you're of a mind to dig out the jug that I know you've got stashed around here someplace for safe keeping, and you'd care to share it and a little time with me—I'll tell you how I've got this thing figured out."

Captain Bonneville smiled at Sam as he headed toward the bookshelves. Almost everyone at the Fort thought that Sam Houston was just a noisy drunk that had screwed up his life, but it was obvious that Sam knew more than Sam got credit for. A little time spent listening to Houston's take on the proposed expedition might come in handy.

"By God, Frenchy, you got the right idea on storing your bottle. They're ain't three men on this whole damn post that would pick up a book, let alone read it. That jug couldn't be safer if you dropped it down a well."

Houston had gathered up two glasses and was settled in at a small table when the captain returned with the refreshment. "The first thing you need to understand is Andy Jackson. He's not like you or me. Hell, he's not like anyone else I've ever known. He's got a lot of parts, but there's one part you need to comprehend. He doesn't believe in just taking things as they come and making the best out of a situation. He believes in making things happen, and once he's set in his mind, it's a hell of a force. It's like his run for the presidency in '24. He won the election but didn't carry a majority. Them Eastern political types were scared shitless. They thought they'd lost control to a renegade from the West, but the house saved 'em when they gave the job to John Quincy. That didn't turn Jackson one degree. By '28 he toasted the Adams-Clay bunch, and Andrew Jackson was the new president of the United States of America. The first one from the West."

"What do you think President Jackson is going for now?" Bonneville asked.

"It has to do with the country," Sam answered. "He believes that the way to shape the States into the nation it was predestined to become is to get people headed West. Jackson is an admirer of Jefferson. Not necessarily Jefferson the person, but for his ability to make things happen. Take, for instance, the Louisiana Purchase and the Lewis and Clark Expedition, both necessary for a Western expansion. What made up Louisiana was not exactly known. It was loosely defined as the Western watershed of the Mississippi River as far north as the British territory, south to the Spanish territory, and west to the Continental Divide, wherever the hell that is. When Lewis and Clark returned it looked as if the United States of America had doubled in size and was now joined to the Oregon Territory. Oregon is the key."

Captain Bonneville had liked Sam from the very first, but it had taken time for him to appreciate his complexities. Listening to Sam at the poker parties had taught Bonneville much about the nature of the Indian, especially the importance of honor. Houston would never say it, but he knew that Sam liked him, and respected the way he handled his men and dealt with the Cherokees. Could it be that Sam had something to do with his chance to lead an expedition westward?

"The general told me he remembered Jefferson saying that Oregon is our country's only attachment to the Pacific, but our claim to it is not solid. We must get there and settle it first." Houston paused just long enough to take another drink and then refill his glass.

"And our first try at settlement, Fort Astoria, was lost to the English during the War of 1812." Captain Bonneville had managed to slip in a sentence. Conversations with Sam tended to turn into lesions of history and philosophy, the length of which being directly proportional to the amount of alcohol consumed. The Bonnevilles had been friends of the Astors for many years, and the captain was well acquainted with the history of Fort Astoria. President Jefferson had encouraged John Jacob Astor to give England some competition for the fur business in Oregon. He formed the Pacific Fur Company and established a trading post at the mouth of the Columbia River. The enterprise hardly had a good start before the United States and England went to war. A young Alfred Seton had been one of Astor's men stationed at Fort Astoria the day a group of British trappers from the North West Fur Company arrived saying that they intended to claim the trading post for England. They backed it up with a British man-of-war in the harbor. Poor leadership, bad luck and timing had ended the venture. Seton said that he never forgot how he felt when he watched "Old Glory" pulled down off the fort's flagpole.

"Exactly." Sam was back. "If Madison would have sent a little military aid out to Fort Astoria during the War, or Astor had picked himself some partners with more loyalty to the States, that settlement would still be there and we'd have control of Oregon. Since the war, treaties between Spain, Russia, Great Britain and the United States have redefined the Oregon Territory. Now it's claimed jointly by the United States and England. Trappers and trading companies are in Oregon, but the English companies control most of the territory. The general believes if we're going to hold on to our claim we must establish settlements in Oregon."

"So opening Oregon to settlement, and thereby expanding the United States west to the Pacific, is President Jackson's grand plan." Bonneville was trying to keep Sam zeroed in on present times. Houston was obviously a man of considerable passion about people and causes that interested him. The more Sam drank the harder it was to keep him directed toward the situation at hand, namely the upcoming expedition.

"Now you're beginning to see Jackson's dream." Sam Houston was up on his feet, addressing his crowd of one. "For better than twenty years this land west of the Mississippi has been probed into by the Americans. Besides Lewis and Clark, Pike and then Long explored different regions of this vast territory for the government. The trappers and traders, following the old Indian traces, learned to move around within what's mostly known as the Great Indian Territory, and established profitable fur businesses."

This was a new experience for Captain Bonneville. Unlike the poker table talk, Sam's actions were as if he was speaking to the Congress of the United States.

"A trail has been pushed out across the territory between the settlements on the Missouri River and Santa Fe." Sam was pointing to the Southwest. "The result is a growing commerce between Mexico and the United States. A wagon trail into the Oregon Territory must be found. A path to the northwest across the plains and over the Continental Divide is well known by the trappers. Can wagons be taken over the Divide and into the traders' rendezvous country of the Green and Bear Rivers? Most think so, but no one has. If you want families to travel overland and pioneer a new country, wagons must be able to get there. Can a wagon move through the territory between the rendezvous areas and the waters of the Columbia River? How would the Indians receive these travelers? Can a safe route across the Great Basin and over the Sierra Nevada Mountains into the coastal settlements of California be established? How would the Spanish settlers, and maybe more important, the Mexican government, react to Americans moving into California, and..."

While Sam was pouring himself another drink, and talking at the same time, he ran his glass over. Apparently any miscue that resulted in wasted whiskey was cause enough for Houston to re-prioritize, and the careful consumption of whiskey ranked ahead of verbal commentary.

"When it comes to getting this migration started, it seems as if our president needs some questions answered." Bonneville seized the moment. It was no secret that President Jackson favored expansion, and he was supported by most of the Americans that lived in the western reaches of the United States. It was not popular in the East, and the vast majority of

Americans lived in the East. They were of the opinion that everything west of the present settlements was Indian Territory. Any movement into that area should be controlled by the federal government and limited to trapping and trading with the natives. A government-supported-and-financed exploration of the way to Oregon would not receive support from the Eastern politicians. The president needed this expedition to help get the people moving, but it must not be perceived to be a prelude to a western extension of the nation, or connected with the government in any manner. "I guess that's where we come in."

The sound of a distant steamboat whistle signaled that a supply boat was coming up the Arkansas River. Both men looked toward the fort's river landing. Before long the boat's signal gun would speak, and all within hearing distance would know the boat had safely negotiated the mouth of the Grand River. An arrival of a paddle wheeler was always received with great anticipation.

"You've picked up the scent, Frenchy." Houston was back. "The general's expedition will have to look like a business venture and be privately financed. It's obvious that the only realistic business in that country is in furs, and one of the wealthiest men in America, John Jacob Astor, is in the fur business. The general is going to take control of Oregon for the States. There's one thing, though, that you need to keep in mind. He's been real careful about who knows what. You won't find any of this written down anywhere, and not many are in the know. The man who lets this become public knowledge has the future of sour owl shit. Just try to imagine what it would be like with both Astor and Jackson coming after you."

An empty bottle set on the table, and Houston left just about as quickly as he had arrived. He'd mentioned looking for another good book, but then turned and mumbled something about getting back to my pretty little Cherokee, Tiana, and was out the door. Sam stopped, turned around and shouted back, "Frenchy, if you need me, I'll be at Wigwam Neosho. Send someone to fetch me."

Captain Bonneville thought awhile about the recent conversation. Had it all been whiskey talk? If Sam had the true reason for this expedition figured out, why would he tell anyone? He could be following the president's instructions, and things did make a bit more sense. Seton was a close and longtime associate of John Jacob Astor. He hadn't mentioned anything about whether John Jacob was or wasn't involved in the new fur company, but he had made a point about the necessity of keeping a complete journal, noting all things in, around, and along the journey. Bonneville knew that his desire for an opportunity to travel into this exciting country was no secret, but Seton handing him this chance had surprised him. Sam just could be right.

When Houston rounded the corner of the barracks he heard the signal gun discharge. The sound of the gun meant that the steamer was only three miles from the fort and would soon put in along the riverbank at a dock that nature had carved out of solid rock.

People were already starting to gather. Excitement always filled the air when a boat arrived. Passengers coming and going, friends to meet and greet, and news from the outside world all made the event captivating and noisy. Sam was interested in a couple of things. He would likely hear from his friends, Jim Bowie or John and Bill Wharton. They were involved with, and had interests in, Austin's settlements down in Texas. They'd been trying to get him to join them. Right now, though, he was more taken with finding out if the boat captain was who he thought it would be. If he was right, then an invite onboard to sample the boat's liquor and toast to a safe arrival would be forthcoming.

Chapter Three

The meadow ahead was nestled in a saddle formed by several tree-covered hills. It was a little larger than Walker remembered. The trees were turning their leaves loose, and the late afternoon sunshine flickered with the red, gold and yellow colors of fall. A small stream twisted its way through the south end of the meadow. Walker enjoyed watching the changing of the seasons, and knew that the meadow would be a perfect spot for tonight. With all the leaves on the ground it would take a real soft foot to sneak into camp.

"By golly, Cap'n, I don't figure man or horse could have it much better than this," Billy B. was saying as he rode up. "Course, a hot bath and a pretty little thing to listen to my travel tales, now that'd put a cap on it."

Captain Walker had motioned Billy forward for a few instructions. Neither Billy nor Swit knew it yet, but this night would probably prove to be memorable.

"Billy, let's see if the herd will ease on down to the creek and take on a good fill," Walker said. "Then let 'em graze their way out onto the meadow. About the time they're in the middle I'll be back and will meet you and Boone out there. I'm gonna have a look around."

Joe Walker moved his horse off to the left, and was soon back in the trees and out of sight. The captain had seen signs all day. Early in the afternoon he had gotten a quick glimpse of two riders. The Indian territory was still a good day's ride away, but it wasn't unusual for a few of the young braves to slip over the line now and then. How else was a new warrior to prove his courage?

"Where's the captain going?" Swit spoke before Billy could utter a sound.

"Said he's gonna look around," Billy B. answered. "We're to let these ponies take on some water and then make 'em think it's best if they feed out to the hub of this here meadow."

"Did he say what he's looking for, or when he'd be back?" Swit asked. "The captain's never rode off and left us to handle this bunch alone before. Did you see any Indians around?"

"He said he would meet us out there in the middle when he got back," Billy answered. "Nope, I didn't see no Injuns, and it ain't my job to look for 'em. I leave all the Injun spottin' up to the cap'n, unless of course fifty of 'em should ride right out on this here meadow. Now *that* I'd notice."

"I guess I'd notice that, too." Swit Boone liked things to stay about the same. Some change was okay, but it was best if he had time to consider any upcoming modification before it all took place.

Swit watched the horses drink from the stream. It had been a long day on the trail, and the animals looked tired. Trailing horses was not like making them first go this way and then another. It was more like trying to let them graze along at their own pace, in a direction they wanted to go—as long as it was your direction too. Captain Walker had told Swit, "The secret is not letting the herd know that they are under any kind of restraint."

Swit had come to the realization that the key to easy trailing lay with the leader. Billy said that you could usually pick them out of the herd, and the first day out an older mare had quickly established herself as boss of the bunch— a kind of a "She" who must be obeyed. The trick was to get the mare started off in the right direction. The main bunch would follow her, and if you kept the group moving along while you gathered up any stragglers or drifters you could laze along behind the herd, and they'd graze their way to your destination. It was nothing to cover ten or twenty miles in a day, sometimes more, and get there with horses that were still in good flesh.

"Swit, would you get the corral rope and the sidelines off the pack horse?" Captain Walker had motioned Billy B. over to where he and Swit where located. "I picked up some stakes. I believe we better hobble most of the horses tonight." When Billy arrived, he and the captain started toward the other side of the meadow.

Swit slowly climbed down off his horse and then just looked at the captain. They had used the sidelines only once before, the first night out on trail. It had been a lot of work to hobble all the horses, but it sure did keep them bunched during the night. Swit was still trying to gather his thoughts and sort out this change in operation when Walker turned sideways in his saddle and spoke. "Go, Boone. I want to get this done before that sun slips behind the hill." Swit headed for the packhorse.

"Billy, you take these stakes and head over there." The captain pointed toward the backside of the herd. Billy B. took the stakes and rode off. He didn't say a word. Billy knew as soon as he looked at the captain that this was business time, not talking time.

Using the rope and stakes, they made a temporary corral. The three men worked like a team. The horses were green broke to the saddle and fairly gentle as long as the men worked quiet and easy around them. Sidelining was restraining a horse by tying a front foot and a hind foot on the same side about eighteen inches apart. It wasn't particularly comfortable for the horse, but it sure kept him from moving very far, very fast. A free-footed horse could be tied to a sidelined one and still be able to walk around as he pleased. However, the hobbled horse was his pivot point of movement.

"Let's leave that flatfooted bay mare, the gray gelding, and the grulla that's standing over there without hobbles," Walker said. "Use this rope to tie 'em to a stout sidelined partner." As soon as most of the work was done, Walker mounted and rode to the far end of the meadow.

"I just don't get it." Swit was confused. "Before, if we hobbled 'em, we hobbled all of 'em; if we didn't, we didn't. Billy, do you think the captain is scared that all these horses are going to run off tonight?"

"I think the cap'n saw somethin' today we didn't see," Billy replied. "I know one thing, he ain't scared a nothin'. He's just bein' the cap'n. Swit, now hear me. You listen close when he talks and do zackly what he says, when he says it. Don't worry about what we don't know. He'll tell us what we need to know when it's time to know it."

Walker was fairly sure that the developing situation could be handled without a great deal of hardship. He'd found the Indians camped and busy preparing a meal. There were eleven young sprouts that couldn't have been more than fifteen or sixteen years old. If no one got crazy or careless, it shouldn't be life threatening, and the experience would benefit everyone. Walker knew how Billy would handle most situations, but he wasn't sure how Swit would react.

"It would appear that we're likely to get some company." Captain Walker had returned to the herd just as Billy and Swit finished with the horses. "There's a small group of Indians that's been playing hide and seek with us all day. They're camped about a mile back, and I expect they plan to pay us a visit. My guess is that they're not after hair. They probably just figure to spook our horses, gather up as many as they can, and head for Indian territory. They're having their supper now, but we won't do any cooking tonight."

Billy was more taken with Boone's reaction than Captain Walker's announcement. Swit never changed expression. He just stared at Walker. It was kind of like he was in a trance. Billy wanted to laugh, but he knew this wasn't the time for that. Swit had sure enough remembered the part about listening close to what Captain Walker had to say.

"No fires of any kind tonight. That means no smoking," Walker continued. "Fill yourselves on jerky and water. We'll bed down on this meadow in a triangle arrangement. Billy, I want you to go over by that big boulder. Tie your horse to that lone tree and then set yourself in tight against the right side of the rock. Put your saddle between you and the trees. It'll offer you a shield if one's needed."

Captain Walker had turned and was pointing to another place on the meadow. "Swit, you can set up the same in that little dugout area over there. You'll have to tie your horse in that scrub thicket."

Swit was in motion before Walker could put his arm down. He had a foot in the stirrup, his rifle in hand, and almost had a leg up before Captain Walker could get him stopped.

"Just a minute." Walker was surprised by Swit's readiness. "Ol' Scab and I'll be situated down by the creek. I only saw two guns at their camp, but they may have more. I expect them to sneak out on the meadow just before daybreak. There'll be a lot of noise and probably some shooting when they arrive. Check your guns, make sure they're loaded and ready for action. If you see anyone trying to sneak out on the meadow, fire in the air. Don't shoot at anything unless it's trying to kill you—then kill it." Walker had never stepped down from his horse. He spun Scab in a one hundred and eighty-degree rollback and headed for his campsite.

"I never have fought any Indians before," Swit said as the captain rode away. "I'd sure feel better if we was all together."

Billy had never seen Swit so intense or move so quick. He felt the same as Swit; there was safety in numbers, but if the captain thought the best way to keep hold of the herd was to spread out, then that's what needed doing.

"It'll be all right. Most likely when they come they'll come down the creek toward the cap'n," Billy said. "Anything walkin' through those leaves will give notice long before they get here. Just do like the cap'n said. Your old horse will let you know if trouble's comin'."

"He didn't let me know nothing today," Swit said. "How does Captain

Walker know they'll be coming just before daylight? If they're coming, I'd just as soon they'd get here quick. It'll be ink black out here pretty soon. I never could see too good in the dark."

"I don't guess the cap'n knows for sure when they're comin'," Billy answered. "He just figured that with them already camped and havin' supper, and it bein' all cloudy and dark tonight, well, it seems most likely they'd try to grab our horses when the seein' is better, and then head for home. Then again, he could be thinkin' somein' all together different. I quit tryin' to figure out which way the cap'n's gonna jump some time ago. I plan to do zackly like he said. I'm headed for that big rock over there to make ready. Best you do the same."

Billy B. started for the boulder. Swit watched Billy and the captain both riding away, then turned toward the spot Captain Walker had pointed out as his place to spend the night. Twilight had started to fade when Swit reached his dugout.

Captain Walker set himself on a little rise just back from the stream. He had a good view up the creek, but darkness was gradually taking that away. His stallion was tied in a little thicket that was behind him and a little to his left. He would have preferred to have Scab in a little closer, but he wanted him positioned where anyone following down the stream wouldn't see him. Walker was sure of one thing: if someone tried to sneak in and untie that horse, things would get real lively. He thought about Billy and Swit. It was already too dark to see how they had deployed themselves. He was confident Billy would be okay, but Swit was untried. Thus far he had handled himself just fine; however, it was unpredictable when you put a new man in harm's way.

Billy B. was swallowing his last bite of jerky. Elk made right tasty jerky, but it was a poor substitute for a hot meal. If he squinted, he thought he could make out the top of Swit's hat moving up and down. In the last several hours Swit had revealed a side that Billy B. hadn't seen or believed was possible. He had developed a liking for his new friend, but thought him a tad slow on the uptake. There had been times when it seemed near impossible to get or hold Swit's attention. That sure hadn't been the case just lately. Billy closed his eyes and thought about this new rendition of Swit. A smile caused a curious twist in Billy's mustache as he settled into the darkness.

Swit had a lot on his mind. He had tried to do just as the captain said. The little dugout area had seemed like a good spot to hide; but when you were lying down so as not to be spotted, up was about the only direction you could look. In a setting position, Swit felt like his head was out in the open for all to see. He tried popping up and looking around every once in a while, but gave that up. It was too dark to see much anyway. He couldn't see the captain or Billy. This Indian business wasn't to Swit's liking. He thought about his dad. Indians had killed him when Swit was twelve years old. No one seemed to know much about what happened, or at least they didn't tell him. All he knew was that his Dad and three other men had headed into the wilderness to look for honey.

The honeybee had been introduced into the States during the time that the East Coast was being settled. Now there were wild bees out fifty to one hundred miles west of the settlements, and a honey hunt was a way to make some extra money after the fall harvest. The bee hunters would get a wagon, some barrels, and then start marking trees with hives in them as they traveled west. When the hunters calculated that they had found enough honey to fill the barrels, they turned around and headed back home. Each tree they'd marked on the way out they cut down, collected the honey and filled the barrels. The Indians called the honeybees white man's flies, and the thick, sticky, sweet honey they produced was a favorite treat. Naturally the Indians looked upon this enterprise as plundering their land, and did their best to discourage its practice.

Swit hadn't noticed so many night sounds before. He was giving exceptional attention to the territory surrounding him, and the situation deserved his alertness; but as time passed, things gradually seemed to grow kind of peaceful. His horse was standing perfectly still. Swit thought he was probably sleeping, and envied a horse's ability to sleep and stand at the same time. They could sleep and still be ready to head for safety at the first sign of trouble. The captain was probably right; not much was going to happen until about daylight.

At first Swit thought it was just the wind. No, it wasn't the wind. Somebody was walking down the hill through all those leaves. He thought he'd better take a quick peek and see how many there were.

Billy heard it too. He eased over on his stomach with his rifle ready. He had almost been asleep when his horse switched direction suddenly. It sounded like more than just one Indian walking down the hill between him and Swit. Cap'n must have been wrong, Billy thought. They ain't waitin' till morning. He strained to see in the direction of the noise, but it was too dark.

Swit couldn't see a thing. He thought it sounded like they were coming straight for him. He knew he should warn the captain and Billy, but he couldn't think how to do that without firing his gun. The captain had said to shoot in the air if he saw them sneaking out on the meadow, or shoot one of 'em if they was trying to kill him, but nothing about firing a warning shot if it sounded like they were coming.

As near as Billy could tell, they were headed more in Swit's direction. He decided to shift a little to his right so he could get a better look, and a shot off, if it came to that. He had just started his move when the noise stopped. It got deathly still; even the normal sounds from the darkness were gone. Billy waited.

Swit was still trying to figure out his problem when it turned quiet. No one was moving. It had sounded as if they were just a short distance up the hill. Surely they couldn't already be out on the meadow? No, the sound hadn't gradually faded away. It stopped all at once. Had they see him?

The horse was still just standing like a statute, and he was about all Swit could see from his dugout. Swit was afraid to move and try to get another look up the hill. He waited for what seemed like a long time, and was just ready to risk taking a peek, when he heard the leaves again. This time they sounded closer. Swit decided that he had to look. Either they hadn't seen him, or they had and didn't care. In any case, he better be ready. Swit eased his head up, thinking how hard it was to see anything in the blackness. Not more that four feet ahead, and just a little to his left, was the biggest doe he'd ever seen. Before he could blink, she was gone, and the other deer flew past right behind her. He could hear them running back into the trees off to his left. His heart was pounding, and it was hard to catch his breath, but he couldn't remember when he'd felt more relieved.

Billy heard them heading his way through the trees. Deer, he thought. Hell, I should'da thought of that. Guess the night's got me a little unsettled. One thing's for sure, if deer are movin' on this side of the meadow, there sure ain't no Injuns around.

Joe Walker could feel their presence before he could see them. He looked toward Scab, and the horse was looking straight up the creek. It was not yet daylight or daybreak, just the first faint flicker of a new day. Walker spotted the leader. He was moving slow and easy along the edge of the stream. He didn't seem to mind the tracks that his horse was making; his intention was to not create any noise. There looked to be three or four of them working their way along the creek in a single file. The rest of the party was moving out on the meadow from another direction, or they were back in the hills waiting to gather in the stampeded horses. Just before the Indians reached Walker's campsite, they turned out onto the meadow. Walker could make out Swit and Billy's horses, and it looked like Billy was where he was supposed to be. Swit was not to be seen.

During the night Swit had worked out a plan for seeing out without disclosing his location. Taking his hat off and lying mostly on his side, he could look over the edge of his dugout with one eye. He'd spotted where the captain's horse was tied, but couldn't tell exactly where Walker was located. The horse herd had drifted over into the line of sight between himself and where he thought Captain Walker might be. Swit's horse turned around. He had his ears up and pointed toward the creek.

Billy had spent a fairly restful night. After the deer episode he had crowded in next to the rock and dozed off, believing the attack would come by way of the little stream, probably in the morning like the cap'n thought.

Three riders, each one carrying a rifle, filed by slowly. Joe Walker waited until they were all out in the open. He leveled his gun and fired, putting the rifle ball in the ground just to the side of the first Indian's horse. The horse jumped four feet sideways in one motion. It left its rider hanging out in midair, but the Indian never let go of the horse's bridle rein. In spite of the confusion created by horses circling, Indians shouting and gun fire, the dislodged Indian swung back up on his horse faster that it would take to tell about it. The rifle fire was being used to help drive the horse herd back into the hills, and despite his horse trouble, the leader of the raid managed to get off one of the shots fired. The little bunch of Indians rode straight toward the herd and Swit's dugout.

Swit saw the fire explode from the end of the rifles before he heard the shots, and it looked as if everything was coming his way. The horse herd was in a panic. Horses were struggling against their sidelines, falling down, trying to buck and rear, anything to run away from danger. His own horse was pulling back on his tie down. Swit hoped the bush didn't give way. He could count three riders, and it looked as if they were all headed straight for him. A riderless horse went by him first. Before he could grasp that the Indians were upon him, they were by him and gone.

For Billy it was like a balcony seat at a barroom brawl. You could see all the action, and at the same time you were in no danger. He hadn't noticed any Indians on the meadow until Captain Walker fired. It had looked as if there were two riders, with maybe a third Indian leading a horse. Then he could see all three riders yappin' out that shrieking sound that Indians seemed to enjoy.

They were all headed for the herd. Billy hadn't seen Swit yet, but he had to be right in the middle of all the turmoil.

Swit popped up out of his hole, hatless and with his rifle in hand. He ran to his horse, leaped aboard bareback, and started out after the marauders. He knew the Indians had gotten at least one horse and probably others that he hadn't seen. His horse was at full speed when Swit heard another shot back toward the creek. He looked and could see the captain waving him back. Most of the horses were still on the meadow. Some continued to fight their restraints, but things had already started to settle down. Billy was saddling his horse, and the captain was walking back to the thicket. Boone rode for his dugout to gather up his hat and saddle.

"I see you still got your hair." Billy dismounted to help Swit saddle his horse. The horse was still skittish and making it unhandy to get a saddle on him when Billy reached the dugout. "I thought one of them Injuns was goin' grab you up outta that hole the same way a magic man plucks a rabbit out of a hat. Figured that's why you took your hat off."

"I took my hat off 'cause I wanted to give each one of 'em a fair chance at the hair my mamma gave me," Swit countered. "It must of been a mustache that they was looking for."

My God, the man was trying his hand at poking a little fun, Billy thought, was there no end to the changes this meadow would bring forth from Swit?

Joe Walker showed up as Swit, and Billy finished getting the saddle on Swit's horse. "Men, you did everything absolutely perfect," Walker said. "I wish you two would ride through the horses and check for any injuries. I didn't see any myself, but I made a quick pass coming here. Let's leave the lines on a while; let 'em settle down some. When you're satisfied, slip down by the stream and start a little fire for breakfast. I'm going to look around a bit. I'll meet you at the creek. I'd say a hot meal would be in order."

"Captain, aren't we going after that bunch? They got away with some of our horses," Swit said, and then wished he could pull back the words and shove them back down his own throat. He was embarrassed and dumbfounded to think he had not only tried to engage the captain in conversation, but was questioning his leadership. "I bet you already know how we're going to get 'em back. You'll tell us when it's time to go," Swit said, trying to put the matter straight.

If we don't get Swit off this meadow, Billy thought, we're gonna leave here with a totally different man than we started with.

"Swit, when you deal with Indians it's helpful to remember how an Indian thinks and what he considers important," Walker began. "All we lost was a little sleep and the horses that we didn't sideline. The sleep was more important than those three horses. In fact, we're better off without that bay. She was just trouble looking for a place to happen."

Billy B. watched in disbelief. Captain Walker wasn't in the habit of explaining himself to his men.

"That group of young braves meant us no harm," the captain continued. "They weren't just stealing horses; that's an act as natural to them as life itself. Their main purpose was honor, courage and success. By the time they get those three back home, especially considering the trouble that bay will give 'em trying to break free and return to us, the story of their raid on the meadow will have grown into a major campaign."

Swit wished that Billy would say something. It wasn't that the captain's tone was criticizing, in fact it was the opposite. Captain Walker seemed set on helping him understand the situation. Swit knew that he'd got himself in this predicament when he questioned the captain's actions. Maybe if Billy would just ask something it would all go away?

"There will be several nights of reliving and celebrating the experience around their camp fires." Walker was pleased by the way Swit had handled himself. "When the talk's over and the fires are all out, we'll be in Fort Gibson finding new owners for these ponies."

Billy B. was in a daze. Swit had completely flip-flopped, and now the captain had just conversed with one of his men. Swit, no less, about Indian logic. Lord, I'll be glad to get to Gibson, Billy thought, maybe things will right themselves. He walked to his horse, mounted and headed for the herd.

Chapter Four

Fort Gibson was home to several companies of infantry soldiers, and with the recent passage of the Indian Removal Act it would soon be the headquarters for the entire Seventh Infantry and a unit of mounted cavalry troops. New horse corrals, stables and barracks for the Mounted Rangers were already under construction. The arrival of Walker's string of saddle horses generated considerable interest.

The corral gates were opened to receive the horses, and once they were safely inside, Billy and Swit were to stay with the herd while Captain Walker conferred with Colonel Arbuckle. It seemed to Billy that things had started to realign themselves. Swit was back in his old mode. When the captain announced he was going down to the fort, he just nodded and turned for the corrals. There'd been no further discussion between Captain Walker and Swit about Indian philosophy.

Swit noticed that several soldiers, an Indian and two men that appeared to be trappers were working their way toward the horse herd as Captain Walker rode off. Billy started up a discourse with three of the soldiers and one of the trappers. The Indian stationed himself apart from the others, but close enough to hear. The men naturally wanted to know all about the horses, who the big guy was and what was going on. It amazed Swit how Billy could answer questions, ask a few of his own, joke, tease and continue a running bull session with all four men—yet, he never really told them much. The men seemed satisfied with Billy's answers, and as far as Swit could tell everyone was having a good old time. Billy B. already had an invitation to join his new friends. They were planning to visit some place that was located a few miles up the river. Swit watched as another man rode toward Billy and his group. He was about Captain Walker's size. His appearance was to some extent road worn, but his demeanor suggested that he was an official of some type.

"From what I've heard about the great and famous Joseph R. Walker I'd guess that these are his horses, and you're not him. How am I doing?" the man abruptly asked Billy as he stepped down from his horse.

"Perfect. You just missed the cap'n, but I'm the great and famous Billy B. Alexander," Billy answered with a smile.

The man didn't return the smile; he was looking over the horses. "I'm Big Al, Famous Billy, are you the one in charge of this bunch of soup bones?"

"I wouldn't zackly say that I'm in charge, Mister Al." Billy still had a big smile on his face. "That'd be Cap'n Walker; however, I am watchin' over this fine group of saddle horses. Now then, if you're of a mind to boil yourself up some soup, maybe you ought'a take a look at that specimen you got your saddle hung on."

Swit noticed that a quietness had descended on Billy's little group, and Big Al's eyes had changed into the same frightening fixed dead glare that a cougar gets just before it leaps for its prey. All of Billy B.'s recently acquired friends had eased themselves back away from their new acquaintance.

Billy knew he had once again let his mouth put him in conflict. Mister Al had size, and Billy was sure he'd need some help if he expected to have at least a sandwich while Big Al was taking a meal. Billy was trying to keep an eye on Al, and at the same time secret a look for some handy equalizer to balance his size handicap, when he felt something rub his arm.

"I don't guess I've had the pleasure," Swit said. "My name is Swit Boone." It was Swit standing at Billy's side. As the others moved back, he had been moving forward. Swit hadn't been a part of Billy's group, but he was listening when Big Al and Billy exchanged opinions about horseflesh and soup production.

"Captain Walker is down at the fort," Swit reported.

There was no doubt in Big Al's mind that the balance in the fight he had been about to start had shifted. "As much as I would like to stay here and talk horses with the likes of you two, I'd better find this Walker fellow that thinks he's a captain. I'd like to know what the hell he's a captain of."

Billy was about to suggest that he thought this would be an excellent topic of discussion at their first meeting, but decided against it. Swit Boone didn't speak, and his facial expression didn't change. His eyes had narrowed their focus down to one thing, the man that was being disrespectful to Captain Walker.

Big Al turned to address the group that had gathered to examine Walker's horses. "If I were you, I'd keep my pay for something better than these used up soap factory candidates. The Army will get you the best horses money can buy." No one spoke as Al climbed on his horse and turned for the stockade.

Some of the same potential horse buyers, along with a few new ones, began to collect back in around Billy and Swit's location after the big man's departure. Billy attempted to introduce Swit, but Swit still had his full attention in Big Al's direction. Discussion about the merits and shortfalls of past and present horses was reintroduced once more, and Billy was again directing the dialogue.

Walker introduced himself as Joseph Walker to the desk sergeant at Colonel Matthew Arbuckle's office. He was treated with courtesy, and when the sergeant announced his arrival to the colonel he was presented as Captain Walker, recently from Jackson County, Missouri.

"Come on in Joe and have a seat," Colonel Arbuckle greeted Walker. "By golly, it's been a spell since I've had the pleasure of your company. We received word, not too long ago, that you were headed our way with a string of horses. I hope your trip was easy. How do you like our new corrals and livery?"

"First rate," Walker said. "Thanks for allowing us to use your corrals. I've heard that you'll soon be quartering some cavalry troops. Some of your men already here might be interested in a saddle horse or two. Would you have any objection to my trying to put these horses into the hands of your officers or enlisted men?"

"I welcome any horses of the quality you're known to handle," Arbuckle answered. "However, Albert Truemain may look upon your enterprise in a somewhat different light."

"I don't believe I know Albert Truemain," Walker said. "Does he have the say about me selling horses here at the fort?"

"Albert seems to have a lot to say," the colonel answered. "He's the government horse buyer for this area. I'm sure that he knows you've arrived with your horses. He has no authority over any affair occurring on this post, or on any other one, as far as I know, but he does seem to command the attention of many of our locals."

"The only time I'm concerned about a horse buyer's attention is when I'm buying. When I'm selling I welcome all buyers," Walker said. "What do you hear of Colonel Chouteau? Is his health good? I heard a while back that he was doing poorly."

Ten years before Colonel Arbuckle was sent west by the Army to set up a new outpost along the Arkansas River, A. P. Chouteau had already established a colony of trappers and traders at the mouth of the Verdigris River. Colonel Chouteau was a graduate of West Point, and a member of one of the most prominent fur trading families in America. He had resigned his commission from the Army to join his family in the fur business.

Chouteau added a small shipyard and soon his settlement extended up the shore of the Verdigris for several miles. Buying, trading and shipping of pelts to St. Louis and New Orleans, along with building and repairing boats, caused the community to prosper. It was Chouteau who recommended the area adjacent to a natural rock landing three miles up the Grand River as an excellent site for Colonel Arbuckle's post. The Grand emptied into the Arkansas about half a mile below the mouth of the Verdigris, and the whole area was called the Three Forks Region. Colonel Chouteau had the respect of all the men that moved in and out of Three Forks.

"Colonel Chouteau's health is capital now," Arbuckle said. "For some time he did suffer from some type of—"

"Sir, I'm sorry to disturb you," the desk sergeant interrupted Colonel Arbuckle. "Albert Truemain insists on seeing you immediately. Shall I ask him to return at a later time, or would it be…"

"I think he'll see me now, Sergeant," Walker turned sideways in his chair, and coming through the door was Big Al Truemain. The sergeant had been elbowed aside. "I suppose this is the Walker that I've been hearing about. I just had a long talk with your boys up at the corrals."

"Is that so?" Joe Walker got up from his chair, turned around and extended his hand. He thought how a long talk with Billy would require a great deal of listening, and with Swit, you'd need to supply most of the verbal parts, and at the same time keep his attention. It was hard for Walker to picture Mister Truemain qualified for either challenge. "I'm Joe Walker, and I'm pleased to meet you. I hope the men showed you our horses. We plan to find them some new owners."

Truemain quickly shook Walker's hand. It seemed to be more of a forced politeness than a how-do-you-do. "I'll give you thirty-five dollars a head for the whole bunch. You won't get better than that anywhere," Albert Truemain calmly offered.

"Thirty-five dollars might buy you a horse somewhere; however, I believe it would take a little more than that to purchase what we've brought down here," Walker said. "These horses were put together with the thought of providing adequate mounts for our men here at Gibson."

"I'll see to the horses the men here ride," Truemain had raised his voice. "The government hired me to do that job."

"The last time I noticed, our government didn't object if a man took responsibility for his own mount." The pleasantness was gone from Walker's voice. "I've sold the government horses before. Any bid you care to make is welcome, but I can tell you now that thirty-five dollars won't buy a quality cavalry mount in these parts."

"Arbuckle," Truemain bellowed, "you better get those horses off government property. The Army don't want no private sales on their land."

"Albert, just calm down." The colonel had experienced Truemain's bullying before. "No one's trying to take over your job here. The captain has brought us down some horses he thought the men would like to own personally. You know it's done all the time. I even have three of my own over at the barn. Sergeant, would you see if you could scare us up a little coffee? Albert, have a chair and let's hear all about your last buying trip."

"You can take your goddamned chair and throw it out the window." Albert Truemain had about lost all control. "Don't think I don't know what you're up to. You turned down the last bunch of horses I delivered here, and now he shows up with these. General Macomb is going to hear about this— you can be damn sure of that."

Truemain realized that he had lost command of himself and the situation. His size and explosive nature worked to his advantage with many men, but the two in this room were not influenced by his lack of restraint. He decided that the best thing for him to do would be to say no more and just leave. He whirled himself around and reached for the door, accidentally catching his toe on a loose board in the floor. Albert Truemain lost his balance and fell into the hall tree that held the Colonel's overcoat and hat. Big Al, tree, hat and coat all snarled together and came tumbling down. Truemain was swinging his arms and thrashing around on the floor in an attempt to untangle himself. It looked as if he was wrestling with a stick man. Finally Albert Truemain ended the fight. He lay quietly with his head still partly covered by the coat. Ever so slowly he climbed to his feet and walked out of the room.

"Colonel, that's a pretty tough guard you've got on that door." Walker was smiling as he spoke. "I believe he could have taken Truemain if he hadn't been wearing that heavy coat." Albert Truemain was leaving the building, but he'd remember Walker's parting words.

"I told you he'd have a lot to say." Colonel Arbuckle watched as Walker picked up the hall tree. "Though I never thought it'd lead to combat. Well now, where were we? Oh yes, you were asking about Colonel Chouteau. He had some kind of blood thing. It turned him as yellow as a lemon. We thought sure he was a goner. It took a while, but he's back now as sound as ever."

Captain Walker and the colonel visited for a while before Walker excused himself and left. He stopped at the sergeant's desk to ask where Captain Bonneville might be found. The sergeant informed him that the captain had just returned from a patrol up the Arkansas River, and showed him where to find Bonneville's quarters. Walker crossed the parade ground at an angle and headed toward the officer's barracks. He was rounding the corner when he and Bonneville almost ran together.

"Damn, that was close, I was just coming to see you," Walker said. "You may not remember me. I'm Joe Walker. Lieutenant Montgomery introduced us back at Fort Leavenworth a year or so ago."

"Of course, I remember you," Bonneville said. "It's a pleasure to see you again. I'd heard of your coming and wanted to speak with you while you're here. You say you're on your way to see me? What can I do for you?"

"Sam Houston sent word to me in Missouri that you're planning a fur trapping enterprise into the northern Rockies," Walker answered. "He suggested that you might be looking for a guide, someone experienced in leading trappers."

"Indeed, I am." Bonneville thought how this chance meeting was perfect. Walker was obviously interested in the expedition. "I'm on my way over to the officer's mess. If you haven't eaten, please be my guest and join me. I'd like to talk with you at length, and in private, about an undertaking that could be both interesting and profitable. I understand you're engaged in a horse-selling venture. When would time permit you to have such a conversation?"

"I'm going to sell the horses at auction on Sunday afternoon, and then follow the sale with a horse race," Walker replied. "I thought I'd ride out tomorrow morning and lay out a course for the race. The two of us could mark the course and have time-a-plenty for uninterrupted discussion. How's that sound?"

Captain Bonneville thought the arrangement was satisfactory. The fact that Walker had searched him out and seemed interested in the expedition had helped ease his concern about hiring Walker. It was another reason for him to thank Sam Houston.

Walking along with Captain Bonneville, Walker looked toward the horse corrals. He could see that Billy and Swit were both preoccupied with the horses and a small crowd that had gathered along the fence.

Billy was once again locked in conversation with the prospective buyers. Swit backed away from the group and the bouncing around of words. He hadn't intentionally moved in any particular direction, but when he looked over his shoulder, the Indian was standing within reach.

The man was bigger than Swit had first realized—taller and more muscular than Billy. His demeanor and the color of his skin told you immediately that he was an Indian, although he was lighter than most Indians Swit had seen. He wore a plain blue wool jacket, cotton leggings, beaded moccasins and a cloth turban. Swit noticed the Indian had a different odor about him. It wasn't revolting, or especially objectionable, just different. He was thinking that not all white men smelled the same either, and was trying to identify the source of this man's aroma, when he noticed that the Indian was looking at him—eye to eye.

"My name is Oo-tse-tee," the Indian said.

Swit almost jumped back into Billy's rabble. He never expected the Indian to talk to him, let alone speak English.

"Your name is?" Oo-tse-tee asked.

Now it was on him. Not only was the Indian talking, but he also wanted to know Swit's name. "Mister Stewart Jarvis Boone," Swit loudly answered, and then wondered why he had spoken in such a manner.

Billy stopped in mid-sentence and looked towards Swit. Swit, who when he did talk barely spoke above a whisper, had resoundingly introduced himself in a name Billy had never heard before. A stillness had suddenly formed. Everyone was silently looking at Swit Boone. The Indian was even startled. Then an unpracticed suggestion of a smile began to creep across the Indian's weathered face. He held his right hand out in the same way that a white man would offer a greeting. Swit looked toward Billy. He didn't know which way to jump. How'd he get himself into this, anyhow? Why couldn't things just stay simple? What was he supposed to do now, with all of Billy's friends looking on?

"Shake his hand, Swit," Billy B. said. "He ain't a gonna scalp ya. Hell, he might be a horse buyer for the whole Injun' Nation. If you run him off, the cap'n will prob'ly send you back to get them horses that we lost out on the meadow."

Swit slowly reached out and took hold of the Indian's hand. He was surprised by the strength of the man's grip.

With one big pumping action, the Indian said, "Happy to meet Boone, Sam is my friend. Do you know Sam?"

Swit felt the hole getting deeper. Talking to Billy was one thing; mainly all you had to do was listen. This man hardly said anything, but it was mostly questions. He even called him by name, and now Swit couldn't remember the Indian's name. Billy had the boys' attention again, and they were back to jawing at one another.

Billy was so busy with his crowd, and Swit with the Indian, that neither had noticed Captain Walker's arrival. "I hope you men haven't sold all the horses yet. If you're hungry you can slip on down to that mess house over there on the right and get yourselves some grub. I've okayed it with the sergeant."

Billy immediately started introductions between his new friends and the captain before telling Walker about someone calling himself Big Al and that he was looking for him.

"He found me," Walker replied as he turned his attention toward Boone.

"This Indian wants to know if I know Sam," Swit reported. "Says he's his friend."

"My name's Joe Walker," Captain Walker announced. "Are you a friend of Sam Houston?"

"Yes, Sam Houston." The Indian nodded when he spoke.

Sam Houston had been a friend to Oo-tse-tee's people for as long as the Indian could remember. His father had told him stories about how Houston had wandered into their Cherokee camp when he was only sixteen or seventeen years old. The tough, unafraid, free spirited youth was soon a favorite with the members of the tribe. The chief even adopted him and gave Houston the name Co-lon-neh.

"What are you called?" Walker wanted to know.

"Oo-tse-tee," the Indian answered.

"Is Sam anywhere around here?"

"Usually at Wigwam Neosho." Oo-tse-tee pointed north up the river, called the Grand by most whites, and Neosho by the Indians. "About three mile. Drunk most of the time." Apparently Oo-tse-tee had said everything he wanted to say. He turned and walked toward the horses.

It was a fair string of horses, Walker thought, but not as gentle as he would have liked. All but two of the horses were solid colored. Walker believed, as did many horsemen, with the exception of most Indians, that spotted horses resulted from inbreeding, and inbreeding caused offspring that were inferior, both mentally and physically.

"I'm glad to see that you're acquainting yourself with the Indians." Captain Walker put his hand on Swit's shoulder. "They're an interesting people, and some of 'em are not as different from us as you might think. You can learn many things from associating with them."

Billy and his buddies were already headed for the mess house, and Billy was waving for Swit to catch up. He used that as an excuse to remove himself from Walker's presents before he messed up somehow. By mid-afternoon Billy and Swit's new associates had given them a royal tour of the post. As they slowly made their way back up the hill to the corrals, Swit was focused on checking to see if the Indian was still around, and Billy was explaining the what's and why fore's of soldiering.

Billy B. and Swit joined Walker at the corrals. "Cap'n, how'd you feel about Swit and me slippin' off for a spell tonight?" It was obvious to Walker that Billy and Swit had been working up to something. Finally, Billy approached the problem. "Some of the boys down at the fort figure to go out to a little spot just off the gover'met ground. They claim that your friend, Sam, plays cards there about every night. They've even got a gambling wheel. A soldier won a hundred and fifty dollars there a while back. We wouldn't be out too late."

"I don't mind you're going, but I'd have to say your timing is bad," Walker answered. "We have some work ahead of us getting these horses ready, and the best time to visit the gambling house would be after the horse race. By then we'll have sold the horses, and you two will have some jingle in your pockets. If it was me, I'd postpone the party a little."

Walker watched Billy and Swit discuss the matter as they walked to the other end of the corral. Billy did the talking, Swit nodded, and it appeared that they were in agreement. As Captain Walker prepared to turn in for the night he saw Billy, Swit, three soldiers and the Indian all settled in around the fire. Apparently they had decided that his advice to delay their outing was sound. Walker guessed that they were probably discussing the gambling wheel and all the money they were about to win. He was sure that part of the conversation would be about the girls that worked there, and others that they had known. Billy had been careful not to mention anything about the girls.

The post bugler woke Walker. Billy and Swit didn't stir until the fort's morning gun banged and echoed through the surrounding hills. Captain Bonneville arrived at camp as they were finishing breakfast. Introductions were made, and they all shared the last of the morning coffee before Walker explained that he and the Army captain were going back up into the hills to mark a path for Sunday's horse race. "Catch up the horses and put 'em in their sellin' clothes. We might be gone for some time, should anyone ask. When we're done, I'll come back here first." The two captains rode off in the direction of the morning sun.

"Those two men seem young but very dependable," Bonneville said. "Have you known them long?"

"This is Swit's first trip with me," Walker answered. "Billy I've known for years. He was really just a young boy when he made his first trip down the trail to Santa Fe. Billy had a hard start in life. His mother died when he was a baby, and his father treated him with neglect. A bunch that I was running with in those days kind of adopted him. Billy B. has seen more in his few years than most do in a lifetime. They're both good men, though. Tell me about your plan for the Rockies."

"Well, I've had this…I guess you could call it an obsession…to travel over the Divide and into the Oregon Territory." Bonneville was anxious to tell Captain Walker what he could about the upcoming expedition. "It's beginning to look like I could get my wish. Some investors from New York want me to lead a fur trapping venture into the upper valley of the Green River, and then on northwest to the Columbia. It's my earnest desire to interest you in coming along with me."

"Do you have any experience trapping or trading in furs?" Walker asked.

"Not really." Bonneville was trying to get a feel for how Walker received the invitation to accompany him westward. "You probably don't know, but I was raised in New York. I've spent the last ten years assigned to frontier posts, leading soldiers in the field and interacting with the Indians. I know very little about trapping, or handling the type of man it takes to be a trapper. If you're interested in investing some money in this enterprise, I would welcome you as a business partner, as well as pay you for your services as a guide and advisor."

"When do you intend to begin this business, and how many trappers are you going to take with you?" Walker wanted to know.

"I'd like to start out from the Fort Osage area as early as possible in the spring of '32 with about one hundred men," Bonneville answered. "Please understand, my plans are not entirely set at this time. Any input you'd care to give would be welcomed."

"Excuse me, Captain Bonneville, I need to mark that oak over there," Walker said as he headed for the tree.

"Please call me Ben." Bonneville wished he knew what Walker was thinking.

Walker tied a red dyed cloth around a limb that was shoulder high, if you're six four and on horseback, before turning to Bonneville. "Ben, I'd like to hear more about where you intend to do your trapping, how long you're planing to stay out, and what arrangements you've made with your investors about selling your furs? Do you plan to contract with free trappers or hire men for wages?"

It was obvious to Captain Bonneville that Walker was, step by step, showing how nonsensical it would be for investors to select a man that had absolutely no experience in the trapping, trading or selling of furs. He hadn't even mentioned how the Army was to be convinced that they should let one of their officers run off into the wilderness and play king of the fur men. Before I end up losing Walker, Bonneville thought, I'd better start talking sense.

"I'm sorry, but I don't have the answers to your questions," Bonneville admitted. "Your friend Sam Houston has told me more about this arrangement than anyone. I don't know if you are aware of this, but Sam is drinking heavily. Although I consider him my friend too, I have some reservations about the reality of his information. Everything I have told you is true. What I haven't told you is that my backers are very interested in my keeping a detailed account of the expedition. I'm not talking about the location of fur grounds. They want to know about terrain, Indian tribes, travel routes, weather. You know, tactical intelligence of a military nature about the country we'll travel through. They want maps."

Joseph Walker had no actual information about the upcoming expedition, with the exception of Sam's pressing him to get on down to Gibson and hire out to Captain Bonneville. A chance to once again lead men into the wilderness, explore new territory and recapture the freedom of that life was the force driving Walker.

"The only investor I've talked to showed more than a passing interest in your coming along." Bonneville could see that he had Walker's full attention. The next couple of minutes were critical to his purpose. "Sam thinks this entire campaign has been secretly cooked up by President Jackson and John Jacob Astor. Their intention is to open up settlement in the West and expand the nation to the Pacific Ocean. I truly don't know, but a lot of what he says makes sense. If you'll join us I'll do my best to see that you can lead a party of forty to fifty men into the California settlements."

"Sam always did drink more than most, but you're the second man since I arrived here to tell me he's a drunk." Walker was pleased that the Army captain had decided to lay his cards face up on the table. "Ben, did your investor say anything about who would handle your furs when you got them back to the States?"

"He mentioned the Cerré family in St. Louis," Bonneville answered. "I'll be in Washington next spring, and while I'm there I plan to go to New York and meet with him again. I hope I can tell whoever I talk with that you've signed on, and give them a skeleton plan of the trip. Joe, I have no idea what they're going to tell me."

Captain Walker was tying another marker on a walnut tree. Drunk, Sam Houston had a better grasp of reality than many men did, Walker thought.

"Michael Cerré may be the man you need to see about handling your furs." Walker's acquaintance with the Cerrés extended back to the time he'd spent trapping in the territory around Taos and Santa Fe. They were a well-known family of French fur traders, and Michael Sylvestre Cerré was probably about the same age as Captain Bonneville. "Michael's family has been in the fur business for many years. When he was very young he operated a trading post and ventured down into the Mexico fur territory. He's honest, closemouthed and a good man to have with you in the field. If you and he can reach an agreement, he'd be a valuable addition to our group."

"Does this mean that you will accept my offer as partner and guide?" Bonneville asked.

Walker had recently advanced money to some members of his family. He had considered Ben's offer to invest in the new enterprise. Sister Jane's husband, Abraham McClellan, always seemed to have money available for speculation, but Walker was convinced that the primary reason for this expedition was to gather information, not profit.

"I've suffered some unexpected family expenses, and I don't feel that I can afford to invest any money," Walker answered. "My fee to act as guide and advisor will be the normal amount paid by any fur company. If that's agreeable to you, then I'm on board."

"Agreed." Bonneville shook Walker's hand. "I will begin to work on obtaining my leave of absence immediately. Like I mentioned, I'm going to Washington and New York next spring to arrange all the financing. After my work is completed there, I'll come West and meet you wherever you say."

Bonneville felt that he had just made his first big step toward the West. Cerré sounded like a good addition, and someone they could trust. "I'll stop in St. Louis and talk with Cerré on my way back from Washington. He's probably just the man to put in charge of handling our supplies. One thing we must all be very careful about is our correspondence. If Sam is right, no one except us should know the true purpose of our journey or the source of our financing. All written communication between us must be destroyed. If information about how and why this expedition is being formed was leaked to the Eastern papers, it would be very embarrassing to President Jackson, and the end of my military career."

Bonneville was all Army, Walker thought. His military mind was racing as he planned and organized his thoughts. It was like he was formulating a battle plan. The upcoming expedition looked to be a well-organized and thought-out excursion. With a little help from himself and hopefully Cerré, Captain Benjamin Bonneville would lead a successful campaign into the West, and Joseph Walker would get his shot at California. He had wanted to make that trip for ten years.

California was where Walker, McKinney, Tuck and Choquette had been headed when they made that first trip into Mexico. Tuck was the one with the idea that they could make more money, and that the girls were prettier in the Spanish settlements. Money and girls appealed to most men, especially young men, and that had been enough to swing the bunch from California to the beaver country in *Nuevo* Mexico. That same attraction would soon pull Swit and Billy B. to the place up river that the soldiers had told them about—but not until after the horse sale.

Chapter Five

A clear and sunny fall day that warmed into the low sixties by the afternoon was perfect for a horse sale. Gathered in and around the corrals were the locals from the Three Forks settlement, travelers off the two steamboats tied up at the dock, all ranks of the military, a few trappers and Indians, and two buffalo hunters. A feeling of celebration and entertainment was in the air.

The procedure for selling the horses was not going to be complicated. Captain Walker put a fifty-dollar starting price on each animal, and the auction began. The highest bidder was the new owner as soon as he paid the clerk. Walker had engaged Colonel Arbuckle's desk sergeant to clerk the sale, and everything went smoothly with the exception of one small snag. When Albert Truemain went to settle with the sergeant, he claimed that he'd only bid fifty-two dollars for his horse. The clerk showed the horse selling for fifty-four. Walker settled the disagreement by auctioning the animal again. It brought fifty-five dollars and went to one of the buffalo hunters.

With the sale over, the race was next. The contest would start from behind a mark that Captain Walker had made along the ground. When Walker determined that the horses were fairly aligned he would fire a shot in the air. The horses were to head for a designated opening into the trees about two hundred yards in the distance. From there they'd follow a marked trail up a hill, down through a draw, over a slight rise, across a small stream, around a prominent large rock and back out onto the flat. Once in the open it was another three hundred yards to the area behind the company kitchens and the finish line. The total distance was approximately two miles. The first rider to cross the finish line would collect the one hundred dollars that Captain Walker had put up, and one half of the entry fees. Fourteen contestants paid twenty dollars each to enter their horses in the race. Colonel Arbuckle was appointed the official judge, and his decision would be final.

Most of the horse race participants were Army personnel. Two women and two men, who apparently had come over from one of the local watering holes at the Three Forks settlement, entered an old buckskin gelding. One of the men, who claimed that he was riding the best damn racehorse in these parts, couldn't stay in the saddle. They finally decided that the tall girl with the squinty eyes would be the jockey.

No one around the fort could remember seeing the horse that Albert Truemain was riding. A story circulated that the horse belonged to some of the gambling element over at Three Forks. Side bets between the spectators were hot and heavy. A dandy who had come to Fort Gibson on one of the steamers was working his way through the crowd giving odds on the different horses.

Billy was leading an unsaddled gray mare when he and Swit walked up to the starting line. Billy had bought the mare in the auction—a credit deal he had worked out with Captain Walker before the sale. The gray was not as big as the other horses in the race. She had small bones and fine features. Billy knew she could run, he'd watched her all the way from Independence, and thought that she'd sell cheap. Most men preferred a big, stout animal. Captain Walker sure did.

Truemain's horse would have brought top dollar if he'd been in the sale. He was a large roan colored stallion that had action a-plenty. The horse was deep through the chest, with heavy muscles over his rump that extended down into his hind legs. Billy felt certain that the big roan was the horse to beat. The stallion would be fast, at least for a short distance. How he'd handle two miles through hill country was anyone's guess. A horse race was more than pure speed and endurance. Timing and luck made winners too.

"Are you sure you wanna ride this race?" Billy asked Swit. "I know you can ride as good as me, but I don't weigh as much as you."

"Don't matter," Swit said. "She won't hardly know I'm on her." First his hat went and then his coat and shirt. Swit was sitting on the ground taking off his boots when Truemain started laughing.

"Well, would you looky over here," Truemain announced to the crowd. "Don't that about beat all? I've heard of putting a burr under the saddle to make your horse run faster, but nobody ever told me that a stripped-off rider with holes in his socks could make a winner out of a stumble, fart and fall down excuse for a race horse."

"Never you mind, Mister Big Al." Billy was coming to Swit's defense. "Swit figures to be so far ahead by the time he hits the creek he may just want to stop and take a bath. This way he'll be ready for the water and all dried off by the time he gets back."

As far as Billy could tell, Swit hadn't heard any of the conversation, and he took no notice of anyone around. Boone was back into his concentration mode. He grabbed a handful of the mare's mane and swung up, landing on her back as light as a fly. Billy had just admitted to Swit that he was his equal as a rider, however he knew inside himself that Swit was a better horseman than he'd ever be.

Almost before Billy realized it was time, Walker fired his pistol and the race was on. The gray mare went straight to the front. When they reached the trees, Swit and the mare had the lead. Truemain was less than a length back, and the stallion was closing the gap. The gray lost a little ground going up the hill, but held her own, might have even gained a little back, going down through the draw. As they crossed the rise and headed for the creek, the powerful roan pulled up alongside the mare. He took the lead when they crossed the stream. The little mare was running one hell of a race, Swit thought, but there was no denying the speed of the stallion. The big horse could run. His rider was a different story. The way he slopped around in the saddle forced his horse to keep changing leads. Big Al's elbows were flapping up and down so far and fast that Swit couldn't help but smile. He looked more like he was trying to fly than ride.

By now the race was really just a two-horse affair. The others were so far back that you could hardly see them through the trees. The roan and the gray were headed for the rock. The mare was losing a little ground with each stride, but Swit knew there was still plenty of race left to run. The last dash to the finish line could make the difference. Swit couldn't believe what he saw next. Truemain cut the trail. Instead of swinging out around the rock and back toward the opening onto the flat, he crossed over and picked up the trail just before it broke from the trees. Truemain and the big roan entered the flat, a good two lengths ahead of Swit and Billy's gray mare. The run for the finish line was exactly that—an all-out run. The mare was gaining a little with every stride, but she was still short when they crossed the line.

Truemain's crowd was shouting, jumping around and hugging each other.

A few shots were fired in the air. As soon as Big Al could get his horse stopped, he circled back, jumped off the roan and grabbed the prize money out of Walker's hand.

"By God, I guess that'll show you who knows horses. When you run against me you better bring something better than that little gray nag." Not waiting for a comment, Truemain turned around to join in with his friends celebrating their victory.

Truemain's quick, bold move had caught Walker off-guard. The enjoyment he'd experienced watching an exciting horse race had suddenly turned into controlled anger as he watched the winnings being carried out across the racetrack. Almost instantly his controlled burn was changed into uncontrollable laughter. Truemain and his group had walked right in front of the last horse to finish the race, the old buckskin with the tall, squinty-eyed rider. Truemain dropped the money. One of his gambling partners was knocked down and rolled fifteen yards down the course. The girl rider caught her foot over the head of another man and finished the race with him face down in the dirt and her on his back.

Captain Walker offered to paid Billy and Swit some of their earnings and hold the remainder of their funds until morning. Walker knew they'd have enough ready cash to have a good time, and this way the gamblers wouldn't get it all—at least not right away. That was agreeable with Billy B. and Swit, and off they went. The sun was low in the sky when Walker saw his men leave the fort accompanied by three soldiers and the Indian.

The three soldiers knew how to get there, and even though Swit hadn't won the race, the group was in a festive frame of mind. Oo-tse-tee didn't have much to say, but that wasn't unusual. Billy had recovered from the disappointment of losing a close horse race, but was concerned about Swit. He hadn't said two words in the last hour. Billy thought that he must have been trying to study out what he could have done to win the race.

The building didn't amount too much, a one-room affair with two tents out back. Inside it had a barrel and plank-type bar along the side opposite the front door. Three round poker tables with chairs were scattered about, and on one end of the room stood a table with a gambling wheel on top. The story that Billy heard was that the wheel came from a riverboat. Some type of misunderstanding between the boat's captain and a Three Forks gambler had brought the device ashore. A back door was set about midway between the end of the bar and the gambling wheel. The soldiers called the building

Paddy's Place. It was named in honor of its owner, a small in stature, tough, hard-boiled little Irishman named Patrick Sean O'Rourke.

They were not the first ones to arrive. Big Al Truemain and his party were playing cards at a corner table. With the bar's help they were in the process of trying to heal their finish line wounds. The newcomers made straight for the bar. Billy got a whiskey, and the rest had beer. Two girls were standing around Truemain's card table trying to generate some interest.

"Look what we got us here tonight, B.B.," Lucy said. "I'll betcha these young pups are here for a good time."

Swit heard one of the card players ask the girl called B.B., or Belle, to bring him another drink. He thought that the other one that they called Lucy, or L.L., looked a little older than Belle did—not old, just a bit older.

"I get that one with the mustache." Belle ignored the order for a drink. Both girls were headed for the bar, and she was declaring her target. "You can have the soldier boys, but you better get started. They'll be closing the door before long."

The entry that B.B. was talking about was two huge gates along one end of the fort's palisade. The enlisted men's quarters were inside, and at precisely nine o'clock every night a drum roll and fife sounded. If you wanted to spend the night in your own abode, you'd better be headed for the fort.

"I don't worry any about them old gates," L.L. answered. "I keep more of the Army tied up and off the fort than any of them Indians they're always chasing. Now which one of you would-be generals is ready to mount an attack?" The soldier standing on Swit's right didn't need a second invitation. He and Lucy marched off toward the back door. Swit thought he looked a little scared. Like maybe he was going off to war.

After Lucy's remark about Indians, Oo-tse-tee wasn't sure of his welcome. Sam had brought him into Paddy's Place several times; he'd even tried to teach him to play poker. But traveling in the company of Sam Houston was different; not many around Sam said that much about Indians. He picked up his beer, eased himself off into a dark spot along one wall of the building, and sat down.

Swit thought how things were just not working out at all like he'd imagined they would. First the soldier pulled out, and now the Indian was moving away. The girl in front of him was standing with her hands on her hips. She'd already declared her attraction for Billy's mustache, but Swit could feel her eyes pour over him.

"Maybe I'll put that mustache on hold and get me a jockey what likes to ride with his clothes off." Belle was headed straight for Swit. "You're the one that rode the little gray today, aren't you?"

Swit just knew that she was going to slip right into the gap that was left when Billy's friend went off to war. "It ain't necessarily that I like to ride without my clothes, it just seemed like the thing to do at the time," Swit answered.

It was Billy's opinion that the evening was off to a perfect start, and Belle was the answer for Swit's doldrums. "I used to get all my wishes answered after I grew myself this here lip hair, but now I see I need to shave it all off and start ridin' necked. I knew I'd be a goner once you gals got a look at old Boone there in his birthday best. Never was a mustache that could stand up to that kinda competition."

"Don't you do nothing to that mustache." Belle threw Billy a quick glance. "My desires can fluctuate from time to time. It's just that after watching a horse race I'm more likely to be drawn down by a jockey with his clothes off."

"I'm not expecting to take my clothes off and do any more riding. It didn't help anyhow." It was just like Boone had feared. B.B. had slid right in beside him. She had her body pressed so tight against his side that he could feel her move each time she took a breath. Swit felt all alone and on shaky ground.

"It was my pleasure to know one other jockey that liked to ride without his clothes." B.B.'s conversation now was a whispered breath meant only for Boone. "He and I use to play a little game all by ourselves out back. You come with me and I'll show you how the game's played."

While they where making their way up the river to Paddy's Place, Swit had thought about meeting the girls that the soldiers were always talking about. He'd considered the possibility of his going out to the tent after they'd had a little time to get acquainted, but this was moving way too fast. He didn't think that one of the girls would get this close to him, at least not this quick. She wanted to go now, and in fact he was inclined to go with her. At first he hadn't been, but now he was beginning to feel like it would be all right. He sure liked the way she smelled. It wasn't like anything he could remember, and he didn't care about trying to comprehend its origin. He just enjoyed the feeling it gave him.

"I do believe I'll take a run at that wheel," Billy B. said as he and the two soldiers moved off toward the table. "I never could gather any luck with the ladies, but gamblin', now that's another side of the coin."

Belle had Swit's hand in hers, and Swit noticed that she sure had pretty eyes. Almost before he knew he was walking, they were hand in hand out the back door. At the same time Boone and Belle went through the back door, the front door opened. Joe Walker and Sam Houston walked into the room. It only took one look to see that Sam was drunk. Walker's state was hard to determine.

"We just fought our way across the river and through the canebrakes to get here before you closed. I hope this wild bunch hasn't drank up all the whiskey." Sam was talking to owner O'Rourke, but loud enough so that everyone could hear. "I'd have never made it if I hadn't had my guide here with me. We'll each have a glass of your best Tennessee sippin' whiskey, mister bar-man, and should it come to your attention that the bottom of the glass has become dry, we will require a replenishment."

Billy B. had just doubled his last wager and won again. Lucy had brought back her first soldier, deposited him beside Billy and left with another. Billy saw Sam and the captain come in, but his attention was enveloped in the atmosphere of the gambling table.

Truemain, however, was watching the whole show. "By God, there was a time before all these celebrities started coming around that a man could bring his friends here for a game of cards and spend a quiet evening." Big Al made his announcement to everyone in the room.

The captain and Sam stood at the bar. To Billy it appeared they hadn't heard Truemain, but he was sure they had—Swit probably heard him out back. Walker said something to Paddy, and he was laughing. It was Billy's moment.

When Billy B. was out for a good time, aggravation was the one thing that he liked better than whiskey, gambling or whores. He truly loved to aggravate. The trick was to work it right up to the point of serious physical conflict, and then at the last minute, slide aside and out of harm's way. There were lots of ways to maneuver your target, but Billy knew the first thing you had to have was an active participant. Truemain had announced his candidacy, and Billy was willing. Suddenly it was clear. Billy hadn't minded losing the horse race so much, it was losing to Mister Big Al that had upset him. He wondered if Swit felt the same, but doubted that right now Swit was too concerned about any old horse race.

"Now if I'd won all that money today, I'd be ridin' that big roan right out in front of the biggest parade this country has ever seen instead a sittin' in a dark corner of this old trapper's cabin with a bunch of skinned-up card players," Billy said. "You musta thought that a parade run you over after you collected your money."

"What the hell would you know about parades, or horse races for that matter?" Truemain answered back. "A little sprout like you couldn't even see a parade unless he was standing on someone's shoulders." The card players were getting true enjoyment from Big Al's comments, and they seemed to be having fun for the first time since Billy and his bunch had arrived.

"The way I normally handle them parades is to look for that tall, squinty-eyed girl. You know, the one that ended up ridin' on top your friend's head." Billy had everyone in the corner's attention. "She's generally standing right on the front row. I just set myself down in front of her, that way I got a view most don't get. Course, you gotta be quick when the parade's over, she's likely to tangle up one of them long legs of hers around your head." The skinned-face friend had stopped laughing. They all looked in Truemain's direction.

"You thought you bought a race horse today, but old Walker there, he just stuck it to ya, didn't he?" Big Al had started to get up out of his chair.

"It's true enough, my little gray mare couldn't totally come up to the mark in this race. I think she might have learned enough though that she'll do better the next time out. It's too bad that Scab couldn't have been in the race today. He would of fairly well stomped the fat out of that chunk of coyote bait you was ridin'," Billy had set the trap. Now it was up to Big Al.

"The only thing that gray bitch learned today was to look up my horse's ass and keep the shit out of her eyes when I went by her."

Truemain's friends thought they knew what was coming next. Big Al was up and looking for a fight. "I don't know who or what Scab is, but if there's any stompin' to do, I'll do it."

Billy B. had gained Walker's attention when he introduced Scab into the conversation. Big Al seemed formidable, but Billy figured he lacked desire unless everything was weighted heavy in his favor. He knew that the captain wouldn't tolerate many disparaging remarks about his horse.

"She learned how to cheat." Swit and B.B. were standing by the back door. No one in the room missed Swit's statement.

"What the hell did you say?" Truemain shouted.

"I said you cheated. You didn't swing around the rock, you cut across in front," Boone answered.

"Why you lying little son of a bitch, I'm gonna split you wide open." Truemain started for Swit.

"No lie, I see it all from the hilltop." The voice came from a dark corner across the room.

This was all new to Billy. His plan to lead Big Al into an unsettling position was developing more twists and turns that he had imagined possible. First, it looked like he would need to defuse a Truemain-Boone explosion, and now Big Al's brain was trying to digest the Indian's information. Billy knew something was about to happen right here and right now, but he felt lost as to what.

"I ain't takin' that off of no damn Indian." Truemain turned and headed across the room toward Oo-tse-tee. Big Al had thrown a chair out of his way and was almost even with the end of the bar. Houston and Walker had turned to face the show.

"Sir, I don't really believe that an Indian engagement is what we need right now," Sam said as Al approached.

Truemain looked crazy. Without a word he shoved Houston and went for his knife. It was a one-punch fight, actually it was a two swing, one-punch fight. When Truemain started for his knife, Sam, although he was moving sideways from the shove, swung at Al. Sam's swing missed, and he fell to the floor, but Joe Walker's didn't. Truemain's head snapped back with such force that Swit thought the captain had surely broken Big Al's neck. Paddy had been reaching for the club he kept behind the bar, but now he was just stunned to see Albert Truemain dropped with one punch. No one moved or made a sound except Big Al. He was lying on the floor, his left leg jerking in a spasmodic movement. You could hear a clicking sound when the heal of his boot tapped the leg of a chair.

It was over, and Billy was glad. This one had almost gone too far. It only took a few minutes before Truemain began to come around. Walker and Houston had gone to the river. Sam claimed that he needed a little splash of water on his face and that his guide and protector should soak his hand. Albert Truemain's friends helped him out the door and into the darkness. Lucy with soldier number two in tow came through the back door, having missed the whole show. She didn't spend any time lamenting her loss, but exchanged number two for three and was gone again. Billy picked up his winnings and headed for the bar. He couldn't see Oo-tse-tee, but guessed that the Indian must still be back in the dark somewhere. Belle had a hold on Boone's hand, and she was doing her best to keep Swit's attention. Swit turned for the bar; all he wanted was to get back to camp before anything else happened.

Paddy's Place was dark, and the fort's palisade gates were closed when Captain Walker passed by. He noticed the glow of a small fire up toward the camp. Riding in closer, he could make out Swit, Billy and the Indian huddled in around the fire. Voices carried on a clear, cool night, especially if a breeze was moving your way. Billy's was the only voice he heard.

"By golly, it's been an unusual day." Walker began to unsaddle Scab and make ready for the night. "Did you men end up winning back that gambling wheel for the boat captain?"

"We didn't zackly get the wheel, but I think old Paddy will need an infusion before they give it another spin," Billy answered. "We took a bit more out than that soldier boy did a while back."

Billy B. had more than made back all the expenses for the evening's activities, both inside and out back. After they left Paddy's Place, Billy shared his good fortune with all hands. He explained that the fiesta was on him, and then handed each one a gold piece sufficient to cover any and all of their expenses. Billy even tried to give Swit an additional twenty dollars. He said it was for riding his gray mare in the horse race. Swit wouldn't have it.

Swit thought it was more relaxing crowded in around the fire. He liked the Indian's company, unless he started asking questions, and he hadn't done that lately. The last time Boone could remember Oo-tse-tee talking was when he told what he had witnessed during the race. It seemed as if Billy didn't mind the Indian either. He probably liked having two listen to him instead of just one. It was better this way, Swit thought, his ears only needed to catch half as many words.

"We did pretty good with the sale today. I've set your wages and your part of the profits aside for you," Captain Walker said. "Have you two made any plans for the future?"

"I haven't decided anything for sure," Billy answered. "I was gonna go to New York and take ol' Boone along, but he's in love now, so I guess we're confined to this area till she runs off with one of them river boat cap'ns."

"I have a mind to ride on one of those riverboats again myself," Walker announced. "I thought I'd head for St. Louis on the one leaving tomorrow. If it wouldn't cause you a lot of extra trouble, I was hoping you could bring Scab back when you come. Billy, I know you have an extra horse to tend. Swit, do you think you and Scab might make it back to Missouri sometime?"

Around Billy B. things just never could stay peaceful, Swit thought. Billy hadn't said one thing about going to New York, and why would he make up a story about him being in love to tell the captain? Swit hadn't thought about what he was going to do tomorrow, let alone what he would do in the future, however long that was. Ever since Billy had told him to stay away from the captain's stallion, he'd wanted to see if he and the horse could work out an understanding.

"I'll take care of your horse, Captain Walker. When do you want him there?" Swit asked.

"When I get home I'll be in no hurry for the horse. If he gives you one speck of trouble just sell him, trade him or shoot him. I'm not married to him. If you men are looking for an adventure to tell your grandchildren, try to be in the old Fort Osage area about this time next year, and look me up. I can't say any more about the why or what for right now. Colonel Arbuckle has your money. It's a fair sum, and safe in his care. You can get it anytime you want it." Walker picked up his bedroll and moved back off into the darkness.

The moon was just rising, and Billy noticed that the Indian was gone. It seemed as if he could come and go like a puff of smoke. Billy thought he could talk Swit into staying around Fort Gibson for a while. Wintering in this country would be softer than in Missouri. The fire was down to its last flicker of light.

Chapter Six

Autumn had a way of slipping in unnoticed. The long, hot, humid summer days that smothered the Missouri countryside were ever so slowly being tempered with cool mornings and pleasant evening sunsets. Joe Walker looked forward to the changing of the seasons. It had been almost a year since he'd left Fort Gibson and made his way back to Missouri. Captain Bonneville had kept him informed, and Walker expected to see him soon. It sounded as if the Army captain had had a busy year.

As soon as Joseph Walker agreed to guide for Captain Bonneville's expedition, Ben reached out to the Army for approval. Colonel Arbuckle supported Bonneville's proposed expedition. He suggested that the best approach would be to get in touch with Major General Alexander Macomb, the commanding officer of the Army of the United States, or General John Eaton the secretary of the War Department.

In May 1831, while Bonneville was in Washington, he contacted General Macomb. The general asked Bonneville to prepare a letter officially requesting permission for his absence. It would be sent through the proper channels. Bonneville thought that it was almost like the general was expecting his request.

While awaiting a reply from his superiors, Captain Bonneville purchased a telescope, sextant and horizon, compass, thermometer, microscope, pocket compass case of instruments, and patent lever timepieces. He took the articles to West Point to hone his skill in using the instruments, and further occupied himself by reading and digesting all the information he could gather from the journals of the explorers: Baron Alexander Von Humboldt, Sir Alexander Mackenzie and William Clark.

On July 29, 1831, General Macomb notified Captain Bonneville that the War Department had approved his leave from the Army until October 1833. The Army's reply to Bonneville's request had percolated through the military red tape faster than expected.

Joseph Walker and Captain Bonneville had discussed the importance of having official documentation for their journey into Oregon, and especially the foreign-controlled territory of California. Bonneville wrote to General Macomb requesting assistance in obtaining approval from both the United States and Mexican governments for traveling in and out of their respective countries. In August, having prepared himself as best he knew and completing the financial arrangements for the trip, Bonneville left New York for the frontier. He arrived in St. Louis in early September.

St. Louis was the primary staging area for most of the merchandise and supplies headed down the trail to New Mexico, or needed in the newly developing settlements along the western frontier. It was the hub where mules brought back from Santa Fe, and pelts and hides that the trappers and traders had gathered in the wilderness could be exchanged for whatever the parties involved thought was of equal value. All matter of dissimilar individuals inhabited and passed through the community. Captain Bonneville searched out anyone that could provide the most current information about the territory that they would soon visit. After working out some details about supplies and equipment with Michael Cerré, he headed for Missouri to meet with Walker.

Captain Bonneville had established areas of responsibility for his men. The expedition would be under his command. He would arrange all the financing and be responsible for gathering and recording the information for the military. Michael Cerré and Joseph Walker were to be his field lieutenants. Cerré would see to the supplies and equipment needed. He would take charge of all the pelts and hides they planned to accumulate, and see them back to the settlements. Walker was to be the guide and advisor. His assignment was to find men appropriate for the trip and the livestock necessary for transportation. Joseph Walker was scouring the settlements of western Missouri for trappers, horses and mules. He knew nothing about the source of the expedition's financial backing, but it appeared to him that money was not a problem. However, finding capable men for their expedition was different story.

A trapper's life was one many men dreamed about, but few had the stamina and courage it took to live in the wild country. The almost unlimited personal freedom and the chance for considerable wealth were more than balanced by ever-present danger and the struggle for survival. The fur country of the northwestern Rockies had proved to be extremely profitable. At one time the British, who owned the Hudson Bay Company, had controlled almost all of the trapping in the area. Now, the United States-based Rocky Mountain and American Fur Companies battled with the Hudson Bay Company, as well as with each other. Accomplished trappers were in short supply.

Most of the experienced men were already contracted to the existing fur companies, or had become involved in the commerce of the Santa Fe Trail. Many of the men Walker selected for the trip were green. He looked past trapping experience and searched for those personal traits that would soon turn inexperience into skill. Joe thought how Billy had more savvy about living in the wilderness than most of the fresh recruits he had engaged. He wondered if Swit or Billy would return before winter set in.

Billy B. and Swit had stayed around the fort after Walker headed back to Missouri. Colonel Arbuckle gave permission for them to make a winter camp at the partially completed Mounted Rangers' quarters. Swit helped some with the construction, and Billy used his talent for hunting. He brought fresh meat to the fort almost every day. Walker's stallion had accepted Swit as his master. At least as much of a master as the captain had been. Paddy's Place had become a favorite spot for Billy and Swit. A welcome remedy for the wintertime blues, was how Billy had put it. Paddy and Billy had become good buddies. Billy had even been asked up to O'Rourke's house, a two-story affair that set on a hill above the river.

"Paddy has a sweet little wife and a house full of young 'uns," Billy told Swit. "L.L. and B.B. each have a room on the top floor. It ain't at all like you'd think; the whole clan treats them whores like they was part of the family. The girls act altogether different at the house than they do down at Paddy's place."

"I don't think I'd care much to be called by letters," was Swit's only comment.

"It was the soldier boys that got to callin' them L.L. and B.B.," Billy recalled. "One of 'em thought Lucy had little legs, so he started callin' her L.L. Another one picked up on that and called Belle B.B., for her big bosom."

"It still don't make sense to me." Swit thought that the soldiers were wasting their time working up initials for people that already had names. "It's hard enough to remember someone's name without making up another one to think about."

Belle would always come around whenever they visited O'Rourke's establishment. She was for hire to anyone that had Paddy's approval, but it was Swit's opinion that Belle preferred the action of a good game of cards to the tent encounters out back. She was a skillful bettor and seldom lost money. Billy couldn't beat her at cards, and Swit watched as she would maneuver him into a game by making comments about his mustache. To Swit it looked as if Billy got what he wanted from B.B., and Belle got what she wanted from Billy B., but it was Billy that did all the paying.

Billy hadn't seen anything of Truemain since he'd been carried out of Paddy's after the fight. Everyone at the settlement seemed to think he was off buying horses for the government. Billy watched the red, white and black colored spinning wheel, with its numbered slots and little white ball, ever so gradually recapturing his previous winnings. He convinced Swit that they should sign on with a party of trappers and head for Mexico. Billy had met two of the men years ago when he was trapping beaver with Captain Walker along the upper Rio Grande River.

All the trappers either knew or heard about Walker's exploits in and around Santa Fe and Taos. The one that Billy seemed to know the best enjoyed telling all who would listen. "I membered Billy when he was just a colt. Rode into Santa Fe just as big as you please—with a damn tough bunch, too." Billy knew that the beaver had been trapped-out in that part of Mexico, and the trappers knew what Billy B. knew. They were determined to push their hunt farther west, maybe clear through to California. Billy B. was bound for Santa Fe.

Swit was ready to get out on the trail again, though it worried him some that the captain wasn't around to lead. By now Swit understood why Captain Walker wanted Scab brought back to Missouri. It was pure pleasure to have the horse under you. Scab drew his share of attention, but there was more to him than just puff. It was necessary to stay alert at all times. Scab was ready to test his rider if there was any indication of a let down. He was just as quick to powerfully respond to Swit's slightest signal. One of the trappers wanted to trade for Captain Walker's big stallion, but Swit explained that it wasn't his horse to trade, and if it had been, he'd be hard put to come up with something that he wanted more than that horse. What bothered Swit most was that instead of returning to Missouri, he and Billy were headed west.

Swit wasn't sure just what Billy had in mind. He'd taken some of their money, along with a couple of deer carcasses that he had aging in a shed up at Paddy's house, down to the river dock and traded for what Swit thought must be things that Indians would like. He got provisions that everyone would need, like coffee and tobacco, but mostly he brought back brightly colored cloth, blankets, shiny trinkets and sparkling stuff. He even had two mirrors. Swit knew that a looking glass was a high-dollar item, and he was sure they'd end up broken or at the very least cracked.

They were traveling along with men bent on trapping, and yet it seemed to Swit as if he and Billy were headed to Mexico to trade. Billy hadn't brought any traps along, but it was hard to tell about Billy—he might trade for traps. Bringing Oo-tse-tee along was another thing Swit couldn't understand. Billy hadn't said anything about the Indian coming with them, but he was there the morning they left. Maybe Billy brought him to help with the trading.

Billy B. was just as confused about the Indian as Swit. He guessed that Swit must have asked him to make the trip. They seemed to enjoy riding along together, although Billy couldn't understand why. Neither man was capable of more than one or two comments in an entire afternoon. Oo-tse-tee had spotted two small bunches of Indians riding in the distance before anyone else in the party noticed them, and as they traveled southwest to where the two forks of the Canadian River join, he found, or already knew about, a spring that surprised even the seasoned scouts. Attacking Indians or a lack of water hadn't been a problem yet, and Oo-tse-tee's discoveries only added to Swit's anxiety about the leadership ability of Billy's trapper friends.

Moving along the south bank of the south fork of the Canadian River, they traveled westward. Gradually the surrounding countryside changed. Swit didn't mind that the hills had stretched out into a broad slowly rolling plain, or that the little feeder streams were fewer and farther apart as they made their way up river. The timber country was behind them now. This was a land of grass and sagebrush. The winding river plateau was flanked by ridges of rocky bluffs and crisscrossed with the cuts and canyons of smaller watercourses. The dry, sandy creek beds and the arid surroundings didn't jibe with the water-carved escarpment they were traveling through. Swit could only conclude that from time to time a great deal of water must flow through this country. He wondered about the settlements of Taos and Santa Fe that he'd heard the trappers talk about. It sounded as if they were located somewhere in the mountains. He had never seen mountains, and this country wasn't at all like what he thought it would look like. Swit knew one thing, though; Missouri was getting farther away.

Oo-tse-tee tried to keep from daydreaming as he rode along. He knew his time was better used paying attention to what was here and now, but he enjoyed thinking about why men acted and did the things they did. It seemed to him that all men, no matter their color, acted in similar ways. Red, white, black and brown were the only colors he knew. He'd heard tell of a yellow colored people, and one time he thought maybe he saw one on board a steamboat—he didn't know anything about them. Oo-tse-tee thought that the men he'd known didn't differ that much when it came to their consideration for someone unlike themselves.

There were a few individuals that just naturally seemed to not notice any color difference. They treated you pretty much in accordance to how you treated them, but more than a few saw only color and reacted, just as naturally, in a hateful manner. All the others seemed to be trying to work out what was natural for them without upsetting already established friendships and at the same time hold true to their own feelings. Oo-tse-tee guessed that he probably belonged to the last group. He was trying to not notice the color difference, but it was hard. White people, as a rule, just acted so different. Many of his Indian friends thought he was crazy to spend so much time with the whites. They had no honor.

The night had brought another beautiful sunset. Swit never seemed to tire of watching the sun go down in this wide-open place. It would gradually slip from sight as you gazed out across the seemingly endless space between where you were, and the end of the day. The light slowly faded until a sharp division started to form between a huge pale blue colored sky and the darkening earth. On the western horizon a pink brilliance slowly captured the sky and spread itself sideways until it was impossible to see it all in one view. As the twilight settled in, the earth changed from a variety of shadows into a common blackness. The daylight continued to fade, and the pink part of the sky changed into an orange-red glow that was brightest just above the spot where the sun had disappeared. Ever so gradually it dimmed into varying degrees of redness as it spread up into what remained of the fading blue sky.

Swit thought about how it was a grand show and took a long time to develop. Sometimes there were fluffy clouds that played with the colors in the sky and created changing shades and patterns of nature's beauty. Eventually the redness was pulled down and disappeared into the dark earth. The sky faded into shades of gray, and the gray gradually became darker and darker until there was no longer a division. The sunset had turned into night, and the sky was decorated in a luminous configuration of stars.

The trail led the men west just before the river started its swing to the north. Billy wasn't sure just where they were; but he told Swit, and hoped he was right, that they were following along an old trace that led from Fort Smith to Santa Fe. He was pretty sure that before they reached the mountains they'd cross the Santa Fe Trail.

"Are you lookin' for the Rockies?" Billy noticed that Swit had been studying the sky to the west. "I member the first time I seen 'em. I was just a tad and had this idea in my mind, you know, what they'd look like. I'd heard the bunch I was with talk about them mountains a lot. Well, anyhow, they weren't nothin' like I figured."

Swit had listened to the trappers' tales, and when he thought about the Rocky Mountains he envisioned a looming, rough, rocky, cold, dangerous, snow- and tree-covered home for bears and mountain lions. "Billy, how are we gonna ride over the top of them Rockies?"

"You ain't gonna ride over no mountains on old Scab," Billy B. answered. "He's a high stepper, but I can see right off that he's no snow horse. Three jumps out in the snow and he'll be belly deep and tryin' to buck. The only way you'd get him across is to shoot him, skin him and make a sled out of his hide. Then most likely he'll get away from ya goin' down the other side and hit a tree."

"Your ol' gray mare won't even make it up to the snow line." Swit could see that Billy was in the mood to go on and on about horses crossing snow-covered mountains. There wasn't any point in trying to find out any real information about getting over the mountains. "That's how we lost the race. She couldn't run uphill."

"Now you see that's where you're confusin' racin' and mountain climbin'," Billy said. "If you was any judge of horseflesh at all you could see that she's built to run on the flat and travel in the snow. In this mountain climbin' business it ain't so much how big and strong you are, it's how quick and light you can move your feet. I 'spect the gray to almost float over snow. She's sure to be good for two, maybe three mountain crossin's a day."

Swit realized it was best to just ride along and listen. He wondered what Oo-tse-tee knew about the Rockies, but there really wasn't much use asking him. He'd just say, "Go up and go over."

The next day Swit got his first look at the mountains. It was like they weren't there, and then all of a sudden they were. At first he thought the barely visible line was a wall cloud way in the distance. As they traveled closer and the line became clearer, he could pick out the ridges. He knew then that it had to be the mountains. All doubt was gone when he could see snow covering the tops of the peaks. Boone thought that watching for mountains was about the opposite of waiting for the sun to set. Sunsets took a while to play out. Mountains popped into view without warning.

The trail westward was redirecting itself more to the north when the trappers decided to leave it behind and head for the Rio Grande River. They planned to follow down the Rio Grande, eventually working their way over into the mountains that produced the feeder streams for the Gila River. The Gila would lead them westward. It was time to bid his friends farewell, Billy thought, from here to Santa Fe it would be just himself, Swit and probably the Indian.

"You figurin' on bringin' the Injun along with ya to Santa Fe?" Billy asked.

"I didn't bring Oo-tse-tee nowhere," Boone answered. "In fact, I thought you was the one that invited him along."

"Now don't that beat all." Billy was shaking his head. "Here we been travelin' along, day after day, through Injun country with a red spy. We're lucky we ain't all been massacred. I guess by now it's too late to try and get on his good side by askin' him to come with us. If he rides off and leaves us I 'spect we can look for an Injun raid."

What beats all, Swit thought, is how Billy B. could think that Oo-tse-tee was a spy. He hadn't done anything but help since they'd known him.

"I'll tell you one thing, if Oo-tse-tee rides off, I'm likely to ride off with him. Especially if he rides away from them mountains."

"It's turnin' out just like I was afraid it might." Billy was doing his best to feign disappointment. "Ever since you buddied up with that Injun, I knew it was just a matter of time before you'd be wearin' feathers and beads. I guess old Scab'll prob'ly end up in some ol' squaw's stew pot."

"Well, I'd rather be used up in a stew than end up as a sled," Swit answered. "You know just as well as I do that Oo-tse-tee is a good friend, and he hasn't done nothing but right by us. If we go on to Santa Fe I'll bet he'll come with us, and I for one will welcome his coming."

Billy B. looked over at Swit and winked. A smile that seemed to spread out from Boone's eyes slowly developed. Santa Fe would be a new experience for Swit, and Billy looked forward to seeing if the old settlement was still the same.

Chapter Seven

Billy, Swit and Oo-tse-tee reached the Santa Fe Trail before noon. The celebrated path from Missouri to Mexico looked much like Billy remembered, except it showed more wear. Billy B. was a running travelogue as they moved along.

"Now over there is Starvation Peak. Way back, a bunch of Spaniards crawled up on top of that peak to keep from bein' wiped out by Injuns. Well, the red men surrounded 'em and kept them black eyes up there till they was all starved to death. Been called Starvation Peak ever since."

"That just don't make sense." Swit thought that the butte was way too big for even a whole tribe of Indians to surround. "I might climb up there to keep from getting killed, but I wouldn't stay to starve. The first dark night I'd slip down and make for the settlements. Besides, there ain't no peak to it at all; its top is as flat as a table."

Oo-tse-tee thought how Billy B. liked to sort people according to their color. The Spaniards were black eyes, and Indians were red men. White men that spent most of their time outside turned darker—some even had a reddish hue about 'em—and in fact his eyes and Swit's were as brown as most Spaniards. He guessed it was kinda like Billy's tale about Starvation Peak. It didn't have to be exactly as Billy told it as long as it made a good story.

The trail led the three riders to San Miguel Del Vado, the first Mexican village east of Santa Fe. In the distance it looked the same as Billy remembered, with continuous adobe houses forming a large rectangular fort that surrounded the plaza. An adobe church, with its twin towers, was the most noticeable structure. They crossed the Pecos River just east of the plaza and entered the village through a large gate that the settlers closed during Indian attacks. Although things had looked the same, there was a difference. Billy remembered how they had been welcomed in the old days. He would never forget the generosity of the villagers, especially the *señoritas*. This had all changed.

Now, there was nothing special about the coming and going of strangers, and the Mexican government had posted officials in the plaza that Billy had to deal with before receiving permission to continue on to Santa Fe. The government collected a tax on all trade goods entering Mexico. The men in charge called it progress, but to Billy the villagers weren't as carefree or even as happy as they had once been. Progress hadn't made their lives any better.

The trio followed along a trail running up the western side of the Pecos River. It took them up and over Glorieta Pass before turning to the northwest and crossing the Santa Fe River. The Santa Fe plaza was straight ahead. It was a hive of activity.

Swit never expected Santa Fe to look like it did. It was an old town, and there were people and all matter of things going on everywhere at once. The plaza was cluttered with trappers, traders, soldiers, Spaniards, Mexican natives, Indians, clergyman, children of all ages, horses, oxen, mules, sheep, chickens, a few cows, dogs, wagons, two-wheeled carts and now the three riders from Fort Gibson.

The activity was unwavering. The adults were busy unloading, loading, buying, selling or just moving around from one place to another. The children played games like hide and seek and chased each other. Animals, wagons and carts moved in and out of the plaza, creating clouds of dust that covered everything, especially the shabby-looking adobe buildings that randomly surrounded the plaza. Some traders were selling their goods in the withered open air of the plaza, while others offered their wares out of rented stores in the rundown buildings. Yet, in the midst of this dusty, drab, confusing background there was one thing that lifted Swit's spirit. Some of the Mexicans of substance adorned themselves in a lively combination of colors.

The ladies dressed in brightly colored full skirts, low-cut blouses and head scarves called *rebozos*. However, it was the men that arrayed themselves in splendor. From their *sombreros* down to their boots and spurs they were a mixture of brightly dyed cloth, tinsel cord, silver, tinkling filigree buttons and embossed leather. Their horses were also decked out in shiny polished saddles, bridles and woven multicolored blankets. It was exciting to see.

"By golly, things has changed a bit." Billy B. was surprised at all the activity. "Last time I was here there weren't half this many people. That big building on the other side of the plaza, that's the governor's palace. Manuel Armijo's was the main man around here then. His lady of the evening deals monte in a kinda private club over where all those horses are tied. In the old days they'd let us in the place. I'm gonna go over and see what I can find out."

"Oo-tse-tee went somewhere, and now you're going off to play cards. I guess I'll just wait for you here in the plaza." Swit felt alone and knew that his inability to speak Spanish was going to be a handicap.

"I'm guessin' that Oo-tse-tee's prob'ly checkin' out the Injuns that's camped down along the river," Billy said. "You know we need to find that Injun another name, somethin' with sort of a Mexican flavor. It'll make for less problems if he's gonna hang out with us while we're here. Them black eyes is real touchy about Injuns. What do ya say to Otis Tejas?"

"I don't guess Oo-tse-tee cares what he's called, but I don't take much to remembering another name for one I already know," Boone answered. "What's Tejas all about? Was it somebody famous?"

"I don't know," Billy said. "I've heard the Spaniards use that word when they're talkin' about friendly type Injuns. Anyhow, it's gotta be better than Oo-tse-tee. Why don't you see what you can find out from the American element around here while I try to get into that gamblin' hall."

Swit watched as Billy headed for a building that had several men lazing around by the front door. He tied his horses to the rail, and it looked as if he had come across someone he knew. After some backslapping and chatter, Billy went through the door and out of sight. Swit was uneasy about leaving Scab and his packhorse tied up while he wandered around the plaza. He rode toward a wagon where several men, dressed like they were from the States, were busy unloading and moving boxes into an old building. One freighter in particular caught Swit's eye. The man was black, and Swit thought he looked to be about the same age that he was. In Swit's experience black meant slave, but the way this man carried himself and related to those around him, you knew he was a free man. Swit guessed that he qualified for what Billy had called an American element.

"Howdy, my name's Swit Boone. I just got here from Fort Gibson. Did you come down the trail from Missouri?"

"Glad to meet you," the black man said as he extended his hand in greeting. "My name's Reginald Harris, but everybody calls me Hog Eye. We got here last night, seventy-three days on the trail from Independence. It was a good thing that there was a bunch of us, too. Them Comanch ain't very neighborly. That sure is a nice-looking horse you're riding."

"Damn it, Hog Eye, quit your jawin' and get to totin'," an older man standing in the wagon said. "You'll have plenty of time to jabber. Let's get these goods inside."

"I better get to moving, but I'll be done here in no time," Hog Eye said as he climbed up into the wagon. "As soon as I get this stuff inside I'll be at that little canteen over there. Come on over."

Swit was heavy in thought about his new friend's name. He didn't know if he could call him Hog Eye. It didn't seem respectful. Reginald was loaded with respect, but it didn't fit the man. He was thinking along the lines of Mister Harris when someone grabbed him by the shoulder and spun him around—hard. A man adorned in the finest Spanish attire had done the spinning. Five more men, all horseback and ready for action, formed a quarter circle behind their leader. The Spaniard was talking in a loud voice, and in a language Swit didn't understand. His men had a rope around Oo-tse-tee's neck, and they didn't seem to mind that their actions were painful for the Indian. Hog Eye peered out of the wagon and shouted to Swit. "He's trying to find out if you know the Indian. Don Carlos thinks he's one of the raiders that tried to burn his ranch, but the Indian says that he's with you."

"He's with me." Swit was focused on the man in front of him. "Tell him his name is Otis Tejas, and he just rode in with me and Billy B. from Fort Gibson. He's got the wrong man, and I ain't liking the way he's treating him."

Apparently the Spaniard understood some English because he immediately had his men free Oo-tse-tee, and it seemed as if he was apologizing. "He says he's sorry," Hog Eye translated. "He's still upset about the Indians trying to burn him out, but he knows now that he made a mistake, and he'd like to apologize by taking both of you over to Doña Tules."

"Tell him it's not necessary. No harm done," Swit said.

By this time Hog Eye was standing beside Swit and whispered, "He's insisting that you come with him. You know, you really should go. Don Carlos is a very important man in this country. He feels bad about the way your friend was treated, and if you'd go with him it'd make him feel better. Besides, I've tried every trip to get an invite into Doña Tule's place, and it ain't happened yet. You can tell me all about it later."

"Thank Don Carlos for the invitation, and tell him we'd be pleased to go if he'll take you with us," Swit told Hog Eye. "I need someone to do my listening and talking for me."

Don Carlos, when he wasn't mad, had a big, toothy smile. It was obvious that he understood Swit's instructions and was completely agreeable to the condition. What Swit wondered was could he talk the language as good as he understood it. Hog Eye hollered to someone named James about going with Don Carlos Suarez, and James reluctantly consented. One of Suarez's men politely brought Oo-tse-tee his horse. Don Carlos was still smiling and gesturing with his arms and hands as they headed for the same building that Billy had disappeared into. Swit tied his horses next to Billy's. Oo-tse-tee said that he would wait outside, but Don Carlos would have none of that. He handed Otis's horse to one of his men and personally escorted the Indian, Swit and then Hog Eye through the door.

From its outside appearance, Swit had expected something along the line of Paddy's Place. As rough as the building looked outside, he couldn't have prepared himself for the opulence inside. The walls were papered in calico, and the windows decorated with colored cloth, all of it in shades of red. The bar and gambling tables were made from carved dark wood and some had marble tops. Numerous mirrors and paintings were hung on the walls.

The place was full, but not crowded, with men that looked to be better off than the average Santa Fe citizen. As far as Swit could tell they were either gambling, drinking, smoking a pipe or all three. One man at the bar had his tobacco rolled into a short sticklike shape. The bartender called it a *cigarrito*. A strikingly attractive, properly dressed Spanish lady seated underneath one of the windows was dealing monte to several of the men. Swit couldn't pick Billy out in the crowd. Maybe this place had a back door like Paddy's, and Billy was busy, how'd he say it, seeing what he could find out.

Don Carlos led them directly to the bar and ordered drinks all around. Hog Eye was trying to tell Swit what everyone was saying, and Oo-tse-tee was doing his best not to look nervous. It was plain that if there had ever been an Indian or a black in this place, it hadn't occurred regularly. When they walked in, everyone turned to see who had entered—the room got quiet. Don Carlos addressed the gathering, and Hog Eye informed Swit that he announced that these three men were his friends. After that it quickly returned too normal. Drinks were set up, and Hog Eye was repeating everything Don Carlos said as he told the story about how he'd made a big mistake misidentifying Otis Tejas.

"My God, Boone, it just ain't safe to leave you alone anymore." Billy had walked up behind Swit and laid a hand on his shoulder. Swit turned, and Billy had a big smile on his face and a pretty young girl on his arm. "I no more than turn you loose on these Santa Fe'ites, and you go and gathered up the biggest cow man in the territory. Now you've broke in here with the first Injun to ever duck under that door. Hell, you even brought along your own slave to interpret for ya."

"Billy B., I knew it must be you that this man said he was traveling with. Welcome back my good friend," Don Carlos was talking and Hog Eye didn't need to translate. The English had a strange sound, but it was plain enough. "I see you didn't waste any time finding *señorita* Delgado."

"First things first is what you always said. Don Carlos, how did you fall in with this motley crew that I'm ridin' with now? I hope ol' Swit didn't come out to the ranch and kidnap ya. Hell, forty to fifty *vaqueros* wouldn't detour him one bit. I saw him take on a whole party of Injuns out on a meadow one time."

Billy was being Billy, Swit thought. Most of the men at the bar stopped talking after Billy's last statement, and they were directing their attention at Swit. It made him nervous, but it was obvious to Swit that anyone that could handle Indians was looked upon with respect—even if it was more story than fact. "I met Mister Don Carlos out in the plaza, and he was nice enough to ask us to this place."

"We have not been introduced." Don Carlos was looking at Billy. "I did him and his friend a great mistake, and for this I'm sorry."

"Well, let me make the introductions," Billy said. "Don Carlos, I would like to introduce you to Mister Stewart Jarvis Boone. I'm sure he would like you to call him Swit. This Injun's name is Otis Tejas. He doesn't talk much, but I've found him to be of splendid character. I'm sorry, but I'm not acquainted with this black gentleman; however, I would like you all to meet Don Carlos Suarez. If you spend your life lookin', you wouldn't find a better man."

"His name is Mister Harris," Swit said. "I asked him to come along cause he talks the lingo." The thought went through Swit's mind how Billy B. was just as relaxed performing in front of a group of people as he was when just the two of 'em rode along together. Don Carlos, Billy, Swit, Hog Eye and the Indian were shaking hands with each other, and anyone else that was close by and cared to make hellos. Violin and guitar music was coming from the far end of the room, and it seemed like everyone wanted to buy drinks. Swit turned to ask Hog Eye what the Spaniard giving him a drink was saying. The black man and the Indian were gone. Oo-tse-tee had pulled another one of his vanishing acts, and this time he took Hog Eye with him.

Oo-tse-tee was confused about why first Swit and then Billy had introduced him as Otis Tejas. It was obvious that most of the men around the bar thought that the Indian was in a place that he shouldn't be. The black man must have felt the same because Mister Harris and Oo-tse-tee both started working their way toward the door as soon as Billy had everyone's attention.

Billy knew exactly how he wanted to sell their supplies when he and Swit left Doña Tules Gertrudes Barcelo's establishment. He found a spot next to the canteen and started to display their trade items. In no time at all they were surrounded by women looking over the bright cloth and shiny objects. Señorita Delgado was still standing next to Billy. The two mirrors had made the trip unharmed, and after the first one sold for twenty times it's cost, Swit just sat down and watched the show. Three señoritas got in a fight over the second mirror, and while they were rolling around on the ground a chicken spooked and flew up under the skirt of the one that looked to be winning the battle. The fracas had drawn a fair-sized crowd, and now half of them were laid back in laughter. In less than an hour Billy had disposed of all the merchandise and replaced it with a skin full of gold and silver coins.

Swit was puzzled over the origin of all the coins they were seeing. Billy explained about the silver mines that the Spanish had discovered to the south, and the placer gold that the Mexicans found a couple of years ago in the dry, scrub-covered Ortiz Mountains. The Spanish had sent most of their precious metal back to Spain, but after the Mexicans took control, they made coins out of the silver and gold and used it to purchase merchandise coming down the trail from the States.

"Instead of tradin' supplies for other supplies, it's customary in this country to trade coins for what ya need." Billy B was trying to clarify Swit's concern. "Carryin' a few coins beats haulin' around a crate full of chickens."

"If I was hungry, I believe I take the chickens," Swit answered. He knew that gold and silver had value, but was unsure of the amount of coins it would take to get what you wanted.

Don Carlos owned an adobe house on the edge of Santa Fe; and he offered it to Billy, Swit and Otis Tejas as a place to bed down while they were in town. Then he invited them all to come out to the *rancho* on Sunday afternoon for a fiesta. When Billy and Swit left the plaza they couldn't find Oo-tse-tee. Mister Harris had a group of traders gathered around his wagon, and Swit waved to Hog Eye as they left the plaza. The black man paused briefly to return the greeting before continuing with what Swit was pretty sure was a full account of his most recent experiences.

Chapter Eight

Oo-tse-tee was blessed with uncommon eyesight. He could determine the identity of a distant spot on the horizon before anyone else, and for this reason the wagonmaster had asked him to ride at the front of the train and keep a lookout. Billy B. was riding his gray mare, and Swit was aboard Scab. They'd positioned themselves, one behind the other, off to one side of the wagon train. A breeze kept them out of the dust cloud kicked up by the wagons. Billy was not himself. For three days they'd traveled through country that he'd crossed many times, but he rarely spoke to Swit—no stories, tales or comments.

Swit was worried about Billy. It wasn't Billy B.'s style to ride along mile after mile and not say anything. He pondered the problem and wondered if he'd done something to cause the slump in Billy's spirit. When they'd first arrived in Santa Fe everything seemed fine. Don Carlos mistaking Oo-tse-tee for one of the Indians that had raided his ranch had kick-started their stay with a certain amount of excitement, and Billy was back with old friends in familiar surroundings. The fiesta at Don Carlos's *rancho* introduced Swit to a new way of life. He'd spent most of the spring and summer out at the ranch. Billy spent most of his time in Santa Fe with Señorita Maria Delgado. Swit and Billy didn't see each other every day, but when they did it seemed to Swit that everything was all right.

Swit wasn't exactly sure how to describe Billy and Maria's relationship. To begin with, he thought it was just kind of a business arrangement. Like Billy had explained, you took silver and bought what you wanted or needed from those willing to sell. Maria sure had what Billy wanted, and it was for sale too—but not to everyone. Many a buyer had walked away still holding his silver.

Maria was an easy thing to look at. Swit could picture the way her black hair danced around her face when she talked, especially when she laughed. It would have been hard to fault her appearance. The Almighty had given Maria his blessing from her hair all the way down to her trim ankles and small feet. Swit thought that he probably took extra time when he fashioned her face, especially the eyes. They would radiate and sparkle with happiness, love, laughter and fun. It was impossible for her to hide her feelings.

Those dark eyes told all of her passions, and they were capable of extreme change—almost immediately. Before Swit could perceive a transformation coming, hate and anger would replace the sparkle, and two black objects would fix on their target. It was not pleasant. Sadness sometimes moved in, but it came slower and stayed longer. As the weeks went by, Maria and Billy spent more and more time together, most of it in Santa Fe, but occasionally they'd visit Don Carlos at his ranch.

Don Carlos was just as Billy had said. A finer man you couldn't encounter. Carlos Suarez looked after the trio from Fort Gibson like they were family. It really wasn't that unusual for Don Carlos, he treated almost everyone in that manner. Everyone except those who tried to do him or his friends harm. When he hung the three horse thieves in the trees east of Pena Blanca, Swit realized that Don Carlos Suarez was the best kind of friend and the worst kind of enemy.

Swit especially enjoyed being around the *vaqueros*. Their horsemanship and ability to handle livestock fascinated him. He tried to establish a friendship between himself and the men, but the feeling wasn't always mutual—especially when Billy was around. Swit thought he knew the reason; Maria Delgado had stopped all sales. At a time when she was Santa Fe's most alluring strumpet, and could turn the head of everyone in the plaza, she made herself available to just one man.

Swit considered himself to be a fair hand with horses, but soon realized he was no match for the *vaqueros*. Scab and Swit's willingness to enter into the games around the ranch brought attention to this strange horseman from the north. Juan Marquez and Francisco Barrera were the first to befriend Swit. They saw in him a natural ability with horses, and they liked the way he tried and lost without complaint. Swit remembered them from the plaza. They had been two of the riders who accompanied Don Carlos. Franciso had brought Oo-tse-tee his horse.

Otis Tejas visited the ranch from time to time, and Don Carlos always greeted him in grand style, but he never seemed to stay around long. As far as Swit could tell he was spending most of his time with the Indians camped along the river. He'd even changed his manner of dress to be more in keeping with their style. Swit and Billy were helping to move cattle one morning when they saw a small party of Indians in the distance. Oo-tse-tee was on a big buckskin horse riding out in front with the leaders. The turban was gone from his head, and he had a wild look about him. The *vaqueros* always got real nervous whenever they saw any Indians on horseback.

"I'm bettin' the Injun has found himself a squaw down there on the river," Billy told Swit. "I spect he'll raise his own little bunch of fighters and take over Santa Fe." Oo-tse-tee hadn't said much lately, but Swit hadn't seen any sign of him taking a wife. Billy could come up with the damnedest notions.

With the help of Juan Marquez and Francisco Barrera, Swit Boone's life was changing. Living out at the ranch was exactly where Swit wanted to be. He started wearing a broad-brimmed hat, boots and spurs. Juan and Cisco brought Swit a forty-foot length of braided rawhide rope that they called *la reata*. He practiced daily with his new lariat. Swit's attempts at roping provided entertainment for the *vaqueros*. He learned to build a loop, throw and snare a cow, jerk the slack, and take a dally without losing his hat, stirrup or thumb. The *vaqueros* had laughed at his inability, but later gave him a new pair of *chaparreras* before taking him with them into the country south of Santa Fe. Without those chaps the brush, cactus spines and mesquite thorns would have chewed up his legs. Swit was learning the workings of a ranch. He felt like he could do this forever, but time was rushing by, and he hadn't forgotten his promise to Captain Walker. Scab would be back in Missouri by fall.

When Swit told Billy that he was getting ready to head back to Missouri. Billy acted like he couldn't remember any plan for them to be in the Fort Osage area before winter. He was plum full of justifications for why they should stay in Santa Fe, and he asked Swit, "Why risk gettin' killed just to deliver a horse?" Swit explained to Billy that he didn't have to go along, there were several caravans that planned to leave Santa Fe before winter. They were always glad to have an extra gun travel along with them, and if you were willing to lend a hand with the work they'd even feed you.

Swit and Billy still had the use of Don Carlos's place in Santa Fe, but the closer it got to leaving time the less he saw Billy. Swit thought that he was making the trip alone, but the morning he was to leave, Billy and Oo-tse-tee showed up, all packed and ready to travel. Swit would never forget the look on Señorita Delgado's face as they rode out of the plaza. Sadness had filled those big beautiful eyes to the point that it spilled over and ran down her cheeks. It was a haunting look of despair.

Billy was quiet from the start. Swit thought that he was probably just not feeling his best. Maybe he even had a pain somewhere. At first he kept looking back, and Swit thought maybe someone was following them. There were two separate caravans moving along the trail together. One was made up of pack mules, and they intended to turn north and cross over the mountains on their way to the Arkansas River before heading east to the States. It was their contention that along the mountain route water was more plentiful and an Indian attack less likely. It was admittedly the longer of the two paths; however, it would pass by the new fort that the Bent brothers, along with Ceran St. Vrain, had started building along the Arkansas River. The post was a welcome break to the daily routine of traveling along the Santa Fe Trail, and a source of supplies for those in need. The other group of traders had wagons pulled by oxen. They planned to take the Cimarron cut-off.

"What do you think, Billy? Which way shall we go?" Swit asked.

"The cut-off's shorter," Billy answered. "Hotter and drier, but shorter."

That's all he would say. Swit wasn't sure if that meant they should go north, or go hot, dry and short. He didn't like the sound of crossing any mountains, so he took the cut-off. They all three took the cut-off.

"Billy miss the señorita bad," Oo-tse-tee said to Swit. "He not want to leave Santa Fe."

Swit didn't answer. It wasn't like the Indian would expect a comment. He was standing right there when Swit told Billy that he didn't need to come along. Maybe Billy's problem did have something to do with Maria.

Swit was surprised how easy it was moving along toward the Cimarron River. They'd left the mountains in the background, but they still crossed creeks and streams of water that flowed down out of the high country, so thirst was not a problem. Swit missed Billy's tales. They moved through some rougher country that the wagoners called the Cimarron Breaks. Somehow the sun seemed hotter. An occasional spring would surface beside the trail, but the watering holes were starting to get farther apart. The Cimarron was a big disappointment to Swit. He'd envisioned a river carrying fresh, cool, clear water, and lined with shade trees and green grass. He found only a few trees, and any green grass that might have been along the river had long ago been eaten by buffalo or animals moving along the trail. What water the river did carry, and that was very little and not too far, was dirty, brackish and not safe to drink. What you found mostly was dry riverbed sand.

Their horses stayed in fairly good condition, so Swit reasoned that the short, sparse dried grass in this country must be healthy for livestock, providing they could get enough of it. Water was the biggest problem, and every time they came to a spring it raised everyone's spirits.

Middle Spring was especially inviting. Clear, fresh water flowed from the ground on the north side of the Cimarron. It formed a pond that some might even call a small lake. The water was surrounded by a nice little grove of trees, and green grass could be found close to the pond's edge. It was a favorite place for travelers to spend some time and rest their animals. When they arrived, a caravan of traders coming from the east was camped at the spring. The news about the death of Jed Smith soon spread to the newcomers. Swit knew the name and remembered that he was famous for something, but wasn't sure just what.

"My God," Billy said. "He's about the same age as the cap'n. The last I heard he was headed for St. Louis. You say that the Comanch got him?" It was the most Billy had said since they'd left Santa Fe.

"A group moving ahead of your bunch was already camped at the next spring downriver when we got there. They told us all about it," one of the traders said. "Smith was leading a bunch out of St. Louis. It's said that they ran out of water, so he struck out on his own to find Lower Spring. He found it all right, but a Comanche hunting party found him. It cost the Indians some, though—Smith killed their chief."

"When'd all this happen?" Billy asked.

"As I got it, just not too long ago," the trader answered. "The man who told us all about it said that he guessed that Smith must had been out of his head from lack of water, and about dead when he found the spring. Otherwise no Indians could have snuck up on Jedediah Strong Smith."

Billy turned away from the traders, muttering, "That man don't know a damn thing about Jed Smith."

Swit and Oo-tse-tee followed Billy when he left the circle of traders. "Did you know the man?" Swit ask Billy. "I've heard of him, but I didn't know him."

"Any man that figures no Injun could sneak up on Jed Smith didn't know him any better than you," Billy answered. "I met him once, a long time back. I didn't much take to him. He thought he knew everything, and he didn't mind tellin' ya all about it. Carried a Bible around with him all the time and told how he was a workin' God's will."

74

"Was he a preacher?" Swit asked.

"Nah, he's a mountain man," Billy answered. "He's a hell of a trapper, or was, I guess it is now. Tuck told me he took six hundred sixty eight pelts all by himself durin' the hunt in '24 and '25. That's some pretty fancy trappin'. He was plenty tough too. On his first trip out a griz tried to chew his head off. His men got to him in time and killed the bear, but part of Smith's scalp and one ear was peeled away. They all thought he was as good as dead. Smith had'em sew his ear and scalp back on. Ten days later he was up and goin' again."

Swit wanted to ask how Jed Smith looked after he got his ear reattached, but was so glad to hear Billy's words that he just nodded and hoped that Billy would keep talking. When he didn't, Swit decided to see if he could get Billy started again. "Did he trap with Captain Walker in the old days?"

"I never heard that." Billy couldn't remember that he had ever heard the captain mention Smith's name. "He must of been a lot like Cap'n Walker when it came to explorin' new territory. He had to love goin' where others ain't been. I heard he traveled all over the western mountains, was over in Californy, and even went up into the Oregon country. If that's true, he was some trailblazer. I'll tell ya what, though, if you was a goin' with him you'd better take a good look around fore ya leave. More likely than not you ain't comin' back. Lot of men that went with Smith found their end somewhere along the trail. He made two trips across the Great Sandy Basin into the Californy settlements, but he couldn't get along with Injuns, the Spanish, or the Mexican government. Them that was lucky enough to survive the trips ended up in jail. They'd prob'ly all still be there too, if they hadn't had help from the cap'n of an American ship that was anchored in the harbor."

"A Mexican jail don't sound too good to me, but I believe it'd beat getting killed." Swit tried to keep the conversation going.

"There ain't no good jails," Billy said. "But it seems to me if your travelin' with Jedediah Smith you'd be a whole lot safer in jail than out on the trail. He led a total of thirty-three men toward the Californy territory, and twenty-six of 'em didn't make the round trip—ten didn't even get to see Californy."

"Did they run out of water crossing the Great Sandy Basin?" Swit didn't know what or where the basin was located, but it sounded dry. "I'd hate to be without water."

"Nah, I heard Injuns killed most of 'em," Billy answered. "It ain't that Smith wasn't a hell of a trapper and trailblazer, 'cause he was. He just wasn't a man I'd a cared to follow. I been in several tight spots with Cap'n Walker

75

and didn't get much more of anything done to me than being scared. Smith said he always made it 'cause God was with him. I guess maybe God don't travel the Santa Fe." Billy turned and headed back toward his gray mare. It seemed to Swit that Billy B. was spending more time fooling with that horse than he used to.

"Billy more like the old Billy B.," Oo-tse-tee said. Swit thought how it had been more like old times to listen to Billy's words.

Swit couldn't see any sign of an Indian fight when they reached Lower Spring. It was a nice little spring, and the water was fresh, but it wasn't a shady place like Middle Spring. One of the bullwackers found an arrowhead and thought he could tell where the killing took place. Another was sure that the Indians had been riding to the spring from the east before they ambushed old Jed. Billy just walked away when they tried to get him involved in the story. The old Billy B. would have had great fun tangling up the wagoners in their stories about Jed Smith, his fight with the Indians and how the chief died—but not today.

The long, dry run was in front of them now. They took all the water they could carry and left the Cimarron, heading northeast for the Arkansas River. Swit asked one of the wagoners how far it was to the next water. The bullwhacker thought it was about a hundred miles. Swit was glad that each wagon had two water barrels. But when you figured that each wagon was pulled by six oxen, and that each one of them could drink fifteen to twenty gallons of water a day, it added up to short rations for both man and beast.

Swit was starting to understand the meaning of hot and dry. Day after day they rode along. The sun pushed down on them like it wanted them cooked, and the wind blew from the south like it wanted them north. All this didn't happen once in a while, it happened every day—all day. The wind continued to blow day and night. Everything was scorched, and each step taken by animal or man brought up a puff of dust. Swit was beginning to understand the look on the faces of the traders when they talked of their trips through the *Jornada*.

Before the caravan stopped for the night they discovered the results of some Indians' handiwork. A burned wagon and a dead mule lay off to the south side of the trail. There were two fresh graves on top a slight rise back behind the wagon. "Comanch or Kiowa," Billy volunteered, "maybe both."

"Why would they want to attack someone just moving along?" Swit asked. "They didn't mean no harm to those Indians."

"The Injun figures different," Billy answered. "It's his territory, and unless you got a right of passage, you ain't welcome. They always tries to hit them trains that has horses and mules. If you're gonna risk gettin' killed servin' notice to the passer-bys, you just as well get yourself a horse or two in the process."

"So only Indians can travel through here safely?" Swit asked.

"Injuns north of the Arrowpoint ain't welcome either. Best way to travel is like the cap'n does. He mostly rides along with the okay of them that lives there. If he can't get that, he's prepared to defend what he thinks is his rights."

"Well, it don't make much sense to me to just kill someone that's not doing you any hurt." Swit couldn't see Billy's point, but it was refreshing to hear him talk like he used to. "Where's this Arrowpoint that some Indians ain't suppose to cross?"

"Flint Arrowpoint is what the Injun calls the Arkansas River," Billy answered. "To the Injun, them that travel this trail are doin' him hurt. You're trampin' out and eatin' off what little grass there is, and usin' up what skimpy water this place provides. That's to say nothin' about the game ya kill and run off. It's a hard country to live in. You might be glad for a snowstorm about now, but if you stay here till winter you'll find all the cold you'd care to handle. I know it seems strange that anyone would kill someone crazy enough to travel through this forsaken country, but they been doin' just that for hundreds a years. It's home to 'em, and they ain't lookin' to share it. At least not with anyone as outlandish as us."

Swit wasn't sure what Billy's last statement meant. It must have something to do with the fact that he and Billy didn't own any land. He could understand what Billy was saying about the Indians protecting their home. Still, it seemed as if there must be a better way than killing those who were not invited.

Swit worried that the Arkansas River would be like the Cimarron. It wasn't; instead it was the biggest river they'd seen since they left the Canadian. There were a few cottonwood trees and some small stands of willows scattered along its course. The water wasn't clear like the mountain streams or the springs, but it was wet. Wet counted right up there when they arrived at the river with all their barrels empty. They'd been that way for the last day and a half. The Santa Fe Trail ran east/west along the north side of the Arkansas, or Arrowpoint. Swit kinda liked the sound of Arrowpoint. Someone was always taking a good name and changing it.

After they had rejoined the main trail and were headed east for the States,

Billy started talking about his trips to and from Santa Fe. When they rode by two large pits dug in the ground on the north side of the river, Billy said. "Them's the caches, the cap'n dug 'em there in '22."

"Was he trying his hand at mining?" Swit was remembering the silver mines Billy had showed him when they were in Santa Fe. "It don't look much like mining country."

"That's cause it ain't minin' country," Billy said. "Caches is what you dig when ya wanta hide somethin'. Cap'n Walker was headed back to Missouri after the fall trappin' and was hit by an early blizzard. He found this little group of traders tryin' to get shelter from the storm on an island out there in the river. Jim Baird and Sam Chambers was leadin' the bunch."

This was even more like the old Billy B., Swit thought. He was stroking his mustache and talking about people Swit hadn't heard of, or ever expected to see.

"They'd just spent eight years in a Chihuahua jail for trapping and trading in Spanish territory," Billy continued. "The Mexicans set 'em free after they kicked out the Spanish. As soon as Baird and Chambers got out of the calaboose they made for St. Louis. When they got there and heard all about the big money bein' made tradin' with the Mexicans, they straightaway headed back down the trail—never mind that it was already November."

"Bill Branch was jailed down in Mexico for a while." Swit wanted Billy to know he knew people too. "As far as I know he never went back after he got out, and..."

"I don't 'spose he did," Billy cut in before Swit could drift clear away from his story. "I doubt he dug any holes along the Santa Fe Trail, either."

"I don't know about that." Swit was trying to remember everything old Bill had told him. "I know he had to break up a lot of rocks when he was in Mexico."

"Anyhow," Billy doubted that he had Swit's mind on track, but he decided to finish his story, "Chambers and Baird's pack animals were loaded so heavy with trade goods that they couldn't handle the deep snow. Cap'n helped 'em to build a cache. They dug the two holes, lined the cavities with cottonwood bark, stored their supplies and covered it all up with sod. That way the Injuns couldn't steal their stuff. Walker led 'em on down to Taos, where they wintered. In the spring they came back, opened the pits and recovered the treasure. Said it was lucky that the cap'n came back with 'em, 'cause it was hard to spot the place where they'd done the buryin'. Them big ol' holes been here ever since."

Billy continued to point out places from his past as they moved along the trail. Swit was once again enjoying Billy's words, even if some of it didn't make sense. Oo-tse-tee was busy taking in everything he could about this new country. Water was no longer a problem, and as near as Swit could tell, after listening to the traders, they had entered a portion of the trail that held no threat from the Indians. Billy explained how a council had been held in a large grove of trees where the trail crossed the Neosho River. The men of the Santa Fe Trail Survey and the Osage Indians had signed a treaty. In return for trade goods, the Indians had agreed to let all the travelers pass unmolested through their lands. Captain Walker had been one of the signers and, to commemorate the occasion, the captain's brother, Big John, was called upon to take his knife and tomahawk and carve the message "Council Grove, Aug. 10, 1825" into a massive white oak tree.

The flat prairie had given way to rolling hills, and the trees were more numerous. Everyone was feeling the coolness of fall in the early morning. Missouri was just ahead.

Chapter Nine

Fort Osage was no longer an active federal instillation. Some of the early settlers had carried the old posts and beams away, and it was in need of repair. Almost all of the travel west of St. Louis had passed by the fort in the early days, and at one time its river landing site was as far west as the steamboats ventured. The fort was still a well-known locality in Missouri, and many of the trappers and traders headed for Independence used it to layover and visit with the families that had settled in the area.

"I brought him back to you, Captain." Swit walked up to where Joe Walker was talking with some old friends. "I would have got Scab back sooner, except I took a roundabout trail."

"It's good to see you again, Swit." The captain shook Swit's hand and introduced his young friend to his old buddies. "The way you're dressed, I'd say your travels must have taken you to Mexico. You have that *vaquero* look to you. What'd you do with Billy, send him on to New York or leave him in Spanish hands?"

"Billy's here in Missouri," Swit answered, wondering if the captain approved or disapproved of his change in wardrobe. "He said he was going down to check on his pa. I didn't even know his pa was alive. I just figured he was like me, without folks. Oo-tse-tee's here too, but I don't know where he went."

"Billy's dad lives in a little shack down by the river. He doesn't deserve or appreciate the kindness Billy shows him, but I guess family's family." Walker turned and reached out to lay a hand on the horse's neck; Scab tried to bite him.

"I couldn't break him from trying to nip you if he gets a chance." Swit felt released from a sense of responsibility now that Scab was back in the captain's hands, but he knew he would miss the horse. Swit was trying to decide if he should bring up what Captain Walker had told the three of them before he left Fort Gibson. They were to look him up at Fort Osage to find out about some kind of adventure they could tell their grandchildren all about. Swit had spent considerable time speculating about what Captain Walker had in mind.

Joseph Walker solved Swit's problem by explaining all about the fur trapping enterprise, and expressing his desire that Swit, Billy and Oo-tse-tee would all go west with the expedition. Swit was ready to go. He asked Captain Walker what he needed to do to join up. Walker invited him over to a little office that Captain Bonneville had set up in what remained of the old fort. At the office, Walker showed Swit an official-looking document. "You'll need to sign this." Walker handed Swit the paper.

"I'll have to ask you what it says." Swit was looking down at the floor. "I ain't had much practice with letters."

"Reading is a handy think to know," Walker said. "But it isn't everything. You have your own attributes. It uses a lot of words, but what it boils down to is that you agree to work for Captain Bonneville from March 1, 1832, until October 1833. You will treat him honest and fair in all ways. He'll pay you at the rate of one hundred seventy-five dollars per year. The money will be held for you at Rene Paul's counting room in St. Louis. If you should steal from or desert him, you'll owe him ninety dollars, and you will receive no wages. If you agree to those terms just make your mark on that line."

Swit wasn't sure what an "at-tree-bute" was, but it sounded as if it was good to have. "Does it say anything about what happens if he wrongs me or steals any of *my* stuff?" Swit asked Walker without smiling or losing eye contact.

"By golly, Swit, you know Captain Bonneville plumb forgot to provide for your care in this here document." Walker was trying hard to keep his smile from turning into out-right laughter. Joe had thought that this man was something special from the very first, and he wasn't seeing anything to change his mind.

"I believe Captain Bonneville to be a honest and fair man," Walker continued. "I've never asked for or been required to sign one of these agreements before meeting up with the captain. Personally, I don't put much faith in this type of arrangement. If a man is going to cheat you, he'll steal and lie no matter if he signed a paper or not. It does, however, put to rest any future disagreement that might come up about the amount of pay and time of service."

Swit had been brought up to believe that keeping his word was an important part of who he was—maybe the most important part. Placing his signature, even if it was a mark, was serious business.

"This paper is just Captain Bonneville's way," Walker explained. "Actually, it's the military way, and Bonneville is all Army. I signed mine, because everything it said I was to do I would have done anyhow. If I feel unfairly put upon or cheated by the captain, there will be an immediate settlement."

Swit put S.J.B. on the line. He wished that he could have written his name, but S.J.B. looked almost like a name, and Swit thought it carried more weight than the X he'd watched other men use. Walker placed the paper in a desk drawer. When they walked outside, Oo-tse-tee and Billy were standing in front of the office.

"This is turning out to be a capital day." Walker greeted Billy and Oo-tse-tee. "It's been more than a year now since I left you three down at Fort Gibson, but I've thought of your whereabouts many times. Swit hasn't had time to fill me in on all your travels. Maybe we could go over to my brother's place. His little Mary is the best darn cook in these parts, and I know Joel would welcome the conversation."

"Captain, maybe Billy and Oo-tse-tee would like to sign on for the trip since we're here where the papers are," Swit suggested.

"We're here about a trip, all right." Billy was looking at Walker. "But I doubt it's the one you're talkin' about. The Indian and me are fixin' to head back to Santa Fe. Captain, our horses need rest. We hoped you could help us get some good mounts."

"Of course I'll help you." Captain Walker was studying Billy B. and Oo-tse-tee. The request was unusual for this time of year, and not at all like Billy. "I realize you're not asking my advice, but I can't help myself. You'd be better off to stay on here. Rest yourselves and your horses until spring, and then start for Santa Fe. Billy, you know better than most about what you can run into between here and Santa Fe in the wintertime. I don't know of anyone leaving until next spring. You two will be alone out there."

Swit was in shock. The captain's demeanor had changed from lighthearted conversation to serious business. Swit felt like Señorita Delgado had looked when they left Santa Fe. This was entirely his fault. He was responsible for Billy leaving Santa Fe in the first place. Now Billy could end up in a little grave along the trail, probably Oo-tse-tee too. He couldn't even go along and help. He'd already signed on with Bonneville.

Billy could see that his decision to go back to Santa Fe had upset his friend. "Swit, this has nothin' to do with you. You know how I feel about ya. It's just that I left a part of me back down there in Mexico. I didn't even know it myself until we was almost here. I have to go back and get myself together. The cap'n's right about me knowin' the trail in winter. He might not say it, but he knows outside of himself that I can get through that country as good as anyone. Why, I might like the trip so well I'll turn right around and come back."

"Billy's experienced, knows the way, and usually has good judgment. That doesn't guarantee he'll make it, but he has a better chance than most." Walker could tell that Billy had his mind made up. "You know the consequences of your actions, and you seem determined. I try to never interfere in a man's decision if those are the circumstances. I'll help you in any way I can. Oo-tse-tee, do you understand what can happen with just the two of you, and winter coming on?"

"We need to go now—move fast," was Oo-tse-tee's answer.

"See, that's the same damn thing he said when I told him that I was goin' back." Billy gave the Indian a disgusted look. "I tried to talk him out of it, even threatened to shoot him. He's determined. Keeps sayin' somethin' about no snow for two moons. He hung out with them plains Injuns so much I guess he thinks now that he knows weather."

"Just one more piece of advice before we all head over to Abraham's and pick you two up some horses," Walker said. "Don't take the cut-off west of the Caches. Follow up the river another sixty miles or so to Chouteau's Island." Walker thought the less time spent along the cut-off, the less likely they were to have trouble with the Indians, and if the weather turned bad they might be able to make it to Bent's Fort. "If the weather's good, head straight south of the island. It'll only be about fifty miles to the Cimarron. You should cross the regular cut-off at, or just before you get to, Sand Creek. If you reach Sand Creek before you cut the trail, you'll be too far west. Angle a little to the east as you head on south to the river, and you'll find Lower Spring. Pay special attention when you get there. It's a favorite spot for an ambush."

The four men went to look at the horses. Captain Walker usually kept some horses at the McClellan place. Abraham McClellan had a hand in several businesses, and the arrangements for the horses and supplies that

Billy and Oo-tse-tee would need for the trip were made. After all the preparations for going to Santa Fe were completed, they went over to Joel's for supper. Billy and Oo-tse-tee were well mounted, but Billy's gray mare was staying behind.

Swit remembered seeing and meeting people during most of the day's activity, and everyone had been friendly and helpful, but it was like it happened in a fog. There was a good deal of talking during the meal, and Swit thought Billy acted and sounded normal. Maybe he still had all his parts and didn't know it.

Swit watched as the two riders headed west. The sun wasn't up yet, and they looked like faint shadows in the dim, early morning light. Swit had helped them to set their packs, but he couldn't say anything. Oo-tse-tee didn't say anything either. He was the first one ready to go. Billy was in good spirits when he swung up in the saddle and told Swit, "Everything is gonna be all right. Now just stop your frettin'. I'll see you in the fall, or not at all." After the two riders had passed from sight, he thought, That's just like Billy. He says that he'll see me in the fall, and I don't even know where I'll be.

Mister McClellan put Swit to work taking care of all the horses he had at his place. It was just the job Boone needed. It took his mind away from Billy, and brought a measure of satisfaction back into his life. Abraham McClellan embraced life in the new frontier settlements in much the same way that Walker took to the wilderness. He was a town leader and had a hand in building and establishing all the necessary businesses and institutions it took to pioneer a new community.

In the latter part of February, Swit began to notice the arrival of a diverse group of individuals. The gathering was taking place in and around Fort Osage. Some of the men looked much older than others did, but Swit soon realized it was hard to determine a man's age by how he looked. They wore all kinds of wardrobe with many different adornments. In general they dressed somewhat like the Indians. A few of the men brought along their wives and lodges. Swit couldn't find one wife that didn't look like she was at least part Indian. Their horses were as varied as they were, and some even brought their dogs along. Each man seemed to pick out his own spot to set his camp. Some stayed off to themselves while others bunched together. The assemblage appeared friendly, and they sure enough enjoyed laughter and an active lifestyle.

***

The sun gradually shifted northward in its east/west track across the sky. It gained strength and put an end to winter's hold. The cold spring rains came earlier than usual, and the dull brown shades of winter gradually changed to various hues of green. New life was everywhere.

The day the wagons arrived everyone knew this was no ordinary fur trapping expedition. Michael Cerré led twenty new, fully loaded wagons into the fort. Most were pulled by four oxen, but several had horses or mules up front. Swit wondered if the choice of pulling power was up to the wagoner. These men looked different from the bullwhackers he had experienced coming from Santa Fe. Generally speaking, they seemed younger, and they dressed more like trappers. Extra horses and mules were brought in from the McClellan pasture as the numbers of trappers grew.

Captain Walker helped Swit put together his string of horses. Swit couldn't find any words when Walker brought Scab and Billy's gray over to him and handed him the lead ropes. "You better add these horses to your bunch," Walker said. "I've got that young stud over there to ride the kinks out of." Swit knew that the horses weren't his to keep, but to just use Billy's mare and the captain's stallion was a treasured gift.

Bonneville, Walker and Cerré were all busy putting on the finishing touches and making ready. Swit watched as Captain Walker made his way through the men. Even the most rowdy and free spirited of the bunch always treated the captain with courteous respect, and any slight modification he might suggest was corrected with dispatch.

Captain Bonneville had gone East to meet with his backers, and after completing his financial arrangements he returned from Washington with a passport and Mexican visa made out in Joseph R. Walker's name.

The day came on May 1, 1832. One hundred and ten men, twenty wagons, and a herd of extra horses and mules left Fort Osage. They headed off in the exact same direction Billy and Oo-tse-tee had taken when they left. As Swit rode along he tried to picture in his mind the difference between Santa Fe's location and the fur territory where they were supposedly headed. Even if by some unimaginable mistake they were on their way to Santa Fe, he didn't care. He'd find out about Billy.

Part Two: Heading West

Chapter Ten

Joseph Walker directed Bonneville's expedition to the Southwest along the same trail used by the wagons headed for Santa Fe. The spring rains had left the ground spongy, and he knew the wagons would have easier going and make better time following along the old path. They would use the easier traveling to ready themselves and become better organized for the tougher times ahead.

Captain Bonneville believed that he was the leader of the finest equipped and best-organized group of men to venture into the West. It was a dream come true. They would open a wagon path for others to follow, and he would chronicle the entire event. It was history in the making, with the added bonus of earning a fortune in the fur business. He had silently questioned the wisdom of Walker's decision to start out following the Santa Fe route, but after they left the trail and turned northwest it was easy to see why the men held Walker in such high regard. Rivers and creek crossings had been made wagon ready along the old trail—now it was different. The smallest stream could slow the caravan to a crawl.

Most of the men in the expedition knew one another. This left Swit on the outside looking in. Captain Walker had called him forward a couple of times and asked him to ride here or there and do this or that, but other than Captain Walker, no one appeared to care if he was part of the group or not. Swit was searching for someone about his age that he could get to know; and had his eye on a tall, rangy-looking fellow that seemed to be acquainted with most of the men, but rode alone most of the time.

Woodrow Willard had his long, lean frame draped around the tallest horse he had been able to find. He hated to ride a little horse. They didn't fit together, and that always caused comment and conversation that he didn't care to deal with. This was not Will's first trip into the fur territory. In 1830 he'd trailed with Andrew Drips into the Bear and Green River country. However, that had been with pack animals, and Woodrow was still trying to decide if pushing and pulling wagons was easier than unpacking horses and mules every night and then packing them again the next morning.

Wagons could carry more supplies, so there was less chance of slim rations before they hit the buffalo country—but still, wagons were trouble. He was busy helping to dig an opening through the deep bank of a lively little creek when he said to no one in particular, "Well, now, I never figured to build a road to the beaver ponds."

Swit was intrigued by the way the tall man working beside him moved. He always seemed to be in slow motion. The surprising thing was the amount of work he could get done. Even though he moved at caterpillar speed, he did as much or more than any man in the outfit. Every movement seemed calculated to require the least amount of effort needed to complete the task, and it was all done in a smooth, fluid rhythm. His manner of speech was exactly the same—slow and unhurried. Swit was pitching dirt off to his right while the man beside him was throwing his dirt to his left. It seemed to Swit that he was heaving at least twice as many loads as the tall stranger beside him, but the piles that heaped up on both sides of the trench were about the same.

"If we use the same trail coming back the road'll be waiting on us," Swit answered the man's comment. He continued digging and didn't take time to see if there was any reaction registered on the man's face.

When both men finished they moved away so the wagons could begin their crossing. Woodrow put down his shovel and stuck out his hand. "My name is Woodrow Willard, but everyone except my mother calls me Will."

"Glad to meet you, Will." Swit shook his new friend's hand. "I'm Swit Boone."

"I see Captain Walker call on you once in a while. Is he everything everybody says?" Will thought that Walker seemed to have confidence in Swit, and yet it wasn't hard to tell that this was his first trip into the wilderness.

"I'm not up much on what everybody says. I'll tell you this, don't ever underrate him. I wouldn't be on this trip if he wasn't in the lead. He don't talk that much, but be sure you listen when he does, it's worth gathering in. Have you made this trip before?"

"Well, not exactly this route, and we didn't have any wagons with us." Will was still trying to make up his mind if wagons, on a whole, were a plus or a minus.

"You have any idea where we're at?" Swit asked.

"I'd say we're just south of the Kansas River, probably be there tonight or tomorrow. You ever make a big river crossin'?"

"Not without a boat, and I ain't much of a swimmer either. Is the Kansas as big as the Missouri?" Swit had respect for rivers.

"Well, now, I'll tell you what, the ol' Kansas ain't no Missouri, but it'll be full, spring run-off and all. Clark says that they could sure use a ferry at the agency. If they ain't got one I suppose we'll have to build a barge for these wagons."

"You mean there's a settlement out here? I never figured to see nothing but Indians in these parts. Who's Clark?"

"Clark is General Clark, the younger brother of William Clark; you know, Lewis and Clark—the explorers." Will had passed by the government agency on his first trip. "It really ain't no settlement, just a couple buildings settin' on the north side of the river. Clark's the superintendent of the Kanzas Indian Agency. He kinda lives like a king out here."

Swit was more concerned with the river crossing than Clark's kingdom. He hadn't cared much for deep rivers since he had decided to teach himself to swim in the Blackwater River back in Missouri. If a big tree stump hadn't floated by at just the right time, he probably would have drowned.

The expedition reached the Kansas River late in the afternoon. It was bank full, and no one had started up a ferry business. Early the next morning Captain Bonneville quickly organized the construction of a raft to carry the wagons across. By days end everyone and everything was safely on the north side of the river and camped at the agency.

Captain Bonneville had the wagons aligned in a square configuration, five wagons to a side, and all the animals were herded into the center of the square. The horses were sidelined, or tied to one that was. Bonneville was discovering that leading these men was considerably different than leading a military detachment. Trappers were an independent and freedom-loving bunch, and they'd take advice and direction from only a few individuals.

Joseph Walker was pleased with Bonneville's command. The captain had shown the discipline of military life, but not in a harsh and dictatorial way. Walker and Bonneville established a routine of discussing the day's march while they took their morning meal. Walker would point the way and explain hazards and obstructions they were likely to encounter. They shared ideas and settle on their plans for the day. Michael Cerré sometimes attended these meetings, but usually he was busy checking on the supplies and wagons. After breakfast, Bonneville would take readings with his instruments and update his journals while Walker rode among the men to get a feel for their cares and concerns.

Swit's latest concern had been lifted when they were safely across the river. Will had finally been able to convince Swit that as long as he could stay on top of Scab he wouldn't have any trouble getting to the other bank. "A horse with a big ol' chest like that will float like a cork," Will said as they entered the water. Woodrow's assessment proved accurate. Scab swam the river and was shaking himself dry before Will's horse was three-fourths of the way across.

"I wish Billy could have been here to see the way this horse can swim." Swit was proud of the horse's performance, and relieved to be on the north shore. "Billy B. didn't figure Scab to be much of a snow horse. Bet he'd be surprised how handy he is in water."

"Who's this Billy I keep hearin' about, and why ain't he here on this trip?" Will had noticed that it was hard to talk to Swit without hearing about Billy.

"Billy is just Billy B. Alexander. He was coming along, but he had to go back to Santa Fe. Said he left part of himself down there."

"Well, I've left my hat in a few places, and one time I forgot my boots when I was in kind of a hurry, but I can't think of ever leavin' a part of me anywhere. What part did he leave?"

"It's not like he really left a leg or something like that; it was more like the part was inside him, you know, like a feeling or an idea."

"By golly, you know if I was to leave somethin' like that behind I doubt I'd know how to go about findin' it. Seems to me it would be darn near impossible to locate, and if you did, how would ya know it was yours?"

Swit couldn't see much point trying to explain Billy B. to Will. It seemed to Swit that lately talking to Woodrow Willard was not all that different than talking with Billy, except Will talked so slow that his words didn't pile up on you.

Swit and Will's attention was directed away from Billy and his missing part when a group of Indians approached the camp. Will explained that these Indians called themselves Kanzas, and they lived and acted pretty much like the Osage tribe. Their chief, White Plume, was wearing an Army coat and hat. Will pointed out that the government had built one of the large stone houses at the agency for the chief, and he lived, wigwam style, inside the structure. The Kanzas were curious in the extreme, and they wanted to know about all the strange new things that these travelers carried with them. It occurred to Swit that maybe they had never seen wagons, or at least not this many.

Bonneville could see that these Indians were farmers. He opened negotiations with White Plume for additional corn. Walker had known White Plume since the treaty signing at Council Grove, and he cautioned the captain that the chief was a braggart and a shrewd dealer. Captain Bonneville traded what Joe Walker believed was an excessive amount of their trade goods for buffalo hides. He had to pay cash for a supply of corn.

After leaving the agency, Bonneville's expedition headed in a westerly direction along the north side of the Kansas River. When they reached the place where the Blue River joined the Kansas, they followed up the Blue in a northerly direction. At the fork of the Little Blue River, they crossed over the Blue and proceeded northwest along the north side of the Little Blue River. They had definitely moved out of the tree country.

Swit had already experienced the vast grassland that lay to the West when he and Billy went to Santa Fe, and again when they traveled from Santa Fe back to Missouri. This wasn't the same. It was spring, and this time Swit found himself entering a seemingly endless expanse of tall grass and wild flowers, altogether different from the hot, windy, dry, short-grass country. Instead of the terrain being mostly flat, like it had been along much of the trail to and from Santa Fe, it varied as you rode along. There were places where the land was flat as far as you could see, but other times you'd find yourself moving along through rolling hills. They traveled by areas of rock outcroppings and skirted along beside canyon country. The farther west they went the fewer the trees.

The topography continued to make its slight adjustments, but one thing remained the same. You were surrounded by grass and dominated by an openness that made it hard for your eye to find anything to focus on. Most of the prairie was covered with the previous year's dead grass, the new green growth of spring and a sprinkling of wild flowers. Occasionally they would ride for hours through places where the old grass had been removed by fire. Swit thought that the fire was probably a result of lighting; however, he had heard of Indians starting fires to help drive buffalo to a killing site. Whatever the cause of the fire, the fresh green blanket of new grass was not hidden in last year's growth. Swit had never seen anything like the splendid array of multicolored blossoms spread out on a green background.

The northwest-bound caravan was one month out of Fort Osage. Traveling in a westerly direction along the Little Blue, Joe Walker directed them to the northwest, away from the river. "We must be changing rivers," Swit said. "You know where we're headed?"

"I'm not exactly sure where we are, but I'd have to say we can't be more than a day's ride south of the Platte." Will was gaining appreciation for Joe Walker as the outfit moved along. He'd heard men tell about the hardships they'd endured traveling between the Kansas and Platte rivers. The path Walker had selected was not exactly easy, especially having wagons to contend with, but it had brought them north with less difficulty than Will had expected. The scarcity of a meat supply through this country was a known fact, and everyone looked forward to reaching the buffalo country. Bonneville's expedition reached the Platte River the next day.

The Platte River was unlike any river Bonneville had ever seen. Walker explained that they had joined the Platte about twenty-five miles above a well-known Platte River landmark, where the river divided into two major branches, creating a large island—marked as The Grand Island on Bonneville's maps. The river valley appeared to be miles across, with no particular hills or breaks leading down into the valley. The river had low banks, and Bonneville's measurement of its width showed it to be twenty-two hundred yards across. The river had a sandy bottom and was shallow, no deeper than three to six feet in most places. Numerous little islands split it apart. A few small cottonwood trees and willows grew on the islands, with an occasional large tree growing along the edge of the main river channel. Bonneville rode to the highest spot he could find to get a better view of the valley. It was a magnificent artery to the west. He was positive that this river valley would become as important to the Oregon settlers as the Cumberland Gap had been to the earlier frontiersmen.

Walker directed Bonneville's assemblage west, following up the south side of the wide river valley. Traveling was easy but game was less than scarce. They passed a place that was littered with many bleached bones, indicating a great buffalo kill had taken place sometime in the past. The skulls appeared to have been arranged in some type of circular pattern. Everyone agreed that following the hunt the Indians had performed a religious ceremony to commemorate the event. The old kill site renewed confidence that they would soon find buffalo, and Swit listened as the older men told stories about earlier trips across the plains, and their participation in previous buffalo hunts

After traveling for two more days with no sign of the great beasts, Walker suggested to Bonneville that they kill a couple of steers to nourish the men and raise their spirits. Having done this, they continued their westerly movement along the Platte River, ever so slowly climbing toward the Rockies.

"We'll soon be to the forks. The way the Platte looks now, I doubt we'll be able to cross there." Joe Walker announced his presence with this when he rode up to where Swit and Will were resting. "I need you two to ride ahead, follow up the south fork, and look for the best place to cross. I expect the South Platte will be carrying a heavy load, so look for a wide, shallow spot where the current's not too strong. As soon as you find a place to cross, head back and meet us at the forks. Will, where'd you cross when you were with Captain Drips?"

"It seems to me we had to go a fair piece up the south fork before we found a spot. We still had to use bull boats to get across," Woodrow answered.

"There's a place that's an easy two days' ride from the forks that might work. Take what supplies you'll need from the wagon, and I'll see you in a few days." Walker headed back toward Michael Cerré's wagon.

"Where's this fork the captain's talking about?" Swit's mind had focused in on this important location.

"Well now, I'll tell ya what, we'll ride right by it on our way up the Platte." Will was turning his horse toward the supply wagon. "You see, up ahead there a-ways, the old Platte breaks into two parts—south branch and north branch. That's called the forks. We'll just ride up along the south part."

"What's them bull boats that you told Captain Walker about?" It hadn't occurred to Swit that they would ever have to crossover the Platte River. They'd been following up the large waterway for a week and now, all of a sudden, Captain Walker was sending him and Will to look for a spot to cross. The river was so wide that it looked impossible to reach the other side without a boat

"You probably noticed that there's not many trees in these parts," Will answered. "It's hard to build much of a boat without timber, but what you can do is make a kinda boat frame outa them willows. Cover the framework with buffalo hides, and you got yourself a bull boat."

"That don't sound like too strong a vessel. I doubt they could float a wagon."

"It'll surprise you how much they can carry, although I'll admit I never saw one under a wagon." Will was puzzled at Swit's concern about crossing the Platte. He'd crossed the Kansas River without mishap. "You won't have no trouble gettin' over. Ol' Scab can probably walk across and not even get his belly wet."

At the forks the north branch continued on in a northwestern direction while the south branch came in more from the west. Will and Swit rode up the south branch and found the spot Walker had described. The river valley looked to be more than a mile across, and the river took up about one-third of the valley. The current was fairly slow, but Will thought that it might be too deep and sandy for oxen to pull the wagons across. They rode on, looking for a better place to cross the river. When they reached the crossing that Will remembered from his last trip, it didn't look to be any easier than the one they'd passed farther down stream. In fact, the water seemed to be moving faster. Swit and Will headed back to meet Walker.

"What happens if we would keep on heading west along the south side of this river instead of crossing over?" Swit wanted to know. "There's no sense crossing a river you don't have to."

"The Platte ain't that hard to cross," Will answered. "If we was to keep on following the south branch we'd soon start swingin' south. If your destination is Taos or Santa Fe, you'd be headed in the right direction."

"You mean if we was to follow up this river we'd come to Santa Fe? I'll bet ol' Billy B. would have some tales to tell us if we was to ride into Santa Fe."

"Well now, you see the thing about it of it is, if the two of us was to ride down to Santa Fe from here, we'd have a few tales of our own. This ol' river don't exactly deliver you straight to Mexico. It swings off kinda southwest till it hits the Rockies, and then it bends more south. Just north of Pike's mountain we'd have to leave the South Platte and travel another eighty miles on down to the Arkansas River. South of the Arkansas we'd be in Mexico tryin' to get over them Rockies by following along the mountain branch of the Santa Fe Trail. All total we would have traversed Arapaho, Cheyenne, Kiowa and Comanche lands, not to mention climbin' over a mountain or two. It ain't no ride through the tulips."

Swit didn't mind the part about crossing the Arkansas; he'd done that. The Indians and mountain climbing seemed chancy. Still, it would have been good to see Billy again.

Chapter Eleven

Oo-tse-tee stopped to visit with the Indians camped along the Santa Fe River. Billy headed for the plaza and Doña Tules's place of business. He had to see Maria, and the sooner the better. It was the reason that he and the Indian had spent the last forty-three days on the trail to Santa Fe. Captain Walker's suggested route to Lower Spring had eased the trip through the *Jornada*, and the weather, while not exactly enjoyable, had been unusually mild. A heavy snowfall on the plains, with its unavoidable wind- created drifts, was a blizzard that every traveler respected; however, the Indian's prediction had held up. They'd only had to deal with two small flurries of snow, which were more aggravating than troublesome. The only Indians they sighted were ten miles west of the Council Grove, and Oo-tse-tee spotted the Osage Hunting party before they saw the two unaccompanied riders. A pack animal suffered a broken leg and had to be put down, but other than that the trip was unremarkable.

Billy took a quick look around when he walked into the club. Some of his old acquaintances were there to greet him, and surprised by his quick return to Santa Fe. The old Billy B. would have spent hours telling about his travels and catching up on all the local gossip, but not today. Billy was watching and waiting for Maria.

Pedro Ramirez managed the bar and about everything else in the establishment. It was common knowledge that Doña Tules Gertrudes Barcelo was Governor Armijo's mistress, and the best monte dealer in Santa Fe. Unlike Doña Tules, Pedro was the product of a poor Mexican family. The revolution had been his opportunity, and although he was hardly more than a boy, he gained recognition as a tough fighter and leader of guerrilla forces. When the Mexican Army drove Spain's appointed officials from power and claimed the government, Pedro became a man of significant resources and respect.

"Has Maria Delgado been in today?" Billy asked Pedro after he had been able to separate himself from his well wishers and speak privately at the bar. "I'd really like to find her as soon as I can."

"Billy, it's a hard tale I must tell you," Pedro answered. "Maria has not been here for many days. In fact, she hasn't been here to conduct any business since you left. She quit her whoring."

Just the word turned Billy's insides. It had been part of the problem that caused Billy to ride away. He held no particular disdain for whores, just confusion. He had known more than a few in his young life, and one in particular had played an important role when he was younger. Never knowing his mother, and having a neglectful father, Billy was raised and influenced at any particular point in time by whatever and whoever made up his environment. This woman had a mother's love for the little boy that was trying so hard to survive. He had her attention for only seven months before his dad moved on to another town, but thoughts of her still engaged his mind almost every day. The young boy knew the word "whore," and he had watched and listened to the men as they entertained themselves. He knew this woman to be a fine lady—a mother to him—and yet she was a whore.

Billy wasn't even sure of her name. He'd always called her Mattie; however, just lately, he remembered that others had used the names Matilda and Lucille when they requested her services. Years later Billy went back to find her, and she was gone. No one seemed to know where she went, or cared for that matter, Billy thought. They didn't know any more about her name than he did. Billy had never been able to resolve the lady-whore conflict within himself, and the discord caused him sleepless nights when he lost his heart to Maria. Billy knew more about Maria Delgado than he did about the lady from his past.

Maria had been a little girl playing in the plaza when Billy first saw her. It was his first trip to Santa Fe. He hadn't given her or her friends any more notice than he did to the chickens that run loose around the big quadrant. Tuck had been the one that had started him playing tag with the Spanish children, and his education about their culture and language was underway. Because Billy rode with a respected group of men and was so young, the Mexicans looked upon him as something special. That was another part of the problem. Billy had been brought up to believe that the black eyes were somehow not quite up to his measure.

During the Mexican revolution Maria had been sent into the hills with a message for the guerrillas. When she returned her village was destroyed, and her family was dead. Maria was compelled to live with the family of her mother's brother in Santa Fe. She was still just a young girl when she started developing a woman's loveliness. Maria found herself being used by her uncle and his sons. She survived in the only way she could devise. Maria learned to get for herself what life had to offer by using what she believed was her one asset. Pedro helped her to move away from her uncle's control, and then introduced her to the business world. It was better than living with her uncle. Especially better for Pedro.

Billy showed Maria that she was much more than that one attraction. He liked her laugh, her ears and the way she hopped around on one foot when she was trying to put on her other shoe. Sometimes he'd get disgusted at some notion she'd take off on, but that never lasted for long. Maria had a delightfulness that Billy couldn't fend off. The very best times were their long talks about all kinds of secrets—past, present and future.

"After you left, Maria changed," Pedro said to Billy as he pushed a whiskey in front of him. "You must have left her some silver, because she had plenty for her needs. You probably know I wasn't happy when she quit her whoring. She was the most popular one here, and we let her pick and choose. Anyhow, that's all behind us now."

"You mean she's left Santa Fe?" Billy asked.

"What I mean is that after you left I tried to get her back, but she told me she was through with that life," Pedro continued. "In fact, she actually said she was through with life. I didn't really get what she meant until later. Maria climbed into a tequila bottle. She never laughed. She almost never smiled. She didn't bathe, wash, comb her hair or eat much either. Hell, she didn't even change her clothes. She stayed in the plaza day and night. It didn't take long for men that would have paid any price to spend just a little time with her to walked out of their way so as not to get too close. I expected to find her stone cold every morning. She already smelled dead."

My God, what have I done, Billy thought. "Is she dead?"

"I really don't know," Pedro answered. "One morning two of Don Carlos's men brought a wagon into the plaza. They picked her up and laid her on some blankets in the back of the wagon. They didn't seem too happy about their task. When someone asked if they were going to get any supplies before heading back, the one called Cisco said that Don Carlos had just returned to the ranch. When he heard about Maria he told 'em, 'Go get whatever's left of that beautiful dove away from that damn pack of dogs.' We got the idea that it might not be too healthy for any of us to go out to the ranch for a while. No one has been out there or heard anything about Maria since that day. A *vaquero* passing through about ten days ago said he'd stopped at the Suarez ranch, but he hadn't seen or heard anything about anyone called Maria."

Billy was headed for his horse before Pedro finished telling about the *vaquero*. It was a short ride to the ranch, but to Billy it seemed as far as Missouri. When he had reached Santa Fe he thought that as soon as he found Maria everything would be fine. It hadn't occurred to him that Maria would be so influenced by his decision to leave. Billy B. rode along in a mixture of worry and regret.

When Billy entered Don Carlos Suarez's *rancho* he was surprised by the absence of activity that was usually present. He didn't see a single person. The strange silence sharpened his awareness as he slowly and alertly rode past the horse barn and granary on his way to the main house.

The Suarez's home was situated on the first rise of a tiered hill that climbed up out of the river valley. Don Carlos could sit on the porch and all of the main ranch outbuildings were within his view. He could see the irrigated ground along the river bottom and the huge garden. The *veranda* was a favorite place to spend time between supper and sundown. About fifty yards behind the house the hill again climbed up to a second bench. This shelf was a large, almost flat, partly wooded area. From its viewpoint you could see up and down the valley for miles. Billy and Maria had picnicked there many times.

Just as Billy was about to reach the lane leading to the house, a part of the upper bench came into view. He could see a large group of people, dressed in their finest, and gathered at a small site that was nestled back in a little grove of trees. Billy rode up the winding path to get a better view. It was what he had feared. Everyone was gathered in the ranch cemetery.

He now knew that his trip back to Santa Fe was too late. Pedro had said that he looked to find Maria dead every morning. She'd made it out of the plaza, but not off the ranch. Billy's original plan to realign his own life had been changed to try and somehow correct the damage he had inflicted upon Maria. He'd failed himself, and he'd failed her. The wear of worry and travel descended on Billy. He felt as if his body was about to give out.

Billy stopped his horse, dismounted, walked back off the lane and sat down under a tree. His love was gone. Life would go on, but he knew that it would never be as good as it had been last summer. Billy's world gradually shrank into the small space around himself and his horse. He looked up now and then and gazed out over the valley, but Maria's face was all he could see. Billy never heard the ranch family coming down the path behind him. Don Carlos was surprised to see Billy hunkered down under the tree.

"Billy, oh, Billy, there's much sadness here today." Don Carlos motioned the others to pass by. "But seeing you brings some happiness into my heart. She was like a flower that you looked forward to seeing at the start of every day. Now she'll bloom no more—at least not in this world. We'll go on, but my house will never be the same again. There's someone that'll..."

"You look just like I remembered. Trail dirty, hollow and smelling like a hot horse. Your mustache is a little different, I don't think you're giving it as much care as you use to." Maria had walked up behind and slightly to the right of Billy's spot under the tree. Billy turned to see who was speaking. She was staring down at him without any welcome in her eyes. "You could have cleaned up a little for the funeral, but then I guess that's your way. Just suit yourself, and to hell with anyone else."

"Don't be too hard on Billy." Carlos hadn't expected Maria's harshness. "It's obvious that he's fresh off the trail. I'm sure he knew nothing of Petronila's death. Go and make a room ready for Billy, you two will have plenty of time to talk later."

"Billy's quite a talker, that's for sure." Maria started for the house. "That doesn't mean anyone cares much what he says."

Billy's collapsed realm was suddenly being pried opened. Maria was alive. Don Carlos had lost his wife. Doña Petronila de Marina Suarez was the finest lady Billy had ever known. She was the perfect mate for Carlos, always gracious and relaxed in her manner, and never unsettled by Carlos's explosions of anger. Petronila was the first to support his actions when she knew him to be right, and the first to confront him with reason when she knew him to be wrong. She had been a loving, caring and protecting wife who had given Carlos seven children. Petronila's love and devotion to her children was second only to her affection for Carlos.

The Suarez children were as different as siblings are in most families. However, they had all learned the value of honesty, understood the virtues of hard work, and endeavored to live like God commanded. The shock of Petronila's death and the pain Billy felt for Don Carlos was tempered somewhat by the relief of finding Maria alive. Slowly Billy looked into the eyes of his old friend.

"It's all right." Don Carlos could see the tears in Billy's eyes. "Maria still holds you in her heart. She had a very bad time after you left Santa Fe."

"I heard," Billy said. "I stopped at Doña Tules, and Pedro told me what happened. When I saw everyone at the cemetery I thought I was too late. I'm so sorry for your loss."

"Death comes to us all." Carlos set down next to Billy. "We had a good life together, and I'll miss her every day, but let's you and I talk about Maria. When you left without her, she thought you didn't want her. Maria decided that she could use the silver coins you gave her to end her life. Pedro was more than willing to sell her all the tequila she wanted."

Billy had never trusted Pedro, and wasn't surprised that he would sell Maria tequila. If she would have gone back to work he would have done his best to keep her alive, but to just stand by and watch Maria slowly kill herself...Billy never figured Pedro would do that.

"Until now I had no way of knowing your true feelings for Maria," Don Carlos continued. "I doubt you even knew them yourself when you left. I'm afraid Petronila and I have changed the way she once thought about you. We had to teach her that life for her was more than just Billy B. Alexander. I told her that I thought you would return for her, but if you didn't, life could still be good. I believe God sent her to us. She and my Petronila were both dying. Petronila taught her about life, and Maria made Petronila's passing easier. They had a very special feeling for each other."

"I thought it'd be all different," Billy said. "On the way back I planned how we'd get together again, like last summer. I was gonna ask her to marry me. What we did after that didn't much matter, if we were together it'd be okay. Now I don't know which way to jump."

"Stay out here at the ranch for a while," Don Carlos suggested. "I can see you need the rest. Give Maria some time to adjust to the idea that you're back."

"She sure didn't seem very happy to see me." Billy stood up. Carlos was leading him toward the house.

"Take your time before you make any decisions about Maria. She has the same love for you as before, but right now it's hidden deep in her heart. Maria almost died because she confused her love for you with life itself. It'll take time for her to learn that she can love you and her own life at the same time." Carlos walked beside Billy. Maria was right, he did need a bath.

***

Maria had an emotional stampede going on inside her. One minute she was mad and ready to lash out, an instant later she was sad and crying. She wished that Petronila were here to explain what was happening to her. So much had happened since the day she'd been brought to the ranch. Her memory of the trip was a collection of bits and pieces. She could remember riding to the ranch, wrapped in a red blanket in the back of a wagon, shivering with a deep coldness. But it was all like a dream. Maria couldn't recall being carried into the house, but Anita had told her how they had carried her to the tub. Steam rising from the water and someone forcing her to drink a terrible broth was pictured in her mind. After that Maria could only remember the big bed with Anita or Lena always at her side, urging her to sit up and drink more broth.

Maria knew that her life with Carlos and Petronila had been the best she'd known since she was a little girl living with her family in a small village that she could barely remember. Petronila talked with her every day. Even in the night if one or the other were in need of conversation they would comfort each other. She had taught her many things about living one's life by example. This special lady made Maria feel about herself in much the same way Billy had. Like Billy, she showed her things about herself, both good and bad. Petronila said it made her the special person that God loved.

Maria could faintly remember her mother talking about God, but she hadn't heard about God's plan for salvation until Petronila brought it to her. Petronila was dying and yet she made it seem like death was not final—only a different part of living. When they were together, talking about God and living and dying, everything seemed certain. Later when Maria was alone, things had a tendency to muddle up and become murky. Her confessor and confidant was now in her savior's hands, and Maria had no one to help her make sense out of confusion. Petronila always seemed to find her answers in the teachings of Jesus, and lately Maria found herself thinking more about what he would say to her problems.

Since Petronila's death it seemed to Maria that her problems had been on the rise. Seeing Billy under the tree had only added to the list. Her cold feelings for Billy seemed strange after she thought about it a while. For so long a time Billy had been the only thing on her mind. If he would just come to her, everything would be okay again. She could remember waking up in the plaza, lying next to a building with a dog licking her face, and thinking that Billy was back. The thought left her feeling foolish. She had never seen Billy B. act like he had today. He sat with his head down, raising it only once to see who spoke to him. He never got up or uttered even one word.

Billy was surprised how dirty and hungry he felt. Maria had noticed it right off, even commented about his mustache. Carlos found him some clean clothes, and Billy did his best to put himself right before they ate supper. When they sat down for the meal he suddenly felt starved and was doing everything he could to correct the feeling when he noticed everyone at the table was watching him eat.

"I guess we threw his manners out with the bath water." It was Maria's only comment to or about him during the meal. Carlos tried to explain Billy's actions to the group, and made light of the incident, but Billy was embarrassed. That night in bed he tried to make sense of the day's events. Sleep took him before he had a chance to put forth much thought.

Chapter Twelve

The South Platte River crossing was to be attempted at the place Will and Swit had chosen. Walker agreed that it was too deep and sandy to pull the wagons across, so Captain Bonneville put the men to work removing the wheels and running gears from the wagon boxes. A mixture of tallow and campfire ashes provided a paste to make the wagons as water tight as possible. The buffalo hides that the Kanzas Indians had traded to Bonneville were used to protect the supplies from the minor leaks. After the wagon boxes had been fashioned into temporary boats, they were pulled, floated and dragged safely across the river.

Walker pointed the expedition northward through the grass-covered rolling hills that separated the two branches of the Platte River. After reaching the North Platte they followed up the south bank of the river. Early in the afternoon of the second day the caravan entered the first stand of trees they'd seen since leaving the eastern woodlands—a journey of more than four hundred miles. The small but welcoming, little grove of ash trees was located in a hollow containing a small spring-fed creek. The spring poured forth a refreshing source of clear, cool water, and the stream's banks were lined with lush grass and bushes full of sweet berries. The expedition took advantage of the unusual surroundings and decided to spend the night nestled in the trees. Swit and Will set their camp under a large tree where they had a good view of the river.

"If we'd had some of these big trees down on the South Platte," Swit began, "we could have built us another raft instead of tearing them wagons all apart."

"I ain't for buildin' rafts for wagons, or boats out of wagons. Best thing to do with a wagon is leave it at home." Will was watching the birds in the trees. He hadn't noticed it before, but there weren't many songbirds out on the prairie. "What's the point of spendin' all your time diggin' roads and floatin' rivers?

"I noticed you didn't mind setting under a wagon when we were caught in that hailstorm," Swit said. "Did you see them big ol' deer scoot out of the trees when we rode in? I'll bet the hunters come back with some fresh meat tonight."

"I sure did," Will answered. "Them's black deer. You'll see a lot of 'em in the Rockies. Mulely eared-lookin', ain't they? I'd sure look favorable on some cooked venison for supper."

"What I'm really hungry for is some buffalo." Swit had limited experience with buffalo meat, but listening to the trappers had stirred his interest. "Everybody says we should have seen buffalo by now."

"Never heard of nobody crossin' the plains and not seein' buffalo," Will admitted. "You don't suppose them wagons scared 'em off, do you?"

"There's not much that beats a good shade tree in summer." Captain Walker had walked up without Swit or Will noticing. "I've got a chore I'd like you two to help me with."

Swit was on his feet almost before Walker finished his sentence. "What can we do for you, Captain?"

"Henry and his bunch found some buffalo today." Walker was leaning against a tree. "They shot three and brought back what meat they could carry, but Henry thinks that there's more of 'em up ahead. Henry knows buffalo, so I expect he's right. I've asked him and Robert to get Woolly Wilson with his wagon and see if they can find the main herd. I'd like you two to ride with 'em. I realize you'll miss the buffalo feast here tonight, but by this time tomorrow I'll bet you find yourselves in the thick of a buffalo hunt."

"Do we need to take anything special?" Swit asked. "I never been on no buffalo hunt before."

"Henry will have everything in Woolly's wagon that you'll need, except your bedroll. Ride your strongest horse. Will, have you hunted buffalo?"

"Well, I've hunted, but I've never shot me one," Woodrow answered. "I've pulled the hide off a few, though. How far away are these buffalo?"

"Henry thinks it'll take several days for the caravan to get there," Walker replied. "My only advice is to listen when Henry talks. At first glance you might be inclined to reject anything Henry says. Don't make that mistake, especially where buffalo are concerned." Walker moved back to where his horse was grazing.

Swit only knew Henry by sight, and like Walker had suggested, Henry hadn't impressed him as someone deserving special attention.

"Thanks for your help." Captain Walker had mounted. "I wish I was going along."

"Well now, that takes care of tonight's feast, might even take care of tonight's sleep too." Will had unraveled his long legs and was starting to pick up his blankets. "I ain't never seen a hunter yet that liked to do anything except shoot. The rest of the work is left up to us squaws."

"They must have done something besides shoot." Swit already had Scab saddled, and his bedroll tucked under his arm. "They brought buffalo meat back with them."

"Sure, and you would too if you wanted to head right back out and shoot some more." Will was aware that Swit was waiting on him, but things just took so much time. "Be sure you take your best rifle along. If we do get a shot off, we'll probably be a hundred and fifty or two hundred yards from the beasts. Unless, of course, Henry figures to run 'em down—better be on ol' Scab if that happens."

Swit couldn't get over how deceiving it was to be around Will. He'd been standing around and waiting for Will to get himself ready. Before he realized it, Will was in the saddle waiting for him to climb up on Scab. They rode over to Woolly Wilson's wagon and deposited their belongings. Woolly was sitting on the wagon seat, smoking a pipe. He was one of the older men in the group, or at least he looked older. Neither Swit or Will, or probably anyone else in the expedition, knew Woolly's given name. Woolly fit the man just fine. He was covered with more hair than Swit had seen on any one human. Swit didn't know about his head. He'd never seen Woolly when he wasn't wearing his little Scotch plaid brimless cap with the red ball on top. Woolly called it his Balmoral.

"Hello to ya, lads," Woolly greeted the two riders. "I'm glad you're a goin' with us. I've watched ya from afar and wanted to make your acquaintance. I'm Woolly Wilson."

"It's good to meet you, Woolly," Will said. "My name is Woodrow Willard, but mostly I answer to Will. This here is Swit Boone. It seems like they fairly showered the two of us with W's, don't it?"

"Aye, that it does," Woolly answered. "We best get to movin', lads. See how far west we can get before dark."

"Where's Henry and Robert?" Swit wanted to know. "I thought they were going with us."

"Aye, they are," Woolly answered. "They left about thirty minutes back. It's us that goes with them. Henry wanted to use all of today's light." With that comment, Woolly ended the conversation by moving the wagon forward through the trees and heading it upriver.

"Do you know Henry or Robert?" Swit ask as he and Will rode along behind the wagon.

"I've met 'em both," Will answered. "Wouldn't say I necessarily know 'em. Robert is real quiet. You could ride to St. Louis with him, and I doubt he'd say more than a dozen words. Henry's older, probably about Woolly's age. I heard he lived with the Indians for a time. Andy Drips said that he thought Henry S. Ismert was the best pure rifle shot he ever saw."

"What's the S. stand for?" Swit asked.

"Well now, ya know I never give it much thought." Will was puzzled by Swit's question and how he could ask the most unlikely questions. "Maybe it's for shooter."

Will didn't reveal any more information as the two men rode along. Swit didn't ask any more questions, he was busy working his head and trying to sort out what he did know. One thing was for sure, it would be dark before they caught up with Henry. Swit didn't like the idea of riding through unfamiliar territory in the dark.

The sun dropped behind a cloud, and daylight turned to twilight. When darkness set in the soft glow from a half-full moon made the North Platte River shine like a polished silver ribbon. Swit decided that as long as he could see the river he wasn't lost. The three men traveled along in the darkness for some time without talking. It was quiet except for the night sounds and the clatter made by the wagon and their horses.

"Do you think that's Henry and Robert's campfire up ahead?" Swit ask Will. "It's hard to tell how far off it is, ain't it?"

"It sure enough looks like a campfire." Will didn't know if it was Henry's, but it was a good guess. "Hey, Woolly, would you say that's Henry's fire ahead?"

"Aye, he'll have supper ready when we get there," Woolly hollered back. "A big chunk of buffalo steak. I'll bet ya Robert'll have the biscuits ready to soak in the drippings."

"How far away would you say we are?" Will's stomach decided to growl a little in anticipation of the coming meal.

"Not far. We'll be there in thirty minutes time," Woolly answered. "I can already taste it me-self, laddie."

"By golly, Robert, I've never seen it fail to happen." Henry was talking loud enough so that the riders could hear the conversation as they pulled into camp. "Just as you're ready to set down to a fine meal, company shows up. It's a good thing we got an extra biscuit buried in the fire. You three just as well scurry on down here and fill yourselves. A hungry man ain't no fun to be around at all."

"Now, if it's a little fun that you're a want'un, maybe a wee nip of me malted barley could help." Woolly pulled a jug from the wagon and headed for the fire. "I can taste Robert's bonny biscuits already. Do you lads know me escorts? The tall one would be Woodrow Willard, and this here's Swit Boone."

"We're always glad to meet two healthy young specimens like ourselves, ain't we, Robert?" Henry stood and took a pull from the jug. "I guess we'll have to feed 'em the whole course, dessert and all, since they brought the wine. Will, I think maybe we've met before. You ever been up on the Green River?"

"We met two years ago." Will remembered being introduced to both Henry and Robert. It had been a brief encounter as they passed their camp, and Will was surprised that Henry recalled the incident. "I was with Andrew Drips. He introduced us."

"I thought so; we had a fine buffalo hunt over on the Bear that summer." Henry shook hands with Will and Swit. "Swit, I see you're still riding the best horse in the outfit. You better watch out for Robert, he's mighty partial to good horseflesh. He'll talk you right out of that horse before you know what's happened—could get your saddle too. Gentleman, this handsome young gent setting down here by the fire is Robert William Albert Morrison. His talents are many, and high among 'em is biscuit making. Will, you probably remember Robert."

"Yes, I do." Will started to reach a hand down toward Robert.

"Howdy," Robert said, casting a quick look up and a nod before he turned his attention back to his cooking.

"I better be seeing to the horses," Swit said as he headed for the wagon. Captain Walker's words about not making a mistake judging Henry's leadership had Swit's focus. Henry was a little old man, and there wasn't much about his physical appearance that would say, "get up and follow me."

He dressed strictly for utilitarian purposes. How he looked meant little compared to how he felt. He was inclined to do a lot of talking, and it seemed more suited for entertainment than guidance. When Swit thought of a leader he pictured Captain Walker. Henry's image wasn't at all like Walker's, although Swit had noticed that both men seemed to radiate confidence and were what Billy B. called quick thinkers.

Robert was the truly interesting one. He appeared to be about the same age as Swit, and seemed to stay completely within himself. He spoke just that one word, and never made eye contact with anyone. Robert had a traveled look about him, kinda like Billy. It suddenly occurred to Swit how much Robert looked like Billy. Both had the same rugged yet groomed appearance that Swit believed the ladies seemed to favor. They each had the same type of mustache. There was enough resemblance that they could have passed for brothers.

Billy and Robert may have looked alike, but their actions couldn't have been more dissimilar. When Swit returned to the fire, Henry handed him his meal. It was delicious. However Henry and Robert had arranged their traveling and cooking duties, it made for good meals and entertaining company. The last thing Swit remembered before sleep took him was Henry and Woolly crowded in close to the dying fire, passing the jug and talking about buffalo.

"Robert, you're gonna have to go wake the ladies up." Henry and Robert were huddle around the fire. It was still dark, and Will was being eased back into consciousness by the aroma and splatter of boiling coffee and meat cooking in a skillet. "I don't mind building the fire and cooking breakfast, but I'll be damned if I'm gonna spend all morning waiting for these lovelies to open their eyes. We got a full day's ride ahead, and I plan to have buffalo in my sights by nightfall."

"Did you and Woolly spend the whole night talking?" Swit and Will arrived at the fire together, and Swit was wondering if Henry had slept at all. "It seemed like you two had a lot of catching up to do."

"Robert, where is that old Scot this morning?" Henry ignored Swit's question. "He tried to kill me last night with that jug juice of his. I almost slept the morning away. Swit, run up there and kick on that wagon a spell. Tell him I'm gonna set it afire if he ain't down here in two minutes." Swit was getting up to go look for Woolly when the Scotsman wandered into sight.

"Top of the morning to ya," Woolly greeted the group. "I see Henry's itching to travel. I'd say my old elixir has stirred his blood some."

"It stirred something up all right," Henry said. "But it ain't my blood, it's my bowels. I'll be a traveling, but mostly it'll be off into the bushes."

"Are we headed for the Chimney today?" Woolly poured himself some coffee.

"Exactly right." Henry was anxious to leave. "We'll get a bead on the buffalo and either be at the Chimney when you get there or meet you there later. You three keep a sharp eye, now. I didn't see any Indian sign yesterday, but Indians and buffalo go together. There's a good spring by the Chimney, and it's a favorite campsite for their hunting parties. If you have to hide out, don't worry, we'll find ya. It pays to be alert. Robert, are you about ready to go or would you like some more breakfast?"

"I'm ready." Robert finished his coffee and headed for his horse. Henry fell in behind Robert. The two men mounted their horses and headed west. Once they left the light of the campfire they were out of sight.

"Where's this Chimney that Henry was talking about?" Swit asked Will. It had to have been close to an hour since they broke camp, and the soft light of the new day finally made it possible for Swit to look around a little. "I figure it must be some kind of landmark."

"That's exactly what it is." Will was pretty sure that as soon as they reached the top of the next little hill they'd be able to get their first view. "It's a rock that kinda looks like a chimney stickin' up out of the prairie. It'll be real faint when you first see it."

Swit was keeping a sharp eye like Henry had suggested. He was watching for a rock formation that resembled a chimney and at the same time trying to spot any Indians or buffalo that might be in the area. All he had noticed so far was a couple of long-eared rabbits that the trappers called jacks, and some squirrel-sized gophers called prairie dogs. When they topped the hill, Will's prediction proved correct. Swit spotted the dim outline of what had to be the Chimney.

"How far from it would you say we are?" Swit asked.

"I don't know," Will answered. "But it'll take us all day to get there. All you can see from here is the top, wait till you get up close—it's a queer lookin' thing."

It was late in the afternoon, and Swit thought the Chimney still looked to be miles away. The surrounding country was beginning to show a roughness. Outcroppings of light colored sandstone formations were visible along the south side of the river valley. A variety of ravines, gulches and canyons had been formed by the small streams and creeks that flowed through and around the hills on their way to the Platte. Swit was thinking about Indians and how they could hide anywhere in the breaks and strike without notice. He remembered the old bullwackers on the Santa Fe telling how they would put the river to their backs and turn over a wagon to use as a barricade when they were under attack.

Swit was putting his what-if plan together in his head when he noticed the little black specks on the hills. He thought buffalo immediately, but it seemed as if there were too many. The specks turned into dots, and the dots into buffalo. They were so thick that some of the hills looked black. As soon as one of the animals moved down the hill out of sight, it seemed as if two more climbed up from the opposite side. It looked the same for miles. Swit had watched buffalo before, but that was no more than a hundred at one time. This bunch went as far back in the hills as you could see.

"How many buffalo do you suppose there are out there?" Swit noticed that he wasn't the only one watching the enormous herd.

"Well now, I'll tell ya, it'd be hard to count them." It was more buffalo than Will had seen in one location. "I've heard 'em tell about hundreds of thousands of 'em in one group. They say that the old bulls hang together and travel along on the outside of the pack, with the cows and calves in the middle."

"I ain't never been up close to a buffalo bull." Swit had listened to the trapper's tales and knew that buffalo could be dangerous. "I heard that bull hides make the best robes."

"Well, they're big." Will's experience with buffalo had for the most part been with dead ones, but he'd heard enough stories about men that had underestimated a buffalo's capability. "Some will weigh up around a ton. They're mean too, and quicker than you might think. Don't take any chances with them. Woolly, there's enough buffalo here to feed every red man alive. Have you seen any Indian sign today?"

"Nay, laddie, nary a trace of our red brothers," Woolly answered. "Ya know that many buffalo could cause ol' Henry to turn dotty on us."

Even Will's inquiry about Indians couldn't shake Swit's thinking away from the buffalo. The bullwackers had talked a lot about the shaggy animals. It seemed as if everyone had his favorite story, but what Swit remembered most was that buffalo had real poor eyesight and apparently weren't too smart. They must be mean like Will had said, because there were lots of tales about some old bull that killed someone, his horse, or both. Stampedes seemed to be common in buffalo herds, and Swit recalled that they had a tendency to tromp down everything in their way. He guessed that they'd all get flattened if this bunch ever decided to run for the river. That is unless Scab could outrun them.

The wagon and riders continued to move in a northwesterly direction, following the North Platte. The buffalo stayed in the hills south of the river valley, and the Chimney grew closer as the hours passed. When the entirety of Chimney Rock was finally in view, Swit had tired of watching buffalo graze in the distance, and directed his attention to the landmark. Rising out of a fairly flat plain was a large, round hill with a peculiar towerlike rock sticking straight up from its center. He hadn't truly appreciated the size of the monument until Woolly stopped the wagon and started to make camp on the southeast side of the hill. The chimney part was somewhat larger at its base, and Swit guessed that it was at least a hundred and twenty-five feet high. If you counted both the hill and the rock it must have reached up five hundred feet above the valley floor. No wonder they'd been able to see it so far away. The Chimney was not something you'd ride by and not take notice or forget.

"It's quite a sight, ain't it, Woolly?" Henry and Robert rode into the camp from upriver just after sundown. Henry had obviously been fueled by the events of the day.

"Aye, never thought I'd see anything like it." Woolly watched Robert dig his biscuit pan out of the wagon.

"I ain't never seen more in one cluster." Henry was still shaking his head. "They're starting to cross over the river a few miles west of here. There's so many, Robert even had to make comment. Looks like they've grouped together from all over to make the crossing. They're fanned out farther than the eye can travel. If this breeze stays out of the south we can move right out in 'em and lay in a meat supply that'll last us a day or two."

"See any Indians today?" Woolly asked.

"No Indians, but what I did see riding back here this evening I'll remember forever. Them great brutes spread out in the hills had us all but surrounded for as far as you could see. The sky was as deep a blue as I've ever seen it, and fluffed with clouds. Just as the sun slid between some clouds behind us, a bright shaft of light struck the face of this old landmark. Woolly, it was really something to see. That ol' Chimney Rock stuck out like a diamond in a goat's ass."

The hunters ate their evening meal with little conversation and turned to the blankets early. It had been a long, hard day, and sleep was welcome. The jug stayed in the wagon. Swit was awakened when Robert nudged him. "It's time," Robert said as he moved over to where Will was sleeping. Swit looked around. It was almost daylight, and he didn't see any sign of a meal being started. Will was stretching out his long limbs. Henry and Robert were getting their horses ready. Swit jumped up and hurried off to catch Scab. Swit was ready, and Will about ready, when Henry and Robert gathered around.

"The four of us are going to ride off to the south and work our way right down into the middle of a little bunch that will be coming in over there." Henry pointed back into the hills.

"What about Woolly?" Swit asked. "Ain't he going along?"

"What for?" Henry answered. "Woolly couldn't hit a bull in the ass with a bass fiddle. Let him sleep. He'll have a meal ready when we get back. I want this hunt to go something like this: We'll get ourselves in among'st the cows first. With the breeze in our faces they ain't gonna smell us coming."

Apparently Woolly wasn't too handy with a gun, Swit thought. He wondered how he'd do when the shooting started. Billy B. was good with a rifle, and now he wished that he'd asked Billy to show him something about marksmanship.

"Just follow along in single file behind me and Robert and do exactly like we do." Henry had no idea about Will or Swit's hunting abilities. "I'll pick out the cows. The best shot is through the lungs in that little bare spot just behind the elbow. You hit 'em there and you'll take out the heart and lungs. After we get enough cows down you can have at all the bulls you want. Shoot 'em from way off, or on the run, whatever turns you on. Don't take no more cows, and no matter what you do, don't kill any calves. Them babies is the future. If you kill half of the bulls you see, which you won't, you'd effect the buffalo's future about as much as a bunch of gnats."

They stayed, for the most part, down in the deeper ravines as Henry slowly worked his way back into the hills. Sometimes they'd get off and lead their horses over a piece of higher ground; other times they'd just lean down close to the horse's neck and continue riding. Occasionally they would startle some old bull, and he'd turn and trot off over the next rise, taking twenty or thirty head with him. The huge clouds of dust kicked up by such a small bunch, and the speed with which the buffalo could get out of sight, surprised Swit. He watched Henry skillfully maneuver his way inside the vast complement of animals. The little old man was a true master of the hunt. Henry stopped the safari just before they were about to climb out of a long notch between two flat-topped hills.

"Robert and I are going on foot from here." Henry handed his horse over to Will. "I think we're gonna find what we want just over this rise. Keep a tight hold on them horses. Our plan is to get some cows down without spooking the bunch but sometimes plans get sideways. If we was to trigger a stampede, them horses is gonna wanta run, and if they do, we wanta be on 'em. If you hear us shoot for a while and nothing happens, ease yourselves on up and take a peek around. Robert, hand your horse over to Swit and let's see if we can get some meat for the table."

Henry and Robert carried their rifles. First walking in a crouched position and then crawling along on their bellies, they moved on up the draw and out of sight. It seemed to Swit that Henry and Robert had been gone too long when he heard a rifle announce its presence. Swit watched and listened. A stampede of buffalo was bound to kick up considerable dust and create enough noise that he and Will would hear 'em coming.

"You'd think the sound of gunfire would send everything in retreat." Swit was trying to settle the horses; they'd noticed the rifle shot.

"Well now, I'll tell you what, buffalo is kinda funny that way," Will answered. "Shootin' noise don't seem to bother them hardly at all. Fact is, in any little group there's generally only one leader. If you can drop that one first, the rest will usually just mill around. They don't really pay much attention to each other unless one spooks and runs. I've seen 'em all picked off one at a time, without any of 'em gettin' excited. But you try to ride up on 'em horseback and they're likely to take off like one horse and rider could wipe out every buffalo alive. They got one big ol' head, but it sure weren't put there to house no hefty brain."

The sound of rifle fire was coming in regular and steady. Swit and Will decided to slowly walk the horses toward the noise and chance a look. When they reached the top, Swit could see that they were surrounded by hills covered with tall grass slowly shifting in a soft breeze. Everywhere, on every hill, there were buffalo. It hadn't occurred to him before, but now he realized he wasn't exactly sure which direction he was facing. The wind and the sun made him think it was south, but the sun was high in the sky and the wind could change.

Henry and Robert were about two hundred yards off to the right. A herd of seventy or eighty buffalo was another hundred yards beyond them. There were seven cows down on the ground, and the group didn't seem the least upset. They took no mind of Swit, Will or the horses. They just seemed confused. Henry would fire, and a cow would usually jerk up its head. Most of the cows that Henry shot seemed to stand at first as if they knew something had happened and they couldn't decide exactly what it was. Then they would just drop. Others would take a step or two, stagger and fall over. When they fell one or two individuals close by might jump sideways, but it didn't seem as if it was from fear; it was more like they were trying to just get out of the way. Each time a cow went down, one or two others would come over and sniff around on her, but they didn't seem to think that her condition was in any way a threat to them.

Robert loaded one gun while Henry used the other. It was teamwork developed from years of hunting together. Robert never missed a move and seemed to anticipate Henry's every need. Swit was thinking that Will, or whoever it was that said Henry was a true shot, had hit the mark. He never missed. It didn't take Henry long to get what they'd come after. When he was finished with his shooting, he stood up and looked out across the hill country. He had one foot resting on the top of a little mound of dirt, and he held his rifle by the barrel, letting its butt rest on the ground beside his other foot.

"Looks like ol' Henry can hit a bull with a fiddle," Swit said softly to Will. "I never saw shooting like that before."

"Just look at him," Will said. "Standin' there like he's in charge of everything within sight, and I guess he pretty well is. Makes you think maybe God put him here for just this purpose, don't it?"

"I don't know why he's here, but he's waving us over." Swit didn't mind if Henry was in charge of everything, as long as he knew the way back to the river.

"As fat a bunch a cows as I ever seen," Henry said as soon as Swit and Will arrived. "Robert had the loads just perfect in them guns. It sure makes your job easy when you got good help."

"How come they ain't hightailing it out of here?" Swit was puzzled. The fact that men and horses were standing in plain sight of the remaining buffalo didn't seem to cause any panic at all. They were slowly grazing off in the opposite direction. "Can't they see us now and what we've done to them?"

"We're standing out here, plain as a pig in a parlor," Henry answered. "It's just that they're not set to do much figuring about what just happened. It's the way they're made. They ain't the best at solving problems. Back in here, where it's mostly cows and calves, they ain't used to that much danger. They're not likely to bolt off in any ol' direction unless you move in too close or too fast."

"Are we suppose to shoot us some of them bulls now?" Swit wanted to know.

"I'm headed on back to camp," Henry answered. "Robert likes to run 'em, so he's gonna stay out a while. You two suit yourself. After we eat we'll work the wagon up this way and start the business of meat and hide preservation. Before we separate, how about giving me a hand opening up the jugulars on them cows so they can bleed out good. If you got the Indian's taste for a hot blood breakfast, be my guest. Myself, I never did learn to appreciate their enthusiasm for that delicacy. Approach those cows careful, though. I've seen so-called dead buffalo get up and charge ya. Have your horses handy."

Will decided to stay with Robert, and Swit thought it wise to go along with the man he believed best qualified to find the river. Before they left, Henry issued a warning. "Don't forget about Indians and buffalo. You keep a close tab on things."

Swit was pleased by his decision to head back when Henry started off in a direction that was about thirty degrees to the right of Swit's calculated path for return. He thought about how the hills could disorient a man's sense of direction. Each hill looked pretty much like another and there wasn't anything to sight on. It was easy to get turned around.

True to Henry's belief, Woolly had a hot meal ready when they rode into camp. "I heard ya blasting away," Woolly said as they met around the fire. "Did ya hit poor old Robert and Will? I shoulda known better than to cook up a mess for all of us."

"Don't you worry any about what I hit," Henry answered. "I got you enough work to put your old Scot heart at ease. Robert and Will is out there gunnin' 'em down on the run. I ain't ever seen the like, Woolly. I'd like to know how far you'd have to ride to get through 'em."

Swit didn't realized how hungry he was until he got a whiff of Woolly's breakfast. He hadn't fired a shot during the buffalo hunt, but he felt pleased that Captain Walker had sent him along with these men. It was an experience he would have hated to miss.

Chapter Thirteen

Skinning buffalo carcasses, collecting and preparing the meat for storage, and drying the hides was work for all hands. Woolly's ability with a knife was an amazing sight to watch. First he'd select the choicest cuts of meat, and then with the skill of a surgeon, dissect it off the bone and slice it into strips for hanging. Henry didn't just hunt and shoot; he could slip a buffalo out of its hide as fast as any man, or Indian squaw, for that matter. Robert's area of responsibility was hide care. As soon as a buffalo was relieved of it's tough outer covering, he was there to stake it down for drying and scrape away any particles of flesh or fat that had accidentally been removed with the hide. Swit and Will were learning about buffalo from men that knew. To Will's surprise, everyone did their share of the work. There weren't any slackers in this bunch.

Captain Bonneville led the caravan into Woolly's camp at Chimney Rock while Joe Walker took a party of five mounted trappers to scout the country upriver. Bonneville could see that Henry's men had been busy, and he enlisted others to help. They strung strands of rawhide from every available pole, wagon part or rock that they could find. Strips of drying buffalo meat hung from all the lines. The hides were pegged down, hair side next to the ground, and spread out all over the prairie to dry. Robert had fashioned a smokehouse from a small cave he found along the base of Chimney Rock. He had buffalo tongues curing in the smoke.

Before Woolly, Swit and Will reached Chimney Rock, Swit had noticed the faint outline of what appeared to be a mammoth bluff off to the northwest.

118

The activities of the last several days had put his thoughts about the unusual formation aside, but now that the expedition was moving forward Swit could see that the river was leading them toward a huge mountain of rock.

As the expedition moved west, the massive barricade on the south side of the river valley became clearer and larger. Swit wondered if it was the beginning of what Will and the other trappers called the Rockies. The unusual rock formation extended four to five miles south of the river and appeared to be the same type of rock, stone and clay that formed Chimney Rock. It looked to be at least two hundred and fifty feet higher than the chimney, and hard to tell how far across. Walker and his men rejoined the expedition as it reached the bluff. Captain Bonneville followed Walker's suggestion and swung the wagons toward the south end of the enormous structure.

"I didn't expect to see a chunk of rock that size," Swit said. "Not here in the river valley."

"The Indians call this place 'Me-a-pa-te' the 'hill that is hard to go around.'" Will was ready to tell Swit everything he'd heard about this place. "Most of the trappers call it Scott's Bluff. You ever hear how it got its name?"

"Didn't even know it had a name," Swit answered.

"Seems that back in '28 a handful of Ashley's men was headed downriver in canoes," Will started his story. "They must a got caught in some rough water, 'cause they all got dumped in the river. Their gunpowder was ruined so they couldn't shoot any game or put up much of a fight if the Indians was to attack. The little group was making their way down the valley on foot, trying to live off what berries and roots they could find. When they reached the mouth of the Laramie River, Hiram Scott was overcome with an illness."

"Was he their leader?" Swit wanted to know. "I wouldn't think too much of boating a river. You could come around any ol' bend and find yourself in tricky water before you realized you was there."

"I don't know who the leader was," Will answered as he noted how Swit could get zeroed in on one little piece of information. "Scott's name is the only one I ever heard. Anyhow, the men decided to layover and wait for ol' Scott to get better. One day while they was a pokin' around lookin' for something to eat, they stumbled on what they thought was a fairly fresh trail made by some other trappers that had passed through the area. They talked it over and decided that the best chance they had to avoid starvation was to try and catch up to 'em. The only hitch was that Scott wasn't well enough yet to travel. Well, they headed down the trail anyhow and left Hiram Scott to do for himself."

"Why didn't they just send the two fastest runners to catch up with the trappers?" Swit asked. "The rest could do their best for Scott and hang on until their buddies got back with the supplies. Two good men traveling alone could make better time, anyhow. They sure didn't have much of a leader."

"Swit, we ain't talkin' about leadin' men down the Platte. I'm trying to tell you about how this bluff got its name. Who was leadin' the group ain't the point."

"If you was walking out here in the middle of nowhere, and all you got is wet boots and powder, it'd be a mighty big point," Swit replied. "Anyone can misjudge a situation, but a good leader ain't likely to follow it up with one bad call after another."

"Well, whoever the leader was," Will tried to bring Swit back to his story, "that's what they did. The men succeeded in catchin' up to the bunch ahead of 'em and saved themselves. They told their new comrades that Scott had died back along the fork of the Laramie."

"You mean they never even went back to check on Scott after they saved themselves?" Swit asked. "Dogs running in a pack take better care of each other than that. I'll bet you that Henry, Robert or Woolly wouldn't leave you to the wolves."

"I expect you're right about that." Will was beginning to regret trying to tell Swit about this bluff. "Anyhow, the next summer some of them same men is travelin' up the Platte on their way back to the beaver. They find a man's skeleton, and they can tell from the scraps of clothes wrapped around the bones that it's Hiram Scott. They..."

"Well, what did they expect?" Swit interrupted "A grave he'd dug and buried himself in?"

"That's not the whole of it." Will had always thought that the story about how Scott's Bluff got its name was interesting, but apparently Swit didn't care how it happened. "They found Scott's remains just on the other side of this mountain of rock. That's a good sixty miles from where they'd left him to die. This place has been called Scott's Bluff ever since."

At first Swit didn't say anything. He rode along in silence for several miles before turning to Will. "It's a damn shame a man that tough couldn't have traveled under Captain Walker. Alone out here you ain't got much chance when things just go against ya. You're just the same as alone if you ain't got a good leader."

"We found fresh tracks this morning. Six riders moving away from the river." Joseph Walker was certain that it was time to reevaluate the Indian signs they were observing daily.

"Do you think it's the same Indians that watched us yesterday?" Bonneville asked.

"Looks like it to me," Walker answered. "At first I thought it was just a small party out looking for buffalo. I doubt that now; don't think they would have hung around this long watching us if they were after buffalo. They're probably a scouting party for a larger bunch, and I think they've returned to report their findings."

"Do you think we should prepare for an attack?" the captain asked. "I've never heard of Indians out here attacking this large a complement of men."

"I have an idea that if we do get a visit, it will be out of curiosity about our unusual travel arrangements." Walker was sure that most of the Indians in these parts hadn't seen this many wagons in one group, if they've seen any at all.

"I'll just keep the men in a little tighter and let 'em know that we might get some company." Captain Bonneville and Joe Walker had finished their morning meal, and Bonneville stood up to leave.

"Let's try and not have any gunplay unless one of us gives the word," Walker suggested.

"That sounds like good advice, Joe. I'm going to find Michael and pass your thoughts on to him. When possible, we'll travel with the wagons two abreast and closer together. Are you planning to take out an advance party this morning?"

"Yes, I think I'll take Henry and Robert," Walker answered.

"Why don't you take that young man that was with you when you were down at Fort Gibson? Bonneville suggested. "I've been watching him. I think he has leadership ability. The experience would be good training for him. What was his name? Boone?"

"Swit Boone," Walker answered. He hadn't considered taking Swit along, but he thought Bonneville's reasoning was sound. Looking for leaders from within his command must be part of Bonneville's military training, Walker thought.

It was the last week in June, and the afternoon temperatures had been reaching into the high eighties. The morning was hazy and felt cool as Swit rode along behind Captain Walker and Henry. Robert was last in line. Swit calculated that by now they were several miles out ahead of the main expedition. Behind Robert he could see the faint outline of Scott's Bluff, and somewhere up ahead was the fork of the Laramie, where Hiram Scott had been left to die. They were following along the North Platte, and it continued to flow in the same northwest to southeast direction. Swit had no idea why he'd been selected as part of the advance party. The Captain, Henry and Robert had acted as if his coming along was a common morning occurrence.

Swit was trying to follow Captain Walker's instructions to the letter— watch for game and any sign of Indians. To be chosen for this duty was an honor, and Swit intended to give it his full attention. He was pretty sure Walker would see any Indians before he could, and he knew Henry could pick out and probably even shoot a deer, elk or whatever before he knew they were anywhere around. To be in the company of these men, out in the open on such a fine morning, riding a magnificent animal in the most pleasant of surroundings, was perfect. That worried Swit. His dad had told him that when everything seemed to be going perfect he should set his feet, get a good hold on things and be ready—trouble's on the way. Scab threw his head up. Walker had stopped the procession.

Captain Walker turned sharply to the left and put his horse into a fast trot. He led his men up a little draw, over a knob, and then pulled up short of reaching the top of a large grass covered hill. Following Walker's lead, they all dismounted and slowly led their horses closer to the hilltop. When they were almost on top of the bluff, Walker handed his horse to Henry and crawled the last few yards. He peeked over the top and saw what he expected. Below him, hidden from the sight of anyone coming up the normal path along the Platte, was a large group of Indians. Some were sitting on the ground visiting, while others just stood around. Each one had hold of a horse. They would all be ready to ride at a moment's notice. Walker motioned Henry forward, and Henry handed the horses to Swit and Robert before he crawled up to the captain's location. They both carefully looked over the situation, then slowly retreated back to where Robert and Swit held the horses.

"I make it out to be about sixty braves," Walker quietly said to Henry. "Looks like they're painted for action. What'd you see?"

"That's about what I counted, maybe a few more," Henry answered. "They're Crows. I think they've been traveling for a while. That paint's old. It don't figure that they're after us, at least not in the beginning. I finally saw their lookout. Is that what tipped you off? Do you think he saw us?"

"I caught sight of him as he was moving over to get a better view of the trail." Walker waved Swit in closer. "I don't think he saw us. If they knew we were here, I think they'd all be horseback and looking for us. Swit, I want you to work your way down that gully over there. It'll feed you back onto the main trail about three quarters of a mile to the east. Once you're deep in the ravine, their lookout can't see you, so mount up and hurry on back to Bonneville. Tell him about this bunch of Indians. There's not much doubt that they mean to surprise us. What we're not sure of is if they intend to do us any harm. My guess is that they'll ride out before the column is within rifle range and put on a big show for us. If it works that way, they're not looking to fight, so I'd advise that we hold our fire. If they wait until the last minute to pull their surprise, expect the worst and be ready to shoot."

"What if he asks me where you are?" Swit wanted to know.

"Tell him we'll be in a position to either watch the performance or send in some rifle balls from a direction that the Indians hadn't counted on. You keep your eyes open; there may be others we don't know about."

Swit, with Scab in hand, headed for the ravine. He didn't look back; he was intent in his assignment. Swit took his time working his way down to the bottom of the washout. He was just starting to climb up on Scab when a startled buck deer that had been hiding along the side of the gully suddenly leaped out of the tall grass. Now it was Swit and Scab's turn to be surprised. Scab jumped sideways, knocking Swit down. The deer was over the next rise and out of sight before Swit could sort out everything that was happening. Scab headed down the ravine. Swit had been able to grab a stirrup with his right hand and hold on to a bridle rein with his left. After about seventy-five yards of Swit bouncing off rocks, getting stepped on and grass-burned, Scab overcame his natural instinct of fright and flight and stopped running. Swit got to his feet, took inventory of himself, mounted, and with Scab running as hard as he could, they headed for the caravan.

Captain Bonneville was at the head of the column. When Swit rode up, Bonneville had halted the wagon train. His first concern was how Swit had received his injury and what had happen to the other men. Swit hadn't realized that his ear had been cut. He had dried blood smeared on the side of his face, along his jaw and down his neck. It was one of those injuries that looked worse than it actually was. He carefully related all of Walker's messages, and Bonneville had the caravan moving again when Swit joined Woodrow along the left flank of the column.

"Did you get attacked by Indians?" Will ask when Swit rode up. "Is everybody else okay?"

"Nobody got attacked by nothing. There's just some Indians up ahead, and I was sent back to let you know."

"Are they friendly or not?" Will was looking at Swit's wound. "How'd you get the cut in your ear?"

"I musta cut my ear on a rock. We don't know if they're friendly or out to take us. We'll know more when we try to squeeze around that bend up ahead."

Will was studying the turn in the trail that Swit had pointed to, and at the same time trying to imagine how Swit could have cut his ear on a rock when the Indians suddenly appeared. They marched out from around the bend dressed and painted for a fight. Three chiefs rode in front of an impressive ten abreast, six deep, column of braves headed straight toward Bonneville's command. By this time the caravan was in the middle of an open plain. Captain Bonneville directed the ranks to tighten in closer as they slowly continued to move forward. The two groups moved toward each other until they were about one hundred yards apart. The chief that was apparently in charge of all others stopped. He split his men into two bunches. One group running to the left, the other to the right. They formed two circles around the column of trappers, one-half moving in a clockwise direction, the others counterclockwise. Bonneville stopped the caravan.

The Indians continued to ride in circles around the column, whooping, hollering and demonstrating their considerable feats of horsemanship. Swit watched and thought how Captain Walker had called it a performance. That was exactly what it was. Both the Indians and their horses were adorned in shiny trinkets and bright colors. They displayed a riding style that seemed to make the horse and rider into one unit. Swit watched in amazement. The thought of firing his gun never occurred to him. After the Indians had exhausted their individual acts of triumph, they stopped circling and a calmness replaced all the commotion. The leader of the Indians slowly approached Captain Bonneville.

The chief and the captain made peaceful gestures to each other, and soon they were smoking from the chief's ceremonial pipe. The other Indians began to move among the wagons to examine all the strange new contraptions. They were particularly interested in a cow and calf that trailed along behind the last wagon. The Indians seemed to think the pair was some form of buffalo that the white man had tamed with his great medicine.

Joe Walker, Henry and Robert returned to the caravan, and Walker was trying to ascertain the intentions of the Crows, while at the same time attempting to covertly caution Bonneville about becoming too familiar with these Indians. The chief told about a band of Cheyenne that had attacked the Crow's village and killed one of their people. The Crow war party had spent the last twenty-five days pursuing the Cheyenne raiders, hoping to avenge their dead brothers. He suggested that the two parties camp together, and Bonneville saw it as an opportunity to become better acquainted with the people that made this country their home. The two groups spent the rest of the day and into the night in cultural exchange. In the morning the Indians and trappers split, each continuing on their chosen paths. Not long after the Indians had departed, Captain Bonneville discovered that many of his men had been relieved of their knives, whatever they'd had in their pockets, and even some of the buttons on their coats. Swit thought that it was no wonder the Crow Indians had all those bright shiny ornaments to carry into battle.

Chapter Fourteen

Billy B. thought about how his actions over the last several days hadn't been normal, at least not for him. He'd always been one to get up and get going, but lately all he felt like doing was sitting in a chair on the porch to view the valley below. He wasn't exactly tired, he just seemed to lack the gumption to move off the porch. It seemed as if almost anything, even getting out of bed, required more effort than he could provide, but he knew it was time to get on with his life.

Maria's place in Billy's future was still a big question mark. She continued to carry out what Billy thought must be her assignments around the house, and it appeared, at least from his point of view, that Maria was gradually becoming more involved in caring for the Suarez children and the management of the household. She was making many of the day-to-day decisions that had previously been made by Petronila. Her take-over and take-charge demeanor didn't seem to cause any problems. In fact, it appeared to be appreciated and expected by both the Suarez family and the household help. Don Carlos wouldn't allow anyone to be addressed as a servant.

The Don had thrown himself into the day-to-day ranch operations. He was up eating his morning meal when the light cracked the eastern sky. Maria ate her breakfast with him, and when he finished eating there were always two riders sitting on the edge of the porch drinking coffee and holding his horse. He left early and returned late. Don Carlos would sometimes join Billy on the porch after supper, telling him all about the amusing things that had occurred that day. He always asked about Billy's well-being, and answered all of Billy's concerns with the same basic advice—rest and take your time.

Billy thought that Maria looked much the same as she had last summer. The ordeal she'd suffered through had not robbed her of any of her beauty. In fact, Maria was more impressive than before: she had developed a confident repose within her. Billy could see Petronila's influence in Maria's manners. The few times Maria had been close enough that Billy could look into her eyes, she surprised him. Those eyes that used to tell a story in one glance were not talking. Billy thought Maria was treating him like she would any other guest. She was friendly, and asked about his needs in much the same way Petronila did during his previous stays at the ranch. Maria seemed to have lost her bitterness toward him, but she showed no desire to restore their past relationship.

Anita was the one person that seemed committed to bring laughter back into Billy B.'s life. She knew nothing about him except stories she'd heard from the other workers. Billy couldn't remember Anita from any of his previous visits. She was not blessed with Maria's outward beauty, but she sure wasn't hard to look at either. He'd noticed that more than a few of the *vaqueros* took an interest in Anita's whereabouts and tried to gain her attention. In some ways she reminded Billy of an innocent, playful child.

"Did you really first ride in here from Missouri when your feet could only hang halfway down on a horse's belly?" Anita asked as she continued to sweep the porch.

"I was ridin' some mighty big horses in them days." Billy chuckled to himself. "Who told you a story like that anyhow?"

"Doña Petronila said you were a man in a boy's body when she first saw you," Anita answered. "She talked a lot about you before she died. I miss her, but I don't think as much as Maria. Doña say she fell in love with you when she first sees your mustache. Did you love her?"

"I loved her in the way I would've loved my very favorite aunt, if I'd had one. Talkin' about love, I've noticed that Juan Marquez has been spendin' his time hangin' out back by the kitchen door tryin' to get your attention. Seems like all of a sudden he wants to do all the kitchen chores."

"What does he know of kitchen chores?" Anita's face showed a little blush. "He's like the rest of them *vaqueros*. If it can't be done horseback, it don't need done."

"I'm not too sure about that," Billy said. "Yesterday I saw him climb down off his horse, dust himself off and clean his boots before he rode around to the back of the house. I don't guess that's a kitchen chore, but it sure looked like he was tryin' to feather his hat a little. Wouldn't have anything to do with you walkin' back toward the orchard with him, would it? I noticed he kept his horse with him in case he had to make a fast getaway."

"We need to get you a job around here," Anita suggested. "How about you go back to the orchard and clean out them dead limbs?"

"You tryin' to get me killed?" Billy said. "If I was to lift one hand around here, Juan and his friends would ride in, rope me off this here porch and drag me all the way back to Missouri. I got to keep on your friendly side. If I was ever to displease you in any way I'd be a goner. I'm busy all day long tryin' to figure up ways to keep you happy."

"I wish you could make her happy," Anita said as she pointed the broom toward the path that led back up behind the house. Maria was slowly walking up the path. "She's on her way to visit with Doña Petronila again. She'll feel better when she comes back."

"Right now I'm tryin' not to make her mad," Billy said as he watched Maria move out of sight. "I doubt I'm up to creatin' any happiness there. I'd say I'm just another chore that she thinks she needs to oversee, about like sweepin' this here porch."

"You're wrong there, Billy B." Anita stared at Billy with her dark eyes. "I seen her sneak a look at you. One night I found her sitting in your room, watching you sleep. She had tears in her eyes. She tried to make out that she was looking for blankets, but I could tell. She thought she was past you, but now she knows that she's not. Maria is afraid of you."

"You better scoot on back in the house," Billy said. Tears were beginning to form in his eyes. "You got so much dust kicked up around here my eyes are startin' to smart."

Anita took her broom and played like she was going to throw her little pile of gathered dirt his way, then flipped it off the porch and went inside.

It was a perfect storybook type of evening. Don Carlos and Billy were parked on the porch and taking in the entire event. Carlos had returned from his day in extraordinarily good humor, and the evening meal was one of good food and enjoyable company. Maria had even joined in the laughter. She poked fun at how weathered Carlos was becoming from being outside all the time. Billy was enjoying the aroma of smoke from Carlos's pipe, and thinking about how long he'd been at the ranch. He'd experienced other low points in his life, and always found a way to pick up and start again. He would head back to Santa Fe. Something was always happening in Santa Fe.

"Why didn't Swit come back with you this time?" Carlos asked. "I sure liked that young man. He had a real way with animals, especially horses."

"He'd made plans to go west with Captain Walker. I miss him, hope the bears out there don't get him."

"How far west was he going?"

"I think they were headed into the Oregon country." Billy thought how that all seemed like a long time ago. "There was talk about trappin' up on the Green River. I haven't thought about Swit or the Indian since I got here. Have you seen anything of Otis Tejas?"

"Lord no, I didn't know he was with you," Carlos answered. "The shape you were in when you got to the ranch, I thought it was best not to ask any questions. Have you given any thought to what you'd like to do now that you're better?"

"I don't really have any plans. I guess I should try and make peace with Maria."

"You need to do that." Carlos swung his chair around so he faced Billy. "Billy B., look at me. I have a plan I want to share with you. I came from pure Spanish blood, and was born not two miles from this spot. My parents taught their children to respect all people, no matter what their origin, in accordance with how they acted and treated others. We were lucky to be born with many advantages that others didn't get, but I never believed that I should give away what I have to someone with less, just *because* they have less. I've always tried to help the ones that were willing to help better themselves."

Billy already knew most of what Don Carlos was telling him. He'd mentioned that he had a plan, and Billy wondered how this plan would involve him.

"I've seen this country change before," Carlos continued. "And I believe it's about to change again. The Mexican people threw Spain out, and now I think the American settlers, back down in *Coahuila y Texas*, might end up throwing out the Mexicans. When the Mexican revolution came, my beliefs caused me to lose some friends and make some others. I've watched your people and studied your country. I'm convinced that before they're through, everything you see around here will be a part of your country."

"You mean the Texacans has got a army?" Billy couldn't imagine this country being anything but Mexico. "I've never heard anybody talkin' about takin' over your country."

"I don't mean now, Billy. I might not even live to see it happen, but I feel strongly that some day it will. I don't necessarily think it would be all bad, unless your people try to take away our land rights just because we're Spanish. There's a hatred against anything Spanish in your country."

"I know there's some that don't think much of Mexico or Spain," Billy admitted. "I never thought of it as hate."

"I've known you since you were a boy," Don Carlos said. "I know the men that raised you. I've never known a better man than Captain Walker. You're still young and lack experience, but you're much farther along than most at your age. You are completely truthful with others, and what's more important, you're truthful with yourself. I believe you to be honest, and I would trust you with my family."

"I would never fight against you or your family," Billy stated. "If anyone tried to do them harm, I'd have to take 'em out."

"I hope it never comes to that," Carlos replied. "What I'm proposing is that you work for me, or more correctly said, work with me. Just before Petronila got so sick the last time, I also went West. I visited our settlements in California. It's a beautiful country, and a perfect place to raise cattle and horses. I worked out a deal for a land grant not far from Monterey. I want you to go there and manage it for us. You will have a half-share in the ranch, but you'll also do most of the work."

"I don't know what to say," Billy whispered. "I don't know how to ranch. I just know how to break trail between Missouri and Santa Fe. I doubt I could blaze a new path anywhere without gettin' lost. I wouldn't even know how to start a ranch."

"That's the easy part." Don Carlos watched Billy's facial expression change from surprise to doubt. "I plan to send two men with you that know everything you'll need to know about ranching. Juan Marquez and Francisco Barrera were raised ranchers and have many of the same personal qualities you possess. They also will have a piece of the ranch. What you three don't know, you'll soon learn. You already know what many men never learn."

"Why me? Why not just send them?" Billy asked. "I don't think the Mexicans would look favorable on me runnin' a ranch in their country."

"Life in California is a little different than living here." Carlos explained. "California is a long ways from Mexico City, and the Spanish people have more influence on the way the government's wishes are carried out. Your talent is the way you get along with people. I've cracked the door open a little, but you'll open it to its fullest. It'll be touchy at first, but in the end you'll have their blessing and respect, just like around here. Juan and Cisco would have a fairly difficult time gaining acceptance in California. Spanish blood is important there. It would be impossible for them if the Americans take over. You'll handle either situation, and I'll know that my family will be cared for, especially if I'm right about what's coming and not around to do the caring."

"Would we need to trail our own cattle and horses to California?" Billy asked.

"Horses and cattle are cheaper in California than they are here," Carlos answered. "A fifty dollar mule here can be bought in California for ten dollars. Any stock we drive between here and California will be in this direction."

"What about Maria?" Billy wondered if Maria knew about Don Carlos's trip to California. "Does she know about your plan?"

"Right now no one but you and I know what I've just told you. I'm not sure what Maria sees in the future, but I can tell you that California is a wonderful place for a new beginning." Don Carlos was standing and turned for the door. "You give some thought to what I've said here tonight. We'll talk about it at a later time."

To say Billy B. gave some thought to Don Carlos's conversation would be an understatement. It completely occupied his mind, except for when he thought about Maria. Anita had said Maria was afraid of him, but to Billy it seemed the opposite was true. With each passing day, Billy had become more convinced that Maria didn't want him. He was afraid to find out if it was true. Billy was setting on the porch when he noticed Maria leave by the side door and start up the path. He wrestled with himself over the wisdom of joining her to see if he had any place in her life. Maria was out of Billy's sight when he finally decided that it was time to find out where he stood. He headed up the hill. When Billy reached her she was sitting beside Petronila's grave.

"She was the finest lady I ever knew," Billy said very quietly. "You must really miss her. I see you visit her a lot. I hope I'm not disturbin' ya."

"I saw you coming up the path. I would have thrown a rock at you if I'd wanted you to stay away. Did you know she talked about you like you were one of her own? I never could understand that. One minute she was bragging on you, and then the next thing she'd be telling me that your leaving was the best thing that could have happened. That's why I come up here so much. Sometimes while I'm here I get some of my questions answered."

"I wanta tell you how sorry I am about leavin' you in Santa Fe." Billy still didn't have any idea how Maria would react to what he was about to say. "It's all my fault. I didn't know how much I loved and needed you. I was all mixed up in my head. It took most of the way back to Missouri for it to come to me. I came right back for ya. I want you to marry me. I know that I was almost too late. That first day, under the tree, I thought it was you they were praying over."

"It could have been." Maria started to cry. "I would have traded places with her, except by then if I'd given up on life Petronila would have thought she failed me."

By now the crying was uncontrollable. Maria's emotional dam had burst. Billy sat beside her and pulled her in close to him. He wasn't exactly sure what all this meant. She could be crying because of what he said, or maybe because she was upset over losing Petronila. He only knew that it sickened him to see her in this kind of distress. Billy held Maria tighter and tried to comfort her. "It's okay, it'll be all right."

"Billy, promise you'll never leave me again. Promise, Billy. Promise that only God will separate us."

Part Three:
Land of the Trappers

Chapter Fifteen

The Bonneville expedition continued its northwesterly movement up the south bank of the North Platte River. Swit enjoyed the beauty of the rolling hill country with its big grassy valleys. For the last two days, rain clouds had formed in the afternoon, and a slow steady shower cleared the air and brought freshness to the countryside. The caravan set camp along the fork of the Laramie River on the evening of June 26, 1832.

Swit remembered Will telling that this was where Hiram Scott had been left to die. He looked around at this group of men and wondered if he had any real friends in the bunch. He tried to think who he might risk everything for, but doubted that he'd really know unless he was put to the test. True friends were rare.

The country was changing, Swit thought, and it brought new and different points of interest every day. The North Platte River had redefined itself. Instead of the broad, shallow, reasonably slow-flowing artery spreading out across the plains, it had now, in some places, become a narrow, deep, cascading torrent carrying water out of the mountains as fast as it could. Their course was still generally to the northwest, but they no longer followed all the twists and turns of the river. Swit watched as the terrain became more difficult for both the wagons and the animals that pulled them. The expedition moved away from the river. They headed north with the Laramie Mountains to the west. Ravines and hills made it necessary for the men to dig here and fill in there so that the wagons could continue their journey. Sometimes when they were on high ground Swit could see the outline of another mountain range far to the north. He felt as if the mountains were slowly drawing him in.

"Are we going to cross over them Laramie Mountains?" Moving the wagons through the foothills had been enough trouble, Swit couldn't see how they could get them over the mountains.

"Nah, we'll meet up with the Platte again when we get a little farther north." Will could see that the captain was still following along the same general direction that Andrew Drips had taken two years before. "She'll be a flowin' straight out of the west then, and that'll take us around the Laramies."

It worked out exactly as Will had said, and Swit felt spared that once more he'd been able to avoid crossing any high mountain passes. As soon as they had put the Laramie Mountain range behind, the North Platte River started a wide swing back to the south. Captain Walker directed the expedition across and away from the river in a westwardly direction. Will assured Swit that they'd reach the Sweetwater River the next day.

"What's that big mound that we're headed for?" The countryside had leveled out, and Swit was pointing to a huge dark boulder that was sticking up out of the open plain ahead. "It looks kind of like a giant turtle, don't it?"

"Sort of, but they call it Independence Rock," Will explained. "The way I heard it, Tom Fitzpatrick cached some furs there on the Fourth of July in '24 and named it in honor of our country's birthday. Trappers been stoppin' and carvin' their names in that rock ever since. I chiseled my name on her."

"I'm not too handy with my letters," Swit said. "But I could put my mark in the rock."

"I'll help you with your name," Will offered. "It's interestin' to see the different names and dates carved in that rock. You wouldn't be the first to have a hand gettin' your name placed there."

"I'd like that. If Billy came by he'd know that we made it this far."

"I thought you said he was down in Santa Fe. Is he gonna join up with us?"

"I can't rightly say what Billy's gonna do," Swit answered. "He said something about seeing me in the fall, but he didn't say what fall or where."

"I'm sure anxious to meet up with this Billy B. person," Will said. "Seems like the type to liven up a trip."

Swit thought that Will's assessment of Billy seemed fair. Traveling along with Billy did tend to have its times, especially when he had himself all together.

Independence Rock was situated on the north side of the Sweetwater River. Almost everyone seemed to fancy putting their name on the huge blacked-streaked rock formation that stood before them. Captain Bonneville placed his name in the stone. He said that the rock's tallest northern end measured one hundred ninety-five feet high, and it was twenty-five hundred feet long. Captain Walker was about the only one who didn't seem interested in placing his name where others could see it. Swit thought that maybe Walker had already carved his name, although Will couldn't find it anywhere on the big boulder. It was like Walker to forgo any notice that he had once passed this way. He almost never talked about his experiences. Everything Swit knew about Walker's adventures and travels he'd learned about from someone other than Joe Walker.

The layover at Independence Rock gave the men a chance to repair the wagons and rest the livestock. For the last two weeks Walker had guided the expedition gradually into a higher, drier and more difficult country for wagon travel. Grass had become sparse and game scarce. The perpendicular creek banks, deep ravines, and high bluffs had extracted its toll from the men, animals, and wagons as they slowly moved closer to the great divide. Some of the men were positive that the dry, thin air was the source of their health problems. Stomach pains, cramps and chapped lips were common complaints. The same air quality and punishing travel had caused the wood in the wagons to dry, split, shrink and come apart. Wagon wheels were particularly difficult to keep in working order. Animals became lame, and a mixture of grease and gunpowder was applied to their hoofs.

The caravan moved west up the Sweetwater River, occasionally switching from one side to the other. It helped keep the wagon wheels from drying out. "Found you a present, Captain." Henry was leading a horse when he approached the leaders of the caravan. "He ain't much to look at, but he'd beat walkin'."

"Where in the world did you find a horse out here?" Walker asked. "You don't often see a horse traveling alone in this country."

"He was grazing all by himself in a little meadow about two miles upriver," Henry answered. "Rode right up to him. He's gentle as a dog. It put me on edge for a spell, though. I thought maybe there might be some Crows in the area. We couldn't find anyone thereabouts, but Robert did pick up a fairly recent Indian trail passing over the river and on up into the hills. I guess maybe the Indians accidentally left him behind."

"Indians generally don't accidentally leave ponies behind," Walker said.

"We'll tighten up the ranks and increase the watch," Captain Bonneville announced. "It won't hurt to take a little precaution."

"Thanks for bringing back the news." Walker was glad he'd asked Henry to ride out ahead this morning. If there were any Indians around, Henry would have found them. "Go ahead and stick him in with our other horses and then head on back to your men. Henry, you keep a sharp eye out while you're moving on up river."

"That's the only kinda eye I got." Henry took the horse and headed for the remuda.

Another great range of mountains blocking the passageway to the west was beginning to show itself in the distance. Swit thought that his luck for sidestepping the snowy mountain passes was running out. The talk around the cooking fires centered on the Wind River Mountains they were now facing, and how the Sweetwater would soon deliver them to South Pass. Swit studied the south end of the snow-covered mountain range, looking for the pass. These mountains seemed higher than any he'd seen before, and they had rough, craggy-looking peaks. It gave meaning to the name "Rockies." Taking wagons over this mountain range seemed impossible to Swit; maybe Will's reluctance to bring wagons into the fur country had been right all along.

The water and grass provided by the small Sweetwater River had made it the ideal pathway through an otherwise dry, barren landscape. When the river made a north turn up into the mountains, Bonneville's expedition crossed over to its south bank for the final time. They moved west, away from the river and out onto a wide, flat, sage-covered plateau. Wagons and riders pushed forward, and when it became evident that they would pass by the south edge of the imposing Wind River Mountains, Swit was relieved.

Benjamin Bonneville and Joseph Walker rode together in front of Captain Bonneville's expedition. Michael Cerré had the wagons arranged four abreast as the fur brigade unnoticeably climbed its way to the Continental Divide. The foothills on the south end of the Wind River Mountain range were to their right, and several miles to their left the Antelope Hills defined the northern edge of the Great Divide Basin, a high altitude plain twenty-five to thirty miles wide and sixty to seventy miles long. South Pass was so large and flat, and the incline so gradual, that it looked like anything but a passageway over the legendary Rocky Mountains.

"I sure never expected to cross the Rockies like this." Swit and Will rode beside Woolly's wagon. "Twisting around up and over snow-covered boulders and cliffs was the way I figured it would be."

"Well now, I'll tell you what, you was so worked up about this crossin' that I just thought it better to keep quiet and let you find out for yourself"

138

Looking ahead, Will could see that they would soon start to gradually work their way down into a big, sweeping valley.

"See up ahead there where Henry and Robert are stopped and looking back at us?" Woolly pointed. "That'll be Pacific Springs. You'll know your over the hump and headed west, 'cause we'll be travelin' with that little trickle of water instead of against it."

Swit thought back to Billy's tales about snowy mountain crossings and how this place was the opposite from what he'd pictured in his mind. Its appearance was much the same as the *jornada* along the Santa Fe Trail, with the exception that you could see mountain peaks in the distance, and a nice cool spring was only a few miles away.

Captain Bonneville was not concerned about exactly where the summit of South Pass was located. He'd taken some measurements and estimated that the divide basin area was roughly seventy-five hundred feet above sea level. "Joe, this is simply an incredible place for wagons to cross," Bonneville said. "We have just created a moment in history. The first wagons to cross the Continental Divide. If Sam is correct about the president's grand plan, thousands of wagons will be making this same crossing in a few years."

"I'd say you just put your name in the school books." Walker smiled at the captain. "This is where all the wagon trails will come together. They'll come in from different directions, and once they're on the other side they'll fan out to all sorts of places. This is the one spot they'll all pass through. It's sure not remarkable for scenery or grandeur; however, I'd be hard put to point out any one place that's more important to the Western development of our nation."

"As I recall, the first white man to find this place was Robert Stuart." Captain Bonneville was writing July 24, 1832, in his pocket journal. "He was on his way back to the States after they'd lost Fort Astoria to the British. That was twenty years ago."

"Some of Ashley's men were the first trappers to use the pass when they opened up the beaver country over on the Green River," Walker added. "Fitzpatrick, Smith and Bridger all claimed to have passed through here in '24."

"I've looked forward to seeing the beaver country for a long time." Bonneville was looking towards a flat-topped bluff south of the trail. He was certain that it would offer a better view of the territory ahead. "I'm anxious to reach the Green River."

Bonneville climbed the bluff he had spotted earlier and surveyed the dry, almost treeless, rolling hill country that lay to the west. The sweeping territory ahead contained the valley of the Green River, or as the Indians and many of the trappers called it, the Seeds-ke-dee. The country between here and the river was not unlike the Great Divide Basin; sage, with a light sprinkling of sparse shortgrass, was the predominant vegetation. Water and forage would be scarce before they reached the Green River.

Along the southwestern horizon, Captain Bonneville could make out the peaks in the Uinta Mountain Range. He'd been told that somewhere beyond those mountains the Green became a part of the mighty Colorado River. He could see the faint outline of the Salt River and Bear River mountain ranges running north-south along the western horizon. Bonneville marveled at being able to see mountain ranges than were more than one hundred miles away. A bright, clear day and the thin, dry air made it all possible.

"We'll get to Little Sandy Creek today. I'd advise making camp there tonight." Walker knew they could follow down Little Sandy to Sandy Creek and then on down Sandy to the Green River about sixty miles to the southwest. "We can follow the streams south to the Green and then go back up river toward the beaver country, but we'll lose several days. If you want to take the cut-off we can cross the Little Sandy tomorrow, head west and easily reach Sandy Creek. The push west from Sandy Creek to the Green River will be hard, hot and dry, but we should reach the Green in less than two days."

When the expedition reached Little Sandy Creek, Captain Ben could see the western side of the Wind River Mountains. They were truly impressive. The mountain range appeared to be twenty to thirty miles in breadth, with several peaks exceeding thirteen thousand feet in elevation. "Joe, the Green River must get its start up in those mountains."

"After we crossed the divide we were almost a thousand miles northwest of Fort Osage," Walker announced. "All the water we'd seen up to that point, except for Pacific Creek, was headed for the Mississippi River. Any rain or snow that falls up on top of those northern Wind River peaks can end up in three different places. If it rolls off on the eastern slope, it's headed back for the Mississippi and down to the Gulf of Mexico. Anything falling on the western side could eventually run into the Columbia River and on out to the Pacific Ocean; or it could drain into the Green and make it's way down to the Colorado River and the California Gulf. You could start up there and travel downhill for great distances in three different directions. Following down the Green River all the way to the Gulf would be my choice."

"The upper Green River is where we're headed. I say we take the cutoff." It was the headwaters of the Green, more precisely the place where Horse

Creek emptied into the Green River that occupied Bonneville's thoughts.

The expedition spent the night along the banks of the Little Sandy before moving on to Sandy Creek the next day. They made camp early so they could rest and prepare for their journey to the Green River. Captains Bonneville and Walker had the men ready for an early departure. Joe Walker showed Ben the direction he should take before he headed off into the barren landscape with a scouting party.

Captain Bonneville had the caravan moving shortly after Walker's departure. By mid-morning most of the men had noticed the distant dust cloud that was rising up from behind them. Someone was following and steadily closing the gap. Captain Bonneville ordered a halt to take council with his men. Many thought that the dust was caused by a large Crow Indian war party that planned to attack before they could reach the Green River. Somehow they connected the impending attack with the lone horse they'd found along the Sweetwater.

"Let's move the wagons into the two column position." The discussion had gradually degenerated into a cause and effect conversation, so Captain Bonneville decided to put the expedition into a defensive alignment. "Everyone take your assigned places and we'll continue moving toward the Green. If we come under attack, swing the wagons into our squared camping configuration, only tighter. Chain a front wheel to the back wheel of the wagon in front of you. Put everyone and everything inside the wagon enclosure. Swit, I have a special job for you and Will."

"You want us to find Captain Walker?" Swit asked before Bonneville had a chance to explain himself.

"His input would be valuable," Captain Bonneville answered. "I expect he's already seen the dust cloud and is headed back our way by now. I'd like you two to ride back and reconnoiter with what's coming up behind us. Remember that they may have scouts out in advance of their main party, so pay attention. Bring us word as soon as you can."

"Do you think its Indians that's kicking up all that dust?" Swit and Will had tied their pack horses to Woolly's wagon and, after checking their supply of ammunition, headed back down the trail. They were moving along at a trot, and Swit wondered if the dust they were creating could be seen by whoever was headed their way.

"I don't rightly know if it's Indians or not. Whoever it is, they got to be seein' the dust from our group too. One thing is fact, they don't care that we know they're comin'."

"What's this 'wreck-in-order' we're suppose to do to 'em?"

"That's just military talk." Will's lips formed a slight smile. "It just means that we're 'spose to find out who's followin' us and what their intentions are."

"Do you think Captain Bonneville sent us 'cause we got better eyesight than the others?" Swit asked.

"I think the thing we got is better horses," Will answered. "If you noticed, this last push for the Green has taken about all that most of our horses have to give. Not countin' Walker, I'd say you and me are the best-mounted pair in the group. If we do meet up with some Indians, and they're lookin' to fight, ol' Scab'll have enough left to carry you back and give warning."

"Whoever they are, they sure ain't tryin' to sneak up on us." Swit Boone kept his eyes busy searching the landscape. He and Will were several hundred yards northeast of and parallel to the trail. Occasionally this gave them a slightly higher elevation than anything that was moving along the main drag. Swit thought they had traveled far enough from the expedition. If it became necessary for them to make a hard run to warn the Captain, he wanted Scab rested. Will must have been thinking the same, because when they moved through a little draw that had a slight rise off on one side, they both stopped. Swit dismounted, handed his horse to Will, walked up to the top of the knob and looked back down the trail.

"They ain't Indians." Swit was waving for Will to come on up. "Looks like another bunch of trappers. Maybe you know 'em."

"Hard to tell from here, but I think it's Fontenelle." Will handed Scab back to Swit.

"Who's Fontenelle, the one out front?"

"Yep, I'm pretty sure that's him. How's about you ride back and tell Captain Bonneville, and I'll go down and renew old friendships?" Will didn't wait for an answer. He moved off toward the pack train. Swit turned Scab in the direction of Bonneville's dust cloud.

Walker was back and riding along beside Bonneville when they spotted Swit and Scab headed their way in an unhurried lope. Captain Bonneville had the caravan back in normal traveling alignment by the time Swit arrived. Boone explained the situation, and it was Walker's guess that Fontenelle was pushing hard to get to this year's summer rendezvous.

Lucien Fontenelle and fifty-seven trappers, each leading at least one pack animal, overtook Bonneville's expedition. He stopped just long enough to explain how they had fallen in behind the wagons after leaving the Platte. It was Fontenelle's view that Bonneville's hunters and wagons were driving away all the game, and they'd been forced to push hard so they could catch up and prevent starvation. He believed that they could make it to the river before sundown. His group was soon ahead of Bonneville's bunch and moving away.

"Did you see any old friends?" Swit asked when Will rode up along beside him. "Looks like that Fontenelle fellow's not going to hang around long."

"Well, I'll tell you what, they're pushin' real hard to get to the Green." Will had renewed a few old acquaintances, but they weren't acting all that friendly. "They been cussing us since they reached the Sweetwater. Figured that it's our fault they couldn't find any game and had to ride long and hard to pass us."

"What game they talking about? Outside of that horse we found, we ain't seen enough critters to support a good-size coyote. If we hadn't laid in that supply of buffalo we'd be starved by now."

"Fontenelle and Drips are still workin' for the American Fur Company. Andy is out at the summer rendezvous, and Lucien's tryin' to get supplies and fresh trappers from their trading post at Fort Union up to him. He's already late. I'd say he's a usin' us as an excuse to drive his men."

"He might be slick enough to drive his men," Swit said, "but he's got most of the drive out'a them horses. If the river's very far, he'll be walking in. Have I got this right? Lucien is Fontenelle's given name? Never knew anyone with a name like that. What's a ron-a-view?"

"You got it right. Lucien is French," Will answered. "I don't know anyone else with that name, and rendezvous is a French word. It means kinda like a gatherin'. William Ashley got that all started in '25.

"I've heard you mention Ashley before," Swit said.

"He was one of the first American fur traders to make it all the way out here," Will explained. "Changed the way things was done. Instead of just trading for pelts, he hired his own trappers and took 'em out to the fur country. Bridger, Fitzpatrick, Smith and Sublette all got their start workin' for Ashley. It turned out pretty good too, except that every year they still had to bring the hides back to St. Louis, pick up more supplies and trade goods, and then head back out to the beaver country. Ashley hit on the idea that instead of the trappers comin' back, he'd bring the ware-with-all they'd need for the next year out to 'em. They'd all meet up at some location they'd previously agreed upon."

"And where they all got together was a ron-a-view?" Swit asked.

"That's right," Will answered. "It usually took place durin' the summer when the beaver fur yielded a poor-quality pelt, so no one was trappin' anyhow. Ashley would unload his supplies, load up the skins, and head back to Missouri. Well, the word got out about how supplies was bein' packed out to the trappers. The Indians and free trappers started showin' up to do a little tradin' and have a little fun. Whiskey got to be an important article of supply, and everyone looked forward to the shindig that followed. It's quite a how-do-you-do."

It was dark when Captain Bonneville called a halt to his caravan. It had been a long day, and they were still surrounded by a dry, mostly flat wasteland—no river in sight. The men could rest, but there was no water to be had. In the morning Captain Walker suggested that they allow the stock to get what moisture they could from the early dew collected on the plants before they moved on.

When Bonneville reached the Green, Fontenelle's party was resting along the river. His men and horses were completely done in. A few of the stronger horses had been able to carry their riders and packs to the river before sundown, but most had struggled in during the night. Bonneville felt a sense of completion. He knew there was much more to do, but they'd made a safe journey from civilization into the fur country. They had arrived, the first ever to arrive with wagons. Both parties spent several days replenishing themselves before deciding to go their separate ways.

Chapter Sixteen

Don Carlos Suarez wanted to give Billy B. and Maria a wedding ceremony and celebration that would bring guests from all around the territory and last for several days. Maria didn't want a fiesta. She asked for a simple little wedding with just a few friends and the ranch family. Anita had agreed to stand beside her, and Maria asked Don Carlos to give her away. "I've got the biggest part in this wedding," Carlos continued to remind everyone. "I'm Father of the bride, and best man."

The betrothed couple set the date for their wedding. Billy B. was agreeable to whatever Maria wanted. He had her love again, and the only thing that interested Billy was showing Maria that she was everything to him. Billy had known Maria many times before last summer without recognizing any deep feeling for her, but that had all changed. Now he had a passion for her that seemed to define who he was. Billy was sure she wanted him in the same intimate way he wanted her, but Maria had no intention of returning to the life she'd lived. Those days were over. As far as Maria was concerned, she and Billy were not the same as they were last summer. Both of them had changed, and the past was exactly where she wanted it to be. Maria loved Billy as completely as a woman in love can, but their lovemaking would wait until her recently accepted religion not only condoned the behavior but also encouraged it as a necessary and needed part of their life together. To begin with Billy felt rejection and was confused. He couldn't understand how their denying themselves now made any difference, but waiting until they were married was important to Maria, and that was enough for Billy.

"You might just as well build you a house up there and plant a garden." Anita had watched Billy and Maria holding hands as they walked down the path behind the house. She knew that they had their own special spot picked out on the bench up behind the house. "No sense wearing yourselves out hiking up and down that hill all day long."

"We gotta go up there to watch you and that *vaquero* sashay off into the orchard." Billy liked having Anita around, but he knew that Maria didn't always appreciate their friendly banter. "You got that poor ol' boy so mixed up I saw him try to put his saddle on one of the pack mules the other mornin'. You liked to got him killed."

"From what I can see, the house could burn down when you're up there, and you wouldn't know it. Besides, I don't spend my time with any poor boys. Now I know what that B. stands for, Billy Boy. Your lucky Maria's taking you back; she'll make a man out of you."

"You two stop scrapping." Maria had had enough. "We've got lots to do to get ready for this wedding."

When the day finally arrived, Maria was thinking about Doña Petronila and how it would have been perfect if she could have just been here to share her happiness. Taking their sacred vows in the flower garden beside the cemetery made Maria feel that somehow Petronila would be watching and smiling.

Billy and Don Carlos were on their way to the San Miguel Chapel to pick up the Padre. They had left before sunup and were riding to Santa Fe in a carriage that Carlos only used for special occasions. Fluffy, popcorn-like clouds floated overhead, and Billy was thinking how Carlos Suarez could never go anywhere by himself. He was a man with almost no enemies; however, his wealth was common knowledge for miles around, and if he traveled with only one or two companions he also put them in jeopardy. Carlos thought it was necessary for at least five riders to accompany him. Today seven men rode along behind Billy and Carlos. They never entered Don Carlos's personal space, but they were always nearby.

"How are you feeling?" Carlos asked.

"Scared. I'm gettin' everything I been wishin' for, and now it seems like a bunch of responsibility. I hope I'm doin' the right thing."

"You'll be just fine," Carlos said. "Maria's a wonderful woman. She'll always be there for you."

"I never really had any blood family except my pa, and he was big on you lookin' out for yourself. I guess the idea of havin' my own family and watchin' how some handle that chore makes me a little shaky. I don't know if I'm up to it."

"You're up to it." Carlos had watched Billy grow into a man with good instincts and a solid sense of what was right and wrong. "You'll make your share of mistakes, but in the end you'll do yourself proud. Right now you're thinking about your responsibility to Maria. If you two build on the love and caring you have for each other, that'll all change from you and me to 'we.' You won't be alone."

"We've talked some about California."

"I wondered when you'd get around to letting me know about your plans. Did Maria think California would be a good place to live?"

"She didn't say that much one way or the other." Billy didn't think Maria understood how far it was to California or where it was located. He wasn't too clear about it himself and was glad she hadn't asked any questions. "Seems like she'd be happy to go, if that's what I want."

"Well, is that what you want?"

"The more I think on it, the better I like the idea of us startin' our life together in California," Billy answered. "I've heard, though, that it's a hard journey and that some men don't make it. It doesn't sound like a trip I should ask Maria to take."

"What do you think she'll have to say about your leaving her behind?" Don Carlos was certain that Maria had no intention of staying behind.

"Hard to tell. I thought I'd get your ideas about takin' her along before I talk to Maria about it." Billy was inclined to think that it would be better if Maria stayed in Mexico until he knew more about California and how to get there. "Captain Walker's out West with a fur company. He's talked some about findin' an easier way into California. If I could ask him, I think he'd know the best way to get there."

Billy was right about Joseph Walker, Don Carlos thought. Joe Walker and the other men that first came to Mexico to trap had been responsible for opening up many of the old trails. In those early days the Americans operated more or less on the edge of the law, so they were pretty quiet about their movements. He wasn't sure, but Walker may have already journeyed through much of the country they were talking about. "It seems to me that you'd have quite a job just finding Captain Walker. How or when you go is up to you, but I would strongly advise that you take Maria with you. She's a courageous woman, and she can endure the hardship. You need to start in California together. You'll need each other. In later years you'll look back on the experience as one of your best times together."

"It's easy to die in the wilderness," Billy said.

"It's easy to die in Santa Fe," Carlos countered.

Billy couldn't argue that point. If it hadn't been for the Suarez family he wouldn't be marrying Maria today, or any day. Billy thought about everything that Carlos had said. Maria would have her own thoughts on the subject, maybe she'd rather move back to the States. He knew the way to Missouri.

"Did you invite Otis Tejas to the wedding?" Although Don Carlos had little regard for Indians in general, he always tried to treat Otis Tejas with respect. When he discovered that the Indian had returned to Santa Fe with Billy, he went to find him so he could explain what had happen to Maria and how it had affected Billy. Carlos always renewed his invitation for the Indian to stay out at his *rancho*, but Oo-tse-tee never visited.

"I did, but who knows if he'll show up or not." Billy had wanted to invite Oo-tse-tee, but he wasn't sure how Maria would feel about having an Indian at her wedding. He was surprised when she mentioned that Otis should be at the wedding.

The wedding went just like Maria wanted. Oo-tse-tee arrived dressed in a new wool suit, hair washed and braided, moccasins decorated with porcupine quills, and carrying a Navajo blanket for the newlyweds. Billy looked for him after the ceremony was over. The Indian had vanished.

The ceremony was short and sweet, and that suited Billy just fine. He felt that the old priest seemed a mite put out, at least as far as he was concerned. Maria had removed herself from almost all contact with the church after she tried to get their help in dealing with her uncle. Once Pedro started to manage Maria's life, she fell completely away. Petronila had brought her back to the church, and now it was an important part of her life, the most important part, Billy thought. Billy, on the other hand, hadn't found time to become involved with many church matters. It was probably his negligence that accounted for the Padre's attitude toward him.

Billy's avoidance of religious affairs didn't seem to bother Maria. Her love for him was boundless. Don Carlos had told him that he and Maria would come together, and a oneness with each other was exactly how it felt. They'd moved into a little home a short distance up the valley from the main house. Far enough to be by themselves, and yet close enough that Anita, Carlos, Juan or any of the ranch hands could easily ride over and stop for coffee and a visit. Maria thought that either California or Missouri would do fine. In fact, it perturbed Billy some that she seemed more interested in curtains for the kitchen window than planning for their future.

Billy was spending most of his time with Juan and Cisco. There was no denying their talents around livestock. He could remember Swit telling him about the remarkable feats both men could do with a horse and a rope. It hadn't particularly interested him at the time, but now he was viewing it with a different prospective. He'd found Juan and Cisco to be excellent companions.

Billy B. had some concern and uncertainty about how Juan and Cisco would react to Don Carlos making him half-owner of the proposed ranching operation in California, not to mention putting him in charge. Carlos had told him that Juan and Cisco would be part owners, but Billy didn't know what he'd told the two *vaqueros*, or what part of the ranch they would own. Juan and Cisco had not indicated that they had a problem with Billy's part in the California venture, but he wasn't sure what they knew or didn't know.

It had been Cisco that seemed to most resent Billy's coming to Santa Fe and removing Maria from public employment. A couple of days before he and Swit returned to Missouri he thought it might get out of control and turn physical, but Juan had interceded and nothing had occurred. It seemed to Billy that Cisco still suppressed some ill feelings.

"We were wondering if you had any problem with me and Cisco owning part of Don Carlos's place in California?" Juan had been waiting for just the right time to approached Billy.

"I don't have problem one about your ownin' whatever part of the ranch Don Carlos decided was yours. I'll honor all commitments that he makes." It was obvious to Billy that they had discussed and practiced this meeting for some time.

"He said it'd be like it is here; we each get ten percent, plus our wages." Juan and Cisco studied Billy carefully. They were trying to detect any sign of dissatisfaction. "We'll be partners. It doesn't matter what kind of agreement you have with Don Carlos, we'll take our orders from you just like we do from him."

"I look forward to all of us workin' together." Billy was pleased that Juan and Cisco felt that it was important to discuss the partnership. "Working together is what it'll take to make it a success. I think the most important thing we can do to prevent any misunderstandin' is to keep everything out in the open where we can all see. My share is to be fifty percent, and I won't be givin' any orders. All the decisions will have to be made by the three of us. I hope this meets with your approval, but if not, take it up with Don Carlos. It's his arrangement.

"Have you made any plans to leave for California?" Up to now Cisco had been content to set back and let Juan do the talking.

"I haven't." Billy thought that Cisco's demeanor toward him had gradually improved since his return to Santa Fe and marriage to Maria.

"Do you know the trail between here and California?" Cisco asked.

"No, do you?" Billy could see that Cisco's way was to get to the point.

"No, we don't know." Cisco had eye-to-eye contact with Billy. "You've trailed before, so we'll follow where you lead."

"We'll need more than me to find our way." Especially if Maria is with us, Billy thought. "I've got some things to work out in my mind, and I'd like to talk to some friends that's been through that country before we go. I'd be glad to hear any ideas that either of you have about the trip."

Neither Juan nor Cisco spoke. They nodded their heads as if the planning for the move West was entirely up to Billy. Then Juan mentioned that he and Cisco needed to ride over to the winter pasture and check the stock. As near as Billy could tell, the three of them were in agreement. Getting to California was something they'd have to work out.

Chapter Seventeen

The shine, feel and smell of newness was gone. Grinding miles and life in the outdoors took its toll on the wagons, harnesses and equipment. It was weathered and worn. Men and animals, on the other hand, were rejuvenated. Their arrival into the Green River valley, along with the anticipated lifestyle as a trapper, adventurer and explorer, had reassured the men of Benjamin Bonneville's expedition. It gave them a sense of accomplishment and new beginning.

Captain Bonneville was well aware that General Macomb had expressed more than a passing interest in finding a good site for an Army post. The government might find it necessary to defend its access into and out of the Oregon Territory. Bonneville's brigade had entered the southeast corner of Oregon when they crossed over South Pass, and the captain had been listening when the trappers talked about how they had summered in the Horse Creek area along the Green River.

Joe Walker knew that Bonneville had something in mind, and that somehow it was connected with Horse Creek. Up to this point there had been an openness between the captain and himself that had served the expedition well. Apparently, the Army captain had decided to keep his thoughts about Horse Creek to himself. Walker wasn't one to pry.

When the expedition reached the spot where Horse Creek joined the Green River, they were following up the Green in an almost east to west direction. The creek had its origin in the mountains to the west, and flowed eastward along a channel that was roughly two to three miles south of and parallel to the Green, before it turned north to join the river. This created an elongated, horseshoe-shaped, flat plateau that was bordered on the south and east by Horse Creek and on the north by the Green River. It was approximately two miles by six miles, and centrally located between the mountain ranges on the east, west and north. It offered an ideal location for an Army installation, and as they were now proving, accessible to wagons from the east.

"This is where we'll build our post," Captain Bonneville said after they traveled about five miles west of the Green River and Horse Creek junction. "We'll set her about three hundred yards south of the river."

"You might want to rethink that, Captain." So this is what's been on his mind, Walker thought. Bonneville wants to establish a trading post here on the Green. "I know it looks good to you now, especially considering the country we just crossed, but everything around here has been pretty much trapped out. In about three months it's going to look a whole lot different. I can't think of a much colder place to spend the winter. There'll be no forage for the horses, or game for us. There's just not much here except wind, snow and cold in the winter time."

"This is the spot," Bonneville said. "It'll do just fine. What do you think, Michael, will this do for a trading post?"

"If you want it here, we'll build it here," Cerré answered.

Michael Cerré knew everything Walker had said was the truth, but he also remembered Alfred Seton's letter. The letter had made some interesting and profitable suggestions for marketing the beaver pelts collected by the Bonneville expedition. This must be what Seton had in mind when he wrote that Captain Bonneville is to be supported in certain liberties of action and movement that might not seem to be in the best interest of the fur company.

As soon as construction of the new post began, Joe Walker could see that they were not building a trading post. This was to be an Army fort. The plan called for cutting down cottonwood trees that were at least a foot thick. They would use the timbers to build a square stockade eighty by eighty and fifteen feet high, large enough to hold at least one hundred men and most of their horses and wagons. Blockhouses were constructed in two diagonal corners of the stockade so they could post lookouts and observe all four sides of the structure. The fort was located so as to give an excellent view of the surrounding territory, and a blacksmith's forge was to be situated in the center of the enclosure.

Although Bonneville hadn't taken him into his confidence about the building of the fort, Walker was convinced that this project was about Captain Ben's arrangement with the military. It was not a decision that would profit a fur trading business, but there was no denying that it was an ideal location from a military point of view. It was smack-dab in the middle of land claimed by the hostile Blackfoot Indians. Located along the Green River it could patrol any movement between South Pass and the Snake River Plateau, which would probably become a future passageway to Oregon. During the summer there was an abundance of game, grass and space. A perfect area to bivouac a small army. Freight wagons could bring out all that they'd need to survive the winter.

Every trapper who had experienced the harshness of winter along the upper Green River knew that Captain Bonneville's new trading post was hell for stout, an ideal site for a summer rendezvous, but not where you wanted to be when winter arrived. Walker was well aware of what the men thought about the fort, and if he was to keep their respect as a leader he needed to remove himself from this project—the sooner the better.

"Ben, I think I'll see if I can't find the free trappers that Fontenelle was expecting to meet out here." Walker and Captain Bonneville were having their breakfast. "You've got plenty of men to build your treading post. I think I'd do more good trying to pick us up some additional trappers."

"I agree wholeheartedly," Bonneville said. "I know this project doesn't make good sense to you, but it's something that I have to do. I'm sure we'll take some badgering about my actions."

Walker was brushing some dust off his hat. "I'm not going to give much thought to what other people say, and if I were you I wouldn't either. I have an idea that while we're out here we'll do some other things a little different than most fur companies. Right or wrong depends a lot on your point of view."

"I'm glad you understand," Ben answered. "I wish you success in finding the trappers; we can use a few more." He was relieved that Joe Walker understood his situation and no conflict of leadership had arisen. The men watched Walker's movements and respected his thoughts on almost any subject. Bonneville was confident that he could hold these men together by himself, but if Walker opposed him he doubted he could keep things intact.

Joe Walker moved off to gather a few supplies for his trip. He had just finished putting the supplies on his pack mule when he looked over the top of the animal and saw Swit standing with an axe in his hand, looking back his way. He waved Swit over.

Swit was undecided as to whether he should bring the axe along. In the hope that Captain Walker wasn't going to ask him to cut down some special tree, somewhere, he left the axe and walked over. "Good morning, Captain. Do you plan to be gone long?"

"We shouldn't be gone more than a few days." Walker hadn't thought about taking Swit along until he saw him standing with the axe. It just seemed like the right thing to do. "I've got enough supplies for both of us. All you need to do is go gather up Scab, and we'll be out of here. Tie your bed roll there beside mine, I'm going to get some extra powder just in case."

Swit knew he was going, but he didn't know why or where. The why or where didn't bother him at all because he was pretty sure the captain wasn't going off to cut any trees. He hurried off to pick up Scab and make himself ready for the trail. The morning was turning out better than he first envisioned. He'd been listening to Woolly complain about cutting down all the sweet cottonwoods in order to build "Fort Folly." Captain Bonneville kept referring to the project as Fort Bonneville, but when the captain was out of hearing range most of the men called it Fort Nonsense.

"Well now, where you off to?" Will wanted to know.

"I don't know where we're headed, but I'd bet it ain't to the river to cut timbers." Swit was cinching up his saddle. "We're not suppose to be gone too long, so I'd like you fellows to get right busy on the building. I'd be plum happy if it's all done when we get back."

"I'd be happy too, if Captain Walker needed another hand," Woodrow said as Swit was throwing his leg up over Scab.

"He didn't say anything about asking anybody along." Swit turned Scab and flashed a big smile at Will.

As near as Swit could tell, trailblazing with just Captain Walker wasn't much different than riding trail with Walker leading a whole group of men. The captain led and you followed along behind in a single file. There wasn't any talking because there wasn't anyone to talk to. Captain Walker seemed completely absorbed with everything around him. Nothing moved or made a sound that he didn't notice. When he did speak it was information to be acted upon immediately or carefully filed away for future use. As they traveled along together, Swit never had a thought that he considered important enough or necessary to reveal to the captain.

Walker had told Swit that they were searching for a group of men that he called "free trappers." Swit wasn't exactly sure what that meant. He guessed that he was probably listed as a trapper in Bonneville's fur company, although so far he hadn't even set a trap. He knew he was a free man, but doubted he had what to took to be called a free trapper.

It was the first part of August, and Walker reasoned that the rendezvous held at Pierre's Hole had been over for several weeks. He knew that Fontenelle had been too late for the gathering and had headed on up the Green River. Walker felt that the free trappers he was searching for had most likely been at the rendezvous and would probably head back to see if they could find the missing Frenchman. If they crossed over into Jackson's Hole and then moved south to the Green River, they had already found Fontenelle. But, if the trappers crossed the Tetons and then decided to follow the Snake River down to the Hoback, they just might follow up the Hoback River and try their hand at trapping in some of the small feeder streams. Anticipating the movements of this group of men was speculative at best, but it was as good a place as any to look.

Finding the trappers had been easier than Swit thought possible. To begin with it seemed to Swit that they were again taking a northwesterly heading, but after they started climbing up into the mountains he really only had a vague idea of their whereabouts. In this gigantic country of the fur trade with its countless valleys, holes, ravines and gorges, it seemed as if you could hide out and not ever be found. But then the trappers weren't exactly hiding, and Captain Walker was doing the looking. Many of the men knew Walker from his early days trapping in the streams around Santa Fe and Taos. They immediately began to update each other on their experiences since they'd last parted. Swit stayed off to one side, where he could listen to the tales and watch the antics of these unique individuals.

Walker's normal economy for conversation allowed him to explain his recent history to his old friends in a matter of a few sentences. The same couldn't be said for most of the trappers. They loved to talk, and did their best to tell a story that was bigger and better than the one they'd just heard. Each man had his own horse or horses, and all other necessities for living in the backcountry. His favorite horse, which might be his only horse, was considered his prize possession and companion. They both were decorated in whatever combination of brightly dyed cloth, ornamented leather, brass tacks, beads, feathers and fringe that signaled their individuality.

As near as Swit could tell, every man had his start somewhere in the civilized Eastern part of the country called the States, but to look at them it was hard to believe they'd ever been indoors. They acted, walked, dressed and lived more like Indians than white men. Their skin was baked brown and hardened by the sun, so some even looked like Indians. Most had been in the wilderness for many years. Many of the men had been back to visit the settlements, but they found that they couldn't stay long. There was not enough freedom. Someone was constantly telling them that you shouldn't go there or do that.

Watching these men gave a new meaning to the word independent. They came and went as they pleased, either alone or in the company of others, and they provided for their own care. Their reason for being seemed to be about living as free from restraints as humanly possible. They trapped just enough so as to have some pelts to trade to the highest bidder, thereby providing the necessities that enabled them to continue the life they so truly loved. The only reason that Swit could think of for their being together at all was their need to have someone around to show off for and listen to their almost unbelievable stories. Protection against the Blackfoot Indians was undoubtedly another important consideration.

The recent rendezvous at Pierre's Hole, and their encounter with the Blackfoot Indians, was fresh in the minds of the trappers. "Billy just about got his everlastin'," one of the free trappers was saying to Captain Walker. "He took a ball through the shoulder that wounded another man in the head. It could have killed 'em both."

Swit immediately thought of Billy B. He asked the captain who the Billy was that got shot. Walker told him that it was William Sublette.

"It was bad business all the way around," the trapper continued. "We'd been at the Hole since June. Billy arrived with his bunch around the first week in July. By then we was all ready for some fun and frolic. At least a hundred Rocky Mountain trappers had been waitin' on Bill to get there with their goods. Andy and Vanderburg had another hundred and seventy-five American Fur Company men with them. They was a waitin' for Fontenelle to show up with their supplies, but he never did get there. Gantt and Blackwell had about fifty trappers with them. They'd wintered over on the Laramie, and when they left they couldn't find some of their men. The ones they brought to the rendezvous was a scruffy-lookin' bunch."

Swit thought he was following the story pretty well, but he hadn't heard of some of these men. Andy had to be the Andrew Drips that Will was always talking about, and Fontenelle had been the subject of his and Will's reconnoiter in the dry country between Sandy Creek and the Green River. Vanderburg, Gantt and Blackwell he hadn't heard about.

"There must of been a hundred and twenty Nes Perces, along with eighty

Flathead, and a few Delaware and Iroquois lodges sprinkled around." The trapper was waving his arms to demonstrate how large a gathering they'd had. "Several bunches of us free trappers was nearby, and Alexander Sinclair had a little group he was tryin' to lead. You can see we was all layin' and waitin' for the supplies to show when Sublette rode in with his crowd. First thing he asked was the whereabouts of Fitz."

Fitz had to be Tom Fitzpatrick. Will had claimed that he was the one that named Independence Rock. Sinclair was another trapper that Swit hadn't heard anything about, but it didn't seem like a good time to ask Walker about him.

"After Billy arrived with his men," the trapper lit his pipe before going on with his story, "we must have had a thousand men spread up and down the Teton River. Sublette, Campbell and Fitzpatrick had left St. Louie with supplies and sixty men. They kept pickin' up travelers all along the route. The first bunch that hooked up with 'em was some fellers out of the New England country. Their leader was named Wyeth, and they was headed for the Columbia River to set up a salmon fishery. Just when you think you've heard it all, something new blows in."

Swit heard several chuckles when the trapper mentioned the fishery, and someone asked why would you need a fishery when you can get all the beaver tails you want.

"Anyhow," the trapper continued, "when Sublette reached the Laramie they picked up what was left of the trappers that Gantt and Blackwell couldn't find. Ol' Fitz decided that he needed to go on ahead to the rendezvous and let us all know that the supplies was comin'. Like I said, when Bill got there, Fitz hadn't showed up yet."

That Fitzpatrick must be a right good man, Swit thought. Anyone who would head up here all by himself from the Laramie had better than average abilities. Of course it didn't sound like he made it, so maybe he overestimated himself.

"Most of us thought that Fitzpatrick had had the misfortune to run into a bunch of Blackfoot and was now a hairpiece in someone's tepee." The trapper had Walker and Swit's attention; however, the other men knew all about the rendezvous, and at least one had a different opinion.

"Fitz is too crafty to be surprised by Blackfoot Injuns," a second trapper volunteered. "I had it figured that he most likely suffered a mishap of some kind and ended up as plain ol' bear shit."

"Did Sublette have any trouble with the Blackfoot on his way to the rendezvous?" Walker asked.

"Billy said that when they were camped along the Green one night they got a visit from the Blackfoot about midnight. He didn't lose nobody, but one man was wounded. Sublette figured that the Injuns didn't fare as well, 'cause they pulled up short of tryin' to overrun the camp. They made off with a few horses, but all in all it was more noise than substance." The trapper felt that he needed to answer Captain Walker, but he was anxious to return to his story about the rendezvous. "You can imagine how we all felt when a few days later two half-breed Iroquois hunters fetched ol' Fitz into camp. He was in hellacious shape; I doubt I'd knowed him if we'd met on the trail."

Swit couldn't help but think about Hiram Scott. No one had been around to help him, but apparently some Indians had rescued Fitzpatrick.

"Injuns had been the source of his undoin'." The trapper liked recounting the events of the rendezvous to someone of Captain Walker's stature. "Fitz had been spotted by a party of Blackfoot braves, but he managed to escape by hidin' out in a mountain cave. They'd captured his horse, so he hid durin' the day and traveled on foot at night until he got away from their daily searches. When he reached the Teton River he figured himself safer on the other side of the river, so he fashioned a raft out of some old logs and started to cross. Bad luck was still doggin' him, 'cause his raft hit a big ol' rock. He lost everything except what he had on his back, even lost his knife. Fitz was hard put to defend or provide for himself. He continued to trek along, doin' the best he could with berries and roots, but was nearly dead when the hunters found him."

Swit thought how river travel had been the undoing of both Fitz and Hiram Scott. Fitzpatrick had one thing that ol' Scott didn't get. You can do all you can do out here, but just pure luck will sometimes decide the outcome.

"There wasn't much love for the Blackfoot about now," the trapper continued. "Two weeks later Milton Sublette, Sinclair and that Wyeth feller took about forty men and headed out for a hunt. They was down toward the southeast end of the Hole when they sighted about a hundred and fifty Gros Ventres Injuns comin' across the flat toward 'em. The chief rode out alone and had extended his hand to make the peace when an Iroquois half-breed by the name of Antoine Godin grabbed his hand and either shot the chief with his free hand or had one of the Flathead's put the kibosh on him. In any case, the fight was on."

Swit was surprised by the matter-of-fact attitude demonstrated by the trappers. They didn't seem to mind that an Indian chief who had come in peace had been killed.

It seemed to Joe Walker that he had heard a lifetime of stories where hatred against a race or tribe had precipitated conflict. Most Blackfoot Indians had hated the whites since they'd suffered death at the hands of the Lewis and Clark expedition. They believed in repaying kind with kind. Before long, how it started and who did what to who was lost. All that mattered was that the Blackfoot killed whites every chance they got, and now it seemed that the reverse was also true. This battle was born in Godin's hatred for the Blackfoot, and the Gros Ventres were not even part of the Blackfoot Nation, just allies of a tribe that he hated.

"The sides exchanged fire, and the Injuns took cover in a little swamp that was an entanglement of willows, cottonwoods and vines." The trapper was trying to finish his story before others started to relate their special feats of battle. "Milton sent word to his brother that they had a bunch of Blackfoot pinned down and to come a-runnin'. Billy showed up with several hundred of us from the rendezvous. The Blackfoot, seein' that they was greatly outnumbered, dug in and prepared to fight to the death."

Swit wondered how many of the reinforcements realized how the fight started, or if they even cared.

"Billy, Campbell and Sinclair decided to lead an assault on the Injuns." The trapper could see that he had the attention of the young man that was with Captain Walker. "Drips took a ball through his hat that snatched some hair off his head, but Sinclair was the first to fall. After Billy was put down they give up the attack."

"Is Captain Drips all right?" Swit asked. Since he'd at least heard of Andrew Drips, and knew that Will would want to know his condition, he'd decided to venture an inquiry.

"He's okay," the trapper answered. "But Sinclair died after we got him back to camp. We continued to throw rifle fire into the marsh until we got word that another party of Blackfoot was about to attack the rendezvous. Most of us headed back to defend our camp, but the story turned out to be a lie. When we returned in the mornin' to check on the bunch we'd left to keep them red devils pinned down, we found out that the Injuns had slipped out durin' the night. They took their wounded with 'em, but left ten dead in the swamp. At last count we'd lost five trappers and eight Injuns."

Swit decided it was hard to determine who won what in the battle. Walker thought that it was a complete waste. Indians had battled each other for hundreds of years before white men entered their territory. The differences between the Indian Nations caused constant conflict. He couldn't see the tribal warfare ending, and now with the introduction of whites into the wilderness, race hatred had developed.

The trappers were ready to head over to Captain Bonneville's fort. It was hard to resist visiting anyone that would build a trading post along that part of the Green River. Joe Walker didn't seem to be in a hurry to return, and that suited Swit just fine.

Chapter Eighteen

"I sure wasn't lookin' for everything to happen this fast." Billy hadn't talked to Oo-tse-tee since the wedding. He found the Indian standing by the river next to where the trail caravans crossed. He wanted the Indian to know about the latest development. "I never thought I'd get so bundled up in responsibilities."

"You'll make a good papa." Oo-tse-tee had seen Maria in the plaza on several occasions, and the development of a new arrival was apparent. "When will you leave for Cal-forn-ya?"

"That's all kinda up in the air right now. Before all this happened I thought I might head up into the Green River country to find Captain Walker, but I don't think that's a good place for Maria or the baby."

"Swit be surprised to see you." Oo-tse-tee could picture the look on Swit's face if Billy, Maria and their new baby arrived at Captain Walker's camp.

"Just about everything surprises Swit," Billy B. answered. "With this baby a-comin' I can't settle on what's the best move. Things is sure changin' for me."

Oo-tse-tee thought about how Billy had changed since Fort Gibson. There was a time when he would have headed for California without a thought about how his leaving would effect anyone.

Billy watched another freight wagon cross the river on its way to the plaza. It seemed as if there were an usually large number of Indians camped along the river. Oo-tse-tee had apparently been welcomed and accepted into the midst of the nomadic, freedom-loving, come-and-go-anyplace-any time followers of the buffalo.

161

"How you gettin' along?" Billy asked. "I 'spect you got everyone of them chiefs wantin' to give you horses to take their daughters." Billy watched three inquisitive Indian girls try to stay concealed and inconspicuous between a tepee and the trees.

Oo-tse-tee's face showed that almost imperceptible smile that Billy enjoyed making happen. "I'm good, but the only horses I have is the one I rode in on," Oo-tse-tee answered. "These people move around much."

"Well, you're welcome to move with us, if and when we go." Billy knew that Maria would be waiting for him in the plaza. "I'll let you know more when I know more."

Billy headed for the plaza, but he couldn't tell if Oo-tse-tee was interested in going to California or not. When he turned back to wave, Oo-tse-tee was not in view.

Don Carlos had been forthcoming with his opinion that Maria and Billy should travel to California together, but now he was just as determined that the baby should be born here at the ranch.

"It don't matter much where I am when the time comes; babies get born everywhere." Maria seemed to consider her pregnancy no more than a slight inconvenience.

"You've never had no baby before," Billy told her. "You just might feel a little different when them pains start."

"I doubt it," she answered. "I've seen plenty of babies born. Helped a few of the girls at Doña Tules with their delivery."

"That's not like trompin' around out in the wildness." Billy couldn't understand Maria's stubbornness. "If we was to take off now to look for Captain Walker we wouldn't get there until after the summer rendezvous. The trappers tell me that's the best place to find the captain, or at least find out where he might be. It'd be almost winter when we got to the high country, and you're not havin' this baby hunched down in some snow bank in the mountains. I ain't a-gonna leave you here wonderin' if I'm comin' back, either. California will just have to wait or go on without us. If things work out, maybe we could leave early next spring and head for the rendezvous."

Maria liked the sound of that, but she wasn't saying anything. All she knew was that Billy wasn't going off anywhere and leaving her and their baby behind.

Billy and Juan were riding together checking cows south of the ranch. Billy was getting a lesson in cowology when they saw Cisco headed their way. His horse was running as hard as it could, and he was pushing him with every stride. Cisco charged in with such haste that he had trouble getting his horse pulled up. The ol' horse was covered with white foam and sidestepping in twirled circles while Cisco shouted, "It's bad, real bad. You gotta get to Santa Fe."

"Oh God, no," Billy said, more to himself than to anyone. He knew that Don Carlos and Maria had headed to Santa Fe for supplies that morning. Maria had said that she wasn't feeling her best, but she'd felt poorly before and always got better.

"Calm down," Juan said. "Tell us what happened."

"Bad accident, Don Carlos is..." Cisco's horse jumped and stumbled. Billy missed what he said. Cisco turned his horse tight to the left and stepped down. "He's dead, you gotta get to Santa Fe, *pronto.*"

"My lord, what happened? Is Maria all right?" Billy asked as he dismounted.

"I guess she's all right, I never asked." Cisco thought how he hadn't even thought about Maria. "Cornelio road back from Santa Fe to tell us about Don Carlos. I just never thought to ask. I'm sorry Billy."

"Jesus, Cisco, what was you thinking?" Juan said. "Did they have a runaway?"

"No, no, it's nothing like that," Cisco answered. "Don Carlos and that Indian friend of Billy's was walking toward Doña Tules. A bullwacker shouted, 'If I ain't good enough to go in that damn whorehouse, then there sure as hell ain't no Injun goin' in.' He jumped down from his wagon and stuck a big skinning knife right in the Indian's back. Don Carlos grabbed the man, but before our *vaqueros* could get there he shot Carlos dead. I don't think Maria was anywhere around. Nobody said she was there."

"What about Otis?" Billy asked.

"He's dead," Cisco answered. "The bullwacker's dead too. That black that they call Hog Eye killed him. He was standing in the back of a wagon and shot him after he killed Don Carlos. We better get to the house. Maybe something else has happened since I've been gone."

Billy, Juan and Cisco rode north in silence. Billy was sure that Maria was all right; she had to be. If she'd been hurt someone would have said something. Cisco kept wondering why he hadn't thought to ask about Maria. Juan couldn't make himself believe that Don Carlos was dead. It never occurred to him that Carlos could die so suddenly; he was always so careful. He might get sick like Doña Petronila and die, but it didn't seem possible that a *gringo* would kill him. Juan looked to the west—storm clouds were building.

Cisco blamed himself for not being able to tell Billy about Maria's condition. His horse had been forced to run at full speed to bring the news of Don Carlos's death, and when the ranch buildings came into view the horse was about done. Cisco couldn't wait any longer to find out about Maria. He put the spurs to his spent horse and headed for the corrals.

"That damn fool's gonna ride that horse straight in the ground." Juan watched the horse giving his all to help Cisco end his torment. "I know what he's thinking. He wishes he'd found out about Maria."

"Maria's okay," Billy said. "If she wasn't, someone would have told him. Juan, I'd like you to head for the corrals. Find out what you can about what happened in Santa Fe. I'm goin' to the house and do the same. As soon as you have a handle on what's goin' on, come on up to the house and we'll talk."

When Juan arrived at the barns, Cisco was saddling a fresh mount. "Maria's all right," Cisco said. "She came back with the boys when they brought Don Carlos home. She's up at the house."

"Did you find out any more about what happened?" Juan asked. Cisco had obviously been energized by the news that Maria was unharmed.

"Not much," Cisco answered. "They didn't stay around Santa Fe very long. Just got Maria, loaded up Don Carlos and headed back. A couple of the boys are digging him a place alongside Doña Petronila."

"What about the Indian?" Juan asked. "Did you find out what they did with him?"

"No one said anything about him." Damn, Cisco thought, will I ever learn to ask the right questions? "I'm headed to the west range. Don Carlos sent some men out there early this morning to gather sheep. His oldest is with 'em. Maria said I should go and get him. I'm sure not looking forward to that chore."

The scene at the house was sadness. Billy was split between the grief of seeing Don Carlos laid out in the parlor, and a feeling of relief as he watched Maria rush to greet him. He'd felt sure that she was okay, and now seeing her hurrying along in an advanced state of pregnancy brought a smile and some happiness. Maria's account of the incident was second hand. She had been on the opposite side of the plaza when it all happened and hadn't seen anything. She'd heard the shots, but the first Maria learned about the killings was when one of the *vaqueros* came to get her. He told her what had happened, helped her up on the wagon and drove the team of horses over to where Don Carlos laid wrapped in a new blanket. They carefully placed the body in the wagon bed and left Santa Fe. When they arrived at the ranch, Lena and Anita had the parlor waiting, and they immediately began to prepare Don Carlos for his final resting place.

All the children except Alonzo were at home. Maria had helped them through the loss of their mother. Now they faced the loss of their Father. Billy was setting on the front porch when Juan arrived. The only new information he heard was that some of the traders in Santa Fe wanted to hang Hog Eye for killing the bullwacker. Cisco and Alonzo came riding up to the house in Cisco's typical all-out style. One more horse with all the run out of him, Billy thought as he watched Alonzo hurry to the house. Maria met him at the door.

"I sure didn't enjoy telling the boy about his daddy." Cisco walked over to where Juan and Billy were talking.

"How'd he take it?" Juan asked.

"He just said he had to get back and see to his brothers and sisters," Cisco answered.

Billy knew that his life had just made another turn. Don Carlos was counting on him to look after his family if something happen. It had, and now Billy felt the weight of added responsibility. "I don't know zackly how this will all work out, but I know Don Carlos had a lot of confidence in both of ya. We need to keep this outfit goin' for his family. I'm thinkin' I better make a trip to Santa Fe and find out what I can about how this all came down."

"Take Alonzo with you." Maria had walked up unnoticed by the three men. "He needs to see and hear all about what happened. He needs you to talk to him too. We all owe this family. It's time to pay up."

"I'll take him along." Billy stood up and put his arm around Maria. "Juan, you and Cisco take charge of the ranch operation until I can find out more about where we stand."

Billy B. and Alonzo drove a team and wagon on their way to Santa Fe. Maria still needed the supplies they'd left behind after Don Carlos's death. Alonzo was almost sixteen years old. When he wasn't busy with his studies, Carlos had the *vaqueros* teaching him the ranching business. He and Billy had never spent much time together.

"Is your papa alive?" Alonzo was remembering the time that his father brought Captain Walker, along with Billy B. and some others, out to the ranch. Billy had been considerably younger than the others, and Alonzo had looked upon the young adventurer with a certain awe. Billy had married the beautiful Maria, and very soon she would present him with a new addition to their family. Alonzo thought how Billy's family was growing—and his had just got smaller.

"Yeah, he's alive," Billy answered. "He ain't been much of a pa to me, but until lately he was all the family I got. Your papa help me more than mine ever did."

"He told me all about your plans for California." Alonzo watched Billy rub his mustache. "Are you and Maria leaving for California next spring?"

"Can't rightly say what we'll be doin' next spring," Billy answered. "You wanta tell me what's on your mind?"

"I'm scared," Alonzo answered. "I know I've got to take over, but I don't feel ready. I'm afraid I'll make a mess of everything. First mama and now papa. There's just us kids left, and I'm the oldest. It's up to me now."

"I don't know that much about your uncles or cousins." Billy watched Alonzo sitting in the wagon seat with his head down, slowly moving it back and forth. "Can any of them lend a hand?"

"The war took my only uncle that papa ever spoke highly of," Alonzo answered. "Papa thought of you and Maria like family. He told me to trust you. He was sure excited about the California expansion."

"We'll help out in any way we can," Billy said. "For now we'd better concentrate on your brothers and sisters and keepin' the ranch goin'. California will have to hold. I took it on myself to ask Juan and Cisco to temporarily take charge of the ranch operation until things sort themselves out. From now on we'll all work together, with you directin' the action. Maria will help with the little ones."

"She already has." Alonzo was smiling at Billy. "She told me to get out of the house and go with you to Santa Fe."

It was just starting to rain and was almost dark when they reached Carlos's little adobe hut on the edge of Santa Fe. Alonzo took care of the horses while Billy carried their bedrolls inside and started a fire under the kettle. It only rained hard for a few minutes, which suited Billy just fine, because the roof let about as much water on through as it carried off. It rained just enough to settle the dust and clean the air. Billy had a beef and bean mixture in the pot, and was watching the first stars beginning to appear in the sky when Alonzo hollered from the corral for Billy to come and look. It wasn't a hurried or troubled type of call—just a come and see.

On the top of a hill over toward the river you could see a fire burning. It was hard to tell exactly what was happening. The distance and the darkness made a clear observation impossible, but it was obvious that the Indians were performing some type of ceremony. The faint sound of their chants came drifting in on an easy breeze. Billy and Alonzo watched and listened while they ate their supper. Alonzo worried that it might be a war dance and the Indians were making ready to raid some ranches. Billy didn't think so. He thought the activity appeared more subdued than spirited. They weren't working themselves up into a fervor for fighting. Whatever the cause for their actions, the Indians continued the ceremony late into the night. Billy soon tired of watching and was quickly asleep. He didn't mention it to Alonzo, but he thought they might have been watching a goodbye for Oo-tse-tee. Alonzo watched and dozed, hoping Billy was right about Indian raids.

Pedro was busy cleaning behind the bar when Billy and Alonzo walked into Doña Tules' establishment. "I thought I might be seeing you today," Pedro greeted Billy. "Is that Alonzo with you? I haven't seen you for...longer than I can remember. Boy, you're growing up."

Alonzo was nervous. "Did you see what happened to my papa?"

Pedro explained that he hadn't actually witnessed the incident, but he'd talked with many that had. The story he told was the same as the one the *vaquero* had brought to the ranch. Pedro said the Indian tribe down along the river had taken Otis Tejas's body off with them. He figured that the big to-do along the river last night was for the Indian.

Billy B. thought about Oo-tse-tee and how his feelings for the Indian had changed since Fort Gibson. He remembered how Oo-tse-tee believed that his presence could make a difference in their trip to Santa Fe. Oo-tse-tee was more that just an Indian that he'd known and liked, he'd been a friend. Billy B. would miss him. He asked Pedro about Hog Eye. Pedro wasn't sure if the black was still alive or not.

"The last I heard the freighters had him chained to a wagon wheel," Pedro answered. "They were arguing among themselves about what to do with him for killing James." That was the first time Billy had heard the name of the man that killed Don Carlos and Oo-tse-tee. Billy and Alonzo turned and started to leave. "I guess you know I own half the ranch now?"

"How's that again?" Billy B. slowly turned to face Pedro. "You own what?"

"I'm half-owner of the Suarez *rancho*," Pedro repeated. "I've got the paper right here. Don Carlos signed it over to me."

"Why would he do that?" Billy wanted to know.

"He needed a big stash of silver, and I had it," Pedro explained. "Said he'd pay me back double this winter, but I guess that's not going to happen."

"I'd like to look at your paper." Alonzo's hand was starting to shake.

"Just when did all this happen?" Billy asked.

"Last year," Pedro explained as he produced an official-looking document, which as near as Billy could tell, gave Pedro exactly what he claimed. Don Carlos had signed it. "Carlos said he needed the extra silver for his trip to the Californees."

Alonzo carefully read the words that transferred title to half of the property that he had been afraid he wouldn't be able to manage for his family. He studied it for several minutes before he pushed it back toward Pedro, turned and walked out into the morning sunshine. Billy left behind him.

Chapter Nineteen

The free trappers loved to set around the campfire and tell stories about their adventures in the mountains. Each tale contained accounts of unusual cunning and courage, and was followed by one anecdote after another until the cunning was almost magical, and the courage superhuman. To begin with, Swit hung on each word, but after a few days all the swagger started to wear thin.

The destination was Captain Bonneville's new fort or trading post on the Green River. Getting there, as far as Swit could tell, would be determined by chance as much as design. No one attempted to lead the group. Each man came and went when he pleased, where he pleased. He might be alone or accompanied by one or more trappers, and their traveling arrangements and direction could change at any time. Swit went where Captain Walker went. That usually meant that they rode with one or more of the captain's old friends. Some nights all the free trappers camped together, other times they were scattered. It was a traveling style that Swit thought lacked direction. There were days when he was certain that they advanced no more than ten miles.

Joseph Walker didn't seem to be in any hurry. It was almost as if he had set aside his authority and was just trailing along behind the bunch as they gradually made their way toward Fort Bonneville. Swit decided that he didn't have whatever it was that made you a free trapper. He enjoyed living in the wild country, but he liked it better when Captain Walker was in charge.

The trading post was nearly finished when they reached the Green River valley. Captain Bonneville was delighted to meet his quests. He showed his hospitality by opening up a keg of whiskey to commemorate their coming together, and as a reward to his men for reaching the Green and building a trading post. The free trappers were eager to hear any news from the States. They listened politely, Swit thought almost reverently, to the information they were receiving from back home, but when the conversation turned to reliving the exploits that had occurred during the westward journey they had no intention of being pushed aside or outdone by any of Bonneville's men. The contest about who could tell the most about what happened where was on. Captain Ben was right in the middle of the hullabaloo, enjoying the free trapper's stories about their latest adventures and escapes from danger and destruction.

"That's an unusual group of men." Captain Bonneville and Joe Walker were finishing the last of the coffee. "I'm not sure how many of their stories would pass for truth, but there's sure no denying that it's engaging. They're a lively bunch, and I was able to get some of 'em to throw in with us. The others thought they'd visit with Fontenelle before they decide where they'll winter."

"If any of the Fontenelle bunch return they'll be under directions to do what they can to upset your trapping effort." Walker thought Bonneville didn't understand about how cutthroat the fur business had become. "I noticed we're short some horses. Did you have trouble with Indians while we were gone?"

"No, I put Matthieu in charge of a brigade of trappers with instructions to pull out the poorest and lamest horses and head over into the Bear River country," Bonneville answered. "I understand that winter pasture is better over there, and the Indians are amiable. My hope is that they can take a few pelts this fall and return to us with some rejuvenated horses. Now that I've got this post built, I'm ready to take your advice and move out of this valley for the winter. Joe, I'd like to cache everything we won't need until next summer inside the fort, and then head on up into the Salmon River country. What do you think?"

Walker thought that moving the horses to a winter pasture over on the Bear was an excellent move. Matthieu was not someone he would have put in charge, but the man was reported to be an experienced trapper and a leader of men. The numerous streams feeding into the Bear River had always produced beaver, and the predominant Indian tribe in that area was the Snake or Shoshone. They were proven friends of the white man, and archenemy of the

Blackfoot. Moving to the Salmon River territory for winter was another story.

"You'll find the beaver scarce and the winter hard up on the Salmon." Walker believed that moving north to the Salmon River made no sense if trapping or trading was the primary consideration. "It's Nez Perce territory. They're known to be a gentle people and easy to live among, but you have to watch out for the Blackfoot. They send out raiding parties to get horses away from the Nez Perce."

"As soon as we make winter camp, I'll keep a few men with me and then send the rest out for some fall trapping or trading with the natives." Bonneville seemingly had no concern about wintering along the Salmon River. "You can pick any twenty men you'd like and head to wherever it suits you. I'd like to get acquainted with the Nez Perce Indians. It's my understanding that their territory extends west into the Columbia River country."

It was plain enough to Joseph Walker that Captain Bonneville was looking for a way to get wagons to the Columbia River. The Salmon River joined the Snake River, and the Snake emptied into the Columbia. No one knew that country better than the Nez Perce Indians.

By the third week in August all the wagons had been disassembled. They were stored with the extra supplies in large holes dug inside the fort. Everything was done to conceal the caches from the curious. The fort was closed, and Bonneville's expedition headed for the Salmon River.

They made their way north up the Green River, climbing ever higher into the mountains. To their right stood the tallest peaks of the Wind River range. When the river made its turn to the east they left the Green and continued north to the headwaters of Fish Creek. Following Fish Creek and the Gros Ventra River, they moved down out of the highlands to a flat, grass- and sage-covered opening in the mountains. Woolly called it Jackson's Hole.

Swit was surprised by its size. He'd heard the trappers talk about Pierre's Hole and had tried to imagine how it would look. In his mind he could see a small circular valley, a mile or two across, located in the heart of the mountains. This almost level plain surrounded by mountains on all sides stretched for forty miles along the east side of a mountain range that Henry called the Tetons. There were no typical foothills leading up to the Teton mountains. They abruptly jutted up from the floor of Jackson's Hole. These peaks stood alone like statues to the magnificence of the mountain country. No matter where Swit was looking, his eyes were constantly drawn back to the rough, jagged, snow-covered peaks framed by the bluest sky that he could remember.

"These holes is a whole lot bigger than I thought they'd be." Swit, along with Robert, Henry and Woolly had arrived at the place where the river that they'd followed down out of the mountains joined another river headed south along the east edge of the Tetons. "Who was Pierre and Jackson to get holes named after 'em?"

Henry was watching Robert get a drink from the river. "Pierre was an old Iroquois chief that got his head blowed off in a fight with the Blackfoot. Ain't that right, Robert?"

"Never knew the man." Robert took another sip of water and then climbed back on his horse.

"That's what I was told." Woolly was willing to support Henry's story. "Don't recall his head bein' removed, but they did say that a bit of his top knot had been lifted."

"Did the Blackfoot kill Jackson too?" Swit asked.

"Don't know that he died." Henry had met David Jackson years before when Jackson was trapping for General Ashley with Smith, Sublette and Bridger. "He always liked the Snake River country. Maybe he found this hole. I don't know why it's call Jackson Hole. Do you, Robert?"

"I have no idea," Robert said.

"So this river is the Snake?" Swit could see why Jackson was so fond of this valley; it was sure likable country.

"Aye, laddie, that it is." Woolly pointed at the mountains to the north. "She starts up in the Yellowstone. There's geysers up there that spit hot water hundreds of feet in the air, and boiling mud with fire and steam shooting out of the ground. The Indians is plumb scared of it. It's sulfury smellin', and they don't even like to travel through the place. Colter was the first one to tell about it."

Swit wondered who Colter was, but since they were turning south, and it didn't look like there was any chance that they'd visit Woolly's inferno, he decided not to ask.

The Snake River pointed the expedition south along the base of the mountains, leaving behind what some of the trappers called *Les Trois Tetons*. Captain's Walker and Bonneville led the men across and away from the Snake River and up through a pass over the southern end of the mountain range. Once they crossed the Tetons they entered Pierre's Hole, the site of last summer's rendezvous. Pierre's Hole was another huge, flat, open prairie.

The free trappers pointed out the spot where the Indian battle had taken place.

I expect you heard all about the fight with the Blackfoot?" Swit and Will were riding along together.

"Well now, I'll tell you what, I heard about all I want'a hear about it." Listening to the free trappers talk about the gun battle over and over again had squelched any interest Will had in the '32 rendezvous.

"Did you get to a rendezvous when you was here with Andrew Drips?" Swited asked.

"Nope, we couldn't find it," Will answered. He hadn't thought about it before, but riding through the site of last year's rendezvous you couldn't help but see all the trash that was left behind. He wondered why Captain Drips hadn't been able to find the rendezvous in 1830. Maybe he couldn't find what he didn't want to find. They'd brought plenty of supplies out with them, and whatever the plan had been, they ended up over on the Bear River. The following June they headed back to St. Louis, and he'd missed both the '30 and '31 rendezvous.

"You got any idea how far it is to the Salmon?" Swit asked.

"Beats me," Woodrow said.

Apparently Will was in no mood for conversation, so Swit told himself they were headed for the Salmon River, no matter what, so what difference does it make how far it is. Henry had said that there weren't any buffalo on this side of the divide; however, Captain Walker had told him that they'd slip over into some real beaver country not long after reaching the river. Swit wonder if the mountains off to the right made up the divide. He decided it was probably best if he didn't ask Will.

Will had heard Henry's assessment of the country ahead. No buffalo meant thin rations. The hunters were coming back empty handed, and even the sun-filled days held a coldness that served notice that the winter snows were due anytime. The expedition pushed northwest for two weeks before they reached a little river called the Lemhi that would lead them down to the Salmon. When they arrived at the Salmon River the rations were all but gone, and the only game to be found was an occasional fish or fowl, with an antelope thrown in now and then.

The first day along the Salmon proved eventful. When they woke up they found everything covered with four inches of snow, and about midmorning a large party of Indians appeared in the distance. Swit had watched Captain Walker leave early in the morning with the hunters, and he rested easier when he saw Walker and the Indian chief separate from the main bunch. They were on their way to meet with Captain Bonneville.

Bonneville soon learned that these men were members of the upper Nez Perce Indian Nation, the exact tribe that he had wished to meet and get to know. They were on their way to make a hunt and where as short of food as Bonneville's expedition; however, they demonstrated complete sincerity in their several offers to share what little they had with Bonneville and his men. The two parties camped together for two days.

Captain Bonneville was continually surprised by the kind, giving and gentle nature of these residents of the Salmon River country. Before the Indians left he asked Michael Cerré to take a few men and accompany the Nez Perce. If they had a successful hunt, Michael was to trade with them for meat for the winter. Following the departure of the Indians, Captain Bonneville's expedition traveled downriver until they were four to five miles below the junction of the Lemhi and Salmon Rivers. It was here that the captain selected his site for their winter camp and immediately engaged the men in the construction of several cabins.

As far as Swit was concerned, he felt relieved when Joe Walker approached him and Will with the news of their upcoming departure. Walker had selected his twenty men, and after only one day at Bonneville's winter camp, he was prepared to leave. Swit controlled his enthusiasm as he packed. Many of Bonneville's men were so tired of travel and the grind of the last five months that they looked upon the men readying themselves to leave with pity. This suited Swit just fine; he tried to look as pitiful as possible, while inside he could hardly contain his eagerness to get away from this place.

"It sure don't look like we're packin' much grub to take along." Will and Swit continued to follow Captain Walkers' instructions for leaving. He was as glad as Swit to be included in Walker's group, even if they were, for the most part, only loading trapping gear on their pack animals. "'Course, if we was to take all the vittles they got, we wouldn't have that much."

"We're packing Robert and Henry," Swit answered. "That accounts for a lot more than you could find sacked up around here anywhere. I ain't looking forward to crossing over them mountains, but the way Henry talked, if you want buffalo you gotta be on the other side."

Woolly was as good as there was when it came to driving horses and mules, but by the time they'd reached the Green River most of his horses needed more than a few days rest. When they left Fort Bonneville, Swit decided to let Woolly ride Billy's gray mare. Swit watched as Woolly put his saddle on the gray. He remembered how Billy had praised her as a horse for crossing mountains, while he figured Scab would end up as a sled. Swit kind of regretted not having the mare to ride when they headed for the pass.

Joe Walker was ready to leave. The men said their farewells, and Walker's group headed back upriver. Bonneville's men moved off into the timber with their axes. Captain Walker backtracked up the Salmon to the Lemhi River fork. They traveled about twenty miles up the fork before Walker turned eastward, following up a stream flowing down out the mountains. Aligned in single file, with Walker leading, they moved up and over Lemhi pass much easier than Swit had feared. It had been a more or less gradual climb until they got almost to the summit. The last couple of miles were steeper, but Scab made the climb as good as any, and easier than some. On the top you could look back out over a beautiful river valley with mountains that stretched as far to the west as your eye could see. They headed east out into an area that Henry called Horse Prairie.

After they'd crossed the mountains and made camp, Woolly notified the group. "That there be the same pass that ol' Lewis and Clark used when they first crossed the divide here in aught five. 'Twas a young Indian lass, with her new baby bundled to her back, that showed 'em the way."

"I didn't know Lewis and Clark took an Indian with 'em." Swit had spent many an evening listening to his father tell about the Corps of Discovery. He was a student and admirer of their expedition, but had never said anything about an Indian traveling with Lewis and Clark.

"Five years before, she'd had the misfortune of bein' stole as a young'un, and ended up out on the plains, married to a French trapper," Woolly explained. "Lewis and Clark hired the trapper on their way up the Missouri River and got her in the bargain. Her name is Sacajawea. She'd been born into a Shoshone clan that summered in these parts, and remembered traveling this country as a youth."

"I heard about the black slave they had with 'em, but never anything about an Indian squaw." Swit was disappointed. He thought his dad had taught him everything about Lewis and Clark.

"Jefferson's men had run out of river to follow, and they needed Indian ponies to have any chance of making it on through to the Columbia," Woolly continued. "The chief of the first Indians they saw turned out to be her brother, and they got the horses they needed."

"I'll bet that was some reunion," Swit said. "After all those years she'd made it back to her people."

"Aye, laddie, but you know she stayed with her husband and continued on with the expedition." You could tell Woolly held the Shoshone Indians in high regard, especially Sacajawea. "Brag all ya want about Lewis and Clark. If it hadn't been for that Frenchman's little lady, they'd probably ended their exploration right here."

After leaving the mountains, Walker headed slightly north of eastward out into a wide-open country of huge sweeping valleys separated by distant mountain ranges. That same day Henry and Robert brought buffalo and elk meat back to the travelers, and the men ate their fill. As they continued moving northeastward, the hunters kept everyone supplied with meat. All the experienced trappers were seeing recent signs of Indians passing through the area, and that meant the Blackfoot. For this reason they stayed constantly alert and pushed the march. They packed away the meat they didn't eat, and arrived at the Madison River better supplied and without incident.

Walker quickly established the routine they were to follow. The men divided themselves into small groups and worked their way up the surrounding feeder streams. First priority was the location of beaver activity, second was finding a good spot to camp and hide out during the day. This was no place to get careless. Traps were set out in the evening and run at first light. The rest of the day they stayed at a site where they were protected from the view of any Indians that might happen by. They passed the time skinning beaver, dressing, curing and putting Bonneville's expedition mark on all the skins. There was to be no burning of any green wood that would give off telling smoke plumes, and no fires of any kind at night.

The trappers treasured the beaver's tail and the secretion from the two small glands hidden inside its body. Most beaver meat was not considered edible, but the tail flesh was praised as a delicacy that ranked with the buffalo's tongue and hump meat. The glands produced an oily substance that the trappers called castorum. Manufacturers would pay for the gland excretion, label it castor, and used it to make medicines and perfume. The trappers utilized the beaver scent to concoct the "medicine," which was each trapper's formula for an odoriferous liquid designed to attract the beavers.

"You'd think you wouldn't forget how cold these streams are or why you'd promised yourself you'd never take up a trapper's life again." Will and Swit dragged two more beaver up from the depths. Trapping beaver was good money and the freest kind of living, but it wasn't without danger, or having your feet and legs numbed by the cold. There was no escaping the fact that you had to endure the cold mountain streams to "measure up to the beaver," as the old trappers liked to say.

Most animals use the land pretty much like they found it. Not the beaver, they changed it to suit themselves. They'll pick out a stream, and build a dam to control the flow; thereby creating a pond that gave them an ideal environment in which to live and continue their daily work. While each trapper had his own tricks and special way of capturing these creatures, the basic premise was the same for all.

A trap was hidden just three inches or so below the water surface along the edge of a beaver pond. One end of a stick was planted in the ground beside the trap, leaving about four inches of it showing above the water line. The trap was baited by applying the "medicine" to the exposed stick. The bait brought the beaver, and while he was stretched upward, engaged in sniffing this alluring stick, he could accidentally place a hind foot into the trap.

That move was designed to start him on his way to becoming someone's new hat. When the jaws grabbed his paw he'd immediately jump for deep water. Each trap was secured by a length of chain attached to a stout stake that had been driven into the bottom of the pond. Once the beaver reached the deep water with the trap, the chain held tight, and he found that he could go no farther. His fate was sealed. He soon tired, the weight of the trap pulled him down, and he drowned.

"We been here about two weeks." Swit and Will were picking up their traps. Their plan was to move upstream to a new beaver pond. "You figure we'll be heading back before long?"

"Well now, I'll tell ya, it wouldn't make me mad to stop wadin' around in this water," Will answered. "All total I bet we got us two, maybe three, packs of skins by now."

Swit had watched the older more experienced trappers pack the hides. The beaver pelts paid the bills, and the men took care to see that the furs were stored so that when they arrived in St. Louis they were in the best possible condition. A pack weighted about one hundred pounds and contained around eighty skins. The choicest ones were placed inside the pack, where they were least likely to be damaged.

"We haven't had much luck the last several days—too much ice," Swit announced. "It'd be good to get out of here before any of them Blackfoot find us."

The constant threat of the Blackfoot Indians was always present in the trappers' thoughts. The Indians considered this part of the Rockies their territory. They would try to kill any American they could find. "Did you believe that story Henry was telling about John Colter and how he escaped from them Blackfoot?" Swit asked.

"I'd say that better than ninety percent of the story is fact," Will answered. "I never knew the man myself, but I've talked to them that did. They all said that he was one tough customer."

"Henry didn't say anything about him dying."

"Well now, the way I heard it, his hide turned kind of a yellow color, and he died in his bed back in Missouri about ten years ago," Will answered. "Henry's story happened not two days ride northwest of here."

"How come Colter didn't see that big a bunch of Indians coming and get himself hid?" Swit wanted to know. "I didn't get if he was all alone or had somebody with him."

"There was two of 'em," Will answered. "Him and a fellow named Potts. They was in canoes over on the Jefferson branch of the three forks of the Missouri and couldn't see out over the high banks. The Blackfoot rode right up on 'em and waved 'em to shore. As soon as Colter was out of his canoe they grabbed him and stripped him of everything, including his clothes. He said he thought that each breath was his last one. Potts wouldn't come ashore. Said he'd as soon die in the canoe. He tried to escape by shootin' an Indian and then paddlin' downstream as fast as he could go. They porcupined him with arrows before he'd gone fifty yards."

"But they didn't shoot Colter like they did Potts?" Swit asked.

"The Indians went plumb crazy after Potts killed one of 'em." Will thought how Colter must have figured that he was a goner. "Three or four of 'em swam out and hauled Potts' canoe to shore. Colter said they chopped Potts up into little pieces and kept throwin' parts of him in his face."

"It sounds to me like them Blackfoot is touched in the head," Swit concluded. "I ain't looking forward to meeting up with any of them."

"About the time Colter figured that they was ready to start on him," Will continued, "the Indians moved off to one side and held a council. After the meeting one of the old men came up to Colter and acted like he wanted him to head off toward the east. At first Colter thought they wanted him to stand farther away so shootin' at him would be better sport. He said he just walked away real slow. When he looked back, all the young braves were takin' off everything that would slow 'em down. They each carried a spear. He knew then that it was gonna be a foot race."

"Can you imagine running stark naked for six miles across this prickly pear country with a bunch of Indians after you?" If the story was true, Swit was amazed with Colter's endurance and fortitude. "Did you hear the story like Henry told it? There was only one in the whole bunch that was fast enough to catch him. The two of them was way ahead of the others, so Colter turned back and killed him with his own spear."

"Same story," Will answered. "Colter had run so hard for so long that a bloody foam was blowin' out of his nose. I'll bet when he turned around and the Indian saw all that blood splattered down Colter's face and chest, he though the devil himself was stoppin' to get him."

"I guess the Indians got what they wanted," Swit interrupted. "They set up the race, thinking it would be easy."

"Colter said that he finally had to stop runnin' 'cause he was completely done in." Will always liked this part of the story. "He said the Indian looked to be in about the same shape, and when he stopped, it startled him. The Indian tripped and fell, and the shaft in his spear broke. Colter grabbed the end with the blade in it and drove it through the Indian's chest. He knew that the Madison River was just ahead, so he took the spear and a light blanket that the Indian was wearin', and made for the river."

"After a six-mile race and an Indian battle I wouldn't think there be much travel left in John Colter."

"He said that somehow killin' the Indian seemed to recharged his system." Will thought that seeing the rest of the Indians still headed his way probably had something to do with the recharge. "When he reached the river he hid out under some drift timber. The Indians spent the rest of the day lookin' for him. When night came he pulled himself out of the water and headed for a fort over on the Yellowstone. It's at least a hundred and fifty miles from the river to that fort. He hid out durin' the day and traveled at night. Said it was a good thing he had that Indian's blanket; without it he'd have froze to death in the high country."

"He had to be some kinda sight walking into that trading post eleven days later with nothing but a blanket and a broken spear." Swit was ready to leave this Blackfoot country behind.

The next morning Captain Walker suggested that they haul in their traps and head for Bonneville's winter camp. He led the men back over pretty much the same trail they'd used to get to the Madison. The night before they were to start climbing their way back up over the mountains they camped in some willows by a little stream that had a nice meadow back in the trees. Walker knew that forage would be hard to find after they crossed the divide, so he had the men stake out their horses on the meadow.

After the men had their fill of Henry and Robert's buffalo meat, Walker got a deck of Old Sledge cards out of his pack. Soon the men had a lively game going. It surprised the entire camp when the Indians tried to stampede the horses. Everyone headed for the meadow. When they got there some of the Blackfoot were already mounted. They elected to abandon their newly acquired but uncooperative horses for better cover in the brush when Walker's men started firing. There was a short exchange of hostilities between the two parties before the Indians quietly slipped off into the night. No one was injured, and only two horses were lost to the Indians. Walker was visibly upset over the encounter. He blamed himself for the whole fracas. Returning to camp he pitched his Old Sledge cards into the campfire before walking off into the darkness.

Over the course of the next few days, as they made their way back to the Salmon River, Swit observed a different Joe Walker. Captain Walker was normally not given to demonstrations or shows of emotion, and other than destroying his cards none had been forthcoming. He just seemed to raise his concentration to a higher level. His entire focus was upon the task at hand. Swit thought that the men gave about as much thought to the skirmish with the Indians as they did to the snow that was beginning to fall. It was just one of those things that happen. Not Captain Walker. He counted the fact that they had been surprised by the Blackfoot as a nonperformance of his responsibilities—entirely his deficiency. Swit thought how Walker might be just human like the rest of us but that he held himself to higher standards than most.

Chapter Twenty

Bonneville's winter camp gave Swit a shock. He had expected that the men would be quartered in tight, cozy cabins, the meat supply for the winter hung in storage, and everyone busy making repairs to the equipment that had suffered much during the trip. Instead, many of the men appeared to be off somewhere else, and those left at camp were busy trying to stay in close to the fire and keep from starving.

They had completed three small, cabinlike structures that were barely tall enough for a short person, and didn't look comfortable, warm or snug. You could have flung a cat out of the leaky cabins about anywhere you cared to, but then a cat, or any other critter unfortunate enough to pass by, ended up in the stew pot. All the meals were coming out of a big kettle that had become the final resting place for any rabbit, weasel or rodent that happened by. Roots, berries and bark filled out the menu.

"Did Michael have any luck with the Nes Perce?" Walker had his men unload and store away the packs of pelts and hides they'd brought. As far as he could tell no one else had made a successful hunt.

"Haven't seen anything of Michael since he left," Bonneville answered. "I sent a hunting party over to Horse Prairie, but I haven't heard anything from them either. Adams led a fur brigade off to trap in the upper Yellowstone River country. He's still out. You brought in several nice bundles of pelts. Did you encounter any difficulties with the Indians?"

"Just a little scrap over our horses." It seemed to Walker that the men were in a daily struggle with cold and hunger, and Captain Bonneville appeared to have little concern for the lack of food or beaver hides. "Why don't I take about twenty more of these men and winter somewhere down along the Snake River? In the spring we'll be handy to the Bear River country and ready to make our hunt down there."

"That makes sense to me. We already have a few Nez Perce and Flatheads moving in and out of our camp. If I can winter with these Indians I can learn a lot about this part of the country and how to travel through it. I'm in the process now of mapping out the upper Salmon River area." Bonneville had sent men and provisions off into different areas with the intent of them returning with beaver pelts and fresh meat. So far Walker's group was the only one to return. "We can all meet back at Fort Bonneville next July."

Joe Walker thought about how the situation at camp hadn't dampened the captain's enthusiasm. "We'll rest up for a few days before we start for the Snake. Ben, just so we understand each other, I plan to pick out about forty men at next summer's rendezvous and lead them into the California settlements."

"I understand that completely, and I'll support your expedition with any supplies at my disposal," Bonneville reassured Walker. "Believe me when I tell you that when your excursion becomes public it will probably become a sensitive political issue. I'll more than likely be back in the Army by then, and will have to tell what went on out here by their standards. Privately I do and always will agree to your trailing off into Mexican territory. My only regret is that I can't go with you."

It was the first part of November, and it snowed at least some almost every day. After spending three nights camped along the Salmon, Walker decided it was time to find a better home for the winter. Picking an additional twenty men, he took his group and headed south for the Snake River. Once they reached the Snake they traveled downstream until they arrived at the junction of the Blackfoot River. Following up the Blackfoot, Walker found a protected little valley that let them use the southern sun exposure to help warm their camp. The men were soon busy putting up shelters. Henry and Robert took charge of the hunters, and although game was not plentiful, they managed to find a few buffalo still in the area. Preparing themselves as best they could, Walker's men set in to wait out the winter and make ready for the spring hunt.

Walker had posted lookouts, so it surprised no one when the eight braves rode into the south end of the little clearing. There'd be no unexpected raids on this camp. Although they were outnumbered, the Indians rode forward with an air of absolute dominance over their surroundings. They were heavily dressed in an array of animal skins designed to protect them from the winter's harshness. Each man carried a weapon and appeared qualified and ready for battle. They rode forward with complete confidence. Not in a noisy, just barely controlled, runaway-style arrival, but in an almost military-like formation and movement. Before entering the campsite itself, the Indians stopped. Their leader rode out ahead of the group, carrying his ceremonial pipe.

"Well now, I guess ol' Woolly was right when he said we should get ourselves ready to receive some dignitaries." Will and Swit watched as Captain Walker walked forward and invited the leader to join him.

"Who are they?" Swit wanted to know.

"They're Snakes. You know, the Indians that Woolly's always tellin' us about," Will answered. "The one with the pipe is Washakie. He's not the big chief of the Shoshone, but he ranks high up on the list. Him and Captain Drips had a long talk when I was here last time, and Andy said he was the smartest Indian he ever met. He wanted to know everything about white men and the place called the States. When they showed up they had furs to trade. Wouldn't trade for whiskey, either; came away with guns, pots, knives, blankets, ball and power—you know, things that count."

"I wouldn't wanta see the Indians get any more guns than they already got." Swit thought that they seem peaceful enough, but Oo-tse-tee always watched other Indians with as much caution as he did the whites. Swit knew that the Blackfoot needed watching. "Woolly's right high on these Shoshone, but I doubt he's met all of 'em. Now just what's the deal on calling 'em Snakes one time and Shoshones another."

"Well now, I'll tell ya how that is. Some calls 'em one thing and another calls 'em the other," Will answered. "The way I get it, the Snakes is the eastern branch of the Shoshone Nation. Washakie's not a full-blood Shoshone himself. His pa was a Flathead, and the family lived with his people until the Blackfoot killed him."

"How'd he get to be a chief if he's only half Shoshone?" Swit asked.

"With these Indians it matters more what you do than who you are," Will answered. "The way Captain Drips told it, the Blackfoot and Shoshones have been kill-'em-on-sight enemies since day one. It seems that about five years ago some Blackfoot slipped down to where Washakie's tribe was grazin' their horses. They stole all the horses and left the young Shoshone boys that had been assigned to keep track of the herd for the wolves and buzzards."

"Killing young boys ain't that easy to digest." Swit was beginning to understand why the word Blackfoot triggered feelings of concern and hatred.

"Washakie had a little problem with that himself." Will liked the way Swit stated his feelings. "He formed up his own war party and took off after the horses. Washakie don't have no quit in him. He followed the horses six hundred miles to the north and caught up with 'em along the Missouri River."

It was Swit's belief that a man that just keeps on coming usually prevails.

"When Washakie returned to his people," Will continued, "he brought back about all of his men, most of the horses and scalps from all the Blackfoot that thought they'd plumb got away with their murderin' thievery. Andy said that other Indians he'd talked with called Washakie the fiercest warrior they knew or had heard about. It's said that if he gets bored he's likely to strike out on his own to just hunt and kill Blackfoot. There are plenty of Sioux, Crows, Cheyenne and Arapaho, as well as the Blackfoot, that hate him. Some's just plain scared, but they all respect him."

"How do we know he ain't fixing to attack us?" Swit's asked.

"As far as I know, the Snakes ain't hurt no white man that didn't try to harm them first." Will watched Walker and Washakie walking toward them. "You're always welcome in their lands or camps."

"Was it because of Sacajawea that the Snakes was willing to help?" Swit wondered why Captain Walker was bringing the Indian chief their way.

"Didn't hurt, but I think guns was the main reason," Will answered. "The Blackfoot could get guns from the British trappers, but the Snakes couldn't. Their lack of firepower had put the whole Shoshone Nation at risk. Lewis convinced the Snakes that if they got through to the ocean and back to the States, white men would come from the East with rifles to trade for furs. The Snakes needed guns to survive, so they took a chance, and Lewis and Clark got the horses they needed. Trappers and traders started bringin' in guns to trade to the Shoshone, and there's been a special feeling between the whites and the Snakes ever since."

"Will, I want you and Swit to go with Washakie," Captain Walker said as they walked up. "He remembers when you and Andrew were down along the Bear River two years ago."

"Well now, you know, I remember that time too," Will answered as he greeted the Indian. "I'm glad to see you're in good health."

"Washakie, this man's name is Swit Boone." Walker turned toward Swit.

"Thank you," Washakie answered. "We have a white man in our camp that's hurt bad. Maybe you help. Found him along with two dead men at Sheep Rock four days ago. Blackfoot attack."

184

Swit was getting nervous. Washakie had not taken his eyes off of him. It was like he was processing and storing all the information he could gather about Swit. It wasn't particularly threatening or fearful, just unsettling.

"The Shoshone camp isn't far from here," Walker said. "This man might be part of the bunch that Captain Bonneville sent this way with our lame horses. Do what you can, and find out what happened. You'll be in good hands with these people. When you're ready to come back they'll see you back to us."

The injured man's name was Jennings, and death took him only an hour before Swit and Will arrived at the Indian camp. Will recognized him and remembered that he had been one of the group that had left Fort Bonneville with Matthieu on their way to the Bear River. Washakie told how two other white men had been captured and put to death. It was apparent that the two men had suffered greatly. Ears, nose, eyes, hands, feet and other body parts had been cut off, torn away and gouged out while the Indians vented their feelings. Swit listened to Washakie's description of how he thought the men had died. It didn't sound like death had come to these men in a swift or easy way.

Washakie continued his theory about the attack by telling how he thought Jennings had escaped the horrors of a Blackfoot soiree. The Indians evidently thought that Jennings was dead and left him until later while they amused themselves with the two live captives. Jennings had been able to pull himself into a thicket next to a rock overhanging the river. Washakie said that a sudden storm had moved through the area two days before they found Jennings. He postulated that the storm must have hit before the Indians finished with their entertainment. They probably went back to relieve Jennings of his body parts, but the storm had covered up his tracks and made any additional playtime along the river unpleasant. It was Washakie's opinion that they wouldn't have found Jennings either if he hadn't been out of his head with fever. They heard him mumbling in the brush.

Washakie wanted to know if Will and Swit wished to take Jennings back to Walker's camp or have him laid to rest in any particular place. Will expressed his opinion that it didn't matter much where the body returned to dust. Swit didn't give an answer. The Indians were confused by this seemingly lack of concern about the interment of the white man. They wrapped Jennings in a buffalo robe and carried him off to rest in a place the Shoshones had reserved for their own people. Swit noticed that the Indians hadn't seemed the least bit shocked by the way the white men had met their death. Yet, when Woodrow expressed only limited concern about what to do with Jennings's body, these same Indians looked at Will and himself as if they were the most primitive of savages, completely lacking in any degree of compassion or decency.

The Indian's confusion about Swit and Will's concern for Jennings didn't diminish their hospitality. As soon as Jennings had been removed from the lodge, two young women made the tepee ready for their new guests. The pair were welcomed and invited to settle into their new abode.

"It seems like the Indians don't understand us any better than we understand them, don't it?" Swit asked Will.

"We both got different ways of lookin' at things," Will answered. "I 'spect that's why we ain't got much respect for each other."

"It could be," Swit agreed. "I was thinking that Indians and whites in general didn't get off to a very good start. We was mostly interested in getting beaver skins from them, and they wanted trinkets and shiny stuff from us. What we considered valuable they thought of as practically worthless, and what they treasured wouldn't get you a smile from our people. If that was all you knew about each other, it'd be hard to build much respect for one another."

Will raised up to looked over at Swit. He laid face up on top of a buffalo robe, eyes open and looking up at the top of the tepee. He took a deep breath, closed his eyes and rolled over. It always surprised Woodrow when Swit would unexpectedly come up with these pearls of plain old common sense.

The reason for Woolly's high regard for the Shoshone Indians was beginning to become apparent. They were proving to be the most gracious of hosts. It seemed to give them great pleasure to share almost anything they had with their guests. This tribe was not intrusively curious about the white man's articles, and they showed absolutely no greed or inclination to steal. The person and clothing of these Indians were remarkably clean, given the time of year when washing and bathing wasn't easy, and smoky fires heated their teepees. The Snakes definitely believed in presenting themselves in the finest tradition of Indian fashion. Their garments were not only made for service, but in an attractive manner that showed pride and quality in the workmanship. Horses were as well cared for as themselves.

Swit was sure he knew what Woolly liked best about the Snakes. The

Shoshone women were the most strikingly attractive of any Indian females he'd seen. Their hair was always clean and combed. If it didn't fall freely onto their shoulders, it was braided into various styles. The intricacies of some of the braids caused Swit to marvel at their creation. The copper colored tone of their skin seemed to highlight the sparkle in their eyes, and their lips always seemed to be naturally eager to bring forth a smile. The physical beauty of these ladies would grab the eye of any normal male; however, it was their demeanor and good-natured friendly disposition that captured and held a man's attention.

It seemed to Swit that the Indian woman's responsibilities were numerous and without letup. They gathered all the food except the meat. The men brought in the game, although it was the women that prepared and turned it into an edible meal. They cooked and preserved all the food, tanned the hides, made all the garments, cleaned, patched, put up and took down the lodges, were mothers to their children, and wives to their husbands. It was miracle enough for Swit to see them accomplish all this, yet they did it all and at the same time seemed to be truly happy in their labor and at peace with their surroundings. The only time he saw one of the wives upset was when her husband tried to encroach on what she considered as her duty to repair a leak in the tepee.

"We've been here about a week now," Swit told Will as they were preparing to bundle themselves up in buffalo robes and sleep away the cold of the night. "Maybe we better head on back."

"Well now, I'll tell ya, one thing's for sure," Will answered. "Walker ain't got nothin' this good at his camp. Washakie comes by every day to talk and smoke. If he wants us to leave I ain't seen no sign of it. In fact, it's just the opposite. Says he'll take us back if we have to go, but several times he's said that we ought to stay till spring."

"He sure likes us to talk about everywhere we been, don't he?" Swit said. "He talks English good too. Kinda like Captain Walker. He don't use many words, but says a lot. Do you feel kinda like Washakie would crawl inside ya if he could, and take everything you know?"

"Well, he sure enough wants to find out everything he can," Will answered. "I guess we're findin' out how an Indian lives. I ain't never been waited on like this before. You think maybe they're usin' us to give some of them young gals practice at keepin' up a good tepee? We get a new one in here about every other day."

"I don't know what they're doing," Swit answered. "But it sure makes living easy. You couldn't have it much better. They take care of everything, and they're real friendly, especially the one with the little scar on her cheek. I can see she fancies you tall, drawn-out types. I'd bet if you was to pull back that old buffalo robe she'd slip right in beside ya."

Swit could hear the snow hitting the tepee. He thought about the young girl that had prepared the evening meal, and his life at the Shoshone village. The buffalo meat and some type of root cake had done more than just satisfy his hunger, it left him relaxed and content. He was warm, sandwiched in between two buffalo robes; still, it was time that they rejoined Captain Walker. After all, they weren't hired to vacation here all winter.

"Do you think Captain Walker will do anything special for Christmas?" Swit asked Will. He hadn't thought about Christmas at all when they were staying with the Indians. Since their return to camp he'd noticed that a few of the men were starting to remember the birthday of the Christ child. One man had made a star out of evergreen branches and fastened it to the top of his lean-to. "Even if we don't, I'm still glad we're back in our own camp."

"Speakin' about Christmas, have you got my present all ready to go?" Woodrow wanted to know. "It ain't but a couple days off. You know, you could give me that ol' Scab horse of yours for Christmas."

"I don't expect you're going to have that good a Christmas," Boone answered. "Besides, he ain't mine to give away anyhow. Them two guys riding in over there ain't part of our bunch, are they?"

"No, that's Warren Ferris and Tom Fitzpatrick," Will answered. "You remember Fitz, he's the man the free trappers was tellin' us almost died gettin' to last summer's rendezvous. The last I heard Ferris was workin' for the American Fur bunch, and Fitz was a partner in the Rocky Mountain Company. I wonder if one of 'em switched over."

The two trappers were welcomed into camp by Captain Walker. They expressed a desire to spend Christmas day with Walker and his men. After that they needed to find Andrew Drips, who they thought was in a winter camp over on Henry's Fork of the Snake River. In the course of conversation over the next two days, the story about the conflict that occurred between the American and the Rocky Mountain Fur Companies during the fall hunt was told.

It seems that the trouble really started just before the breakup of last year's rendezvous at Pierre's Hole. Jim Bridger and Tom Fitzpatrick of the Rocky Mountain Fur Company had offered Andrew Drips and Henry Vanderburgh of the American Fur Company a deal. Each company was to have exclusive trapping rights to designated parts of the beaver country around the Three Forks area of the Missouri River. Drips and Vanderburgh refused to bargain, and both companies knew then that they were locked in a battle with each other to make a successful hunt.

To begin with, Drips and Vanderburgh had to go find Fontenelle since he hadn't made it to the rendezvous with their supplies. They found him on the upper Green, and picked up the supplies they'd need for the fall hunt. Drips and Vanderburg knew that they had John Jacob Astor's powerful organization behind them, and that the Rocky Mountain company was on shaky ground. Once they were refitted, their plan was to find Bridger and Fitzpatrick and follow them into the prime beaver country. If Drips and Vanderburgh took some beaver, so much the better, but the main thing was to keep Bridger and Fitzpatrick from having a good hunt. If the Rocky Mountain Company could be forced out of business, then the American Company would more than make up for the bad fall hunt with a free-wheeling uncontested trapping season next spring.

When Fitzpatrick and Bridger discovered what the American Company men were up to, they developed a plan of their own. Bridger and Fitzpatrick were well acquainted with the Three Forks area, and two of the most experienced men in the wilderness. They led their followers deeper and deeper into the seldom-traveled homelands of the Blackfoot Indians. Once inside this hostile territory they split into smaller groups, shook loose from their tormentors and began to remove themselves from the land of peril. They'd let the Indians deal with Drips and Vanderburg.

Vanderburgh and Drips finally realized what the Rocky Mountain men were up too and began to carefully move away from their hazardous location. Drips was able to get his men out without mishap, but Vanderburgh was not as fortunate. His inexperience cost him his life, and the life of one of his men. Warren Ferris, who had been with Vanderburgh and was now traveling with Fitzpatrick, had been wounded. Bridger didn't get out without incident. He took two arrows during an encounter with the Blackfoot. Fitzpatrick said that Bridger still carried one of the arrowheads in his back.

It surprised Swit that these two men, who had been on opposite sides of an affray that had tried to destroy each other's companies and caused two men to die, were now, less than two months later, traveling around together like they were the best of buddies. It was hard for Swit to understand these men of the wilderness. Their loyalty seemed to be to the trapper's way of life and not to any particular individual or company. Interaction between the men or fur companies was a competition for furs, and once over with, forgotten. Without question they had their personal friends and people they preferred to partner-up with, but their individual freedom was all-important.

Chapter Twenty-one

Billy B. thought that the drive back to the ranch always seemed longer than the drive to Santa Fe. Today was no exception. Alonzo thought that it seemed as if his troubles just kept mounting. After he and Billy left Doña Tules place, he'd headed straight for the governor's palace while Billy B. went to pick up the supplies.

Jose Antonio Chavez had replaced Manuel Armijo as provincial governor, and Alonzo was confident that the governor would straighten out this business about who owned the Suarez ranch. The signing date listed on the so-called deed was not possible. Pedro had picked poorly when he chose June 4, 1831. That was the day Alonzo had turned fifteen—he and his father had spent the day together. He knew that the signature on the document was not his father's; however, the paper had been witnessed by one of Chavez's generals. The governor explained to Alonzo that while he had no personal knowledge of the transaction, everything seemed to be in order.

"I guess ya didn't get much help from the governor?" Billy asked after they had traveled along in silence for some time.

"No, and I'm sure that's not my papa's signature."

"I doubted that myself. I have a feelin' that Don Carlos turned a few heads when he brought Hog Eye and Otis Tejas into Doña Tules place, not to mention rescuing Maria and takin' me in. Hard to say if it had anything to do with the killin', but Pedro was sure quick with his claim to the ranch. Do you have any papers that says your family owns anything?"

"We have an old Spanish land grant and some other papers that we got from the Mexican government." Alonzo couldn't help feeling like it was all slipping away, and he was powerless to stop the slide. "Do you think Pedro will want to come out and live at the ranch?"

"I doubt it, but I 'spect we'll hear more from him after he lets us chew on this news for a spell." Billy B. watched Alonzo's gloom deepen. "I'd say we need to put all them papers away in a real safe place. Don't worry too much about what might happen. We'll just take care of things as they come. Let's just pull in tight them that's closest to us. The ones that the Suarezs can't count on will float to the top and spill over real quick."

"Did you hear anything about what happened to the black man?" Alonzo didn't know the man himself, but he remembered that Billy had been concerned about his outcome.

"When I was gettin' our supplies I heard that the wagonmaster had him chained in the back of a wagon. They're takin' him back to Missouri for trial," Billy answered. "It don't look like it'd be a crime to shoot a killer, does it?"

Alonzo never offered an opinion about what might or might not be a Missouri crime. He rode along in silence with his head down. Billy could see that Pedro's announced one-half ownership in the ranch, and the governor's support for the claim, had put a fatal blow to Alonzo's coping with the sudden violent death of his father. The young man began to sob. It started with just a few tears, but the sense of loss and hopelessness quickly captured his whole body and caused him to grab breaths in short, jerky movements. He tried to stop, but there was no gaining control.

"Don't try to hold her back. Let it all out." Billy felt uneasy watching Alonzo cry, but he knew that the release would help. It was hard not knowing how to comfort the boy as the pain poured from his body. Billy rode along in silence. When it seemed as if Alonzo had relieved all the sadness that he could, Billy reached over and put his hand on Alonzo's shoulder. "I know it don't seem like it now, but it'll get better. It'll never be the same, but it wasn't gonna be the same anyway. Things is always changin'. This is one of them changes we wish hadn't happened, but it did. Now we just gotta pick up and go on." Billy knew he was right about changes being the way of things, but he hadn't expected this many this fast.

The day after they put Don Carlos to rest, Pedro Ramirez rode in with two men and announced that they were the *jefe vaqueros*. That night Maria brought Matilda Petronila Ysidora Alexander into the world.

"I guess she's about the prettiest baby I ever seen." Billy B. watched Anita carry the new infant over to meet her daddy. "'Course, I ain't been around that many babies. How's Maria?"

"She's doing just fine," Anita answered. "I've seen my share of new ones. I can tell you that she's not only beautiful, but healthy as they come."

"She sure has her mother's hair and eyes, don't she?" A smile moved across Billy's face and pushed his mustache into that curious twist it sometimes took. "Would it be okay if I slipped in and saw Maria for a second?"

"I'd say you better be thanking her for this little one." Anita thought how good it was to see Billy B. smile again. Things had been grim for too long. "Besides, I better carry little Mattie over to where the light is better. It almost looks like I can see some real fine hair on her upper lip." Billy turned to look, but Anita had already started down the hall. He couldn't see her face, but he knew that she'd have that ornery sparkle in her eyes.

Maria was resting easy when Billy walked up to her. "She's the best baby I ever seen." Billy bent down and kissed the new mother. "Are you all right? You want me to leave you to rest?"

"No, I want you to set down here beside me," Maria answered. "I guess we got a start on our family tonight, didn't we? Isn't she a pretty little thing?"

"That she is." Billy kissed Maria again. "Looks just like her mother. I'm so happy and proud right now that it's hard to hold. With all the sadness we've had around here lately, it's good to get a gift like this. You look tired, Maria, are you okay?"

"I'm fine. Like you say, I'm just tired," Maria answered. "What are we going to do about Pedro and his new men? It looks to me like he's going to move right in and take over everything. He's got the governor's blessing."

"Takin' charge around here will call for a little more than just sayin' so." Billy B. thought back to the two toughs that Pedro had moved out to the ranch and set up as the head *vaqueros*. "I 'spect Juan and Cisco will have a thought or two about who's in charge."

A thin, gray line had just started to bring light to the eastern sky when the two new *vaqueros* entered the bunkhouse. Juan and Francisco were already up and getting dressed for the coming day's work. The other men were still in bed, captured by varying degrees of sleep. Some dead deep and snoring, while others twisted and turned, postponing the eventual rise to meet the new day.

"By God, it's time you señoritas was up and going," the tall *vaquero* loudly announced to the bunkhouse group. He had a left eyelid that drooped until only a squint of eyeball showed. "Get ready for things to change around here. There ain't gonna be no more sleeping the morning away."

"They're a pitiful sight, ain't they, Ojo?" the other *vaquero* added.

"You're pretty new around here to be…" Cisco spoke as he turned toward the source of the second comment. This man was shorter. He had a round-shaped head that seemed to small for his body. An old scar started just under his right ear and ran forward, almost into his mouth. The scar had caused a fold along his right cheek that gave him the appearance of continually wearing an ugly half-smile. Ojo cut Cisco's statement in mid-sentence. The tall *vaquero* had moved in from behind Cisco and hit him just above the right temple with the handle end of his quirt. Cisco dropped immediately to his knees. Then he pitched forward, smashing his face into the floor. He rolled over and didn't move.

"Anyone else care to voice their opinion?" Ojo asked. The room was silent, but everyone was wide-awake.

The sudden unexpected violence caught Juan by surprise. He was astonished at how quickly the tall, bad-eyed one had dispatched Cisco. Juan had observed Cisco in more than a few skirmishes, and had found few his equal in combat. Now he was lying in his own blood on the floor, maybe even dead. Juan only had one boot on. He started to move toward Cisco. The intruder with the part smile stepped in front of him, sticking the point of a big knife just below the level of Juan's breastbone.

"Boys, listen up. This is how it's going to be from now on. Me and Cicatriz is like your *compadre* there on the floor was saying," Ojo paused, then turned and kicked Cisco in the side. "We're new. We're also in charge."

"Don't guess anybody minds." Cicatriz pushed his knife, poking it through Juan's shirt and cutting the skin just enough to produce a small blood spot.

"You boys talk it over," Ojo said as he motioned Cicatriz toward the door. "If you don't think you can work under the new management you better ride on out. That is, if you own a horse. Otherwise, you can walk."

As the two new *vaqueros* left the bunkhouse, Cisco made his first sound. He coughed, spit out a bloody tooth, and then moved his hand to wipe the blood off his face.

Two men rode out on their horses before breakfast was served. After breakfast two others rode out double on an old horse they'd bought from the oldest *vaquero* that worked at the ranch. The old man had been born on the ranch and had worked there all his life. He said that he considered himself to be part of the Suarez family. He didn't like what was happening, but thought that he was too old now to change anything or move. Besides, he didn't want to live anywhere else. He sold his horse to remove any temptation.

Alonzo, Billy, Juan and Cisco had been meeting almost every night in secret. Life on the ranch had changed. Cisco thought of little now except how and when he would end the life of the tall *vaquero*, Ojo. Alonzo stayed around the house most of the time. It was the one place that Pedro and his men hadn't pushed their new influence. The resigning *vaqueros* had been replaced with Pedro's men, and more than a few of the old hands had already spilled over into the new camp. Even the old *vaquero* seemed at ease with the new ownership arrangement. Juan and Billy had continued to fight for the Suarez children, but it was a losing battle.

"Where do you go tomorrow?" Juan asked Cisco as the four men sat under a dying peach tree in the orchard at the back of the house.

"How would I know?" Cisco answered. "They never tell me nothing until it's time to go. I'll tell you one thing, if that Ojo and I go off together, I'll be the only one coming back."

"He ain't gonna go nowhere without Smiley." Billy was noticing how neglected everything was becoming. The orchard, once a place that Don Carlos would show off to every visitor, was dying and full of trash, weeds and dead limbs. "You just as well forget about gettin' even with Ojo. Them two almost always ride with four or five of their own. If we ever had any chance at 'em it was early, and we missed that."

"I'm not talking about getting even. I'm telling you that I plan to kill the greasy bastard." Cisco continued to sharpen his knife on a little whetstone. "He'll slip up, and I'll be there when he does."

"You better watch out for that quirt," Juan suggested. "He might be harder to take than you think. He looks like he's seen his way through several battles already."

"You ever notice that none of the new men are very good with horses or cattle?" Billy B. asked. "I know they're better at it than me, but compared to you they ain't much. Alonzo is handier with a rope than they are."

"I might have some advantage in the saddle, but I'm losing the *rancho*," Alonzo replied. Billy B. brought Alonzo to all their meetings, but all he seemed to be able to think about was how he'd lost the ranch.

"Damn it, Alonzo, how many times do I have to tell you? You haven't lost anything." Juan was tired of hearing about how the *rancho* was lost. "Pedro and his hired fighters are stealing it. They got the law, what little there is of that, on their side. There's not much you can do about it right now."

"Did Pedro pay you for that band of sheep he sold?" Billy asked. "I saw him sell 'em to the supply caravan headed for Mexico City."

"Paid me some," Alonzo answered. "He said it was my half, but I know he cheated us. We both had to sign papers that okayed the sale and payment."

"Did you get a paper with his signature on it?" Billy asked.

"He can't sign his name," Alonzo answered. "He makes a mark that he's real proud of—stares at it when he's done."

"Somebody showed Pedro how to steal legal, usin' words on paper," Billy B. said. "You just collect all those pieces of paper you can and hang on to 'em. The day may come when we can turn 'em against him. We'll ride out this rough spot together."

"Why not ride it out in California?" The voice came from out of the darkness behind them. "You four set here every night planning, and Pedro could be listening to everything you say. You wouldn't even know it." Maria walked up carrying little Mattie. "What holds us here anyway? Don Carlos has given us a foothold in California. All we have to do is go."

"It's not quite as easy as all that," Billy answered. They had all been startled by Maria's quiet approach. "It's a tough, long haul to California, and filled with danger and hard times."

"I feel danger and hard times coming fast right here," Maria said. "Wouldn't it be better to risk ourselves for a fresh start?"

A limb snapped in the dark off to the right. A dull thud and a moan followed the sound of the limb breaking. Someone was moving through the orchard. It sounded as if they'd tripped and fell. The little group silently watched, listened and waited. They could hear someone moving back in the trees. The intruder was headed in their direction. Maria had slipped in without their knowing, Billy thought. Now someone else was out there in the darkness. Maria thought she could hear whispering, but she couldn't understand what was said. Maybe there was more than one.

"Billy B., is that you?" A faint voice drifted over the nervous group. "Billy, I got news, and I need help. I'm about done in."

"Who are ya?" Billy asked. He still couldn't see anyone.

"Hog Eye," The man answered. "I've traveled a ways. I need help. I'm coming in, don't shoot." Reginald Harris limped close enough so the group could see him. He looked beat.

"Are you alone?" Billy asked.

"Yep. There's only me," Hog Eye answered. "Don't you shoot, now."

"I heard you was headed back to Missouri," Billy said. "Not necessarily of your own accord."

"You heard right." Hog Eye moved closer to the group. "My Missouri friends didn't think much of me shooting ol' James. Somehow James got a whole lot more popular after he was dead. When he was alive he was a mean, hard to get along with, seersucker-lipped cheater that killed two men in cold blood right there in the plaza. He wasn't worth as much as a kiss-my-ass until I shot him. Now all of a sudden it's me that's the killer."

"We got a couple around here that needs killing." Cisco got up and helped Hog Eye over to where he could sit down. "How'd you get loose from them traders?"

"Slipped the chains first night out and high-tailed it off into the darkness," Hog Eye answered. "Hid out during the day. Traveled at night. It seemed to me that if I could find Don Carlos's ranch I might get some help."

"We'll start with getting you cleaned up and fed." Maria took Mattie and headed for the house. "You four help Mister Harris back to the house. It's time he was rewarded for his actions. It looks to me like we'll all need each other to handle Pedro or California."

"I thought that was Pedro I seen riding this way yesterday." Hog Eye recalled how he had covered himself with brush and spent the day in a little wash beside a creek. A group of five men had ridden by about midmorning. He was sure that one of the men was Pedro Ramirez. "What's he got to do with California?"

"Pedro has half the ranch now," Juan answered. "He brought in his own men and pretty much does as he pleases."

"If you're of a mind to let the life out of a couple more," Cisco added, "we could pull out early tomorrow and thin out ol' Pedro's troops. If we could hit Squinty and Smiley, the rest would scatter fast."

"Yes, and by nightfall you'd have a troop of soldiers looking to thin you out," Juan said as he helped Hog Eye to his feet. "Pedro pulled a fast claim to half the ranch, and he has the governor's backing."

"The short of it," Billy B. said as the group headed for the house, "is that it's not like it used to be around here. We've thought some of movin' to California."

"Here's something else you can think about," Hog Eye said. "One night, about three days before the killings, I went around to the back of Doña Tules

197

place to relieve myself. Pedro and James was having a big confab. I couldn't hear anything. I just took a leak and left, don't know if they saw me or not. I never thought much about it until everything came down on me after I shot James. Makes you wonder though, don't it?"

"Makes me more than wonder," Cisco answered. "Pedro just nominated himself for the bone pile."

Chapter Twenty-two

Benjamin Bonneville was discovering what living was like along the Salmon River in wintertime. Snow, cold and hunger was a daily concern. Two small tribes of Nez Perce and Flathead Indians had set their camps close to Bonneville's cabins. The captain had less than twenty men, and they were essentially living and working together with the Indians to try and outlast the winter. Combined hunting parties ventured out in search of meat and shared their limited success.

The Indians had arrived with a large herd of horses. Bonneville estimated that at one time there were forty horses for each warrior, but that count was falling fast. The Nez Perce were careless when it came to protecting their animals, especially at night, and reluctant to try and recover their losses. The Blackfoot were tenacious in their efforts to separate this peaceful band of Indians from their horse herd.

Captain Bonneville was busy gathering information from his new Indian friends, taking topographical measurements of the countryside, and using everything he was learning to develop a map of the area. Wintering in this valley was not easy, but Bonneville felt that he was truly becoming a mountain man and took pride in his accomplishments. In the distance he could see a small party of men riding his way, and he thought about all the men he had strung around the country. The trappers under Walker's care had passed through and were wintering somewhere along the Snake River. Cerré and his men were with a Nez Perce hunting party. He'd sent his best hunters over into Horse Prairie to look for buffalo and see if they could find Michael, but they hadn't returned. David Adams had led a group of trappers over into the upper Yellowstone River country, and Matthieu and his bunch were supposedly down along the Bear River with a sizable herd of horses. They were all instructed to report back to the winter camp along the Salmon River after their fall hunt. He'd only heard from Walker. Captain Bonneville hoped that the group riding in was some of his men.

The hunters that Bonneville had sent over into Horse Prairie, along with Michael Cerré and his men, filtered back to camp in small bunches over the next two days. They brought back very little in the way of meat and pelts. The Blackfoot Indians had forced them to take refuge with a tribe of Flatheads. Bonneville had collected valuable information about the territory, but unless Adams or Matthieu's men return with news of successful hunts, his company had very little to show for their first trapping season.

The Nez Perce and Flatheads informed Captain Bonneville that they intended to move farther north, hoping for less trouble from the Blackfoot. The captain agreed to catch up with them in a few days. After the Indians left, Bonneville supervised the construction of a cache to hold their trading supplies for the upcoming spring beaver campaign. Following the completion of their hideaway, they began their march to rejoin the Indians. Taking great care to secure their horses, and sending out scouting parties, Captain Bonneville overtook the Nez Perce without any trouble from the Blackfoot. The same couldn't be said for the Indians. A recent raid had carried off another forty of their horses.

Seeing his Indian friends' what's-done-is-done attitude, and their reluctance to try and recapture their losses, Bonneville offered to try and negotiate a peace between them and the Blackfoot. This precipitated a council of several days that ended with the Nez Perce announcing, "War is not good, and leaves both sides bloody. It also keeps our chiefs alert, and our young men strong and ready to fight. If the Blackfoot come we know they are our enemy, and we are ready. If we say we are at peace the eyes of the chiefs grow sleepy, and our young men become weak and lazy. Horses stray into the mountains. Women and children go unattended. No alarm is given. The Blackfoot tongue will lie, and when he claims peace he means war. If we are not prepared he will kill and steal. We can have no peace—let there be war!"

The mixture of Indians and trappers continued moving north down the Salmon River. Captain Bonneville had information showing the Salmon joining the Snake River, the Snake joining the Columbia River, and the Columbia flowing into the Pacific Ocean. He'd hoped that the Salmon River valley would provide a way for wagons to move westward to the Columbia, but had been told that travel down the Salmon was impossible. When the Salmon River started it's swing to the west, it took Captain Bonneville only a short reconnaissance westward to confirm what he'd been told. Deep canyons, rugged mountains and a turbulent cascading river eliminated any chance for wagon travel down the Salmon.

A stream flowing out of the mountains to the north joined the Salmon as it turned westward. The Nez Perce led Captain Bonneville's party up this tributary about fifteen miles before entering a deep, narrow gorge. This was the entrance into the Indian's new winter camp. Militarily it was an ideal opening to defend against any intruders. A few men could hold off an entire war party. Once inside the mountain stronghold, Bonneville discovered that the Indians hadn't exaggerated the advantages of the area. The lower hill country was covered with bunch grass for the horses, and herds of elk and bighorn sheep were scattered throughout the countryside. In short order the camp was well supplied. Settled inside the Indian's hideaway, Captain Bonneville's men felt well protected from both the roughness of winter and the menacing Blackfoot. The last month of 1832 offered peace and reasonable comfort.

The day after Christmas, Captain Bonneville led a group of fourteen men away from the safety of their mountain retreat. He had decided to search for Matthieu's party. Adams knew the location of the first winter camp on the Salmon, and Bonneville had worked out a system of blazing trees in a precise manner that would show him the way to their new encampment. Matthieu and his men had been sent two hundred miles south of Bonneville's current camp, and all he knew was that Captain Bonneville would be wintering somewhere along the Salmon River.

Bonneville followed the Salmon River south past the first winter camp and the fork of the Lemhi River until they reached the Pahsimeroi River fork. He followed the Pahsimeroi deeper into the mountains before moving through a pass and down to the beginnings of the Little Lost River. Following down this stream they moved out onto the great lava plain of the Snake River Basin—a land of desolation and lost rivers. The Little Lost River soon disappeared into the rocks and crevices. Pushing southward, the group continued to move out into the river basin until they reached the Big Lost River. Three large buttes rose up out of the vast plain to the south. Captain Bonneville lead his men southwest, following up Big Lost River until it started to turn northward back toward the mountains. Leaving the river they headed for the largest butte. It was located west of the other two, appeared to have more of its snow swept away by the wind, and offered the best chance of forage for their animals.

Wind, snow and paralyzing cold seemed to be the order of each and every day. The great river plain of the Snake stretched as far as the eye could see. Past volcanic violence had created a sixty-mile crossing that seemed impossible to travel through. Lava dominated the area. It was everywhere you looked. Chasms four to ten feet wide would suddenly appear, some so deep that it was impossible to see or even hear a rock hit bottom. Just to circumvent one of these crevasses could cause a convoluted side trip of forty miles. Major streams and large rivers like the Big and Little Lost were swallowed up within a short distance. Grass was at best sparse and scattered, while the occasional tree was small and stunted.

When the sun was allowed to shine, its rays reflected off a multitude of ice and snow formations interwoven with the black lava rock. It produced a show of dazzling crystallized sparkle and reflection. A truly magnificent demonstration of nature's beauty, but only partly appreciated and observed by these men who were suffering much from cold and hunger.

Captain Bonneville could see that the horses and men had become too weak to break a trail through the snow and reach the Snake River. A mule had already frozen to death. He regretted having moved out into the harshness of this land. The hunters went out daily in what had become a futile search for any game that might still be in the area. Bonneville knew they were in trouble. One morning a fresh trail made by a recent hunting party passing through on their way south was discovered, and not far down the trail a single buffalo bull was spotted standing off to the right. A release from the winter's snare had been provided.

With the men feeling the benefits of a buffalo meal, and the horses somewhat rested and not required to break a new path through the snow, Captain Bonneville and his men followed the trail south. Just before reaching the Snake River, Bonneville was able to talk with an Indian brave that they had spotted riding all alone. It took some parrying back and forth before everyone was convinced that no harm was intended to anyone. The Indian was a member of the Bannack tribe, camped not far down river, and informed Captain Bonneville that at least two camps of whites were in the area, both farther upstream. Spurred on by the news, the men pushed forward, and at the first camp found some of Bonneville's trappers waiting for Matthieu to arrive.

On February 3, 1833, Matthieu, with his remaining men and horses, arrived in camp. The combined group of thirty-two men welcomed each other like relatives gathering at a reunion. Both groups had suffered their share of hardship, and there was an extraordinary feeling of camaraderie between the men. Bonneville's men knew the harshness of winter and starvation. Matthieu's group had found easier weather and more game, but they had been unable to join up with any band of the Shoshone Nation, and found themselves constantly at odds with the Blackfoot when they attempted to bring meat into their camp. The result was an almost daily apprehension of starvation. It was while hunting for game that Jennings had his run of bad luck.

"Jennings, LeRoy and Ross won't be comin', Captain," Matthieu informed Bonneville. "There ain't gonna be any more horses, either. What didn't get dead or run off we had to eat to stay alive."

"I take it you had trouble with the Blackfoot?" Bonneville asked.

"First off, we had a hell of a time findin' our way through the mountains between the Green River and the Bear," Matthieu started. "Never did find one friendly Injun to help point the way. Found me plenty of them damn Blackfoot, though. We had to be on guard all hours. They'd just wait for any let down and then slip in and get a horse or two. Hell's fire, we couldn't get much more done than guard them horses. Wasn't long and we was out of meat. The Injuns weren't about to try no face off, but I knew that the red-skinned sons of bitches would attack a few hunters in a heartbeat. I hated to split our ranks and send out a huntin' party."

Captain Bonneville was pretty sure what was coming next. Matthieu had sent out three men that he wished now he hadn't. It was a bad decision, and he knew it. No good could come from belaboring the point. Everyone that had to make choices made a few bad ones; it came with the job. Ben wondered why, in this country filled with friendly Indians, Matthieu hadn't been able to join up with someone.

"Jennings just couldn't take to eatin' horses," Matthieu continued. "He got four men to agree to go with him. I should have stopped 'em, but buffalo was soundin' real good to me too. The five of 'em took nine horses and headed for a place called Sheep Rock. One of 'em, and I don't remember which one now, said he'd been there before, and if there weren't no buffalo there'd be mountain sheep. By now mutton didn't sound all that bad to me either. Anyhow, that's where the Injuns jumped them. It wasn't no surprise, neither. Ross was ridin' point and spotted the red buggers before they was

203

ready to pounce. They might all have got away too, 'cept Jennings just had to sneak back and take a look for himself."

Damn, Bonneville thought, sounds like poor leadership all around. I made a bad pick with Matthieu.

"Jennings got caught sneakin'." Matthieu slowly fingered the blade of his knife. "By God, I've yet to find an Injun that didn't need killin'. Anyhow, they shot Jennings before he could get aboard his horse. He was yellin' for help, so LeRoy and Ross went back to lend a hand. The Indians got them three, and the other two hightailed it back to camp. They said they chased 'em fir thirty miles 'fore they cut off and went back. After that we mostly just watched and et horses. We were just startin' north to find your camp when you found us."

"The horses you brought in seem to have recovered nicely from last summer's trip." Bonneville was looking at Matthieu and wondering if he had always hated all Indians, or if it was something he'd developed on this trip. "We'll make camp here along the Snake to allow our horses a few days rest. That'll give us an opportunity to lay in a good supply of meat before we head back to the Salmon."

Captain Bonneville needed beaver pelts if anyone was going to believe this expedition was a fur trading company. Returning to his cache on the Salmon River and preparing for the spring hunt was his new priority. Outside of the skins brought in by Walker, there had essentially been no fall campaign, unless Adams returned from the Yellowstone with the results of a successful hunt. The Captain decided to split his group of men. He would take half the men and the horses that were in the best condition back with him, leaving the other half down here on the Snake to begin trapping along the streams of the Salt River as soon as the ice was off the ponds. Everyone was to rendezvous at Fort Bonneville in July.

Satisfied that his men were ready, Captain Bonneville led sixteen men across the Snake and out onto the enormity of the river plain. Wind and cold still dominated the area. Snow was now about three feet deep and frozen solid enough to support men, but not horses. They had started with the best mounts, but by the time they reached the Big Lost River, the men and horses were trail-worn.

All of Captain Bonneville's men, with the exception of those with Adams, and the men down along the Snake River, were at the old winter quarters on the Salmon when Bonneville arrived. He opened the cache and distributed the supplies needed for the spring hunt. In mid-March Michael Cerré took a few of the men and headed out for the neighboring Indian villages to trade for horses. Bonneville asked Hodgkiss, who had been tending to his duty as clerk, to take some trading goods and go along with Cerré. He was to spend the spring trying to swap with the Indians for additional pelts.

Captain Bonneville was making ready to leave with the remaining trappers. He had in mind to head southwest to explore and trap the country along the Wood River. Everyone was to meet back at the Salmon River cache in June. No one had heard anything about David Adams or the twenty men he had with him.

Bonneville was feeling the pressure of competition for the ever-decreasing number of beaver. They had found their way back to the Big Lost River with very little hardship. However, just before they reached the pass that would take them over the mountains into the Wood River valley, they encountered a group of Rocky Mountain Fur Company trappers. Milton Sublette was leading twenty experienced trappers, and was headed for the same beaver country. The two parties camped together while they waited for the snow to go out of the pass. Bonneville was able to use the time to his advantage. His horses needed rest and forage, and his men had time to lay in an additional supply of meat.

Toward the end of April the fur men crossed the pass and entered the land of the Wood and Boise Rivers. The trappers went to work, and experience began to show. Sublette's men got to the best spots first. They'd quickly take the easy pickings and then move. Bonneville's men got the leftovers, if there were any leftovers, but the captain was gathering a bounty of information about the area around him.

West of the Wood River, Captain Bonneville found the Boise River country to be the most inviting and agreeable place he'd experienced in the West. It was beautiful. Streams flowed down out of the distant mountains and gave life to the plush meadows. It was a land of abundant wildlife and pleasant breezes.

With June approaching, Bonneville gathered his men and headed back to the Salmon River. When they arrived at their old winter quarters, Cerré was already in camp. Hodgkiss was now traveling with a handful of free trappers, and they stayed behind with a tribe of Nez Perce to try and trade for some pelts. He and the trappers arrived a week later. There was still no word from Adams and his men. Cerré had been able to trade for a few horses, but none that could be considered prime stock. The entire company of men had acquired pitifully few beaver skins to add to the ones Walker had deposited at the camp in November. The captain cleaned out the cache and prepared to leave for the rendezvous at Fort Bonneville.

The group of free trappers could make no sense of this. It was a long trip to the Green River through troubling Blackfoot country. They threatened to quit the hunt if they didn't get supplied immediately. They were determined to head for the upper reaches of the Salmon River and prepare for the fall campaign. Captain Bonneville, feeling a need for pelts to make even a poor showing, and wishing to keep all the trappers he could in his employ, issued the men their supplies. He sent Hodgkiss with twenty-one trappers and five camp men off into the mountains to ready themselves for the next go around between the fur companies. They would hook up again next winter.

The loss of the men headed up the Salmon River weakened Captain Bonneville's brigade. Each man would lead two or three pack animals. When the terrain permitted they could form two or three parallel lines instead of lining out in a single file behind their leader. Each night, or if they should come under attack while they were traveling, the line was to be wheeled into a circle. The packs were to be unloaded and used to form a breastwork along the perimeter of the enclosure. Every man carried a hammer and a picket line that was attached to a metal stake. The stake was to be driven into the ground inside the circle, and the horses and mules tied to the picket line with their forefeet hobbled. Using this arrangement, a small number of men could put up a considerable fight against unfavorable odds. Bonneville led his men into the valley of the Green without mishap.

On July 13, 1833, Bonneville's scouts returned to the expedition with three men that had gone south with Walker, and a couple of Snake warriors. They informed the Captain that Joe Walker and the rest of the men were at Fort Bonneville awaiting his arrival.

Chapter Twenty-three

Joseph Walker's plan had been simple. Get his men to the best beaver streams ahead of the other fur companies. Ferris and Fitzpatrick's visit had convinced him that the overall beaver population was falling fast, and the major fur companies had not taken enough pelts last fall to be profitable. Competition between the trappers for this spring's catch would be unprecedented. Walker broke their winter camp early, headed south to the Bear River, and deployed his men along the various feeder streams. For the most part the trappers were young and lacked experience, but as soon as the ice was off, they'd be ready.

Washakie had told Walker that his people would be camped around Bear Lake. They could hunt in harmony and then travel together to the summer rendezvous. Walker knew that the trappers from the established fur companies would be arriving soon, and their reaction to Bonneville's men already in place would probably lack the compatibility that the Indians offered.

"You'd think that in the springtime the water wouldn't seem as cold as in the fall, wouldn't ya?" Swit and Woodrow had finished running their traps. The pond was situated in a little saddle between two hills. Most of the low-level snow was gone, and it seemed to Swit that the trapping was off to a good start. The only other men that they'd seen in the last week were four Snake Indians that rode into their camp two days ago. The Indians had been friendly. In fact, they'd stopped and shared a smoked buffalo tongue with the two white men. Swit was surprised at how relaxed he'd been, even though he and

Will were outnumbered. It must have had something to do with their stay at the Shoshone camp last winter. It sure beat hiding out from the Blackfoot all day long.

"Melted ice feels about the same as water fixin' to freeze," Will answered. "It don't bother Mister Beaver, though. Henry says that the cold water's what keeps his hair thick. I suppose a thin-haired beaver ain't worth much, but I'll bet he's still happy if he can gnaw a tree down now and then."

"Do you recognize the three trappers ridin' in over there?" Swit asked.

"Nobody I know." As they approached the pond Will thought that two of the men were not unusual in their appearance, but the one riding in the middle was hard to ignore. All trappers varied somewhat in their attire; however, as a group they were men that usually looked trim and athletic—not so with this specimen. To be polite, he would have described him as heavyset, but actually he was pure lard.

"Havin' any luck?" Tubby not only carried more flesh than most trappers did, he also had the ugliest set of teeth that Swit could remember seeing. Not one tooth had escaped untouched. If it wasn't already a memory, it was twisted, broken and coated with a yellow-brown film.

"A little," Will answered. "How you boys doin'?"

"I'd say our luck is about to improve, wouldn't you, Charlie?" the man in the middle rolled his bulk slightly to his left to question his partner.

"You boys are gonna have to move on," Charlie announced. "This here beaver pond belongs to our fur company. You ain't welcome here."

"Don't guess I knew anything around here belonged to anybody, except maybe the Indians." Swit had already pulled his rifle to where he could bring it into action if it became necessary.

Will had his gun cradled in his left arm. "Would you men care to step down and share some of our coffee?"

"If you's smart you'd get your coffee and traps and get the hell out," the third man announced. Each trapper carried a rifle across the saddle in front of him. No one had made any threatening move with a gun. "There ain't but two of ya's."

"Well now, I'll tell you what. Sometimes things ain't always what you think they are," Will said. "If you was to turn real careful to your left and look about half way up that ridge, you'd see that things has changed a bit. The man that's got that big ol' buffalo gun leveled your way would be Henry. The other one's Robert. Now if I was you, I wouldn't make any move that ol' Henry might think was troublin', 'cause the one that does is gonna get himself dead.

Before either one of you that's left can make a play, Robert will have rearmed Henry, and he'll likely drop another one of ya. Swit and me, we'll handle whoever's left."

Swit hadn't seen Henry or Robert ride in. He was in his concentration mode and had all his focus on the three riders and their guns. If anything happened he figured to take out the one on the right, because where Will was standing he didn't have a clean shot at him. Swit thought that Will would get one of the others; after that, he didn't know.

"Make your play, or leave. You better be showing some teeth so's Henry don't get confused," Swit said.

Will couldn't tell if any of the men were smiling after they turned to ride away. No one had smiled as they considered their next move. The man on the left had looked scared, the one on the right stupid, and the fat hog in the middle was just plain mad. He'd considered making a fight of it, but must of thought that he better not. The three turned slowly and rode away from the pond, not looking back until they thought they were out of Henry's range. When they did look back, Henry's buffalo gun was still leveled in their direction.

"Where in the world did you come up with that teeth bit?" Will was surprised at the things Swit would say.

"That big tub of guts sure had a mouth full of snags, didn't he?" Swit wasn't sure why he'd said what he did. "Acted kinda like he wanted to bite too."

Woodrow turned his attention to Henry and Robert when they arrived. "You two happened by at just the right time."

"Wasn't no happen to it," Henry said as he stepped down from his horse. "We been trailing them since this morning. Them three devils slipped down on us in the night and tore up four beaver dens. Hell, they even found some of our traps and tossed 'em out in the pond. When I saw that they were riding your way, I knew exactly what they was up to."

"How come you didn't hear 'em busting up the beaver huts?" Swit asked.

"It's my own fault," Henry answered, "or at least partly my fault. With nothing but friendly Indians around, Woolly and I was pulling a little on his jug before we settled in for the night. That stuff causes kind of a deep sleep. Ol' Robert is known for his sound sleeping."

"What happened to Woolly?" Swit wanted to know.

"He stayed to gather our stuff." Henry turned toward Robert. "Told us to follow the buggers. Said he'd head toward the lake and spread the word. Ain't that right, Robert?"

209

"Sounded something like that," Robert answered.

"I wasn't wanting to start no trapper's war," Henry said. "But if that bunch had made one wrong move, I'd have stuck a ball right through 'em. The way Robert had this here rifle set up I think one ball would have got two of 'em. Maybe all three the way they was lined up."

"It's a good thing then that Swit had 'em show you their teeth." Will winked at Henry.

"I did notice that one of 'em was all smiles when they turned around," Henry admitted. He looked over at Swit for some reaction, but none was forthcoming. "If you two don't mind, Robert and I will stay around and trap with ya. If we're gonna start having trouble with these other fur companies, I know Captain Walker would want us to group up in bigger bunches. I ain't about to shag ass until the captain says so. We came here to get beaver, didn't we, Robert?"

"We're better shooters than trappers," Robert answered. "Woolly can find us here as easy as anywhere."

Everyone on the pond was having good luck trapping beaver except Woolly Wilson. He hadn't taken a pelt in four days. Will had just finished setting a trap when he saw Woolly walk downstream from the pond and start a fire. It wasn't long before he began to carry rocks up from the creek and place them in the flames. Will flipped a stick over in Swit's direction to get his attention, and then pointed down toward Woolly's project.

Swit watched Woolly's as he continued to feed the fire. Then he cut some willow branches and used them to construct the framework for a small hut that he placed over and around the fireplace. When the rocks were red hot, and the fire had died down to a bed of coals, he covered the willow branches with buffalo hides.

Woolly had taken off all his clothes and was crawling into his hut with a pan of water when Swit walked up to Will. "Has Woolly got a chill this morning?" Swit asked. "A man covered with that much hair ain't likely to chill very easy."

"Set down here and watch this; it'll be somethin' to see," Will said.

Within fifteen minutes Woolly broke from his hideaway. His body was covered with sweat, and he began to dip cold water from the creek and pour it over himself. After a few minutes he went back into his little lodge.

"It must be mighty hot in there." As near as Swit could tell, Woolly's plan was to first get himself heated up and then cooled down again as fast as he could. "Has he got some kinda sickness?"

"The idea is purification," Will answered. "He dribbles a little water on the hot rocks, and that fills the inside of his hut with steam. It gets mighty hot in there; it'll damn near cook ya. You probably noticed that Woolly ain't been havin' the best luck with the beaver. He figures he's got a bad scent in his body, and Mister Beaver picks up on it when he sets his traps. He's tryin' to drive it out and wash it away."

To Swit it seemed as if it all made sense, but he thought he'd hold judgment until he had a chance to see if Woolly's trapping improved. Woolly repeated the exercise several times before he dismantled the hut, let the remaining heat dry him off, and dressed.

Two things had happened following the purification. Woolly was taking more beaver, and the bear population was on the rise. An occasional bear would wander by their camp from time to time, but lately they'd been popping up a little too often to suit Swit.

"Any self-respecting bear that had any chance at all would go far out of his way to avoid contact with a man." Henry had this theory that bears of any kind looked at men as being kind of dumb and lazy. "The trouble is them damn bears can't see for shit. They can smell a dead carcass buried in the ground four miles away, and can hear as good as a dog. But they couldn't tell if that big boulder over there was a rock or a buffalo unless it farted."

Robert could be around for days without making a sound; it was his nature. When he did talk, and that wasn't very often, it was sometimes so soft that you'd have trouble hearing what he said. This silence made him an excellent hunting partner for Henry, but put him at jeopardy if bears were in the same locality. When Robert was down wind he could walk into a bear's personal space before the bear knew there was anyone or anything within striking distance. That could prove fatal to man, bear, or both.

This territorial overlap had happened before with Robert, but Henry had schooled him in bearology. "The one thing you must never do is run. Ain't a man alive that can outrun a bear." Henry had seen horses that got too close and couldn't get away fast enough. "If you're afoot, you got to hold your ground. If you'll face him and don't move, there's a better than even chance that when Mister Bear sees that you ain't no threat, he'll go his own way."

Robert had been there; it was easier said than done. A big grizzly bear in full-out attack was a terrifying sight. Even a little bear standing on his hind feet could scare the bejesus out of you.

"While Mister Bear is making up his mind, your ol' asshole's likely to pucker up tighter than a bull's ass at fly time." Henry continued his lesson.

"But if you run, he's a-comin' for ya, and it ain't gonna be good. A sow with her babes, or a bear that's been hurt, is probably gonna come anyhow. Still won't do you no good to run. They look slow, but they ain't. Bears have been killed in close with knives, and I met an Indian once that claimed he killed several with an old rusty sword. I'd say a gun shot through the head is your best bet. If ya don't make a head shot, be damn sure you're horseback or got a safe place to get to. I've seen shot bears charge the smoke of gunfire when they couldn't even see who did the shooting. Been more than one trapper killed by a dying bear—shot through the heart."

Robert was making his way around a little arm of the pond, looking for the best place to set his traps. His first indication of trouble was the sound of brush breaking off to his left. He turned to see fury in the form of an adult grizzly bear break out of the brush, headed straight for him. It was a huge animal, but mostly what he noticed was its mouth.

It was wide open, exposing teeth that Robert knew were meant for him. His lower lip flopped up and down with each step, and his tongue hung out, throwing saliva side to side with every movement of his head. He was coming for Robert in what looked to be a slow-motion lope-type gait, but the gap between them was closing fast. The hair along the bear's back was standing up, and a giant swarm of flies hovered over him as he made alternating sounds of sucking in air and exhaling a throaty growl.

This bear had no intention of stopping to put on any show. His only thought was to clamp his jaws around the first thing he could reach. Robert sat down. He was afraid his legs would run or collapse under him. The grizzly didn't stop. He had his head stuck out ready to grab when Robert fired.

The time from first sighting to gun shot was only seconds. Just before Robert pulled the trigger, the bear made a jump that would take him to his prey. He caught Robert shoulder high, a little to his left, and crashed down on him with his full force. The rifle load had hit the bear dead center in the mouth. Robert was smashed backward onto his left side and covered with seven hundred pounds of twitching, jerking bear. But, unlike the bear, Robert was still alive.

Will and Swit looked up when they heard the shot. They were only about two hundred and fifty yards away, but a small thicket filtered their vision. It looked like a bear had Robert on the ground! When they reached him he was trying to get himself out from under the lifeless animal. Flies were everywhere.

"My arm's broke. You better get Henry."

Swit and Will rolled the bear off Robert, and like he'd announced, his arm had a decided bend between the elbow and his shoulder. Will headed off to find Henry.

"If you feel up to a move, I'll help ya get back away from this stinking bear and all these flies," Swit said as he kneeled down beside Robert. "Damn, he's a big one. Are you hurt anywhere else?"

"I don't think so. I'll hold on to my arm and let's see if we can't get back over there." Robert pointed to a little clearing.

"Hold your arm as still as you can," Swit said. "We don't want no bones sticking out if we can help it."

They moved over to the little grassy area. Swit helped Robert get stretched out on the grass as comfortable as possible, even though he could tell that Robert was experiencing pain each time he had to move his arm. They heard a tree limb snap and looked back toward the bear. It was Will, Henry and Woolly coming around the other end of the pond.

"Robert, Robert, how many times I got to tell ya, it ain't smart to sneak up on no bears." Henry dropped down beside Robert to examine his arm. "The only thing left to do is hang a bell around your neck. You hurting anywhere else?"

"I think I'm fit everywhere but here." Robert placed his right hand over the fracture in his left arm. "That one didn't wanta run away."

"No, he wouldn't. He's got a festered arrowhead in his side. Probably had a fever and was hanging in close to water." Henry wondered if the bear had killed whoever put the arrow in him. "Woolly, pull the cork on that jug and get Robert started. We're gonna need to do a little work on that arm. I'm headed back to camp to pick up some things we'll need. Try to get at least as much of that jug juice in Robert as you do in yourself."

"You know I don't like the taste of that stuff," Robert said to Woolly as Henry and Will headed towards the campsite.

"Aye, laddie, but this be one time you best put a wee bit of the ol' elixir down in your innards," Woolly advised as he held the jug to Robert's mouth. "After the first few sips she'll begin to taste just grand. Here, Swit lad, you join in. We'll all have a party to celebrate Robert's successful defense of ye ol' Mister Bruin."

Swit didn't want to drink Woolly's mixture either, but he felt obliged to enter in since it appeared that Robert needed the tonic, and besides, Woolly made it sound as if they were celebrating.

Will and Henry were on the opposite side of the pond when they first heard the singing. Woolly was teaching Robert and Swit an old Scottish ballad. There was no mistaking Woolly's scratchy voice, or Swit's not quite in tune version, but Robert's pure tenor sound caught both men by surprise. Woolly would from time to time accompany the younger lads on his mouth harp.

The music had ended by the time Will and Henry reached the trio, and Robert, who could go for days without issuing a single word, was now controlling the bulk of the conversation. He was in the middle of giving, for the fourth time, a second by second account of his recent conflict. Each new version seemed to contain additional revealing information that the previous rendition had omitted. Telling the story about the charging bear now took at least ten times longer than the actual attack, and several rounds of the jug. Swit wanted to know everything about everything, and Robert was supplying answers as fast as Swit could ask the questions. Henry sat back and enjoyed the conversation while he waited until it was time for him to go to work on the arm.

Captain Walker rode into camp the next morning. He'd heard all about Robert's encounter with the bear. "Robert, how's your arm feeling today?"

"My arm's okay," Robert answered. "It's my head that hurts."

"Well now, I'll tell you what," Will suggested, "it's got to be somethin' that's catchin' and goin' around, cause Swit's been complainin' all mornin' about his noggin."

Joe Walker thought they'd had a good spring hunt despite their trouble with the other fur companies. The men he'd taken over to the Madison River last fall had measured up well against the more experienced trappers. They had learned the art of fur trapping and how to protect themselves from any intruders. Walker was ready to head for the rendezvous at Fort Bonneville, and everyone was to meet at the Shoshone campgrounds at Bear Lake within the next few days. The Snake Indians knew about a pass through the Salt Mountains that would cut two days off the trip back to the Green River, and planned to accompany Walker's men with one hundred Indian lodges.

The first week in June, Captain Walker, with his men and the Snake Indians, arrived at Fort Bonneville. They were the first trappers to reach the site for the 1833 rendezvous. The captain opened the cache buried inside the fort and began to trade with the Indians for pelts.

Part Four:
Breaking the Crust

Chapter Twenty-four

Francisco Barrerra grew up wanting nothing more than to be a *vaquero* on Don Carlos' *rancho*. The ranch and the people that lived there was the only home and family he'd known. Pedro and his men were destroying everything he valued. Each day brought additional humiliation to his family. The missing front tooth that he'd lost when Ojo drove his head into the bunk house floor was a constant reminder of a festering hatred for Pedro Ramirez, Cicatriz and especially Ojo. The only treatment was retribution.

"They're coming." Maria was rocking Mattie. Her vivacious little bundle didn't welcome sleep, and she was persistent.

"What do you mean they're comin'?" Billy wished that Maria would ease back a bit with the rocking chair. How was a baby suppose to get to sleep when she was flung back and forth like that?

"I mean the tall one with the bad eye," Maria answered. "I've seen him watching Anita. He watches me too. That smiley little toad is never far away either. He'll be with him."

"They haven't bothered anyone or anything up here at the house," Billy said. "I doubt Pedro wants them messin' around here. The ranch is his interest."

"Pedro has other interests than land," Maria answered. "I remember him well from my Santa Fe days. He's reckless when his privates take over his brain. I haven't seen him hanging around, but it wouldn't surprise me if he comes when the others do."

"Are you sayin' he's comin' for you?" Maria had Billy's full attention now.

"All I'm saying is that the tall one is coming." Maria didn't like talking about this, but she could see that it was going to happen. "I don't know who for, probably Anita. Maybe they're all coming for whoever they can get. It just looks to me like this house is about to lose its off-limits status."

Billy hadn't known about these new developments. He doubted that either Juan or Cisco had any idea that Pedro's *vaqueros* were eyeing things here at the ranch house. Ojo was keeping everyone busy gathering in the stock so Pedro could sell it. Cisco hadn't even had time to formulate any new plans of retaliation.

Hog Eye had been hiding out in the house since his arrival. No one seemed to be looking for him, but Maria wasn't taking any chances that Pedro might secretly be trying to find him. Billy made his mind up that in the morning he and Alonzo would head for Santa Fe. There was no need to wait any longer.

Billy and Alonzo had been gone four days. Vicente, the oldest *vaquero* at the rancho, died the day after they left. Anita carried an armful of flowers as she made her way up the path leading to the little cemetery. She was thinking about the time Vicente sold his old broken-down horse to the two *vaqueros* that left after Pedro's men took over. He had been her mother's favorite uncle, and she knew her mother would have wanted her to honor his grave.

Anita planted the yellow cactus flowers in the fresh dirt that covered his grave before moving over to where Don Carlos and Doña Petronila were buried. She started to bend down to decorate their graves when Ojo grabbed her. Anita never saw him or heard him until he had her.

"I guess this is as good a place as anywhere," Ojo said as he held Anita from behind with one arm and ran his other hand down the front of her blouse. Anita dropped her flowers as she tried to get away. All she could see was a dirty, scabbed hand slip under her blouse at the neckline. "It's time we got to know one another. You might just as well get used to this. You and me are gonna be partners. I figure on movin' into the big house."

Anita twisted and slipped away from the arm that held her. As she turned, she dropped all her weight down and fell free. The front of her blouse tore away in Ojo's hand, but she was on the ground and out of his grasp. She kicked out as hard as she could, aiming high between his legs. Anita rolled, scrambled to her feet and ran down the path. Ojo was bent over in pain.

"Shall I grab her for ya?" Cicatriz hollered. Anita's first sight of the ugly little man with the scar on his face was when she ran by him. She didn't hear Ojo answer, and Cicatriz didn't try to stop her.

Maria was looking out the window at the back of the house when she saw Anita running down the path. Anita was already in the house and sitting on the kitchen floor crying when Maria got to her. Her blouse was torn, she had only one moccasin, and her skirt was smudged with dirt. Sand burrs clung to one side of her arm. "Are you all right?" Maria wanted to know. "What happened? What were you doing up at the cemetery?"

"I guess I'm okay," Anita answered between sobs. "I just went to put flowers on the graves. I was over where Don Carlos is buried when he grabbed me. I didn't know anyone was around."

"Who grabbed you?" Maria asked. "Was it the tall one?"

"Yes, but they're both up there," Anita answered. "He said we were going to be partners. He's moving into the house. When will Billy be back?"

Maria didn't know when Billy B. would be back. She wished he was here. Ever since Don Carlos's death, Billy had accepted the role as head of the household. His performance, in a position he really hadn't wanted, had been excellent, and he was daily gaining respect from those around him. Now, at a time she had told him was coming, he was off roaming around with Alonzo. Both of Pedro's men would be headed for the house. Maria knew she had to take action. She asked Hog Eye and Lena to hide the children in the orchard. "Stay low," Maria told Lena before they left. "Try to keep from being seen. If they come looking for you, you'll know they got us. You and Mister Harris should take the children and head up the irrigation ditch. Try to hide out until dark, then head for my place. Billy usually has a horse or two in the corral." She kissed Mattie on the cheek.

"Why didn't you grab the bitch?" Ojo asked as he struggled to his feet. He had spent the last few minutes rolling around on the ground with his knees pulled up to his chest.

"I ask you if ya wanted me to catch her," Cicatriz answered. "You never said nothing. How was I supposed to know you wanted me to grab her?"

"You try to talk with your balls kicked up in your belly, you little wart." Ojo made his way over to where Cicatriz was sitting with his back against a rock.

"What are we gonna do now?" Cicatriz asked.

"We're gonna do just like Pedro said," Ojo answered. "We're taking over the house, and all that's in it. There ain't nobody but them women and kids around. Everyone else is down at the south range. Pedro said that Billy and that kid of Carlos's was headed for Taos. I'm going in and take Maria. You leave her to me."

"I don't know if I want that kicker or not. Ain't that them kids headed for the orchard?" Cicatriz pointed toward the side of the house. Hog Eye, Lena— with little Mattie in her arms, and the Suarez children had left the house by the side door. They were carefully working their way back into the orchard. "Looks like that house maid and a nigger is with 'em. You think he's the one that shot old James?"

"Might be, but who gives a shit." Ojo had other things on his mind. "After we're done in the house we'll waste his black ass, and then nail her and anyone else that looks ripe."

Anita and Maria knew where three guns were in the house—two rifles and a pistol, all unloaded. Anita could load firearms, but there was only enough powder for two shots. She remembered her brother telling her that a rifle shot truer than a *pistola*, so she loaded the two rifles. They turned over a table and a bench in the middle of the dining room. Maria pulled down the window blinds to darken the room before positioning herself behind the table. Anita pushed the bench to the opposite side of the door leading into the kitchen and took cover. They could both see into the kitchen.

Ojo was the first one through the back door. He walked across the kitchen and was starting into the dining room when Maria fired. She was surprised how tall he looked coming through the door. The ball sliced his right side just above the hipbone, and caused him to jump to his left. When the rifle fired, Cicatriz dove to the right of the doorway.

"The bitch shot me," Ojo said.

"Are ya shot bad?" Cicatriz asked.

"I don't think so." Ojo was checking his wound. "You better rush her before she has a chance to reload."

"I ain't goin' through that door," Cicatriz said. "The other one might be waitin' to shoot me."

"You better get through there before I shoot ya," Ojo told Cicatriz.

Anita could see the small-headed man with the half-smiley face crawling through the entrance into the room. She waited until he was inside before she fired. The rifle ball tore a hole through his dirty, faded serape. The kick from the rifles had surprised both Maria and Anita, and the force had caused them to drop their weapons. Anita had been knocked backward.

At the sound of the second shot, Ojo lunged through the doorway and landed on top of Maria. He slammed his left fist into her stomach, driving the air from her lungs. With his right fist he pounded her in the face. Maria's world became a foggy haze with everything moving in slow motion.

Cicatriz sat with one leg on each side of Anita and pinned her back to the floor. She twisted, turned and tried to scratch out at his scarred face, but the man was too heavy.

He slapped her twice, then took out his knife, sliced open her already partly torn blouse, and laid the cold blade across her breasts. Anita froze.

Ojo used one hand to hold Maria around the neck while he tore her blouse down the front and then ripped off her skirt and underpants with his other hand. She was gasping for air; there was no way to fight back. Ojo was positioned between her legs, had exposed himself, and was ready when the lead ball from Cisco's gun caught him just back of his right ear. It cut through his head, taking parts of hat, hair and skull in one blast. Every part of Ojo's body collapsed instantly.

Juan had insisted that they ride back to the ranch. He was worried. Everyone was at the south range, even the bunkhouse cook. The ranch had to be deserted except for those at the house. When he couldn't find Ojo or Scarface, he grabbed Cisco and they headed back. They were at the barn putting up their horses when they heard the first shot. Cisco with Juan right behind him was almost to the back door when the second shot was fired.

The sound of Cisco's rifle startled Cicatriz. He raised up on his knees and looked back toward the doorway. Juan's *pistola* was leveled at his head. This man that purely loved the feeling he got when he could use his knife to carve on his victim's flesh knew that he faced death. He heard two shots, almost at the same time, and saw Juan spin to his left and fall back against the wall. It caused Juan's shot to go wild. Cicatriz now had his *pistola* in hand.

Pedro was almost in front of the house when he caught a glimpse of Juan and Cisco running to the back of the house, so he detoured to the side entrance. He had been easing his way up onto the side door porch when he heard the third shot. He looked through the door, saw Juan, and fired.

Cicatriz raised to his feet and turned to see who had shot Juan. Pedro stumbled sideways. A lead ball had entered just under Pedro's left armpit and exited his chest with a piece of his heart sliced away. Just like in the Plaza, Hog Eye Harris had made another superb rifle shot.

When the fat-headed man with the permanent half-smile cut into his face turned back toward Juan, he felt the full nine inches of Juan's knife blade bury itself just under and to the left of his breastbone. Cicatriz wanted to raise his *pistola* and fire, but the weapon was too heavy to lift. He tried to squeeze the trigger, but the gun dropped out of his hand. The scar-faced man looked down to see what had happened. His eyes focused on the handle of Juan's knife. He took one step sideways and fell to the floor.

Cisco dragged Ojo off of Maria. She managed to get to her knees, but she was shaking badly. Cisco helped her to her feet, and Maria started down the hallway to her room. She needed something to cover herself. When Cisco reached Cicatriz he wasn't dead yet, but his time was near. He was trying to talk, but all he could do was gag in the blood that poured from his mouth. Cisco threw him to one side.

"Are you all right?" Hog Eye asked as he carefully examined the room through the side door.

Juan had sat down on the floor with his back to the wall. "I've been shot," he said.

"Let's have a look." Hog Eye knelt down over Juan and examined the wound. "You was lucky, it passed clean through. No broken bones, so you're gonna heal fast. My God, it looks like you been butcherin' in here."

"I don't guess Ojo'll be quirtin' anybody now." Cisco started to drag the bodies out through the back door. When he took hold of Cicatriz's now-lifeless body, he jerked Juan's knife free and handed it to him. "That was one hell of a throw."

Anita had made her way over to Juan. She was holding her blouse together with one hand as she helped him to his feet. "Let's get you over here where we can clean that wound," she said. "We don't need no blood poisoning."

"Who shot me?" Juan asked.

"Pedro," Hog Eye answered. "If I'd just shot a little sooner. I saw him sneaking up to the side door. It hurried me some to get to where I had a clean shot."

"I don't guess we'll have to worry any more about these three." Juan was relieved that they were all alive, and his wound was minor.

"They never did worry me." Cisco had been waiting for this day, even though it wasn't one of his planned attacks. He looked over at what used to be the one they called Ojo, and smiled. "I'd say it looks like you might have lost a tad more than just a tooth, old buddy."

"We've got to hide all this before the others get back," Maria said as she reentered the room. She'd put on fresh clothes, but a few spots of Ojo's dried blood still covered her face. "We need to put them bodies where no one can find them. These three will be missed, especially Pedro. They'll be looking, and they'll be looking soon. You three take care of the bodies. Anita and I will put the house in order."

Cisco and Hog Eye, with Juan helping as best he could, started dragging the dead men away from the house. Maria had remembered Doña Petronila telling her about an old well that hadn't been used for years. Cisco knew exactly where it was, almost straight south of the house, and covered over with bushes.

Maria and Anita carried in water and started to clean. It was several hours after the sun went down before the chores were done and the children back safe inside. Lena had followed Hog Eye's instructions to the letter. "Stay put until I come and get ya."

They all wanted to know what had happened. Maria explained that when the men tried to break into the house she and Anita had fought to keep them out. When Juan and Cisco returned unexpectedly there were some shots exchanged, and Hog Eye said that after he fired at the man sneaking up to the side door, they all rode away. Maria justified leaving them in the orchard for so long because she was afraid that the men might get more help and return. Everyone should now act as if nothing had happened. Tell the story to no one. That night Maria tried to sleep, but her mind kept asking, Where are you, Billy, when I need you?

Billy B. and Alonzo rode in just ahead of the army patrol. They had been stopped by another squad of soldiers about ten miles out, asked for identification, and questioned concerning the whereabouts of a Pedro Ramirez. Billy had been anxious to tell Maria his news, but now he feared for her safety. The soldiers would tell him nothing. Maria met Billy on the front porch. He was stunned and shaken by her battered and bruised face. She was crying, hugging Billy and trying to explain what had happened. Billy was having difficulty understanding the story when seven soldiers led by a young lieutenant rode up to the house.

"Have you seen Pedro Ramirez?" the lieutenant asked Billy. "I understand he owns this *rancho*."

"He has title to half," Billy answered. "I haven't seen him, but I just got here myself. Have you seen Pedro, Maria?"

"Not for several days; it might even be a week," Maria answered. "But that's not unusual. He very seldom comes up to the house. Ask the *vaqueros* around the corrals. They see him every time he comes here."

"How did you receive your injuries?" the officer wanted to know as he carefully studied Maria. She was a beautiful woman, even with the bruises. "If someone did this to you, you must point him out to me."

"No, it's not like that," Maria answered. "We had a bad accident a couple days ago. We were headed to Santa Fe and had a runaway. The wagon flipped, and Anita and I were thrown free, but I landed hard. Juan hurt his shoulder. I was sure glad I'd left little Mattie with Lena. It could have killed her."

That was more information than the lieutenant really wanted. His instructions had been to find Pedro Ramirez, not to involve himself in any domestic problems that might or might not have happened. Pedro had last been seen leaving Santa Fe and heading toward his ranch. "My orders are to search every inch of this *rancho*," the lieutenant announced as he raised himself by standing up in his stirrups. "If he's here, dead or alive, I'll find him." The soldiers turned their horses and rode toward the corrals.

"What's the deal with Pedro?" Billy B. wanted to know as soon as the soldiers were beyond hearing their conversation. "Do you know anything about all this?"

Maria, Billy and Alonzo sat down on the porch, and Maria started to tell her story again. When she had finished, Billy stared straight ahead in silence for several minutes. It was as if he couldn't believe what he'd heard. He'd returned to the ranch fairly busting to tell Maria about the plans that he and Alonzo had made.

They had been to Santa Fe and Taos. While in Santa Fe, Billy and Alonzo obtained a government clearance for a trip to the California settlements, and Alonzo had contracted for the supplies and equipment they'd need. At Taos, Billy found an old friend and made arrangements to travel along with a small pack train of traders headed for California. They would leave within a week, two at the most. He was trying to think like Captain Walker, take plenty of horses, pack extra supplies, and prepare. He hadn't planned on what Maria had just told him.

Maria listened to Billy's explanation of the last several days. "I'm glad, Billy, let's just go on and go. Pedro or no Pedro, either way the struggle for this ranch is not over. Pedro wasn't acting alone. We need a fresh start, especially the children."

"If they find Pedro we won't have a choice," Billy assured Maria. "We'll be stayin' then. Most likely right in front of a firin' squad. You ain't gonna get much help from them other *vaqueros*. They've already showed where they stand. Let's make ready. We may need to leave in a hurry."

More soldiers arrived, and to Billy it looked like the young lieutenant meant to do exactly what he'd said. He was going to search every inch of the ranch. Billy, Cisco and Alonzo collected and made ready the horses and gear they intended to take with them. Maria, Anita, Lena and the children packed and prepared for travel. Hog Eye helped out in the house. He was still following Maria's instructions to stay in the house and out of sight. He didn't think the Mexican government cared that he'd escaped from the traders and was still in their territory, but Maria felt it was foolish to risk detection until they were headed for California.

It was definitely time to leave. The army was searched out. They were preparing to head for Santa Fe. Cisco had convinced the ranch *vaqueros* that Pedro, Ojo and Cicatriz had most likely gone south on the trail to Mexico City to find buyers for the livestock. They probably would be back in a couple of days. The *vaqueros* all headed out with a plan to collect all the livestock of any kind that they could find and bring it back closer to the ranch buildings. The group headed for California had only a few last-minute chores before they would be ready to leave. By sunset it looked as if the only one left at the ranch would be the bunkhouse cook.

"They found the well," Maria hollered at Billy. She had been sitting with Juan on the front porch. They were talking about how the breeze was picking up when she saw a soldier push his way out of the bushes that surrounded the old well and run toward the corrals.

"Damn," Billy said. "We just about made it. This changes everything." Billy had been in the house helping Alonzo pack some personal family remembrances. He could tell Alonzo was torn. One part told him to go, and the other said stay and fight for what you know is yours.

"It don't change nothing," Juan told Billy and Maria. "They ain't gonna find anything in that old well. It's too deep."

"Just the odor will give us away," Billy countered. "Unless you covered 'em with a lot of dirt, or some lime, they'll know there's dead bodies in that dried-up old well as soon as they stick their head over the side."

Juan, Billy and Maria watched from the porch as the soldiers pulled some of the brush away from around the well and made an examination of the burial site. The wind was blowing hard enough that they couldn't hear anything being said, but it was obvious from their actions that a great deal of discussion was taking place about the well. There seemed to be disagreement about what to do next. When the young officer arrived, a decision was made. A small man was selected and fitted with a rope around his chest and under his arms. He was handed a lantern and then lowered into the well.

Billy was working on his next move. When they came with the news that they'd found Pedro, he would…well, nothing came to mind. Run for it? That was foolish. Try to make a stand in the house? They had food, water, weapons and powder. Everyone was already at the house except Cisco. Billy could see that he was down by the corrals, but it looked as if he was headed for the house, although he sure wasn't in any hurry. If they could barricade themselves in the house, maybe they could hold off an assault until dark and then get away during the night. California had suddenly become more of a dream than a possibility.

It seemed like hours before the little man was pulled up out of the old well. He handed the light to one of his comrades, talked to the lieutenant for a few minutes, and then headed back toward the corrals. They all headed for the corrals. In what seemed like minutes the soldiers were mounted and on their way to Santa Fe.

"I don't know what happened," Billy said. "But let's get out of here before they decide to take another look." After thinking that the trip was over before it could begin, everyone hurried to leave. Anita made a quick trip up to the cemetery to visit the graves before they left, and Alonzo asked to stay behind for a while. He'd catch up before dark. When he rejoined the bunch it was twilight, and everyone had noticed a red glow back down the trail. They asked him if he had seen a fire along the way. He told about how he had watched the Suarez Ranch go up in flames.

"The wind must have blown some hot coals out of the fireplace after we left," he said. "The house went quick. The wind carried the fire over to the roof of the bunkhouse, and then on to the barns. Cookie was the only one there to fight the fire, but he could see it was hopeless. He watched for a while and then saddled up and rode off. One lucky thing, though. Someone had turned all the stock out of the barns. Never lost an animal."

"What do you think happened?" Billy and Hog Eye were stretched out for a smoke after supper.

"I'd say Alonzo wanted to put a final touch to the operation," Hog Eye answered.

"No, I don't mean that," Billy continued. "I mean at the well. I thought we was goners."

"They could spend a week checking that well." Hog Eye smiled as he looked over toward Juan. "There ain't nothin' there to find. We buried them three on top of that old *vaquero* in the cemetery. Juan made us promise to not tell, 'cause he said it would upset Anita. Cisco got a real kick out of it. Said she didn't know it, but her flowers would be gettin' all the fertilizer they needed."

Chapter Twenty-five

The valley of the upper Green River, with its lush meadows and clear mountain streams, was invaded and forced to play host to the 1833 rendezvous. Bonneville's expedition gathered in and around Fort Bonneville, or Fort Nonsense, depending upon the point of view. The men of the American Fur Company, lead by Andrew Drips, selected a campsite on the north side of the river and about five miles east of Fort Bonneville. The Rocky Mountain Fur Company established their headquarters another five miles down river from the American Fur Company bunch. Jim Bridger, Tom Fitzpatrick, Milton Sublette, Henry Fraeb and Joe Meek were ready to trade and join in on all the whoop-de-do. Scattered in and around the main fur companies were numerous small groups of free trappers, men separated from fur companies that had failed, and the lodges of the friendly Snake, Nez Perce and Flathead Indians. The 1833 rendezvous brought three hundred and fifty white men and five hundred Indians together in an area along the upper Green River valley that started around Fort Bonneville and spread downriver for a distance of ten to fifteen miles.

Bonneville learned that the men he had left down on the Snake to trap the streams of the Salt River in the spring had found their way to the rendezvous after meeting up with Warren Ferris and Andrew Drips. Ben finally knew where everyone was except Adams and his bunch.

David Adams walked into the rendezvous alone to tell his story to Captain Bonneville. He had led his twenty men to the Yellowstone River country without mishap. They established a cordial relationship with the Crow

Indians that inhabited the area, and were making a successful hunt when half of his men took everything they could steal and deserted Adams to live and hunt with the Crows. When Adams attempted to recover his lost pelts and property, the Indians drove him out of their camps. It was foolish to try and return to Bonneville's winter camp with his weakened brigade, so he and his loyal followers wintered at the American Fur Company fort located at the mouth of the Big Horn River. When spring arrived, they decided to try their luck trapping in the upper Powder River country. While they were so engaged, the Arikara Indians stole all of their horses. Discouraged with the results of their labor, some of his men built canoes and headed downriver for the settlements, while others hired on with fur companies working in the area. Adams felt an obligation to report his failure to Captain Bonneville. Empty-handed, he made his way back to the rendezvous.

The first order of business at any rendezvous was to break out the whiskey. The traders had learned that they not only could make a handsome profit selling alcohol at five dollars a pint, but its effect on many of the trappers would cause them to trade their pelts for frivolous items that they would soon squander during the festivity of the gathering. A year's earnings could easily be spent in one month at the rendezvous, leaving the trapper back in debt to the fur company for the next year's campaign.

Swit, Will, Woolly, Henry and Robert were settled in for the night, unless another drunk trapper stopped in to get Henry for a shoot off. Woolly, Robert and Henry had returned to camp about an hour before sunset carrying a bundle of hides, three blankets, five pairs of moccasins and two jugs of whiskey. Henry had won it all.

Joe Walker was not spending much time at Fort Bonneville. He moved all through the rendezvous area visiting with old friends and joining in on some of the hoopla—especially the horse racing. He was finding out just who was at the rendezvous and beginning to put together the men for his trip into California. Almost everyone at the rendezvous knew about his planned expedition. There were some that held no desire to make the trip; however, many of the men wanted to go along.

To be part of the group that blazed a trail into the California settlements would be a feather in your hat. Some men held back, hoping they'd get asked, while others quietly let it be known that they were interested. A few like Bill Williams and his cronies simply announced that they were going. That was their style, but they knew they wouldn't make the trip unless Walker gave his approval.

Williams was a man a lot like Walker in some ways, but exactly opposite in others. He was a big man, but not in a well-proportioned way. He had long arms and legs that caused him to walk or set a horse in an uncoordinated, gangly manner, and he walked with a long, striding, side-swinging carriage that would have brought laughter, except no one even considered laughing. Bill had moved with his family to the Missouri frontier when he was eight years old. Besides growing up exploring the frontier, he had been a preacher and a soldier. When he was in his twenties he married an Indian woman and lived with the Big Hill band of Osage Indians, helping them in their dealings with the whites. He wrote an English-Osage dictionary as well as a manuscript dealing with the anthropology of the Plains Indians. Bill Williams had a keen intellect and exceptional courage, strength and endurance.

Old Bill, or Crazy Bill, as some had lately started to call him when they knew he couldn't hear them, had been one of the first to venture out onto the open plains and over into the beaver country of the Spanish Southwest. He had been a free trapper along the Columbia River as early as 1824. As civilization and the relocated Indians crowded in, Bill became more and more a loner. He was given to monumental bouts of drinking and womanizing. He took several wives in the tradition of the Indians, and yet he would disappear by himself into the wild country for long periods of time. Williams could commit savage acts of violence against anyone that happened to cross his path at the wrong time. This rough, rawboned, rather grotesque-looking man that was eleven years Walker's senior had lately been given to walking around and talking to himself. Joseph Walker knew that Bill Williams still had the stuff it would take to reach California, but Bonneville silently questioned Joe's ability to control the man.

Captain Bonneville spent almost all of his time at the fort. He was helping Cerré get the pelts ready for shipment to St. Louis. Bonneville's expedition had collected only twenty-two and one-half packs. Walker's men had returned from the Bear River country with more pelts than Captain Ben had anticipated, but the total count was still not nearly enough to justify the expenses. He thought their poor showing during the '32-'33 season could be explained because many of his men lacked trapping experience, and by the misfortune that Adams suffered at the hands of the Crow and Arikara Indians. The lack of beaver pelts was not Captain Bonneville's major concern.

Bonneville had decided to continue his exploration of the West, and that decision presented the Army captain with a special problem. His leave from the Army would be up in October. He needed more time. The free, adventurous life was infectious, and he was not ready to go back. Benjamin Bonneville spent many hours working on a letter that Michael Cerré would hand deliver to General Macomb in Washington.

The letter had to be exactly right. His future Army career, along with next year's financial support for the expedition, could depend on his literary effort. Bonneville began the correspondence by explaining how he had underestimated the vastness of the area. It would take more time to explore and gather the necessary information to make his trip a military success. He expressed his hope that the general would not consider his decision to remain and complete the exploration as an infringement upon their friendship. He then filled several pages describing the fur country, including a history of the fur companies working in the area, and information he'd heard about the Columbia and Oregon Territory. Early in this part he expressed his opinion that if the United States of America was serious about taking possession of Oregon, they should begin to do so immediately.

In the next couple of pages Bonneville explained much of what he knew about the Indians. He wrote about the different nations, their home territories, numbers of warriors and their attitudes toward each other and the white man. Next he detailed all the happenings that took place during the trapper's rendezvous, giving special attention to the prices charged for supplies.

Captain Bonneville saved the last half of his report to give the general a description of his trip from Independence to the Green River, and the exploration of the Salmon, Snake, Wood and Boise River country before reaching the rendezvous. He explained his plan to escort Cerré, along with their beaver pelts, to the Big Horn River before proceeding northwest to the Columbia. He informed the general that he had made plans to meet Michael Cerré the following June, and should general Macomb care to send word back with Cerré, he would comply with all of the general's instructions. He signed his letter, Your Most Obedient Servant, B.L.E. Bonneville.

Bonneville knew that Walker thought he was too concerned about how the general would receive his request for an extended leave from the Army. He saw Joseph Walker as a natural leader of men. He could have been a great Army officer, but it took more than leadership in the Army. It took politics. Benjamin Bonneville knew he was a good soldier and leader. He hoped he was a good enough politician. Captain Bonneville was also busy helping organize supplies for Walker's jaunt into California. They had decided to outfit forty men with four horses each, and sufficient provisions to get them to California and back.

"Dammit, Walker, I'm gonna go to the Californias." Bill Williams tipped his jug, rolled the whiskey around in his mouth, and then swallowed, causing his large, knotted larynx to move up and down his long, bony neck.

"Never said you couldn't." Joe Walker reached out as Williams passed the jug, and he took a swallow from the container.

"You haven't said nothin' one way or the other." Bill was determined to push the point. "Bonneville looked like he damn sure didn't want me or any of my bunch along, and I sure as hell wouldn't want him along. He's a damn fool. Who else would build a trading post here?"

"Captain Bonneville is not going to make the trip." Walker handed the jug back to Williams. "He didn't comment one way or the other about you going along. I'll tell you what, Bill, after we leave the rendezvous we'll spend a spell over on the Bear before heading west. You can meet us there if you feel you're up to traveling all the way to California and back with forty men."

"By God, I'll be there. You can bet on it. It's a place I've wanted to see for a long time." Williams turned to get a better view of a rider headed their way. "Looks like that damn Englishman's headed this way. You hear about what happened to ol' Holmes?"

Walker could tell that the rider was William Drummond Stewart by the way he set his horse. He had learned to ride in the style of his native Scotland, and was an ex-soldier in line to inherit wealth, land and a lordship. He had no interest in trapping or trading. His only expectation was to share in the excitement and adventure of the rendezvous. Stewart had the same courage, self-reliance and love of freedom that characterized the trappers, and was accepted and respected by most of the men.

Stewart and Williams were an unlikely mix, yet the two seemed to enjoy each other's company. Stewart had the advantage of a formal education that challenged Bill's considerable mental faculties, while Williams possessed greater physical strength and endurance than Stewart had ever known in one individual. To associate with Bill Williams was to experience daily unpredictable adventure.

"I never heard anything about Holmes," Walker answered as Stewart joined the two wilderness veterans.

"Top of the morning, gentleman," Stewart greeted Williams and Walker. "I presume the pair of you were spared last night's attack?"

"I was just fixin' to tell Joe all about your tent mate," Williams said as he spit a wad of tobacco juice that landed three inches from Stewart's left boot. "The way I got it you kicked poor ol' George out and then replaced him with one of them festive little Shoshone gals. The wolves got him while he was tryin' to get a little sleep."

"As usual, Mr. Williams, your information is superficial at best." Stewart examined the location of where the tobacco juice had landed. "I simply asked Holmes if I might have some private time to entertain my guest. I had previously done as much for him."

"Are you two saying that George Holmes was attacked by a wolf pack last night?" Walker had never heard of wolves being aggressive enough to come into the middle of a fur company camp, not this time of year.

"Not wolves. One wolf, and a mad one at that," Stewart answered. "I fear that it was infected with the hydrophobia. George was sleeping out in the open about thirty meters down from the tent. I heard him scream during the night. When I got out of the tent he was rolling around on the ground, trying to fight off a wolf. The light was poor, but it appeared that the animal was trying to chew off Holmes's ear. I was afraid to try and shoot the wolf, fearing that I might hit George, so I placed a shot in the ground off to one side. The wolf didn't appear to notice the noise or see the dirt kicked up by the rifle shot. I was running their way, intent upon using my gun to club the creature, when it turned from Holmes and disappeared into the darkness."

"Shit fire, Stewart, you'd done better shootin' the damn wolf." Williams again hurled a spitball that landed midway between Walker and Stewart. "So what the hell if you did hit ol' George. He's a dead man anyhow. You'da saved him all the sufferin'."

"A wolf with rabies means an infected pack," Joe Walker said as he stood up. "We need to get the word out to all the camps. There's a lot of men sleeping out where they'd be in danger. You get one sick wolf in camp, you're sure to have more."

"This one wharn't the first," Williams said, sending another mouth full of tobacco juice toward the nearest tree. "I went down to the American camp about daybreak to pass the word, and Fontenelle said that they'd had two men bitten at their camp the night before last. The worthless bastard didn't even let anyone know about it."

"I woke Joe Meek up this morning." Stewart watched Walker placing his saddle on his horse. "He'd slept right where he dropped after spending yesterday trying to romance all the ladies and drink all the whiskey in camp. I explained what had happened to George and the hazards of his sleeping arrangement. His response was, 'I ain't in no danger a'tall.'" Stewart was trying to imitate Joe Meek's manner of speech. "'I'm at my best when I keep my body filled with this here medicine.' He took a long drink from a half-empty bottle that had been lying beside him all night. Then he said, 'You know, if that ol' wolf would have been lucky enough to bite me, this here potion would have protected me, and at the same time it most likely would have put a cure on him.'"

Walker was headed back toward Fort Bonneville to see if they had learned about the rabid wolf attacks.

As he rode away he could hear Stewart tell Williams, "Bill, you should stop all that spitting. It's very unsightly."

"I'll tell you somethin', fancy pants." Williams was cutting himself another chew of tobacco. "You're in America now, and we got ourselves two sexes here. One spits and the other don't. The one that don't ain't got no call to. The other ain't about to be stopped by no damn Englisher."

On July 27, 1833, Joe Walker left Fort Bonneville with forty men. They traveled south down the Green River, then followed the same trail through the mountains to the west that the Snake Indians had showed Walker on their way to the rendezvous. The Bear River ran north and was considered the western edge of the great buffalo ranges. They made camp and began their hunt.

Bill Williams and his followers found Walker's camp. Joe Walker knew every man to be an experienced trapper and hardened to the life. They would be unwavering in a tight spot, but hard men to control. Within a week they had dried and packed away Walker's required sixty pounds of buffalo meat per man. Bill Williams and his men didn't think much of spending all that time drying and storing meat. They were more inclined to stuff down every bite they could when meat was plentiful, then do without when none could be found. Walker insisted that everyone put up their sixty pounds each or stay behind.

"I'm surprised the captain asked us along on this trip," Swit said to Will. "I figured him to take Henry, Robert and Woolly if they was of a mind to go, but we ain't got the experience that most of these others have. You've been in and out of this country before, but this is my first trip."

"Ain't nobody been in and out of where we're goin'," Will answered. "At least not the way we're goin'. How many times I gotta tell ya? It's our horses that gets us picked for these duties. If we was ridin' a pig-eyed, ewe-necked, roman-nosed killer like that one over there, we wouldn't get invite one."

"Billy said that Scab was a killer until Captain Walker got hold of him. He still bares watching, but it ain't like he once was."

"The captain may need to tame a few of that new bunch before this is all over." Will thought that Williams and his group could be trouble.

"That Leonard fellow that the captain hired on as clerk, did you know him before the rendezvous?" Swit asked.

"No, but Fitz had praise for him, and he don't much hand that out," Will answered. "Seems he started out in '31 with Gantt and Blackwell. I heard he did some clerkin' for them, too. Anyhow, they left Leonard and some other men over on the Laramie River."

"You mean on purpose?" Swit asked.

"Well, to me it sounded more like they lost track of each other," Will answered. "They ended up wintering along the Laramie while Blackwell headed back to Missouri for more supplies. Gantt split the men up in groups of twenty or so and sent 'em out lookin' for beaver. Leonard fought off starvation, freezin' to death and Indian raids, while he learned the trappin' trade. Then Gantt took his pelts and divided them with the men that couldn't measure up to the beaver."

"He got himself mixed up with some bunch, didn't he?" Swit thought he'd heard the names Gantt and Blackwell before.

"He could've done better," Will answered. "Anyhow, Fitz and Sublette picked 'em up on their way to the '32 rendezvous. Leonard was right in the middle of the fracas with the Blackfoot. He spent some time livin' with the Crow Indians, was captured by the Arikara—managed to escape—and was shot in the side with an arrow. You might say that in the last two years he's had a lifetime of experience."

"You might, but he never says much." Swit was watching Captain Walker talking with Zenas Leonard and two other men. "He's always writing stuff in that journal. I guess that's what a clerk does."

Joe Walker led his assortment of individuals toward the Great Salt Lake. Most of the men had previously hunted for beaver along the rivers and creeks that came down from the north, and were familiar with the countryside. The farther west and south they moved, the flatter and drier the land became. By the time they reached the northwest corner of the lake it was the middle of August, and new territory for everyone.

Swit knew it would be a big, salty lake, because everyone kept saying so. After all, it was called the Great Salt Lake. Swit's mental picture of a lake was one of gentle waves rolling up on a rocky or sandy shoreline. It had grass and trees growing close to the edge of the water. It was restful.

This body of water looked more like he'd imagined when he heard people talk about the ocean. It seemed as if your sight just dissolved in the water. You could see that there were hills beyond the lake, but it looked like the only way you could get there was to cross the water. All the talk about oceans that he'd heard described great stretches of sand beaches. This wasn't exactly sand, but no vegetation grew for several hundred yards between him and the water's edge. He was standing in the hot sun on a dry, white-streaked, crusty, barren ground, trying hard to see the lake's nearest shoreline.

Walker spent several days exploring the lake. A couple of drainage ditches that funneled a little lake water to the west, where it spread out in a basin and evaporated, was the only water headed toward California. A small amount of thin, skimpy grass sprinkled around on dry, salty flats with a few hills far in the distance was all that Swit could see. The way to California looked to be hot and dry, with limited forage and water. The group was working their way back toward the northwest corner of the lake when Henry rode in with the news that an Indian hunting party was headed their way.

Walker, Henry and Robert rode out to parley with the Indians. It turned out that they were a group of Bannocks, an allied tribe of the Shoshone Nation, headed east to hunt buffalo. Walker soon had a common campground formed, and he was busy exchanging trinkets for information.

The old Bannock chief said that there was a river to the west, but confirmed that there was nothing much in between except sand and salt. If they would follow the paths used by the Indians, water could be found off to the southwest. The small water holes were usually good in the spring; however, the rest of the year they had a tendency to dry up or turn salty. A single large, round peak would soon show itself, and Walker should make for that landmark. Traveling west away from the mound they would find small streams that would lead them to the river. A sizable group of natives lived along this river, and it was the chief's opinion that they would not be friendly. The river would lead them west before it eventually spread out into a large sinkhole. From there they would be able to see the giant mountains that always had snow in their highest peaks. The old chief had never been on the other side of the mountains.

The two companies of men spent a day smoking and eating some of the dried buffalo before they parted and headed their separate ways. Walker thought about how Jim Bridger hated the Bannocks and called them all thieves and murderers. Maybe they were liars too.

Walker led his men southwest through the harsh wasteland that the Indian chief had described. They found one spring with drinkable water and the rounded peak. It led them to the river. Swit was confused about the river's name. Leonard insisted on calling it The Barren; others labeled it The Mary. One thing was for sure, it was not like the clear, cool mountain streams and rivers. This river had a murky, whitish-like color, and it flowed along in a slow, meandering way. Swit didn't care; it was better than no river at all.

"Hurry up and get your duds off," Will hollered at Swit as he pulled off his shirt. He and Swit had set their camp on a little ledge overlooking the river. "That swimmin' hole back there is just a waitin'. You ain't gonna find a hole like that very often in this river. Craig's already down there, so let's get goin'."

"Do you think it's very deep?" Swit was careful about any water that could be over his head.

"I figured it was a pretty good hole until now," Will answered. "Look at ol' Bill. He's walkin' in and the water don't look to be any more than a couple a foot deep. Pulls up a wagon full of mud every time he takes a step."

"The deepest part is barely up to his crotch." Swit watched as Bill moved out to the middle of the hole and set down. "There goes Captain Walker."

Will turned to look. The captain had stripped to his birthday suit. He was headed for the swimming hole on a dead run, jumping every little bush and sage he came to. "He better slow up before he hits the mud, or it'll take a horse to pull him out." Will had looked forward to a refreshing swim, but now his enthusiasm had dwindled.

Walker stopped at the edge of the pond, and was talking to Craig, who was still sitting in the pond up to his neck in the milky water. Then Walker dove in headfirst.

"Oh shit." Will could hardly believe what he'd just witnessed. "If the captain didn't break his neck, he's gonna kill Craig."

Swit and Will watched as Walker fought his way out of the muddy bottom. Craig had already started to remove himself from the opposite side of the pond. Captain Walker was completely covered from the top of his head down to his waist with a bluish-colored mud. He made his way out into the middle of the pond, either looking for Craig, more water, or both. Walker wiped the muddy globs away from his eyes and was trying to wash the sticky mess out of his beard while Craig was hunched down in some brush, peeking out to see the results of his joke. Walker looked around as he continued to wash himself off, then walked out of the so-called swimming hole and headed for his tent.

The captain put on his clothes and pick up his rifle. He fired a shot in the direction of the pond, reloaded his gun, and then announced loud enough that Craig could hear him. "Craig, you show yourself and you'll get the next lead ball coming out of this gun."

"I ain't never seen Captain Walker act like that before." Swit was watching Bill Craig crouched down in the bushes. "I wouldn't want to trade places with Craig about now. What do ya suppose he told the captain before he dived in?"

"Hard to tell," Will answered. "Whatever it was it weren't too smart. One thing, he sure didn't tell the captain about how deep the water is. It's a good thing that bottom's filled with mud. If he'd hit a hard spot he'd have broke his neck. Craig better stay hid-out until Walker cools down some."

The sun was low in the sky when Captain Walker asked Henry to go find Craig and tell him that it was all right to come into camp and take mess with the men. Henry knew exactly where to look. He told Bill, "This just might be the end of your trip to California. It's okay to come in, but keep a low profile."

Bill was uncharacteristically quiet as he approached the men gathered around the buffalo hides that had been spread out to hold the meal. He helped himself and sat down. When he looked up, Captain Walker was setting directly across from him. The sun's last glimmer of light was shining off of a small chunk of the blue pond mud that was still stuck to the side of Walker's nose. Another little piece was hanging from behind his ear. Bill Craig couldn't restrain himself, and he started to laugh.

"What the hell are you laughing at?" Walker asked.

"It's just that I thought that gentlemen generally washed before eating." Craig knew he was asking for trouble. Everyone had noticed the mud, but no one was about to say anything. Now everyone burst out in laughter.

Walker felt his face and discovered the leftovers from the pond. He flicked a piece toward Craig and then laughed. "One more trick like that and you'll be the late Mr. Bill Craig."

The men that had never seen Joe Walker's temper take control now knew that this normally gentle giant of a man could become dangerous if he was provoked. Henry wondered if Bill Craig realized just how lethal his little prank could have been for Captain Walker or himself. He must have had some inkling, because he'd been smart enough to stay hid until the captain sent for him—even though it couldn't have been very pleasant hiding out in a thicket of thorny rose brier.

Chapter Twenty-six

Billy B., like almost everyone else he knew, had heard plenty of stories about California. Only a few trappers had actually seen the old Spanish settlements, but those who hadn't made the trip usually knew a trapper who had, and the telling about their own or someone else's experiences was a favorite way to pass time and amuse themselves. In 1830 the first pack train carrying wool and woven goods from Santa Fe arrived in the California settlements. Commerce between the two Mexican populations was growing every year, and the trail connecting the two territories changed whenever easier and safer routes were discovered. Everyone thought that before long you would see pack trains strung out for up to a mile, and herds with as many as two thousand mules and horses moving between the settlements. American traders hauling freight between the States and Santa Fe had developed a solid market in Missouri for the big mules that arrived from California. They called the link between the two Mexican settlements The Old Spanish Trail.

The family from the recently vacated Suarez ranch was to meet the small trading caravan at a place called Abiquiu. Billy had visited Abiquiu when he was traveling under the direction of Captain Walker, and was confident that he could still find the way. The old outpost northwest of Santa Fe had been around for about one hundred years. A group of Indians from various tribes had observed the lifestyle at the Spanish settlements for years before deciding to join together and try to live like the whites. Their little colony on the northernmost edge of Spanish civilization survived and prospered. Abiquiu was a favorite place for the Ute Indians to exchange fur pelts, tanned hides and dried buffalo meat for items that made their life a little easier, such as pots, pans, blankets and horses. The trade item that the Spanish valued most were the Paiute slaves.

Billy's family, Anita, Lena, the Suarez children, Hog Eye Harris, Juan and Cisco, along with extra horses, a milk cow and the thirty Mexican traders with their caravan of seventy-five pack mules headed north up what was called the old Ute slave trail. Everyone rode horses or mules except Mattie. She was bound up like an Indian's papoose and tied to a mule that one of the old traders said he would trust with his life. Mattie swung back and forth as the mule walked along. She napped off and on, and seemed completely content when she was awake. Maria was always nearby, but as far as she was concerned if any mishap was to come to Mattie the old trader had already established the cost.

They followed up the Chama River until they reached a place where the river entered a deep, rugged canyon. The old slave trail pointed the caravan more north than west, away from the river. Two days later they rejoined the Chama above the canyon, crossed the river, headed off in a northwesterly direction and gradually climbed to a little lake situated in the south end of the Rocky Mountain range and just east of the Continental Divide.

"By golly, Mattie's makin' the trip better than I thought she would." Billy watched his daughter trying to learn to walk. The grass was tall, and she fell. Before Maria or anyone else could reach her, the old trader had her by the hand. He had appointed himself her guardian.

"I know what he's after," Maria said. "And I'm happy to oblige him, as long as he keeps a close watch on her."

"What's he want?" Billy wondered if he would ever understand Maria.

"He wants me to fix his meals." Maria had noticed that one of the other items Mattie's mule carried was a large stone that the traders used to grind Indian corn into flour for their tortillas. Having the stone tied to the same mule that carried Mattie gave Maria some sense of confidence that the mule was reliable. No Mexican trader wanted to go all the way to California without his tortillas. The traders took turns preparing their favorite meal of tortillas, frijoles, chile colorado and coffee. The old trader had found a way to remove himself from those duties.

Billy B. had insisted that his group prepared for the trip by drying thin strips of beef. Besides the dried meat they brought along a supply of grain, beans and coffee. Maria had added brown sugar and cinnamon to the list. If it became necessary to prepare a quick meal without the benefit of fire, she could make *penole* by mixing dried ground corn with the sugar and cinnamon. When water was added it would almost double in volume. A small amount would satisfy a man's hunger, at least for a while. Anita and Lena made something they called *atole* that the old trader seemed to relish. It reminded Billy of a cornmeal mixture that his dad used to make. He called it fried mush.

The old trader's name was Mauricio Jose Antonio Garcia. He answered to Jose, and had obviously spent most of his life outdoors—leaving him with leathery and wrinkled skin. It was hard to tell what kind of a life he'd had, but whatever his fate had been he must have accepted it with good cheer, because the lines in his face were those of someone that enjoyed smiling, and his dark eyes fairly twinkled when he watched Mattie play. Jose called the mule that carried Mattie, Nene, and divided almost all of his spare time between Mattie and Nene. He was always trying to get Mattie to call him Jo, and Billy noticed that when meal time rolled around, Jo was usually on hand.

Maria and Billy had decided to talk to Mattie, and each other, in both Spanish and English. Billy's Spanish was better than Maria's English, so Maria usually spoke to Mattie in Spanish and to Billy in English. Cisco tried to discourage the practice, believing that it would confuse Mattie and she wouldn't be able to talk to someone without using both languages, which was how it sounded when Billy and Maria talked to one another. Mattie's first word was mama, her second word was papa.

The caravan crossed over the low altitude divide and entered the San Juan River Basin. The trail led northwest. Water and grass was plentiful, but the Spanish Trail was not suited for wagon travel. The mules and horses had all they could handle threading their way along a twisting route that wove its way through and around the low mountains and foothills of the Rockies. When they reached the San Juan River it was flowing to the south. They crossed the river and continued northwest to the Big Bend of the Dolores River. The Dolores had its beginning in the mountains to the north, and flowed southwest before bending off toward the northwest on its way to the Colorado River.

"Look over there, along the south side of the river." Jose was pointing at what was left of some old ruins. "That was an Anasazi village."

Hog Eye and Billy B. were riding together. On this particular morning they had volunteered to stay close to Mattie, and if you were around Mattie you were within the sound of Jose's voice. "What's Anasazi?" Hog Eye asked.

"Anasazi is what the Navajo Indians call the ancient ones." Jose rode along beside Nene, and he had positioned himself so the shadow he cast prevented the morning sun from shining into the little girl's face. "They lived here before anyone else got here. No one knows where they came from, when they left, where they went to, or why."

Billy didn't know any more about the Anasazi than Hog Eye. Whoever they were, they were gone now and wouldn't play any part in their journey to California. It was a curiosity, though, to think that a people had apparently lived, flourished and then left here long before the present settlers arrived.

"The Indians have stories about the Anasazi, but what's true and what isn't is hard to tell. There's quite a few places like this around here." Jose had dug around in the old ruins ever since an Indian at Abiquiu had showed him one of the sites and told him about the ancient ones. "If you poke around in 'em you can find all kinds of stuff. Pieces of pottery and baskets, spoons and tools made from some kind of animal bones; I found a bowl one time that was painted around the top. It was full of different colored beads, and it only had one little crack in it."

"I ain't never heard no talk about Anasazi before." Hog Eye thought that he had it all figured out. The Indians were here first, the Spanish came next, and those that were born here with mixed blood were called Mexicans. Now it looked as if someone was here ahead of the Indians. He thought about asking Jose if he knew anything about what they looked like, but decided to let it go. It didn't seem like much was known about the Anasazi anyhow. Wouldn't it have been something, though, if they were black?

The caravan followed the Dolores River until its flow was more north than west. The Ute trail left the river, continuing northwest away from the mountains. The countryside gradually opened up into a dry, hilly, barren landscape. Water was becoming scarce, and forage for the animals harder to find. They moved along in a more or less northwesterly direction for more than two weeks. Billy was certain that the traders knew the way, but the trail had taken them farther north than he had expected.

"I always thought the way to California was mostly west," Billy said to Juan and Cisco. They were all watching Maria get Mattie settled for the night. Billy tried to picture where they were in relation to Santa Fe and the West Coast settlements. "It seems to me we're goin' north about as much as we're goin' west."

"The problem with heading straight west, outside of the lack of available water, is the Indians that live in that country." Juan's main concern about making this trip was the Indian tribes that lived between Santa Fe and California. "The Navajo and Apache territories are to the west. We lost stock, crops and good men and women fighting off their raids."

"I use to hear trappers tell about their clashes with the Apache when they headed west along the Gila River." Billy wanted to avoid any conflicts with Indians if at all possible. Maria or Mattie in their hands was something he didn't like to even think about.

"Heading straight into Apache country is pure foolishness." Cisco decided to make his feelings known. He had stopped hating all Indians just because they were Indians, after Don Carlos and Billy's friend, Otis Tejas, died in the plaza. That didn't mean that all Indians could be trusted. It just meant that Indians deserved the same consideration you would give anyone else.

"They'll allow no passage without a fight." Juan didn't trust any Indian, no matter what tribe they claimed. "They raided, burned, killed and stole from us for as long as anyone could remember. We tried to make peace with them once, but we soon learned that Apaches don't make peace with anyone. Their religion teaches that they and they alone are "The People," and everything here or anywhere is a gift from their god—meant just for them. It's strictly forbidden for the Apache to kill or rob each other, but considered a virtue to kill and rob everyone else. After all, everybody else is stealing what God placed here for their use alone."

"Sounds like it's a good thing we're swingin' north," Billy said. "Ridin' into the middle of Apache territory don't sound too smart."

The traders said that the upper Colorado River was just ahead, and it would have to be crossed. The trail led the little caravan to a place in the river that, as far as Billy could tell, was the only possible crossing for many miles in either direction. The Colorado River was at least two hundred and fifty yards wide, with a small island in the middle. The traders explained that it was important to reach the Colorado before or after the spring runoff, when the island was visible. Any other time you would need to build a barge to get across, and floating this river was risky and dangerous.

They crossed the river and continued traveling northwest, passing through a dry but fascinating country of unusual red rock formations. The place was full of stone arches, spires, cliffs, balanced rocks, caves, alcoves and windowlike openings that had been sculptured out of the colorful stone by wind and water. All along the trail large bowl-shaped watering holes had been scooped out of the red rock by nature's handiwork, and they held water that must of flowed down through the rocks when it rained. A much appreciated find in the dry country between the Colorado and Green Rivers. The Green River was almost as wide, but not as swift, as the Colorado. Like its bigger sister, it also had an island midstream, and firm footing on the river bottom. Hog Eye and Cisco crossed both rivers side by side.

"If you was to git here, and the island was all covered up, would you build a raft and try to cross her?" Hog Eye couldn't swim, and floating to the other side seemed chancy.

"If I got here and can't see any island, I'm either heading back or staying put till she goes down." Cisco didn't like the looks of either river. They were forced to twist their way through rough canyon walls and over and around huge boulders. Sometimes the river was wide and slow, and then suddenly it was pushed into a narrow cascade of water. "You could put your raft in right here, but who's to say where it's going before it reaches the other side—if it reaches the other side."

After crossing the Green, the pack train and riders climbed up on a high plateau. The trail continued northwest through canyons and dry washes, around mesas, buttes, monoliths and knobs until they reached the southern end of the Wasatch Mountain Range. The caravan then turned southwest along the eastern side of the mountains, crossing over the streams that flowed down out of the foothills, until they eventually reached a place where the trail pointed west between two mountain peaks.

The country drained by the Colorado River was left behind when the caravan crossed over the mountains and followed a stream down into the valley of the *Rio Severo*. The river at this point was flowing north, and the traders turned south up the valley. The Sevier River was the recognized boundary line between the Ute and Paiute Indian tribal lands.

So far the Indian encounters that the caravan had experienced traveling through Ute territory had been for the most part friendly. Most of the Indians they came in contact with had simply walked into camp in twos or threes and asked for food or to just spend the night with the travelers. One group of Indians had intercepted the pack train at the Green River crossing. They claimed that a tribute was to be paid for crossing their river. The traders had anticipated the toll, and purchased the right of passage with a large cooper bowl and two knives.

Billy was concerned, because Paiute country lay ahead, and he'd heard that they were treacherous to deal with and wouldn't hesitate to kill intruders if the opportunity presented itself. He'd been told that they would follow along beside a caravan, and at night they'd steal horses, mules or anything unguarded. If they couldn't get their hands on any livestock, they'd shoot arrows at the pack train from the high bluffs that lined the trail, hoping to kill or at least wound an animal that would have to be left behind. Alive or dead was all the same to them. Animals were food, not transportation. Captain Walker had said that even from a distance you could usually tell a Paiute Indian by the way that he walked. He would swing his head from side to side like a prairie wolf. If the Paiutes found anyone alone or without adequate protection, they killed them. Billy liked the looks of the Sevier River valley, but he knew that from here on he'd need to watch and keep track of everyone—especially the children.

"California's gonna have to go some to beat the Sevier River valley." Billy wanted to cheer up Maria. Mountain peaks flanked both sides of the valley. Elk, deer and bighorn sheep were plentiful in the surrounding foothills, and the river was full of some type of large trout. There were thousands of acres of river bottom land that looked to be as productive as any Billy had seen. Grass seemed almost unlimited, and the water was clean and pure. The only negative he could find was a shortage of trees.

"It is beautiful." Maria hadn't taken notice. Her mind had been on the rain they'd ridden through the last two days. It was cold as a fresh mountain stream, and she knew that any day now they could see snow falling in the high country. The traders threw a square piece of matting over each pack to protect their trade goods from the rain, and Jose had rigged one up to keep Mattie dry. It seemed to Maria that everyone in the entire caravan was miserable with the wet, cold conditions except Mattie and Billy B. Mattie would splash her hand down into every puddle she could get at, and then laugh and splash some more. Billy didn't seem to even take notice of the weather. He was riding off first in one direction and then in another, like he was expecting to find someone.

"The ancient ones must of liked this valley too." Billy said. "There's some old Indian drawin's on them rocks over there. Jose said they was left there by the Anasazi."

"Maybe they liked California better than here, and went there." Maria didn't care about any scratching that the Ana-whatever-they-were-called left on some old rocks. She just wanted the rain to stop so she could dry out.

The rain stopped during the night, and morning brought forth sunshine and smiling faces. Everyone agreed that this would be a good place to stay for a couple of days to let the animals replenish themselves. Billy shot two Elk, and the gang got busy cutting and drying strips of meat to replace their dwindling food supply. The scarcity of timber made it impossible to find enough dry firewood for cooking, so brush was used as a poor substitute.

The pack train and riders continued making their way up the valley until they reached the head waters of the Sevier River, where they turned west to follow a feeder stream that the traders called Bear Creek up into the high country. Moving over and out of the mountains in a southwest direction, they traveled through numerous little valleys, past a lake and down into what the traders called Big Mountain Meadow. This would be the last chance to enjoy pure, clean water and an abundance of grass before pushing out onto the eastern edge of the Great Basin. They left Mountain Meadow, heading southwest, following along and crisscrossing several small feeder streams on their way to the Santa Clara River. The pack train followed the Santa Clara until it turned eastward, where they crossed the river and shortly picked up Beaver Dam Creek that led them to the Virgin River. Each day the country that they passed through was hotter and drier than the one before. The water in the Virgin had a brackish taste, but there was no choice—drink it, or go without.

The Paiute Indians were almost always around, but usually in small numbers. Billy thought that they acted more skittish than threatening. He figured that their uneasiness had to do with the long history of being captured and sold as slaves to the Spanish. The caravan traveled southwest, following along the Virgin River. The sand was deep, and they were forced to cross the river several times, slowing their progress. Juan was concerned about the increasing numbers of Indians that they were seeing.

Three of the traders, who had worked as muleteers for a large California-bound pack train the year before claimed to know a shortcut that would get the caravan to the Mojave River quicker and safer. The next morning the caravan moved away from the Virgin River and spent most of the day winding its way west-southwest, through a waterless waste that was void of grass. They stopped and rested after they reached a valley with a swift stream of water running through it that the traders called the Muddy. A large number of Paiutes lived along this desert oasis, but they appeared to be friendly and offered to trade some of their corn and beans for a helping of the dried elk meat. The Elk hadn't turned out like Billy had planned. The lack of wood for a good fire, rainy weather and their brief stop along the Sevier River hadn't allowed sufficient time for the drying process to do a good job of preserving the meat. A lot of it was moldy. Some was rotten. The Indians seemingly didn't care; they made the trade and devoured the elk like it was the best meal they'd ever had.

"They seem peaceable enough, but it's hard to tell about a Indian," Billy said as they began setting up their camp.

"I don't like being surrounded by hundreds of Indians." Juan felt uneasy. He was helping with the fire, and looked forward to the corn and bean meal in much the same manner as the Indians had anticipated the elk meat.

"When that sun goes down, let's be sure everyone's far enough from the fire that Injuns sittin' out there in the dark can't see us. I ain't interested in makin' myself a target so's some digger can slip an arrow into me," Billy B. advised the group.

"The traders are posting lookouts tonight," Juan said. He was glad to see that someone else was concerned about the Indians. "Jose said that the best sentry you can have is a mule. He claimed they can smell and hear an Indian before you'll know they're around. Said that when they get fidgety and start snorting it's best to keep a lookout in the same direction they got their ears pointed."

The next morning a mule lay dead with an arrow in its neck, and one of the horses was missing. Juan, Cisco and Alonzo rode out to find the horse.

"It looks like the horse is gone for good," Cisco told Billy. The three men had returned before the caravan was five miles southwest of the Muddy. "We tracked him off into the brush, but the track petered out, so we couldn't find him. There's plenty of Indian signs, but you can find that about anywhere around here."

"I 'spect he's headed for an Injun's stew pot." Billy was willing to bet that the horse wasn't the only addition to the Paiute menu. The dead mule they left behind was probably already cut up and divided by now.

The traders labeled this so-called shortcut the *Jornada de Muerto*. Billy thought about the Cimarron cutoff along the Santa Fe Trail and how the teamsters had called that waterless stretch between the Arkansas River and the springs along the Cimarron River the *Jornada*. There was something about the word *Jornada* that killed any enthusiasm Billy might have had for traveling this trail.

The caravan was headed southwest for a place called Las Vegas Springs. When they arrived it was a welcomed relief from the fifty miles of travel through the dry, hot, reddish dust-covered brush country. The springs were in fact a series of four large springs pouring water into a natural basin that was twenty to thirty feet across. The water was clear, but not cool like mountain springs. It flowed up out of the ground with such a force that when you jumped out into the deep water the pressure from the incoming flow would pop you to the surface like a cork. If you walked out into the pond, it was impossible to sink above your armpits. Cottonwood and willow trees shaded the grass that grew around the springs, and a swift stream, five feet wide and two foot deep, watered a meadow of mesquite trees that covered an area three miles wide and twelve miles long. It was an ideal spot to rest before pushing on to the Mojave River.

It had been two days and nights since the caravan moved away from Las Vegas Springs. They had spent their last day at the springs stretched out under the shade trees. A mild desert breeze supplied fresh, dry air, and Maria would have voted to stay longer if there had been a vote. The traders decided that the caravan should travel at night and rest during the day until they reached the Mojave River. She didn't like the change, but she understood their reasoning. By traveling at night they were spared the force of the desert sun, and that made what little water they had go farther. The pack mules didn't suffer as much.

"I don't know how a country could have less than this one's got," Maria barely whispered.

"It ain't got much to offer, that's for sure." Billy B. and Maria rode together beside Mattie's mule. Traveling at night was a tradeoff, because Billy had trouble sleeping during the daytime. It was more like a series of short naps, and after a couple of days he noticed that he wasn't the only one that was tuckered out. "Kinda eerie out here at night, ain't it?"

"I don't like it." Maria watched Mattie sleep as Jose's mule made his way through deep sand. For some reason it seemed as if the sounds of travel had somehow been muffled by the sunset. They moved along in an unnatural quietness. Everyone was covered with the blanched clay dust whipped up by the desert wind, and the moonlight gave the California-bound caravan a ghostly appearance.

Billy didn't like the idea that the Indians were following their journey across this desert like hungry coyotes waiting for a chance to grab anything they could. They stayed back away from the trail, but every now and then he'd get a glimpse of one moving over a ridge or running from one hiding place to another. During the day smoke would rise from the tops of nearby bluffs, and Billy knew that the Paiutes were passing the location of the caravan to other members of their tribe. The Indians were waiting at Bitter Spring when the pack train arrived.

"How many do you figure there are?" Hog Eye watched the ridge above the spring. It was hard to tell what was hidden in the brush. He could count at least twenty, but he felt sure there were others.

"More than we can see," Cisco answered. "Did Billy and Juan get all the kids gathered?"

"Yeah, everyone's over by Jose and Mattie." Hog Eye was watching an Indian move down the hill toward the spring. He was waving his arms in the air and shouting something that Hog Eye didn't understand. The man wasn't caring any kind of weapon, and it looked as if his intentions were completely peaceful.

A Mexican trader who Jose said was the *mayordomo* of the pack train accompanied Billy B. when he went forward to meet the Paiute coming down the hill. The Indian continued to give assurances of his friendly intentions. When he got closer, Billy could see that he was an old man, and the agility that the Indian had demonstrated descending the hill surprised Billy. When the three men came together and no hostilities occurred, some more Indians begin to show themselves.

"Good lord, there must be more than a hundred of 'em," Cisco said. He and Hog Eye had joined the rest of their bunch.

"I wouldn't bet that's all of them." Juan wanted everyone to know he thought a fight was coming. He wished the traders would have used their mule packs to form a protective breastwork, but they hadn't. "They could have that many or more hid where we can't see 'em."

It was obvious that Billy was trying to make a point during the dialogue with the old man. The trader turned and headed for the caravan. When Billy shifted his rifle over into his other hand the Indian begin to back away from their meeting. Billy didn't take his eyes off the Paiute until the Indian was halfway up the hill.

"What gives?" Cisco was the first to meet Billy when he returned.

"They're hungry and wanta come in and eat," Billy said, but he was still watching the group of Indians on the ridge. "I think they sent the old man to check us out, figurin' if we killed him it wasn't much of a loss to them. I told him they could have a horse to eat."

"What'd the head trader have to say?" The last thing Juan wanted was to camp with a hundred Paiutes.

"Didn't say much, just shook his head. I don't think he's for givin' 'em anything."

"Is he for letting the Indians come down to the spring?" Juan asked.

"I'm not sure what he thinks," Billy answered. "I never gave him a chance to offer an opinion. It don't matter, I ain't lettin' that many Injuns get that close without a fight. When I told the Paiute that we'd give 'em a horse, you won't believe what he wanted."

"Whatever it was, they must be discussing it now." Hog Eye had been watching the Indians confer with the old man.

"The milk cow." Billy smiled when he talked. He was dead serious about doing whatever was necessary to keep this group of Indians away from the caravan, but he was not without a sense of humor when he thought about the Indian's request. Billy counted it a miracle that the cow had lasted this long. Maria had wanted to bring the cow along, and it hadn't mattered what argument Billy used, the cow was making the trip. She had dried up long ago, and it was common for her to be a mile behind the other animals. Billy couldn't imagine why the Indians hadn't already killed her. The cow's future had become a nightly topic of conversation for several members of the caravan. When the Indian asked for the cow instead of a horse, Billy thought it could be that the Paiutes had never seen a milk cow, and somehow they had decided that this one-of-a-kind unusual animal deserved special consideration. Maybe it was a religious thing.

"Maria ain't gonna like that." Hog Eye could picture all the little children crying. "You've seen her put Mattie on that old cow's back and then have me lead her around while she holds on to her."

"Yeah, I know." Billy hoped his plan would work. "Juan, would you and Cisco pick out a couple of our poorest animals? Take 'em about halfway up that ridge and stake 'em out. Don't get within arrow range, and keep an eye on them Paiutes."

Billy watched Juan and Cisco select two horses that probably wouldn't last more than a few days anyway, especially if the next several days were anything like the last two. Cisco cut the hair off their tails and cropped both their manes. Hog Eye took his rifle and made a stand part way up the ridge. He was in position to backup Juan and Cisco if it was needed. It was a good move, and Billy wished he'd thought of it.

The horses were delivered without incident. At first the Indians seemed confused. They acted as if they couldn't decide whether a donated horse was as valuable as a stolen animal. Whatever the problem, they soon had it settled, and six warriors descended upon the offering. The two horses were led back up the hill, and the Indians followed the entourage over the ridge and out of sight. The last Paiute to leave was the old one. He stood at the top of the ridge, shaking his arms and yelling as if he was making a proclamation. Billy had no idea what it was all about. His hope hung on the premise that this bunch of Paiutes who had at least pretended friendly intentions had respect for the caravan's firepower and would be satisfied with something to eat.

Maria arranged the children so she could watch over them while they slept. The caravan had arrived at the spring just as the sun was coming up, and they had spent most of the day dealing with the Indians. When night settled in everyone was ready for sleep. Maria fought to stay awake, but she was asleep when Cisco shook Billy. Along with Juan, Hog Eye and Alonzo, they were keeping watch during the night. Billy was back when Maria woke up, and she vaguely remembered hearing someone wake Billy during the night; at least she thought she remembered Cisco and Billy leaving together.

"I don't think the kids made a sound last night," Maria softly spoke to Billy. She was watching the children still sleeping. "Did anything happen during the night?"

"Everything was quiet," Billy answered. "The only thing different this mornin' is that your cow's gone."

"Gone where?"

"I don't know." Billy watched Maria, waiting for some indication as to how she would take the news. "She's just gone. There's not even a trail to follow."

"How can that be?"

"Beats me. We didn't see or hear nothin'." Billy felt somewhat relieved that Maria was more matter-of-fact than emotional about her missing cow. "The traders had their lookouts posted, and they didn't see anything either. If someone took her, they was invisible and mighty quiet about it—wiped out all the tracks too."

"What do mean 'if' someone took her?" Maria looked over at Billy. Sometimes she couldn't understand him at all. "Do you think she grew wings during the night and flew away?"

The caravan packed early and headed for the Mojave River. Two horses and a milk cow had apparently satisfied the Indians. Usually Billy could spot at least one Indian watching them prepare to get underway, but this morning he didn't see anything. "I don't know what to make of these Paiutes." Juan was looking back to see if they were being followed when he spoke. "They was able to get that milk cow without us knowing anything was going on. I guess if they wanted to get us they could have."

"There couldn't have been more than one or two of 'em." Billy was surprised that even one Indian could come into camp without being noticed, but there was no denying the fact that the cow was gone. "Jose's idea about mules makin' the best lookouts ain't workin' out like he said. So far them Injuns has killed a mule and stole a horse and a milk cow without as much as a snort."

It was Jose opinion that they would make it to the Mojave River before dark. Juan hoped that this prediction proved better than his evaluation of mules for lookouts. Reaching the river didn't necessarily mean they were free from attack, but following up the Mojave would put the desert behind and lead them to the settlements.

Jose's prophecy was accurate, and they reached the Mojave River as the sun was setting. It wasn't exactly what Billy had expected. The banks of the shallow river were mounds of sand, and any forage for the animals was thin and hard to find. A few weak willow trees struggled to survive along the riverbank. At first light the caravan followed up the river channel.

"What happened to the river?" Hog Eye had never seen a river such as this. "First you got water, and then you don't got water."

"She went underground on us." Cisco was ready for better surroundings. "Jose says that we'll hit another little pool before long. The farther we go the better she'll get."

The Mojave River valley gradually grew in size as the travelers from Santa Fe moved southwestward. The river developed into a clear stream sixty feet across and several feet deep that watered a nice stand of willow and cottonwood trees along its bank. The sparse grass slowly improved. It provided the needed forage for the livestock. Thirst was no longer a problem; however, game to replenish the almost-empty food containers was hard to find. When the trading caravan left the river and headed toward an opening through the mountains, everyone knew that they were almost to the California settlements. The desert was left behind as the pack train with its traders and ranch family crossed over Cajon Pass. The group had successfully weathered eleven hundred miles in the last seventy-seven days.

Chapter Twenty-seven

"When Walker finds out, there'll be hell to pay," Craig said as he and Bill Williams made their way down a little feeder stream of the Barren River. "That makes five less Paiutes. I'da bet my gold tooth that someone would have told the captain about the two you killed yesterday, but he didn't act like he knew nothin' last night."

"The hell with Walker," Williams answered. "Them filthy, poor excuses for Indians been stealing our traps for too long. It's time we thinned them bug-eatin' sons of bitches a little."

"Yeah, but Captain Walker said to leave 'em be." Craig knew trouble was coming. "The word's sure to be out tonight. I ain't looking for no more faceoffs with Joe Walker."

Williams didn't answer Bill Craig or even look his direction. Joe Walker had made it clear. There would be no revenge against the Indians that lived along this river unless they initiated an attack.

At first the Indians had stayed back and just scavenged the trash Walker's men left behind, but as time went on they started to prowl the edges of the camps and would dart in and grab anything unguarded before disappearing into the brush. When they started stealing traps that the men set to try and catch what few beaver they could find, Bill Williams decided to introduce a measure of fear into their thieving little hearts. So far he'd caught five Paiutes stealing his traps, and rendered his form of justice to all five.

God, this is miserable country, Williams thought. This sorry little stream that feeds that pathetic river we've been following for weeks is typical. We haven't found enough timber along this waterway in the last ten days to build a decent fire.

Conversation at camp that night was light and to the point. Everyone knew about the killings, but no one talked about them. Joe Walker had the next move. "Bill, grab your gun. Let's you and I walk down river a piece." Walker lifted himself to his feet and turned toward The Barren. "Let's see if the Paiutes are planning any surprises."

"I'm with ya." Williams slowly got his long legs gathered in under his lanky body, picked up his rifle and followed Walker into the sunset. "If anyone gets surprised I'd say it'll be the damn diggers."

Craig had called it. "Hell to pay." But Bill doubted that he was that indebted. He held no fear of any man, and respected only a few. Walker had his respect, and Bill had heard that he could be tough and unforgiving in a fight. Williams hadn't experienced defeat in battle since his teens, and that was at the hands of an older and larger man. Walker had the size, but did he have the fortitude?

"I guess you know you've created a problem for me, the men on this expedition and yourself; not to mention the sorrow you've caused to that poor bunch of Indians." Walker continued to lead the way along the river. "How long have we known each other, Bill?"

"Ever since you was wet-nosed down the trail to Santa Fe," Williams answered. "I don't see I created any problem, except maybe for them damn bug eaters that think our traps are theirs for the takin'."

"You're an accomplished man, and you're not stupid." Joe Walker turned and faced Williams. "Bill, you know yourself that many times survival out here hangs on help from the natives. Hell, we might not have even found this river without help from that old Bannock chief. Your killings have changed all that."

"What kind of help could ya get from the likes of them?" Williams asked.

"I never looked to get much help from these poor people, but I had hoped to move down this river without conflict. I'd say that's not too likely now. It's hard to see how anyone could live in this land, and yet these Indians been doing just that for hundreds of years. It's true, they haven't advanced much past the stone and stick times, but if they decide to end our exploration, and there's enough of 'em, our time has run out. It's kind of down to how many and how determined they are."

"I see your point," Williams answered. "I just don't see your problem. If the little farts want to cause trouble we can kill enough of 'em to send 'em back into their holes."

"If it comes to that I'd say you're probably right," Walker agreed. "The thing is, it's entirely unnecessary. My problem, and your problem too, is whose leadership is this group of men going to follow? Everyone knew my feelings about reprisals against these Indians, yet you chose your own course. How would you handle that, Bill?"

Bill Williams was trying hard to size up the moment. There was no doubting Joe Walker's resolve. He'd been called out—the talk was over. It was obvious to Williams that Joe Walker was ready for any movement in any direction.

"I'll make it right." Bill turned to his left and headed back toward camp.

Walker wasn't sure what reaction to expect from Bill Williams. He never conceived that Bill would end their encounter in a peaceful manner. Joe Walker watched one of the most formidable men he'd ever known cross over a ridge on his way back to camp. The moonlight silhouetted Williams' long legged, arm swinging, gangly gait. Walker smiled; it was a stride that always brought a smile.

"Crazy Bill's back," Will quietly said to Swit. "I don't see the captain. You think Bill knifed him?"

"Not likely," Swit answered. "It wouldn't surprise me if Williams and some of his buddies went their own way in the morning. Billy B. always said that Captain Walker expected his men to do what he says, when he says it." With that testimony Swit retired for the night. Woodrow Willard watched Bill Williams head over to where the men he rode with were camped.

The morning brought a new day, and Swit immediately noticed a change in the routine. The best hunters generally left camp first. This gave the expedition the best chance for fresh meat. Henry and Robert were always the first to leave, but usually Williams, and then one or two of his bunch departed soon after. Every man in the expedition aspired to be included among these early departures. It was an honored and privileged position, and they were spared the chore of breaking camp. This was the first time that Bill Williams and his associates stayed behind to help in the tedium of camp life. The first day was not the last, and the message was clear. Captain Walker was to be obeyed.

"Captain, we're picking up more Indians every day." Henry and Walker rode together as the expedition headed toward a skimpy wetlands, where the river spread out into a flat basin of small, shallow lakes. The sink was as far as the river would travel, and it contained an abundance of some type of thin, bladed grass. The horses eagerly grazed the new forage. It was the best they'd seen for some time.

"There's just no way that many could be eking out a living along this river," Henry continued. "I know they can live on damn near nothing, but there's just too many of 'em. They got to be calling them in from somewhere else."

This group of Paiutes had brought new meaning to the concept of living off the land. Both the men and women were, for the most part, naked. The only covering they wore was a small loincloth made from woven grass. Some of the men had considerable body hair, and they were all thin, small and dirty. Being forced to make their homes in little dugouts covered by piling grass and dirt on top of what few limbs they could find hardly made for clean living.

They seemed to eat about anything except each other. Bugs, frogs, lizards, snakes, worms, grubs, flies and larvae topped off with grass seed, berries and roots was the daily menu. Fish and rabbits were scarce and considered special treats. The men made fishing spears by sharpening the end of a sand hill crane's leg bone. They were very adept at taking the few fish that were available. The women formed their cooking pots from dried mud. After only a few exposures to the fire they crumbled and a new one was needed. Crudely made bows and arrows were their most effective weapons. It was little wonder, Joe Walker thought, that these people showed such interest in the traps and camp supplies.

"You're right, and we both know why they're here," Walker answered. "Tonight we'll need to set up camp with this little lake to our backs. We'll use the packs to build a half-circle breastworks between us and them, and picket all the horses inside."

"Lord have mercy," Will said as he looked up after placing one of the packs on the fortress that he, Swit, Robert, Woolly and Henry had been constructing. "There's hundreds of 'em."

Henry looked around. No one else was ready to defend an all-out attack. The Indians had suddenly lifted up out of the brush and tall grass. They were coming from every direction except across the lake. Henry estimated that there were at least five hundred Paiutes walking toward them.

"Has anyone seen Captain Walker?" Swit asked.

"Out front there, laddie," Woolly answered. "Wouldn't ya say it's a sight? Him in all his grandeur facing off hundreds of naked aborigines."

"I don't know about 'ab-or-gees,' but I can see that they all got a bow and some arrows." Swit watched as the Indians stopped their march and then set down. They were about one hundred and fifty yards away. Five of the Paiutes had remained standing. They came forward and begin to sign.

"Anybody know what's up?"

"They wanta come into camp and puff the pipe," Henry answered. "Captain Walker won't allow it. Says he'll meet halfway with anyone they care to send."

"Whatever he said didn't make them little fellers very happy," Woodrow added. "Look how they're stompin' around."

"The chiefs have rounded up some more help." Swit counted somewhere between thirty and forty Paiutes in this bunch. They signed something to Captain Walker, and he answered. The Indians looked at one another for a while and then all started to laugh.

"Well now, don't that beat all," Will said. "The captain must of cracked a good one."

"They said that they were coming in, no matter what Captain Walker wants." Henry motioned for Robert to bring two extra guns. "The captain told 'em not to come any closer or it'd cost them their lives. That's what they think is so funny. They wanta know how that's gonna happen at this distance."

Joe Walker turned back to his men and instructed everyone to take cover. He picked twelve of his best marksman and position them on top of the partly assembled breastworks. It occurred to Walker that this isolated tribe of Indians might not have ever witnessed the use of firearms. There was no doubt they had sufficient numbers to overrun the camp. What wasn't known was whether they were prepared to pay the price. Maybe they didn't even understand how great the cost would be.

When the Indians started their forward movement, Captain Walker turned toward Henry. "You and George take those ducks off that little pond to their right."

Walker had barely finished his request before Henry shifted slightly to his left and fired. A duck exploded in the water. The flock took to the air. A shot from Nidever sounded, and a duck in flight went limp. Robert had been ready; Henry's second shot dropped a third duck.

"Well now, don't that just about make you wanta quit carryin' a gun?" Will marveled at the two men's ability. The first shot startled the Indians, and the second sent them to the ground for cover. "Too bad the little fellers didn't get to see Henry's wing shot."

The Paiutes retrieved the birds and were studying the results of the last few minutes. It was obvious that there was considerable speculation about what had happen. They quickly produced a beaver pelt, hung it up as a target, and moved away.

"Take out the pelt." Joe Walker turned and walked back behind the barricade. Immediately the twelve shooters sent lead balls slicing through the target. The Indians were excited, but this time they didn't dive for cover. They collected the beaver hide and studied the damage before retreating back into the surrounding brush country with the destroyed pelt and dead birds.

"I guess they got the idea." Swit shook his head. "You'd have to be pretty slow not to see what could happen to you. Them birds ain't gonna fly no more."

"Hard to tell what they'll make of it," Will said. "They're probably busy tryin' to figure out how to split up three ducks between five hundred bug-eaters."

Captain Walker doubled the guard. The night passed peacefully. Walker had his men moving down through the basin before dawn. When the first light of the new day improved their vision, it was evident that they were passing through a concentration of unfriendly Indians. Paiutes were visible in every direction. The early movement of the expedition had surprised the Indians. However, it was not long before groups of fifteen or twenty warriors would dart across in front of the riders, causing Captain Walker to exercise additional caution, and slowing the column's advance.

"I ain't liking this one bit." Swit could see that Captain Walker had stopped the procession. "There must be close to a hundred men in that bunch up ahead. They act like they're itching for a fight, and there's Indians all over this country."

"Well, I'll tell you what, it don't look like the shootin' demonstration yesterday had much effect." Woodrow was as concerned as Swit. "We better be gettin' ready to fight off an attack."

"All you men that's been set on killing Indians, prepare to ride," Walker announced to his group. "We have to hit 'em hard, fast and now. We must deliver a blow that will take away their willingness for battle."

Thirty-one men equipped themselves and rode forward with Captain Walker. They made one pass through the gathering of Indians that blocked their way—thirty-nine warriors lay dead on the ground. The California-bound expedition moved forward, leaving behind the sorrowful sounds of an anguished people.

"Seems like a hard way to learn." Swit and Will rode side by side. They hadn't actively participated in the massacre. They'd followed Captain Walker's instructions and stayed behind to help set up a defensive retreat just in case the attack didn't produce the intended results. "I don't think any of us even got a scratch. For a while, though, I was scared. There was Indians everywhere."

"Well now, I'll tell ya somethin', you wasn't alone." Will looked toward Captain Walker. "That's about as excited as I've seen the captain. You know, when you think about it, if they was to all come in one big bunch, and we kill one of 'em with every shot, there'll still be plenty left when we was done shootin'. A bow and a handful of arrows is a better weapon than a gun when that gun's been fired and you ain't got time to reload her."

"I know Captain Walker did what he had to do." Swit agreed with Will's assessment. "I guess the Indians were doing what they thought they had to do, too, or at least what their leaders thought they had to do."

Walker led his men south, away from the Barron River's hostile inhabitants. They continued to travel through a dry, sandy, rock-covered country that had all it could do to support a patchy growth of sage. There was almost no grass or edible forage of any kind. When they passed over the small ridges that broke up the otherwise flat terrain, they could see tall, white-topped peaks off to the west. As they moved farther south, the imposing range of mountains gradually pushed closer

Walker's men had nearly exhausted their supply of buffalo meat when they arrived at a lake being fed by a river that clearly had its beginning in the high mountain country. The lake was ten to fifteen miles north to south, and about five miles across at its widest spot. It had one thing in common with the Great Salt Lake; there was no river outlet. Mountainous slopes bordered its western side, and Swit knew that they would soon be climbing their way toward the snow-covered peaks of the Sierra Nevada Mountain range.

Captain Walker wasted no time following the river upstream. He thought it might lead them to a pass through the mountains, and the river valley offered the best chance for them to replace their dwindling rations. Some of the men referred to the river and the lake it flowed into as Walker's Lake and River. Each morning Captain Walker sent out hunters to look for food for the expedition, and after they had climbed higher into the mountains, he dispatched scouts to find a passageway through the ever-expanding Sierras. With the exception of an occasional rabbit, there was no game to be found. A pass through the towering high country was not revealing itself either.

"Did you hear about Nidever shooting two Indians today?" Swit and Will were preparing to bed down for the night.

"Another fight with the natives is about all we need right now." Will couldn't explain why, but a feeling of doom about crossing these mountains had started to come over him. "Didn't anybody learn nothin' from our bout with them diggers? Here we are startin' to sleep with our ass in the snow, no more buffalo to eat, and we got no idea how to get over these mountains. Did it occur to George to try and find out from the people that live here how to get to California? He probably just wanted to show 'em what a shot he is."

"Fact is, it was a better than average shot." Swit was tucking his blanket in around his feet. "But it wasn't like you think. Nidever feels real bad about the whole thing. Captain Walker, Zenas Leonard and George were out scouting. They got to a place too steep for their horses, so they took off on foot. Nidever got separated from the other two and was working his way back toward them when he sees these two Indians running as hard as they could go, headed straight for him. Henry said that Nidever must have been thinking about how the Arapahos had killed his brother a few years back, and he figured these two had got Walker or Leonard. He just raised up and fired. The ball went right through the first one and into the other'n. Two dead with one shot. Turns out that the Indians had just spooked when they saw Captain Walker. They was just trying to get away."

"Just tough luck all around," Will said as he settled down for a night with his hunger. "They're dead, and we're stuck here on this mountain without food or any idea of how to get to the Promised Land."

"Swit, what seems to be Will's problem?" Henry asked. "He's sure been crabby lately. Acts like a man walkin' along in tight shoes."

"I guess he's just cold and hungry," Swit answered. "He don't say much to me anymore, but I know he don't take to these mountains. When he does talk, it's mostly about how good it was back on the Bear River."

"He ain't wrong there," Henry said as he stopped and looked back. They had climbed high enough that they had a panoramic view out over the great void to the east. "You know, it's country you'd have to be born in to like. Show me a spot where there ain't no buffalo, and I'll show you a place to stay away from."

It was now well into October. Exactly what day was a nightly debate. The mind was too busy dealing with the cold, snow and hunger to spend much energy keeping time. Every day brought the same battle with the mountain. Snow, rocks, ice, gorges, cliffs, hills, valleys and the ever-present cold and feeling of starvation were constant challenges. Walker continued to send out scouting parties daily, hoping to find a way through the mountainous maze. The scouts experienced the same success as the hunters: No game, and no easy pass leading west.

Cloudy days were the worst. The cold seemed to dig deeper into your body. The wind blew the snow off some spots and buried others so deep that passage was impossible. Some of the horses fared better than others, but they were all stiff in their movements and unpredictable in their actions. Even Scab was losing his senses. The constant exhaustion, freezing temperatures and starvation pulled at the mind and body of horse and man alike. Each day they gained only a few miles. It had been almost a week since the men decided that they were on top of the mountain range, and still no indication that they were over and headed down.

Swit was worried about Woodrow. He was still making night camp with Henry, Robert, Woolly and himself, but he spent most of the day with three other men that Swit didn't really know that well. In the evening Will would set around the campfire and stare off into the darkness. He rarely made a comment or offered an opinion. Rations were now down to whatever could be found for the stew pot. Swit noticed that Will wasn't even eating his share of that mixture.

"Captain, me and a few of the men are headin' back in the morning," Will announced one evening. "We wanna take our horses and some lead and powder back with us."

"Just how many of you are sure that's the answer to our dilemma?" Walker asked the seven men that stood behind Will.

"If we don't turn back, I know I'll die on this mountain." Woodrow was looking at Swit. "I know there's others of ya that thinks the same way. It's time to get off this mountain while we can. We gotta get out of this cold and snow. I know I can find my way back to the Bear."

"I don't doubt that you can, Will," Joe Walker said. "But, I know you can't make it. Think about how hard the trip was coming this way. Going back you'll have no supply of buffalo to draw on, and there isn't a horse in this bunch that could make the trip, not even yours. If by some miracle you made it to the Barren, the Paiutes would end your journey right there. We all want out of this, but our only choice is to cross these mountains and reach California."

"If we all went together, I know we could make it back," Will countered. "Sure, we'd be hungry, but we're hungry now. At least we'd be warm. There's no guarantee that things are any better in California. No one here has been there. All we know is just stories told about how great it is. I'm for goin' somewhere I know is good."

"You know how it works out here in situations like this." Captain Walker was through trying to convert anyone to his way of thinking. "The majority has the say. All of you that think Will has the right idea, speak up."

Swit knew that Woodrow was right about one thing. Many of the men had been thinking exactly what he was saying. It was beginning to look as if they wouldn't make it across, and when death and hopelessness prevailed there was a consuming survival instinct that called out, "Go back and get out while you can."

"That's the dumbest shithead idea I ever heard." Bill Williams turned and headed for his horse. "Hunger's done gnawed a hole in his brain, if he ever had a brain. I'm goin' on with the captain. The rest of ya can do as you damn well like." No one else spoke.

"At least give us a few horses and some powder and lead," Will requested. He was wishing now that he hadn't even started this conversation.

"I'm afraid not," Walker answered. The other men were starting to make camp for the night. "There's no point in me helping you men commit suicide. Henry, take Robert and Woolly and put down those two horses standing over there. I doubt they'll make the morning anyhow. Swit, you and Will get a fire started. It's time we put something besides weak soup in our stomachs."

The lean, tough, dark horse meat brought new enthusiasm for continuing the push through the punishing country. Further exploration had revealed that the group was following along a ridge that separated two giant chasms. On the days that warmed above freezing, small streams would twist their way to the edge of shear rock cliffs, then plunge downward before striking another ledge, collect themselves back into a ribbon of water, flow a short distance, and again fall hundreds of feet until they disappeared into the mist in the valley below.

The men reasoned that if they could only find a way down to the floor of the valley, their predicament would be solved. There wasn't any place that a man could climb down, let alone a horse. The men continued to struggle along the ridge, searching for a way off the mountain. Horses died and were eaten, and yet the passageway out of this conquering country remained hidden.

"Well, it don't look like anyone found a way off this mountain today," Swit said. Will, Swit and Woolly had a fire going, and were preparing a chunk of horsemeat for their evening meal. "Henry and Robert ain't back yet, so maybe they had some luck. I'd sure give quite a little for some of Robert's biscuits and a cup of coffee about now."

The traveling hadn't been any easier, but it seemed to Swit that Woodrow was improved. No one favored the eating of horseflesh, but the addition of meat to their diet had helped Will, and almost everyone else. Henry was the exception. He claimed that his gun had rusted shut from lack of use. Henry hated horsemeat, and Captain Walker was the only one who could get him to eat it.

"Here comes Henry and Robert now," Swit said as he watched them walking toward the camp. "Is that a basket they're carrying between 'em?"

"Aye, 'tis a basket, all right," Woolly answered.

Henry and Robert walked straight to Will's fire and set the basket on the ground. "Robert and me figured that you horse-eating savages just might like a roasted acorn for supper tonight. I believe there's plenty to go around, don't you, Robert?"

"They're big ones too," Robert added.

Will reached into the basket. "Look at this, Swit! I've seen taters that ain't this big."

"Where'd you find acorns around here?" Swit asked. "I can't remember the last time I saw an oak tree."

"It was Robert that gathered these nuts," Henry answered. The other men were arriving at the campfire and starting to roast the acorns in the hot ashes. "We'd split apart some so's we could scout more territory. An Indian was a-hotfootin' it up the trail with this here basket of goods on his back. You know all about Robert and his sneaky ways. Well, the Indian didn't see Robert until he was damn near on him. Scared the ol' boy so bad he run right out from under the basket and scurried off into the rocks. Hard to tell where he was coming from or going to. The trail he was following seemed to run mostly north and south, but one thing's for sure. Somewhere out there are some mighty nice trees popping out these acorns."

Everyone agreed that this particular type of acorn roasted up better than any chestnut they had ever eaten. Zenas Leonard pointed out that maybe men who'd been starved and living off horsemeat for several weeks just might not be capable of making a fair comparison. The fact that an Indian carrying food had passed this close to their camp gave the men renewed hope for their trip to the Pacific.

***

"Look up there ahead." Swit had spotted Captain Walker setting on top of a huge boulder, and looking west through his spyglass. "The captain's got something in his sights."

When they reached the granite slab, the reason for Walker's westward gaze became evident. Before them was a flat, sweeping plain that stretched to the west as far as the eye could see. Looking down, it seemed almost perpendicular, and the height was so great that it caused Swit to catch his balance. They weren't out of the mountain's grasp yet, but they were definitely across. That night the hunters again returned without game, but they had seen fresh deer and bear tracks.

There was less snow, and the countryside was not as rough and rocky as it had been; however, the steep descent forced the men to zigzag their way down out of the mountains. After several days they found a place where they could get the horses down, but they'd have to use ropes to ease the animals and packs over the edge to the hillside below. Before the horses could be lowered off the ridge, one of the hunters walked into camp carrying a small deer on his back. It was the first wild game larger than a rabbit that they had brought back to camp since leaving the Great Salt Lake. Every man received his share of this special kill, and after savoring his morsel he was convinced that they had truly made the crossing, and a land of plenty lay just ahead.

The snow was quickly left behind and replaced with bushes, trees and a few patches of grass. That night the hunters returned with two large deer and a black bear, all fat and prime specimens for eating.

"What kind of a tree would that be?" Swit asked. The men had been discussing what month it was, and while no one was positive, the majority thought it was the last day of October. The territory spreading west from the base of the mountains was crowded with trees. They had seen several unusually large specimens.

"Woolly thinks they're some kind of a redwood," Will answered. The tree Swit was looking at was unlike any tree they'd seen. It was remarkable in its enormity. Not only was it tall, but also big around. "Look back over there, there's another one. I'll tell you what, whatever them big trees are, that one's done outgrowed 'em all."

"Lads, I'd say you've not sighted the master," Woolly added. "Look way yon and to your left. There's the biggest yet. The others look like a wee bit of a thing beside it." Walker had spotted the same tree that Woolly had pointed out, and was leading the way toward it. The men all gathered around the great monarch and marveled at its size. It took eighteen men with their arms extended and holding hands to surround the tree's base.

"This here tree sticks up so high that it strains your neck to see the high branches." Henry was watching Woodrow and Swit. They were stretched out on the ground in order to get a better look up to the top of the tree. "Ain't that right, Robert?"

"It's tall all right. Look how thick this bark is." Robert was examining the tree's bark. It had been darkened and damaged by fire, or maybe a lighting strike. The tree was nevertheless alive, and outside of the wound that had been gouged into its trunk, seemed hardy. Robert was still pondering the tree's age and its ability to withstand fire, or maybe even lighting, when they left the big trees behind.

The group continued to push westward. They traveled almost twenty miles before the trees thinned and gave way to the prairie before them. Deer, elk and bear were plentiful. "I can't believe there's no buffalo." Henry was still skeptical. "Never saw any better buffalo country anywhere, but they're not here. Robert and I have scouted every direction, and it's the same. No buffalo. Not one sign that any ever passed this way."

The strain of just staying alive had lessened considerably for the men; however, travel was still slower than normal. The men and horses had suffered severely while making the crossing. It would take time for them to heal. Attitude seemed to adjust and recover first. The men were relieved to have survived the ordeal through the mountains, and were filled with a sense of accomplishment. Not one man had been lost. Joseph Walker had led them across the Great Basin area west of the big salt lake, and over the Sierra Nevada Mountains. Not many men had traveled through that territory. Fewer still were the ones who arrived and returned to tell about their journey. Captain Walker had the respect of all these independent, freedom-loving men before the start of this expedition. His stature as a leader had only grown.

Part Five:
Alta California

Chapter Twenty-eight

Walker moved his men along a river that rushed down out of the towering mountains behind them. The river's rapids soon gave way to a gentler flow, and Walker eased his men into a rhythm of trapping and traveling. Men and horses both needed time to regain their strength. They'd paid the price required to reach California; now it was time to enjoy the experience. November in California, at least this part of California, was like spring in Missouri—rain showers, warm weather and green grass.

"Well now, I'll tell you what." Woodrow had been trying to get Swit involved in conversation for the last two miles. "I think I'm gonna make California my winter quarters from now on. We ain't got the attention we had when we stayed with the Snake Indians, but you can't beat this for weather. Do you think we could get them same Indian gals to take care of us here?"

"I 'spect so, if you can meet Washakie's price." Swit had been riding along listening to Will and thinking how he was acting more and more like his old self. The hardship suffered crossing the Sierras had somehow changed Will and forced him into a bad decision. Will, and everyone he took with him, would have died trying to go back if Captain Walker hadn't made their leaving impossible. "There's plenty of Indians around here. Why not hire them?"

"Too flighty, ya can't hardly get up to 'em." Will and Swit rounded a turn in the river, and not fifty yards ahead stood five small Indian huts. Captain Walker was already trying to establish some line of communication. Swit counted twenty-five men, women and children. The sudden appearance of twice that many white trappers riding into their midst caused considerable excitement in the little Indian village. Some were running away, searching for a hiding place, while others huddled together by their huts, ready to accept whatever fate awaited them. Two men had come forward to meet with the intruders. They didn't seem to understand sign language, or any of the Indian words that Captain Walker was using. The one thing they had in common with other Indians was the ceremonial custom of smoking and sharing a pipe to demonstrated peace and friendly intentions. Walker soon dispelled the anxiety and successfully achieved a limited exchange of information. The trappers were invited to spend the night. Joe Walker was busy learning all that he could from this first contact with native Californians.

"I guess that there answers my question." Will always spoke slowly. He had watched Captain Walker leave camp with some red cloth and a couple of knives. "Looks like the Captain's traded for five new horses."

"We can always use a few more horses," Swit said. "By my count we lost twenty-four head crossing the mountains—ate seventeen of 'em." Swit didn't say it, but some of those were in better shape than the five new additions.

"I'd say Captain Walker is more interested in sending a message to the natives around here that we're willing to trade than he is in acquiring prime horse flesh." Henry was thinking the same thing as Swit.

Captain Walker continued to follow the same river until it emptied into a stream that was flowing in a northwesterly direction. According to the Indians, this river would deliver them to the Pacific. The night of November 12, 1833, was unforgettable.

"I don't give a damn what you say," George Nidever told Zenas Leonard as he grabbed two rifles and dug around in his stuff, looking for an extra horn of powder. "The whole place is full of 'em, and I think they're gettin' closer. I'm wakin' up the captain."

"I'll tell you again," Leonard said, "we're not in any danger. You've seen 'em before."

"Hell yes, I've seen one or two at a time before. I ain't never seen hundreds comin' in all at once." Nidever headed over to where Joe Walker was sleeping. "If you're so sure everything's okay, tell it to them horses. They're fidgety as a bunch of snakes."

"Captain, we got ourselves some trouble." George carefully tried to coax Walker from his slumber. By now several men were at Captain Walker's camp, and they were as concerned as Nidever about the activity.

"What is it, George?" Walker turned and started to set up. "What's all the ruckus a...? My word, look at that sky. It's alive with falling stars."

"Damn right it's alive," George answered. "They're gettin' closer, too, and there's more of 'em all the time."

"I'm mighty glad you woke me." Walker couldn't take his eyes off the heavens. "I'd hated to have missed this show. There must be thousands. I've heard of star showers, but I've never seen one. There's no need to get upset. You can see that they all burn up."

"I ain't too sure about that," George continued. "I think maybe one or two might have hit the ground back that way. It's got our horses all spooked up."

"You could be right," Walker admitted. "There's bound to be some that'll make it. If you were unlucky enough to be in the exact wrong place, at exactly the wrong time, I guess you could get hit. It's kinda like lightning in that way. I don't know where that's gonna hit either. There's no sense worrying about something you can't control, so just enjoy the show. This is something you'll be able to tell all your grandchildren about."

The Walker expedition continued to follow the river. They knew they were getting closer to the ocean when the tide water pushed up into the normally crystal clear river water, giving it a salty taste. The surrounding countryside was low and swampy, but it was the ever-increasing presence of Indians that troubled Walker. The men and older boys were busy fishing the river. Walker tried to communicate with several of them, but was unsuccessful in his attempts. They weren't threatening, just indifferent about the newcomers passing through their territory. As their numbers grew, so did Walker's concern. He headed southwest, away from the river.

The caravan of trappers was working its way over a range of low mountains or high hills, depending on how you cared to describe the territory. They topped a little rise, and suddenly the vast blue Pacific Ocean spread out before their eyes. Swit knew that he would never forget the sight. Many nights he had gone to sleep thinking about the ocean. It had not prepared him for the enormity and magnitude of the experience.

Caution was Swit's first emotion. A smooth, flat, unbroken sheet of water stretched beyond vision. He'd always respected water, but this was different. Swit had a feeling that if he was to wade out into this body of water, even if it was only up to his knees, it somehow had the power to grab and pull him further and further out into its depth. Viewing something this size was a little frightening. They camped that night by a fresh water spring located on a small point of land that reached out into the sea.

The noise caused Swit to open his eyes. He remembered being stretched out in his bedroll under a cloudy night sky, and thinking how the sounds of the ocean were without letup. Somehow this morning's volume had been stepped up a notch. The sun was barely up, and Robert and Henry were crowded in next to the fire. They were wrapped in blankets to protect themselves from the sharp breeze coming off the water.

"The ocean ain't near as peaceful," Swit announced as he joined the men. "Something musta stirred her up during the night."

"Went to bed calm, woke up in a rage," Henry agreed. "Look at the size of them waves. She speaks right out to ya too, don't she?"

"Oh, would ya look at her, lads," Woolly said as he slipped in next to the fire. "Is she not just grand in all her fury? Ya need to be out there in her middle with not one wee bit a land in sight to really feel her passion."

"I ain't lookin' to know her that well." There had been a lot of conversation about the ocean the night before, but this was Robert's first comment.

"I don't believe I wanna go out to her middle either," Swit said as he looked over at Robert and then asked Woolly. "I guess you crossed her when you came to the States?"

"Aye, that I did, lad," Woolly answered. "It wasn't this ocean, though, it was the Atlantic. One minute she can be as soft and sweet as your mother, the next as wild and tangled as the Scottish highlands. A darlin' and the devil, all wrapped in a wet blanket."

"I made the crossing myself," Henry announced. "'Course, I was wrapped in my momma's arms and got no recollection of the trip. 'Spect I could do it again, if the buffalo was to give out."

"Well now, I'll tell you what, just 'cause there ain't no buffalo here don't mean that there ain't no more." Will had made his way down next to the fire. "We seen enough buffalo over on the Platte to cover every place we've been in California."

"And I guess you'd be the one to drive a few of 'em over them mountains, wouldn't ya?" Henry was sarcastic in his tone.

"That'd be quite a challenge for anyone." Swit knew that Henry's evaluation of Will had suffered after Will's attempted to turn back when they were crossing the Sierras. "Buffalo would already be here if they could make it across the desert and over them mountains. They've been about everywhere else I've been."

Henry looked toward the Pacific. Everyone was silent as they watched the big waves roll over and throw themselves onto the shore. "Would be some sight, though, wouldn't it, Robert? Buffalo grazing off in one direction as far as you could see, and over the other way nothing but the Pacific Ocean."

After breakfast, Captain Walker sent out exploring parties. They were to watch for any unusual activity that might indicate a change in the behavior of the local Indians, and to try and make contact with some of the Spanish/ Mexican settlers.

The Indians that lived along the ocean treated Walker's men in much the same way as the ones they had encountered along the river. They fished and raised large gardens of melons, pumpkins and corn, but showed no interest in communicating with the trappers. There were plenty of signs that the Spanish had been around for years, and Captain Walker concluded that somehow that influence had caused the Indians to reject any overtures he tried to make.

Walker thought it would be best if they made contact with the government authorities as soon as possible. He hoped to obtain official approval for their entering into California, and permission to explore and visit the region. When the trappers returned no one had anything new to report about the Indians, and no Spaniards had been sighted. One group had found the remains of a whale on the beach. They estimated that the big fish was more than ninety feet long. Discussion about how and why the whale ended up on the beach was the main topic of conversation during the evening meal.

"Look again, lad, very carefully." Woolly and Swit were up at first light, and Woolly was pointing out to sea. "Sight yourself midway across't the dune, and slowly look farther and farther out into the water. Her sail, 'tis like a faint line."

"I see it." Swit thought how it was kinda like looking for distant mountains. "It's so small. I thought it would have to be a lot bigger to sail on an ocean. Is it headed our way?"

"Aye, she'll look bigger when she gets in closer," Woolly answered. "Let's get some help. See if we can signal her in."

The expedition had been camped on the beach for three days when Woolly and Swit carried back the news about the sailing ship. Everyone was eager to make contact with men who would venture out upon this great body of water. Two white blankets were fastened together and raised as high into the air as the longest poles they could find would permit. The sailing ship adjusted her course slightly, and it was obvious that she was headed their way. The excitement of her arrival was elevated to a new high when the ship was close enough that the men could see that she was flying the Stars and Stripes.

The *Lagoda* anchored several miles from shore. Her crew immediately lowered a longboat into the water and headed for the beach. Captain Bradshaw was in command of the two hundred and ninety-two ton brig out of Boston. He wondered what type of men these were, and what their business was. His business was to travel the coast of California and trade the tons of supplies and merchandise stowed away in the *Lagoda* for all the cowhides and tallow he could collect.

Usually Captain Bradshaw would put in at one of the several main ports along the coast where his shipping company maintained an agent to handle the task of trading his cargo to the local citizens. Harbors at San Diego, Monterey and San Francisco were all safe ports from November through April. Santa Barbara, San Pedro and San Juan were risky places to drop anchor during the "Season of the Southeastern." It was always best, in unprotected water, to be out at least three miles just in case a violent southeast wind suddenly developed. Those winds could put a ship on shore in no time if you weren't prepared to slip anchor and sail out to sea. More than one captain and crew had found themselves landlocked when they failed to respect nature's harsh breath.

The Spanish called this place along the coast *Año Nuevo*, and Bradshaw knew he was anchored in unprotected water. However, these men may have hides, and dealing in hides was his business.

Swit watched the men in the longboat gradually moving closer. The wind was brisk, and he thought it was intimidating the way a huge swell of water would roll forward until its top finally broke over itself, and the wave crashed upon the beach. At times the little skiff looked to be on top of the wave, and then it would fall out of sight as it dropped into the trough between the swells. He wondered how a boat could move through such a collision of water without being swamped.

"This'll be a grand show, laddie." Woolly pointed toward the incoming craft. "See how the Jack Tars are waiting? In a minute now they'll catch 'em a princely tide."

Swit didn't have time to ask or answer. The sailors started to row with increased fervor until a swell of water seemed to grab the boat from behind. The men began throwing their oars as far out into the ocean as they could, while the officer at the back of the skiff fought with the tiller to keep the craft square with the wave. The longboat was propelled and carried to the beach by the sea. The instant the boat touched the sand the men bailed out and, grabbing the gunwales, they ran it up on the beach. The sailors gathered the oars as they floated in, and then stood ready by the longboat for further orders. Captain Bradshaw and Captain Walker greeted each other.

As soon as it became known that both companies were composed of countrymen a joyous celebration started. Captain Bradshaw immediately signaled his ship, more boats were launched, and the brig fired a cannon salute to honor the meeting. Bradshaw invited everyone to come aboard the *Lagoda* and toast to the coming together of what he called "American's finest progeny." He would not take no for an answer. A few of Walker's men carried an unrelenting fear of exposing themselves to the risk of sea travel, and they elected to stay and tend the camp. Forty-five boarded the longboats and made for the ship.

The skill of the sailors surprised Swit. Two men, one on each side of the bow, held the vessel where it would float when one of the biggest waves pushed up on the beach. The sailors took to their benches with their oars ready. Walker's men climbed on board. Swit maneuvered himself so he could get into the same craft that was to carry Captain Walker. He couldn't see how they would ever be able to break out through the continuous bombardment of waves.

After everyone was onboard, the sailors waited for the next big comber. As soon as the boat had water beneath it, the two stout men on each side of the bow ran her out into the sea until they were up to their armpits in water. The oarsmen reacted with the forward movement and immediately began to scull the longboat out into the next incoming wave. As soon as they were in deeper water, the two sailors pulled themselves up into the boat. It was all accomplished with such coordination and teamwork that they were through the breakers, and rising and falling with the movement of the ocean's waves before Swit could realize how it all happened.

Woodrow and Swit moved around the feast that had been laid out for the trappers. "It's been some time since I seen any bread, butter or cheese. I ain't that high on the salted pork, but I'll tell you what, these sailors know their business when it comes to throwin' a party."

"They're pretty handy when it comes to this boat business too." Swit was watching a man climb through the sail's rigging, high above the deck.

"This here ocean is tossing us around pretty good, and that man is scampering up them ropes like a squirrel would shoot up an elm tree."

"Looks to me like a good old time is in the makin'." Will was helping himself to another drink from the keg that was being passed around between the adventuring men of the sea and the exploring men from the land. "That bunch of free trappers and them sailors over there are already tryin' to outdo one another."

"They might be headed for a good time." Swit pointed to the back of the ship. "But what about Leonard?"

The dusk of evening had settled over the ocean, and Zenas Leonard was hanging out over the rail. Every time the ocean tipped the aft of the ship down, he was offering up to the sea a mixture of cheese, bread and anything else he'd consumed. The man had taken on a facial color that Swit hadn't seen before. Leonard had nothing left to deliver into the water, but he was still trying when Captain Bradshaw had a boat lowered, and Zenas departed for firmer footing. Several toasted his departure, but no one showed any indication of ending the banquet.

When the bright morning sunshine reflected off a calm sea, the soiree was still alive. Some of the sailors and trappers had been forced to call a time out to their participation, but no one had called a halt to the festivities. The men were more alike than they had first thought. After exchanging stories about storms at sea and mountain adventures, the trappers were ready to take to the ocean, and the sailors were headed for the high country.

Both Walker and Bradshaw seemed to enjoy each other's company. Each man joined in the celebration, but at the same time kept a eye on things at hand. Walker watched for any sign of violence from his unpredictable group. He looked to the shore now and then in case the Indians decided to confront the small number of men he had at camp. Bradshaw kept a close watch on the weather. He had no intention of letting a "southeaster" sneak in and catch him unprepared. They both allowed their men to cut the wolf loose.

The men reveled in the camaraderie, so a decision was made to take to the beach where the trappers would lay out a feast of fresh meat for the men who had been at sea for so long. The sailors attacked the bear, deer and elk meat in much the same way the trappers had savored the meal aboard ship. The remainder of the day was spent resting, relaxing and recovering.

"My advice would be to head for Monterey." Captain's Bradshaw and Walker were enjoying the late afternoon sunshine. "If you show the governor your request from the State Department, and he's convinced that your visit is peaceful, you'll have no trouble."

"I hope you're right." Walker had heard that the Spanish were nervous about foreigners coming into their country.

"I guess if I was Spanish I'd be a little concerned about strangers moving in myself." Bradshaw leaned back and gazed out toward his ship. "You know, this is a remarkable place. The Spanish have been here for better than sixty years, and they hardly have more than a foothold. If they didn't have the Indians to do the work around the missions, they'd have starved out long ago. Life is fairly easy here, unless you're a mission Indian. They're more like slaves than converts."

"What about an army?" Walker asked. "They surely have an army to patrol their territory."

"There's not but four presidios in all of California," the naval captain answered. "They're at San Diego, Santa Barbara, Monterey and San Francisco. At one time they had plans for a whole string of forts up and down the coast, but they can't even keep up the four they have. I doubt there's four hundred soldiers in the whole country."

"Are all the Indians as peaceful as they seem to be?" Walker thought that there must be some tribes in this country that wage war on each other.

"Pretty much," Bradshaw answered. "There are some that live in the hills and mountains farther east that will occasionally raid and steal, but they're few and not well armed. Before long, someone's going to throw the Mexican government out and claim a mighty sweet place for themselves. The Russians and British are already moving in from the north. If we intend to make this land our western shore, we need to bring some families here to settle this country. There's a real need for craftsman; these people hardly know how to make anything. That's what makes it possible for me to make a living. Even the simplest items have to be made somewhere else. We sail away with thousands of cowhides and bring back some of them in the form of shoes. Transportation and tariffs make footwear a little expensive around here. My guess is that the Mexicans would welcome anyone that intended to settle in and become productive. Of course, you'd have to swear allegiance to the Mexican government, and join the Catholic Church."

"It does seem to be a land just waiting to be developed." Joe Walker thought how wagons could make the trip down the Barren River, but an easier crossing over the Sierra Nevada Mountains would have to be found

"Cattle ranching must be established pretty well if they have that many hides to trade."

"The missions have some large herds, and there's a few private ranches scattered around." Captain Bradshaw thought that it was time for him to gather up his men and return to his ship. "I'll be headed for Monterey in the morning so his excellency, José Figueroa, can collect the taxes on my trade goods. When you get there, look me up. I'd be pleased to help you deal with the head honcho." The crew of the *Lagoda* was quickly assembled. Joe Walker watched as the sailors from Boston made their way back to the ship. It had been an unusual two days. The men's backgrounds, lifestyles and future plans were as different as night and day, but because they were all Americans meeting in a foreign land, they were connected and willing to stand shoulder to shoulder.

Chapter Twenty-nine

Billy B. imagined that the San Gabriel Mission would be a small chapel supported by a modest community of Spanish/Mexican settlers. The buildings standing in the distance indicated that it was a much larger settlement than Billy had expected. The mission church walls were five feet thick, thirty feet high, and over one hundred fifty feet long, with capped buttresses and high, narrow windows. Unlike other mission churches that Billy had seen, this one was made from stone, brick and mortar instead of adobe, and it lacked the traditional bell tower. The church bells were hung inside six different openings in the wall above the door leading into the sacristy. The main entrance into the church was positioned along one side of the building instead of on the end. From a distance Billy thought that San Gabriel looked more like a fortress than a mission, and he hoped for a peaceful introduction into the new territory.

The other buildings at the mission provided private living quarters for the priests and Indians, a winery and numerous rooms used for dining, storage, food preparation and other workshops. Four huge fire pits with tallow vats used in the production of soap and candles, and several long tannery tanks for turning cowhides into leather, had been constructed within the mission compound. A part of the grounds along one side of the old church had been consecrated as a final resting place. It was obvious that much of the mission had been erected some time ago and was in need of repair.

Large fields of beans, corn, melons, squash, pumpkins, chilies, tomatoes, grapes, herbs, potatoes, peas, onions and olives, including an orchard containing a variety of fruit trees, flourished by using a system of irrigation in the semi-arid farmland surrounding the mission. Beyond the buildings and fields were thousands of acres of grasslands devoted to the production of livestock. The San Gabriel workers cared for twenty-six thousand cattle, fifteen thousand sheep, twenty-four hundred horses and numerous mules, goats and hogs. It took more than one thousand converted Indians, and about fifty clergy, to accomplished the necessary tasks to sustain the community.

The sun was low in the sky when the group from Mexico entered the mission compound. The workday was ending, and more Indians than the new arrivals had ever seen in one bunch were walking in from the fields and gardens. Everything was peaceful, but Juan could not shake the anxiousness he felt.

Maria was busy watching the women carry out their various domestic responsibilities. Some made baskets. Others were weaving cloth or washing a seemingly unending supply of soiled clothes. Children, dirty and without a stitch on, laughed and played games in the courtyard. Dogs ran loose everywhere. It looked as if the workers, priests and Indians were all well versed in self-denial. Any riches generated within the mission were for the advancement of the church, not intended to make life easier for its members.

Most of the men at the mission went to the fields to care for the crops, or to the pastures to supervise the livestock. Horsemen rode in and out on fine-featured, deep-chested horses that moved with a spirited action. They didn't appear to favor any particular color for their horses, but a long flowing mane and tail was popular. Billy was reminded of the little gray mare he'd left with Captain Walker. She had the same small, intelligent-looking head with large eyes and short, alert ears. The gray would have fit in here just fine; he wished he had her with him.

Billy's desire for a peaceful introduction to California had been answered when one of the priests welcomed the caravan and ushered everyone into the mission's large dining hall.

"A hot meal beats a massacre anytime." Hog Eye had watched the large number of Indians moving about and, like Juan, they had his attention. "This many Indians will take some gettin' use to."

"We're not exactly used to eating in this style either." Maria was wiping Mattie's face. Each table setting consisted of a silver bowl, spoon and cup. "I think we'd do better to polish our manners instead of questioning their kindness."

"I'll sure try to do my best." Juan removed his hat and playfully pretended to dust off a spot where Anita could set down. The bench and table extended the entire length of the hall, and they were constructed in a simple, straightforward manner that forecasted strength and not comfort.

"I've never eaten off of no silver dishes before." Cisco watch several Indian women pour some type of soup into the trader's bowls and fill their cups with water. The men with the pack train had been enthusiastically received, and it appeared that the hosts were eager to trade for the merchandise arriving from Santa Fe.

"Don't believe I'm up to this kinda treatment." Billy stroked his mustache before giving Maria a wink. "That old trail dust has faded some of my shine."

"All I'm saying is that someone has put a little time in to feed a motley bunch like us," Maria said. "A little politeness and courtesy would show our appreciation."

Maria had noticed that none of the rooms in the mission had stoves or fireplaces, and all the cooking was done outside in the courtyard. Whenever the Mexico summers were unusually hot she liked to cook outside if the wind wasn't stirring up clouds of dust. It helped keep the house cooler. Apparently California stayed warm most of the year and didn't require much indoor heat. Maria was sure that the meal headed their way had been prepared in the huge pot she'd seen in the middle of the square. Three Indian women had been roasting what looked to her like barley, and then dumping it into the pot. She was impressed with their ability to swirl the grain around in bark baskets with such expertise that the kernels would swell and burst without setting the baskets on fire. It seemed likely that a liquid roasted barley mixture would be the menu for tonight.

The food looked plain, but it was surprisingly tasty. The barley gruel had been enhanced with vegetables, chicken, fish and elk meat. A bowl of wild berries and nuts was passed down the table for the guests to enjoy. Everyone at the mission was gracious in their manners and habits. It was obvious that the priests were uncommonly educated, and they were eager to converse with anyone arriving from outside the confines of the mission.

"Is this your first trip to California?" the friar asked the little group that had accompanied the traders from Santa Fe. He was short, Billy guessed slightly less than five feet, but bulky. A pair of sandals that had seen better days and a worn but clean gray robe was the standard apparel for all the padres at the mission. Billy judged that this man's robe was stretched around a body that must weigh over two hundred pounds. His voice had a quiet, soft quality, and when he spoke, a friendly smile was as much a part of his face as his dark eyes. Billy thought that he looked more Spanish than Mexican.

"We're all newcomers," Billy answered.

"Welcome, I'm Father Carrillo," the priest greeted his visitors. Trading caravans following the trail from Santa Fe were not uncommon at San Gabriel, but this little group that had accompanied the pack train looked more like a family of settlers. That was unusual. "If I can be of any help to you, please ask."

"I'd like to have my little girl baptized," Maria announced immediately. With all the turmoil at the ranch in New Mexico, she had postponed the sacrament.

"We'll take care of that right away." The padre placed his hand on Mattie's head. "Bring her over to the church tonight. You're all welcome to join us."

Billy didn't have a church background. During his formative years things seemed to happened more by chance than choice, but Maria's renewed involvement with the church had caused Billy to make some choices about religion in general, and himself in particular. Maria was committed to living with Christ in her life, but she hadn't insisted that Billy become involved with her beliefs. As far as he could tell, her connection with religion, and his disconnection from it, had little effect on their relationship. Billy was pleased with the changes that the church had brought to Maria's life. It had made both of their lives better. He wanted to learn more.

"Are you going to bed down in them little rooms they offered us at the mission?" Juan asked. Juan, as a matter of course, started his search for a place to spend the night immediately following supper.

"You can sleep with the fleas and bedbugs if you want to," Billy answered. "Myself, I believe I'll stretch out under the stars in my own bedroll. I never cared that much about spendin' my day scratchin'."

The little rooms had looked inviting to Juan. The bunks were made from bull hides that had been stretched and fastened to two walls in a corner of the room while the free end of the hide was supported by a post in the floor. Clean, coarse blankets covered the beds, and Juan saw it as a chance to sleep without trying to mold his body to fit the earth's cushion. "How come you think they got bedbugs and fleas? Everything looked clean and well cared for."

"Clean as you can expect with dirt floors and open windows," Billy answered. "Damp, whitewashed walls and dogs runnin' around everywhere makes a dandy flea farm."

Juan decided that Billy could be right about the fleas. They situated their camp outside the mission compound, where they had a good view of the church. The Suarez girls found their Christening dress and, in spite of Mattie's objections, had put it on her. Billy didn't understand all the hoopla surrounding Maria's determination to have Mattie baptized immediately, but it was obviously important to her. That made it important for him too, but he was unsure as to whether he was suppose to go to the church with them or stay behind. No one had asked if he was coming or told him what to do, so he thought it was probably best to stay put and not risk making a big blunder during the service.

"It looks like everyone but us is headed over to the church." The sun was setting, and Billy could see Maria carrying Mattie, Alonzo, Anita, Lena and the other Suarez children hurrying toward the mission. "Maria said it's called vespers, but I ain't sure what that means."

"Vespers is after sundown," Juan answered. "Mattie's sure cute in that dress. Women folk seem to put a high regard on things like that."

"It seems to me you'd be just as baptized if you didn't have any more on than your all-together," Cisco said. "I guess us heathens know more about cleaning guns than cleaning up to go to church."

"I ain't no heathen," Juan announced. "I been baptized. I'm just saying that dressing up for church is a women's way of showing how important it is to 'em."

"Guess I ain't no heathen either then," Hog Eye stated. "My mammy told me never to forget that I was baptized Reginald Harris. She never said anything about what I was a wearing at the time. I expect it was pretty nice, though. She put a lot of weight on church 'tending."

"I've known a few baptized heathens." Billy B. pulled a little at his mustache.

"It ain't up to you to say who is or who ain't a heathen." Juan regretted his decision to stay at camp. He should have gone to church with the others. His mother had taken him on a regular basis when he was young, and he was troubled some knowing that he had gradually drifted away from his religion. Anita had asked him to go along. He almost did, but when the other men stayed he decided to skip the service.

"I 'spect you're right," Billy admitted. "It ain't up to me to judge what a man is or isn't. I got all I can do tryin' to figure out if what he does or don't do is right or wrong."

Maria was so taken with the inside of the church that she had trouble whispering, and normal speech was impossible. The long, narrow structure was adorned with a treasure of holy images. When she was asked to bring Mattie to the baptistery with its hammered copper font and sterling silver shell, she prayed that Mattie would show her best behavior. The little girl was surprisingly calm during the ceremony. The priest let the holy water slowly run over the top of Mattie's head. Maria thought she was prepared for any move Mattie might make. She wasn't. Mattie carefully wiped the water from her eyes. Then she looked up at the priest and gave him one of her irresistible smiles. Maria couldn't hold back the tears. When Mattie noticed her mother's expression change, she started to cry. The short, stout Father Carrillo maintained a smile, but when Maria looked into his eyes they were bathed in tears.

"I expect the four of you have been setting here discussing the Bible while everyone else attended church." Maria and Anita walked up to the campsite.

"As a matter of fact," Billy answered, "our conversation was of a religious nature. Prayers look to be the standard evenin' entertainment around here."

"Yes, and they'll be the standard again at sunrise," Maria announced.

"I expect the barley soup will be standard around here too." Cisco was particular about what he ate. "Any time you got to start adding water to food, the eats is growing short, or you need to slick 'em up some to get 'em swallowed."

It worked out pretty much the way Cisco had it figured. The barley mixture hit the mission table more than once in a while—it was regular. After an hour of morning worship, everyone stopped at the big pot and collected about three pints of an unseasoned blend to start the day. Around noon, or a little before, they'd hit her again. By this time a little beef or mutton with a few vegetables had been added to the mixture. Following the noon meal it was the custom for everyone to rest until about two in the afternoon. Then they'd go back out and work until five before coming in for the evening. During the hot afternoon, buckets of sweetened vinegar were carried out to the fields so the workers could satisfy their thirst.

Billy B. couldn't think of a time that he'd been thirsty enough to drink vinegar, no matter how sweet. He couldn't complain about the food or the lifestyle offered by the mission. No one went hungry, and it seemed that they were satisfied working and worshiping together. It was the everyday sameness about it that Billy thought needed a boost. He'd heard about a new community called Los Angeles located a few miles west of the mission, and a port twenty miles to the south called San Pedro. Several large, privately owned *ranchos* were scattered around between the sizable land grants held by the church missions. It was a land of temperate climate filled with lush grass and cattle. It made San Pedro the best source of cowhides and beef tallow on the West Coast.

The population at San Gabriel had been eager to acquire some of the Santa Fe traders' goods. The problem was they didn't have much to trade. The bulk of their trade goods consisted of soap, candles, some dried food and a few tanned hides. There was some wine available for trade, but fermented elixirs had a way of being consumed before the traders could exchange the wine for more durable goods in Santa Fe. The trading caravan decided to head for the little village named for the angels. Billy thought it was time they started for Monterey. The group had traveled together long enough that parting was hard. They wished each other good health and fortune. Mattie cried when she saw Jose and his mule start down the trail without her.

Billy was trying to sort out the activities of the last several days. They were moving north along a road call *El Camino Real* that connected the twenty-one missions the Franciscan Priests had established along the western coast of California at about the same time the East Coast was winning its independence from England. If they followed the road north they would eventually come to Monterey.

"Maybe if the traders had headed north with us we would have got a better welcome at Santa Barbara." Juan had adjusted to the large number of Indians living at the California missions, and he had thought that they would get the same friendly reception at Santa Barbara.

"It was a good thing Alonzo was carrying that paper signed by the Santa Fe governor." Billy agreed that their introduction to Santa Barbara lacked hospitality. The mission itself might have welcomed their group, but they had been seized by the army and escorted to the garrison before they reached the mission. "I thought we was sure enough headed for the calaboose. The old presidio wasn't much, was it? I doubt that there's fifty soldiers stationed there. That jail couldn't hold a old woman."

"You ever see so many cattle and horses running loose before?" Cisco asked as he charged into Billy and Juan from behind. "We're not gonna have any trouble starting a herd here. That is, if we can stay out of jail."

"Alonzo has a California land grant and a travel permit in his pocket," Billy reminded Cisco. "When we get to Monterey we'll check in with the governor like they told us to in Santa Barbara. We won't be visitors after that.

Besides, who's gonna throw a cute little girl like Mattie in jail?"

Mattie had worked her way with the soldiers like she seemed to be able to do with about everyone she encountered. A stranger was something Mattie didn't understand, and she was fearless in her pursuit to know everyone and everything. Billy wondered if it was Mattie or the papers that had the most to do with the soldiers letting them go on their way.

"You're right about this bein' good cow country," Billy added. "The problem I see is, what do you do with 'em? There's already way more cows than people. It looks to me like a cow critter ain't worth much more than it's hide. The meat's not even worth cuttin' off the bone. Anybody can kill a beef when they need to. All they ask is that you skin it and leave the hide for the owner. It ain't no crime at all."

"We noticed that too," Juan agreed.

"I don't see why they favor all that barley mush when they got cows all over the place," Cisco added. "Remember the morning that me and Juan went off to help gather cows with the *vaqueros* at San Gabriel?

"Sure." Billy was pleased that Juan and Cisco had taken the initiative to learn all they could from the local horseman.

"Well, they're about as good as any we've seen, and they ride first-rate horses." Juan was sure that most of the *vaqueros* were descendants from a past Indian-Spanish marriage.

"Ever so often they'll go out and round up a bunch of cows. Then they sort off the young, fat bulls and kill 'em." Cisco and Juan had both been surprised by the size of the mission herds. They were much larger than anything they'd seen in Mexico. "As soon as they get the bulls down they skin 'em, fold the hides lengthwise and hang 'em flesh-side out to dry in the sun."

"After they're done with the hides they go after the tallow," Cisco added. "The fat that's just under the skin is kept separate and used to make soap and candles. The rest is rendered down and then poured into bags made by sewing fresh cowhides together."

"They'll tan a few hides to use at the mission, but all the rest, along with the bags of tallow, are either sold or traded," Juan reported.

"What do they do with the meat?" Billy asked.

"Save some for their own use. But there's no market for what they can't eat," Juan answered.

"If it was up to me, fresh meat would hit the table a little more often than it does," Cisco added. "We rode out to their last kill site. You could smell the stench of decaying carcasses long before we got there."

"I'll bet there not a hungry coyote for miles," Juan added.

"I ain't seen that many coyotes around here," Billy noted. "But you can't turn your head without lookin' at a dog. Every settlement, rancho or mission we've passed has been dog heavy. When you two was off with the *vaqueros* I followed one of the mission carts that was chucked plum full of hides and tallow as it made its way down to the harbor at San Pedro. Dogs trailed along behind that cart for half a mile."

"Did you get to go out to one of them sailing ships?" Juan ask.

"No, I didn't," Billy answered. "I watched the sailors bring in the trade goods from the big ship, though."

"What kind of trade goods did they have?" Juan asked.

"All kinds of things. Silk, linen, wool, cotton, dress patterns, cashmere shawls, silk stockings, shoes, boxes of *rebozos* and *serapes* that had come from somewhere in South America, gold and silver lace, hoes and rakes, furniture, window glass, nails, iron pots and kettles. About anything you could think of. I don't believe they make anything in this country."

"You'd think with all the hides they got they'd make their own shoes," Cisco said. "I guess if you got enough hides you can trade for everything you want."

"Once they had everything ashore," Billy continued, "the sailors had to carry it up to the top of a hill overlookin' the beach. That's where all the carts filled with hides and tallow were parked. As soon as a trade was made they unloaded the hides off the cart and then filled it back up again with the trade goods. The Indians drivin' them carts didn't lift a hand. They just set on their haunches until the sailors had the work all done. Then they'd poke the oxen pullin' the cart in the side with a sharp stick and head toward home."

"How'd they get all them hides back out to the ship?" Juan asked.

"Instead of carryin' 'em down the hill they threw 'em over the edge and tried to fly 'em down to the beach below," Billy answered. "Most of 'em made it to the beach, but there was some that only got part way on the first try. After they got all of 'em down on the beach, each sailor would take a hide, balance it on top of his head and carry it out to the boats that they used to get back and forth between the beach and the ship. They took special care to keep the hides dry. Once the boats were loaded, the sailors rowed back out to the ship. I couldn't see how they handled the hides out there, but to me it looked like a long day and short night setup for those men."

Cisco was wondering how many hides it would take to fill up a big ship, and that was exactly what Billy had been thinking when he introduced himself to the trade agent for the company that owned the ship. He was from New York and had been in California for sixteen months. It was obvious that he was enjoying the opportunity to converse in English. Billy tried to learn all he could about the hide business.

"The ship I watched had been sailin' up and down the coast for almost a year tradin' for hides and tallow," Billy B. continued his story. "They take all their hides down to the port at San Diego and store 'em in a hide house next to the harbor. The shippin' company has a crew stationed there to cure out the hides and get 'em ready for the trip back to the tanneries."

"Where's the tanneries at?" Cisco asked.

"New York City," Billy answered.

Juan wasn't sure where New York City was or how Billy gathered all this information, but Billy had a knack of finding out things from complete strangers.

"Each man working at the hide house is responsible for twenty-five hides a day," Billy started again. "At low tide they carry the hides down to the beach and tie 'em there so that when the tide comes back in they'll soak in the sea water. They leave 'em like that for two days to soften and clean as the tide moves in and out. Then the heavy, wet skins are wheelbarrowed back up to the curin' vats. The vat's full of a brine mixture of ocean water and salt, and the hides soak in the vat for another two days. I 'spect that'd pickle 'em pretty good."

"I like the cow business, but I don't think I'd take to handling hides." Cisco had already figured out that the hide business wasn't for him.

"It ain't easy, but that's not all of it." Billy had witnessed a few buffalo hides being prepared for robes, but he had never considered what it would take to handle thousands of cowhides. "Each hide is spread out on the ground, stretched, smoothed and staked down flesh-side up. Then the men trim off any pieces of meat or fat that the skinners had neglected to peel away. This has to all be done by noon, 'cause by that time the sun is cookin' the grease and brine out of the hide, and it's startin' to dry."

"You're not thinking about us getting into the hide-curing business, are you?" Juan was getting a little nervous.

"You never know how things might turn out. A cured hide is probably worth more than a raw one." Billy couldn't see himself or any of his bunch doing that kind of work, but he was enjoying Juan and Cisco's reaction to the information he'd learned from the trade agent. It'll give Juan and Cisco something to talk about on their way to Monterey.

"The next step is to scrape away the grease, pull the stakes and carefully fold the hide double with the hair side out. In mid-afternoon they flip 'em over to dry the other side. Then they stack 'em up at night. If the hide's not completely dry by the next day, they unfold 'em and dry 'em some more. At night, after the hides are good and dry, they're hung over a long pole and beaten with flails to get the dust out. Anyhow, when they got enough hides ready, they pack 'em back on board the ship and sail away."

"Just how many hides does one of them ships hold?" Juan asked.

"A three hundred and sixty ton, three mast schooner like I was watchin' can hold thirty thousand hides."

"That kinda explains all the bleached bones we seen. I believe I'd rather push cows than sail the seas," Cisco said. "I guess after we make Monterey we'll start piling up cowhides."

"I guess so, if we're gonna be in the cow business." Billy first concern was meeting the governor at Monterey. How that went would have a lot to do with their future as ranchers.

Chapter Thirty

Everyone had managed to acquire new moccasins at last summer's rendezvous, but by now the travel had worn away the newness. Henry was handing out pieces of deer hide with Walker's suggestion that everyone should rework their footgear. Swit knew that his moccasins were worn through in a few places, but he thought they'd have to last until they reached a settlement. When Henry showed up with the hide, he announced, "You only got about two steps left in them slippers," and rode away.

Swit was left with a piece of leather in his hand, wondering how to proceed, when Robert took charge. Doing most of the work himself, he soon had Swit's feet rescued. "Do it like that," was all he said before heading over to help Will.

The men had just finished upgrading their foot apparel when the Spaniards arrived. "Well now, I'll tell you what, I kinda like travelin' in new footwear and with Spanish guides." Woodrow was looking down at the results of his first attempt at moccasin construction. Swit Boone and Woolly Wilson were riding along beside him. Captain Walker was in the lead as usual, except this time he was accompanied by eight Spanish *caballeros*.

"Did you know that ol' Robert could whip up a pair of moccasins faster than most squaws?" Will ask.

"I know it now," Swit answered.

"Aye, it was bloody well time for me feet to be covered," Woolly announced. "Robert's right handy when it comes to a wee bit of tailoring."

"Did you save your old Mexican boots?" Woodrow asked. Swit had switched to his moccasins when they were crossing the Sierras.

"I still got 'em," Swit answered. "They're okay when you're horseback, but they ain't built for walking over mountains."

"I'm surely glad that the gray mare survived that terrible mountain crossing." Woolly said. "She seems no worst for the experience, and it's a grand ride when she's under ya."

"Scab handled the crossing without complaint." Swit reached down and gently rubbed his horse's neck while he looked over at the gray mare and pondered Billy's whereabouts. When they parted, Billy had said that he'd see him in the fall or not at all. It looked as if "not at all" was the way things had worked out.

"I learned me a little Mexican the summer I was in Santa Fe, but I couldn't make heads or tails out of what them Spaniards was trying to tell us," Swit said. "Billy could talk it, though."

"Captain Walker must have figured out some of what they said, 'cause we've been ridin' along with 'em, and it sure ain't the trail that Captain Bradshaw laid out for Monterey." Will was looking forward to seeing the California settlement. "Just when is this Billy B. feller due to show up? I 'spect we'll be needin' his help when we meet us some señoritas."

"He's skilled when it comes to señoritas," Swit answered. If he squinted he thought he could make out what looked like a set of ranch buildings in a distant valley. "I'd say we're about to visit our first Californy *rancho*. Ain't that a house and corrals over there?"

"Aye, laddie, it's someone's dwellings for sure," Woolly agreed.

The Spaniards, after attempting to and suffering only limited success at establishing some line of communication with this English-speaking group of invaders, had decided to steer them to the home of John Gilroy. He was the closest English-speaking Mexican citizen that they could think of.

"This is some of the best ranching country I've ever seen." Joseph Walker and John Gilroy drank coffee and watched the sun break the eastern horizon. Gilroy was a handsome man with an easy, pleasant manner. Walker had liked him immediately. He stood almost eye to eye with Walker and looked to be no more than four or five years older. "You know, I've heard stories about the year-round mildness in this country. Is it like this every winter?"

"The seasons here are divided more toward wet and dry than hot and cold," John Gilroy answered. "It can get powder dry at times. We suffered through a severe drought a few years back. Most of the wells and even the spring over at Monterey dried up. Over forty thousand head of horses and cattle died from lack of water. It was bad."

291

"My word, that's a terrible loss." Walker's seasonal clock was set on winter, but looking at the California countryside surrounding him, it seemed more like spring. "When is your dry season?"

"It usually starts around the first of August and lasts through October," John answered. "The country turns brown. Looks like winter, but it's not cold. The rains generally start in November, and things begin to green up again. We can usually plant our wheat and rye in January or February and harvest it in June or July. Last year I started that little gristmill over there. We turned out some pretty good flour, if I say so myself."

Walker watched his men gathered around Gilroy's horse coral. Comparing and discussing horseflesh always seemed to entertain most men—no matter the country or the language. "Do you ever have any trouble with the Mexican government?"

"No more than any other citizen," Gilroy answered. "I became a naturalized Mexican citizen earlier this year. I don't know, sometimes it seems like I'm more Spanish than Scotsman. I was trying to remember the last time I spoke in English. Joseph, I can't tell you how grand it is to have you here. Your coming has been a real lift for Clara. Her father died a few months back, and ever since then she's carried a sadness that's not like her at all."

"I'm sorry to hear about her father." Walker couldn't see how the arrival of this large a group of strangers would pick up the sprit of anyone; however, John Gilroy's wife had been more than gracious welcoming them to California. She did seem to enjoy having them around. "It looks to me like you're about to increase the size of your family." Walker and Gilroy were both looking back toward the house where Maria Clara was busy with the children.

"You're right. She's due in about a month. John Gilroy turned to look toward a nearby hill. "We're praying for a healthy baby. See the three little crosses back over there? Some of our little ones were called back before we hardly got to know 'em."

"How'd someone from Scotland end up living in California?" Walker could see the sadness in John's eyes and decided to try and redirect the conversation.

"It was almost twenty years ago. I was a sailor aboard the *Issac Todd* and working for the Hudson Bay Company. We were at anchor in Monterey Bay. The short of it is, I had an altercation with one of the ship's officers. In my mind, he overstepped his authority, and I knocked him down. Aboard ship it doesn't much matter what's right or wrong if you hit an officer, so me and another man jumped overboard and made for the shore before they had a chance to put the cat across our backs. That's when I became a Gilroy."

Joe Walker didn't say anything. John Gilroy was looking past him toward the horizon. It was as if John hadn't thought or shared the story about this past experience for a long time.

"My given name is John Cameron. My mother's maiden name was Gilroy. Deaf Jimmy and I walked to the San Juan mission, and I told them my name was John Gilroy in case the Hudson Bay Company sent someone looking for me. We made our way over to the little village of San Ysidro. I stayed, and Jimmy headed on north. I never did hear what happened to him."

Walker thought it was likely that Jimmy had been directly involved in whatever had happened on board ship. John hadn't given any details about the so-called altercation; however, Walker saw in John Cameron/Gilroy a man who would stand up to anyone if he thought an injustice was taking place. There was still sadness in his eyes.

"What made you stay when your friend decided to keep on moving?"

"I'd say it was the country and the people," John answered. "It was February, and the place was just beautiful. The folks at the village were the most hospitable and friendly I'd known since leaving Scotland. The community was part of a thirteen thousand acre *rancho* called San Ysidro. The land had been granted to the Ortega family by Spain some time in the past, I'm not sure just when, but I know the Ortega's have been here since the first Spanish explorations. At first I considered trying to make my way back to Scotland, but this place just kept growing on me. I rented some acres from Don Ortega, borrowed some cows, and was soon in the cattle business."

"What do you mean you 'borrowed' some cows?" Walker was confused. No one admitted to borrowing cows. It was the same as saying you stole them. "I never heard of anyone just borrowing cows."

"Me either, till I came here," John answered. "There's nothing much cheaper than a cow in these parts. If you need to start a herd, most ranchers will let you take a few cows and use 'em for a few years. Once you've built up your herd you return the same number of cows back to the ranch that helped you to get started. The missions will even do it for you."

"How did you get in that good with the people here?" Joe asked.

"I learned the language, befriended my neighbors, and fell in love with Maria Clara. Did I mention that she was Don Ortega's daughter?" John Gilroy and Joe Walker both laughed. "Three years later I was baptized Juan Bautista Maria Gilroy, and I asked Mexico City for permission to get married and stay in California. In 1821 Maria Clara de la Asuncion Ortega and I were married at the old San Juan Bautista Mission. We like to have our share of fun in this country. I hope you and your men can stay around here for a spell. I think you'd find it interesting, Joe."

"We'd planned to lay up here and rest for a while, but early next year we have to head back." Walker took a stick and started scratching out a rough map on the ground that traced the route they followed getting to California. "Captain Bonneville is expecting us to be back in the Bear River country next July. I'll need to find an easier pass over the Sierra Nevada Mountains."

"I'm afraid I can't be much help when it comes to mountain passes." John watched Captain Walker sketch rivers and landmarks, some of which he'd never heard of. "I'm not much of a traveler. Never really saw the need; everything I ever really wanted is right here. So now you're on your way to meet with the governor, is that right?"

"It's my intention to cooperate fully with the Mexican government," Walker answered. "I thought if we voluntarily presented ourselves to the authorities and showed them our papers we'd have the best chance of getting permission to stay a while."

"I can't see you having any trouble, but the military can be unpredictable." Gilroy thought about all the changes that had taken place since he'd landed in California. Even then the Spanish system of church missions and military presidios had already started to fade. They had become victims of the fight between the Spanish leaders and the Mexican rebels. The government had been forced to use the largest part of its resources to support the army. This left almost no financial aid for the missions. The expanding mission presence in California was over.

When the Mexicans finally pushed the Spanish out in 1821, the California missions hoped for a return to the days before the rebellion. Instead the decay continued; in fact, it grew worse. There was no government subsidy for the church missions, and almost none for the military presence in California. Instead of renewing financial aid, the new government called upon the missions to help sustain the presidios.

The old missions were still impressive enterprises; however, they were struggling to maintain themselves economically. The latest talk was that within a year the mission lands and property would be taken away from church control and divided between the civilized mission Indians and local Mexican citizens. The priest's authority at the missions would be limited to church matters. John Gilroy believed that the upcoming secularization of the missions would mean that a few appointed Mexican *administradores* would get rich. The Indians and most of the Mexican locals would gain little from the change.

"There's some unrest within the military, especially when visitors are involved," Gilroy continued. "As far as the California government is concerned, Mexico City is worth about as much as bumps on a pickle. By the time we hear about some new law or regulation, they've most likely already changed it. Myself, I'd welcome some neighbors from the States. Some of the ranches have already lost horses and cattle to Indian raids. The army believes that the renegade Indians are getting their firearms and ammunition from the trappers that secretly slip over into California looking to trade for stolen livestock and hides."

"All the Indians we've seen have looked like anything but fighters," Walker said. "Where are these hostile tribes located?"

"They're to the east, back away from the settlements," John answered. "Over the years the Indians that the missions were able to convert have been little more than well-treated slaves. After their conversion to Catholicism they were led to believe that as soon as they developed the skills of agriculture, the mission lands would be theirs. I expect by now they're a little tired of waiting. Most of the Indians that raid are converts that ran away."

John Gilroy believed that more trouble with the Indians was headed his way, and the army was not prepared to protect him. A growing number of dissatisfied Mexicans citizens were already talking about forming their own local governments. California, as he had known it for years, was headed for change, and not that far in the future.

"I'd like to keep you around a little longer, but you seem determined to move on." John liked his new friend. "I have a suggestion for you. A few miles south of here is the mission of San Juan Bautista. I'm sure you'll receive a friendly reception at the mission, and it would be a good place for your men to camp. I think you'd find an easier encounter in Monterey if only three or four of you go over to the presidio. Forty to fifty hardened, well-armed Americans riding into the garrison at Monterey might make the Mexican troops a little nervous."

"I'd say that's good advice," Joe Walker answered. He knew he'd found a new friend in John Gilroy.

They picked up the road that John called *El Camino Real* shortly after leaving the Gilroy ranch, and it led them to the mission settlement. The mission showed its age. It had been established in 1797. Zenas Leonard was trying to determine the number of saved souls at the mission. He estimated that it was somewhere around eight hundred.

Everyone at the mission was friendly and helpful, just as John Gilroy had predicted. They seemed willing to share anything from food to information with their visitors. Captain Walker was given permission to establish a camp on a choice piece of mission land where water, timber and forage was plentiful. The district *Alcalde* provided Walker with a permit that the Mexican government required. All non-citizens now needed to have a passport in their possession when they traveled from district to district.

Joseph Walker and his men followed a road leading to their new campsite. As they rode along, Swit was remembering how they had cut a wagon path from Missouri to Fort Bonneville. All he'd seen in California were two-wheeled carts; wagons were scarce or completely missing.

"You'd be stranded in this country if you didn't own a horse," Swit said.

"I don't know about the ownin', but you'd sure need to know how to ride." Will was surprised at the number of horses he'd seen running loose, dragging a short piece of rope. "It wouldn't be any trick to catch one of those horses with a rope around his neck, but then I guess you'd get hung for stealin' horses."

"They don't call it stealing if you leave a horse behind dragging a rope," Henry explained. "They regard that as a trade."

Swit was considering Henry's latest piece of information. He'd need to be careful when he turned Scab loose to graze. Apparently the Spanish had peculiar notions about horse ownership.

Two *vaqueros* had been instructed at the mission to bring in fresh meat for their quests. Swit was watching the men carry out their assignment. It was obvious that they were up to the task. The leader had dropped his *reata* over the cow's horns while the man following behind had somehow slipped his loop up one of the cow's back legs. He held his rope above her hoof—but not so tight that she couldn't walk, just snug enough so that it didn't fall off. The *vaquero* that controlled the cow's head used himself and his horse as bait to encourage a forward charge. The man holding the leg rope provided incentive by popping her across her hindquarters with a leather quirt. Sometimes they moved forward in short jerks, other times it was an all-out running advance that lasted for a mile or more.

The leader and his horse determined the direction of movement. The vaquero in the best position quickly squelched any attempt by the cow to turn and attack in any other direction. His hand would fairly fly as he dallied his end of the *reata* around a large, flat saddle horn. With the cow secured to his horse, he could pull her back on track and get her headed off in the right direction.

Swit noticed that the cow was fat. Not fat like a bear, but fat using the standards of the longhorn type of cow brute. She had probably run free and wild for years, raising a new addition for the herd every year. But now her udder had shrunk, and she showed no evidence of recently nursing a calf. The cow no longer produced calves for the herd, and because of that she'd laid on a nice layer of body fat. Both good reasons for selecting her for Captain Walker's men.

When the *vaqueros* arrived at camp with their captive, Swit was astonished by the speed and method used by the men to dispatch the less-than-willing hostage. The cow was fighting mad and looking to plant her considerable spread of horns into a horse, man or anything else she could reach. She would never get the chance. The men gradually backed their horses apart, stretching the cow between them. Unable to stand in this position, she fell on her side. She had hardly settled on the ground before her captures had dismounted and, using their knives, opened her jugular veins while the horses maintained their holding position. In less time than it would take to tell about the technique, it was over.

"It seems to me that if we could learn to handle a rope like the men that brought us that cow last night, our meat wouldn't be all shot up." Woodrow thought how masterful the two *vaqueros* had been with their *reatas*.

"That's not as easy as you might think," Swit said. "I did a little of that roping when I was down Santa Fe way. It takes a heap of practice to make that loop land where you want it."

"I didn't notice you complaining about any shot-up game when we was tryin' to get you over them Sierras," Henry said. He hadn't forgotten about Will's attempt to turn back. "How do you like that, Robert? When we came carrying in that basket of acorns we was all chicken. Now, because we can't rope we're just feathers."

"There's no denying they was handy with them ropes," Robert added. He wasn't interested in trying to make Woodrow feel bad about his decision to head back to the Bear River country. It always seemed to him that in the midst of a calamity there was a fine line between being courageous and stupid. About anybody could step over the line.

"Well now, I'll tell ya what, I was just makin' talk." Will turned to face Henry. "I didn't mean anything by it. No matter what you might think of me,

I hold you in high regard. I made a bad call, but I can't change that. I'm just thankful that Captain Walker was there to turn me."

"I'd say we're all indebted to the captain." Swit had wondered how long Will would take Henry's jabs. He thought Will said everything that needed saying. Now it was time to change the conversation back to the *vaqueros*. "I'd sure like to be able to handle cows the way those two can."

"I notice you've dug out your ol' Mexican boots," Will commented. "Are you plainin' to join up with one of them missions? Cause if you are, we better start braidin' you up one of them rawhide ropes."

"Robert could whip one up out of buffalo hide," Henry added. "That shouldn't be no trick at all for an old moccasin builder."

"A little more trick than I know," Robert answered.

"I ain't figuring on joining up with any mission, no how," Swit announced. "One thing, though, if you was to take up the cow-man's life, you sure ain't required to do much walking. The only thing I've seen them *vaqueros* do that wasn't from the back of a horse was when they got down to cut that cow's throat."

"You got that right," Henry concurred. "Saw one yesterday gathering firewood. Looked like he'd rode out, roped a tree and was dragging it home."

"Bet I can guess who had to turn it into kindling," Will added. "If they can't do it horseback I doubt that it gets done regularly.

"They ain't much on walking," Swit said. "But I guess I'm a little that way myself. I'd rather ride than walk."

"I'd rather walk than run," Henry said. "Knew a man one time that claimed he walked everywhere. Wouldn't ride or run. Ain't that right, Robert?"

"He mostly limped after that snake bit him." Robert was more interested in going to Monterey than discussing the merits of riding, walking or running. He'd heard Captain Walker talking about the territorial capital, and now that they had their camp set up he knew the Captain would be heading that way. Not everyone would get to go. Zenas Leonard had said that only a couple of men would be going along, but he didn't know who it would be.

Swit watched as Captain Walker rode out of camp followed by Barrel and Muddle. He'd hoped that he would be chosen for the trip to Monterey, but instead Walker had picked out two individuals that Swit thought to be the most unlikely candidates in the entire bunch.

"I sure didn't figure those two would be the ones that got to go," Robert said.

"Hard to tell what the captain's thinking," Henry declared. "I never knew them two before this trip—still don't."

"I can't say much about 'em one way or the other," Will added.

"They've done their part and made the trip as good as any of us, I guess."

"I never knew a man named Muddle, or Barrel either, for that matter," Henry said "You ever try to talk to 'em?"

"Walked up to 'em once when they was talking to each other." Swit watched Muddle ride off on a plain bay horse that looked like he couldn't carry a man out of sight, but he knew the horse was more than it appeared, because he remembered the horse had looked about the same when they left the Green River country. It was still breaking brush when other better-put-together horses were all done. "I asked 'em if they knew where Captain Walker was, and all I got back was a faraway look from Muddle and a stupid smile from Barrel."

"I know that look," Henry said as a grin took over his face. "You can look 'em both in the eyes and wonder if anybody's home. Outside of each other and the captain, I can't think of ever seeing them two talk to anybody. It beats me why they're even along on this trip, let alone riding off to Monterey with Captain Walker."

"'Cause the captain asked them both times." Robert was disappointed that he wasn't going, but glad that Henry had stopped throwing up the Sierras crossing to Will. Both men were acting more like their old selves. Will's spirit was definitely on the rise, and Henry had never been one to hold a grudge.

Joseph Walker rode along the road to Monterey in as easy and relaxed a manner as he had allowed himself for some time. It was all new country to him, but nothing about it was particularly wild or threatening. The Indians had showed no cause for alarm. The Mexicans he'd encountered had all been friendly and helpful. The reaction of the military was his main unknown. Walker thought he had all the necessary government paperwork to satisfy the governor, and Captain Bradshaw had offered to help smooth the meeting between himself and José Figueroa. The visitors from the States certainly were not presenting themselves as a threat to anyone.

Barrel and Muddle were many things, but it would be hard for anyone to mistake anything they did as menacing. Joe Walker thought about his first encounter with his two companions. He'd been riding around to the various scattered camps at last summer's rendezvous, giving warning about the presence of rabid wolves in the area when he spotted their tent. As he rode in Joe could see that the two loners were in the thick of what appeared to be a loud, animated discussion. The one called Muddle was hopping around on first one foot and then the other while he tried to make his point. Barrel didn't move his bulky body during his part of the conversation, but from time to time his arms were flung around in a thrashing action. Whatever the problem, it was an entertaining and lively controversy that ended suddenly when Walker's approach was detected.

Barrel stood with his arms folded in front of his thick, round body. His face was covered with a wide toothless grin. Muddle had squatted down by the fire and pretended to be busy leveling the coals while he arranged the skillet and coffeepot. He would glance upward at Walker every few minutes, peering out with his right eye from under a hat brim that something or someone had taken a bite out of. Both men were dressed in buckskin that bore the effects of sweat, grease, dirt and smoke from many a fire.

"Greetings," Walker announced himself as soon as he was within hearing distance. "I'm Joe Walker, and I thought I'd drop by and make sure you were aware that we have a pack of rabies infected wolves in the neighborhood. We already have had a couple of men bitten. I just wanted to let you know so you can be extra careful."

Both men gave Walker their full attention while he was talking, but to look into their faces it was hard to determine if any of the information was being absorbed. The vacant facial cast of Barrel made it hard for Joe Walker to maintain a serious expression on his own face, let alone concentrate on the message he was trying to deliver. After completing his notification of possible danger, Walker expected some form of recognition, and hoped for an invitation to share some of the hot coffee that sat ready on the fire next to Muddle. Neither man spoke a word. Having completed his task, Walker was preparing to leave when Muddle decided to break the silence.

"Captain Walker, do you think it's correct for one religious group to force their morals upon the will of all peoples?"

"You just don't get it, Muddle," Barrel said before Joe Walker had a chance to recover from the shock of the question. "We are not a collection of peoples. We are one People—God's creation. He instituted discipline for us to delight in, and it is essential we strive to follow his commandments."

"I've heard all that before." Muddle stood up and started to hop around on one foot before switching to the other. "How is it that you're so infallible? You and only you comprehend exactly what God wishes all of us to do? Don't tell me it's because you have a copy of his good book, and in it all is revealed. You don't even have such a book, and you never did."

"I did until you threw it over into that deep crevasse we encountered coming over the Sierra Nevada Mountains." Barrel punctuated his statements with thrashing arm movements. "It doesn't matter that the book is gone. I've read it through and through several times. I am sure Captain Walker has also read our Lord's words and will validate my findings in this matter." Barrel and Muddle both turned and waited for Joseph Walker to speak.

"I can see weight for both points of view," Walker said as he attempted to dodge the controversy. "It would seem to be more a matter of faith."

"Exactly," Muddle announced before Barrel could grab the initiative, "and faith is precisely the essence of the dilemma. Some individuals sustain their faith by deluding others into believing that they have all the answers. Barrel thinks that the beaver and buffalo will always be plentiful. If he had a little more faith in his eyesight, he would see that the beaver have already thinned considerably since the Europeans developed a fancy for the beaver hat. As soon as they discover the warming quality of buffalo robes, you can expect a similar result."

"Once again you have completely distorted a divine manifestation," Barrel said as he folded his arms. "You can never..."

"Excuse me, men, but did you notice any unusual wolf activity around here lately?" Walker was hoping to change the topic of conversation and determine if his warning about possible rabid wolves was received.

"Barrel shot one yesterday," Muddle answered. "It had hydrophobia. We transported it down to the camp south of us and tried to explain the potential nocturnal danger to anyone sleeping out in the open. They didn't seem to grasp the gravity of our concern."

"And why would they?" Barrel started throwing his arms into the air again. "There you were with a deceased and infected animal cradled in your arms, and at the same time trying to persuade a group of men that it had been the bearer of a contagious disease. One that could cause their death."

"If you would recall Zinke's findings you would know that in order for that animal to infect anyone he would have to deposit his saliva directly into an exposed lesion on that person's anatomy," Muddle answered.

"Can't you see that isn't the point?" Barrel asked. "The point being that those men are..."

Joe Walker missed the remainder of Barrel's commentary. He'd removed himself from the reach of Barrel and Muddle's oratory. It was apparent to him that Muddle and Barrel were aware of much more than their facial expressions indicated. Both men were educated and more prone to reflective thought than their appearance revealed. As entertaining as they were to watch, and interesting to listen to, they still gave special meaning to the saying that "silence is golden."

Walker thought how he had never heard Barrel and Muddle in debate again. He had watched from a distance many times, and could tell from their actions that the discussion was lively. Trips to their camp had produced the same comical expressions and direct, informed answers to almost any question he could put before them, but no animated discourse between the partners.

Walker's meeting with Captain Bradshaw and Governor José Figueroa was friendly and beneficial. He received permission for his group of men to stay until spring. They could travel freely, hunt and kill whatever wild life they needed to sustain themselves. The Mexican government had no problem with the trappers trading in the Spanish settlements, but they would not be permitted to engage in any trapping or trading with the Indians. Any hostile confrontation with any of the locals, Indians included, would result in their immediate removal from the territory. Walker completely and fully explained each detail of the arrangement when he returned to camp, and he was pleased by the way that his men had accepted the conditions of their stay.

Leaders of Spanish society, ordinary Mexicans and Indian laborers visited Walker's camp. The men were invited to attend the local horse races, cockfights, dances, hunting trips, bull and bear encounters, fiestas and rodeos. The interaction seemed to bring enjoyment to everyone involved, and with the California folks, enjoyment and entertainment appeared to rate close to the top on their list of things to get done. Pleasure before business prevailed, and no serious discords had occurred. The men had unexpectedly found themselves in the midst of a rendezvous-like atmosphere, only better— the señoritas were abounding, dazzling and benevolent. Life was good, and no one had broken the agreement.

Governor Figueroa and Captain Bradshaw invited Walker and anyone he wanted to bring along to help them celebrate the New Year. It turned into a two-day affair reminiscent of the gathering that had occurred shortly after they arrived along the coast. The party moved back and forth between boat and land, and 1834 had been ushered in in grand style.

Walker and his men returned to their San Juan Bautista encampment during the first week in January, and the first real trouble developed a few days later when six of their best horses turned up missing. Most of the men were for finding the perpetrators and handing out the appropriate justice. Walker decided that it would be best if they moved the camp farther east. He picked a spot in the San Joaquin River Valley.

Swit, Henry, Robert, Woolly and Will had settled in around the fire, drinking fresh-brewed coffee. Nidever, Craig and Weaver where just beginning to meet the new day. It had been more than two months since the group of exploring trappers had first gazed out upon the Pacific Ocean. They knew their time in California was about over, and they watched Captain Walker and Spook in the distance.

Walker shifted his left leg slightly forward so it was easier to turn in the saddle and get a better view off to his right. His horse made a quick side-step, causing Joe to gather in the bay stallion. The men had named the horse Spook. Walker called him Wink, because he had a habit of flicking his right eyelid; however, it was Joe's opinion that the horse was probably doomed to be called Spook. Scab was living proof that a group of men could hang a tag on a horse and make it stick. Spook thought he saw something move, and switched directions. This time he'd spun so Walker was looking toward Monterey.

"Well, I'll tell you what." Will was saddling his horse. It had taken them three days to reach Monterey from their new campsite. "It looks to me like it would have been a whole lot easier to get these supplies before we moved our camp."

"I'd say Captain Walker thought that moving Crazy Bill and his boys farther away from the settlements needed doing first." Henry answered.

"After we tracked the stolen horses back to the settlements, we knew it was Mexicans and not Indians that took 'em. It was just a matter of time before ol' Bill took vengeance on someone he judged responsible for the theft. He just can't grasp the Spanish concept of horse exchange."

"I don't understand that too well myself." Swit was making Scab ready for the ride into Monterey. "I can see 'em exchanging one horse for another now and then, but two men riding off with a small herd don't seem like no trade to me."

"Captain Walker didn't agree with the local magistrate either," Henry continued. "He just didn't think it was the right place and time to prove that we know stealing when we see it, and if you take what belongs to us you'll pay the price. Leonard said the captain told them Mexican officials that he understood what they meant when they said that six good horses in this country was only worth about sixty dollars. What they needed to understand was that where we come from that don't matter. A horse thief can expect to find himself hanging from a tree. The Mexican government, and their way of thinking, is why Captain Walker refused the governor's land offer."

"Well now," Will said, "I didn't hear about any land offer."

"You would have if you'd been in Monterey for the New Year's party." Henry had forgot that Will missed Bradshaw's gala. "The governor ask Walker to bring fifty families into California. He wanted citizens that were skilled in the crafts and of good reputation. If the captain would lead the settlers, he could pick out any unclaimed seven-mile-square chunk of land that he wanted for his colony. All they had to do was declare allegiance to Mexico. Captain Walker said it was a once in a lifetime chance at great wealth, but he just couldn't accept the Mexican's concept of government."

"Now that's a gift that would be hard to set aside," Will said. "I doubt there's many that would place any principle they got over a piece of real estate that size. Hell, fifty hard-workin' pioneerin' families from the States might be enough to take over this whole country."

"I sure wouldn't mind moving here," Swit announced. "I like the country, and I think I'd like tendin' cows. I don't guess I'd have qualified anyhow, though. I ain't no family, and I got no craft."

"It wouldn't be that big a trick around here for you to get to be a family," Henry added. "I been watching the way the young señoritas eyeball you and ol' Robert. Captain Walker would only need to haul back forty-eight more households if he decided to build a town."

"He better get forty-nine," Robert announced. "I'm ready to head back to the wilds. Enough is enough."

Robert was geared to leave, but he had to admit that the Alta California females were hard to resist. The one thing that all the ladies he'd observed had in common was the attention they gave to their appearance. It didn't seem to matter if they were born with pure Castilian Spanish, fair-skinned bloodlines and great wealth or embodied a darker complexion that was common when the Spanish blood was mixed with that of the native Indians and they only had meager resources. Either way, each woman displayed herself in the very best accessories she could manage.

Their gowns were made from calico, crepe and silk. They were cut with short sleeves, low-neck lines and loose around the waist. Shoes were made from kid or satin, and sashes or belts from bright colored cloth. A necklace and earrings were popular items of jewelry, and when necessary she'd use a *rebozo* to cover her head and shoulders.

They usually allowed their naturally colored dark brown to ink-black hair to flow free if it wasn't worn in braids. Señoras were inclined to arrange their hair on top their heads and hold it in place with combs made from a colorful tortoise shell or horn material, depending upon her circumstances. The fairer skinned ladies from the more wealthy Castilian families could be seen protecting their complexions by wearing a wide brimmed hat when they were horseback, and using parasols when they were out walking in the sun. Robert soon learned that California gals could make themselves especially inviting if you were selected for their extraordinary focus.

He didn't understand why he'd been singled out to received Josefa's attention. Somehow she'd managed to become acquainted with Henry, and then she got Henry to make the introduction. Robert liked the throaty way she rolled her words, especially when she called him her Roberto. It was about the only word that he could easily understand. Josefa wasn't from a pure Castilian family. Her mother was the result of an Indian's love for a trapper, and her father was descended from a Spaniard that had been sent to serve in the army. It seemed as if Josefa knew what he was thinking. He couldn't deny that he liked being with her.

Robert felt special when she took him to her parent's house. They treated him respectfully and seemed pleased that she had invited him into their home. Josefa and her parents used the few English words they knew, and he'd picked up a few Spanish words, but still it was hard for him to stay connected to the conversation. At night, when he was awake and thinking about how and where their relationship was going, he was surprised how much he had learned about Josefa and her family without the benefit of a common language. It was Robert's first experience with female intimacy—scary, exciting and confusing.

He guessed he never would understand why everything changed so fast, and without notice. He thought about it a lot, but no answer ever popped forth. She just turned off the allure. It was probably something he said, or maybe didn't say. Whatever it was, it had been plain enough that their time together was over. When Robert looked toward Monterey he could see Josefa's house.

The community of Monterey had grown up around the presidio square because it was the safest spot to live in the early days. Apparently no one, past or present, was concerned about the capital city developing in a planned and structured fashion. There were no streets, and the only fences had been erected to protect small gardens from any livestock that happened to drift into town. The one hundred or more houses that defined the community had been placed at random around the presidio. The houses were almost all one-story affairs constructed from adobe bricks. They usually consisted of two or three rooms, dirt floors, windows without glass, and had only one door. It opened, and was generally left that way, into a common room that was used by all members of the household.

A modest house would have one or two beds, a couple chairs and a table. Usually there was a looking glass, a crucifix and several small paintings hanging from the walls that represented some church martyr or miracle. All the cooking was done in a small outdoor kitchen, so chimneys and fireplaces were absent. The exteriors of most of the homes were whitewashed. The panorama of white houses with their red-tiled roofs casually sprinkled around over the green grass that surrounded the Monterey Mission and presidio was striking.

"I'd just as soon we'd get our supplies and get going," Swit said. "I'm not looking forward to crossing those mountains again, but I'll be glad to get it over."

"You know, young Boone, I believe I'm right with you on that one," Henry agreed. "It's good enough country, but without buffalo it's a dry well. Robert says that oceans and buffalo just don't hook together. Could be that he's right."

The men had experienced a land and culture that most Americans had only heard about. The trip back to the Bear River was fast approaching, and they all knew that the challenge of the Sierra Nevada Mountains would again have to be met. No one had forgotten the trials of that mountain range or would soon forget the ease of life in this western Mexican territory. Captain Walker could sense a restlessness developing in his men.

Chapter Thirty-one

Maria kept a good hold on Mattie. They were standing at the top of a steep hill overlooking Monterey Bay, watching a ship anchored in the harbor run up it's full complement of flags and pendants before firing a cannon salute. Billy thought that all the hullabaloo probably had something to do with one of the religious festivals that the Catholic Church always seemed to be getting ready for, rejoicing in, or bringing to a close.

When Billy B. and his bunch reached Monterey it appeared that the merriment following the wedding ceremony that had taken place that morning was primed to go on for several days. Billy had heard about wedding fiestas that lasted for a week. Guests would come, go and then return again as the party continued. It seemed that no one received a formal invitation—it was a community celebration to be enjoyed by all. Close family members and special guests were sometimes asked to stay with the parents of the bride, but it was commonly accepted that everyone was invited to commemorate the occasion by attending numerous outdoor festivities.

Alonzo and Billy went directly to the governor's palace. Governor Jose Figueroa was absent. Like almost everyone else, he was still attending the wedding of Don Pablo Bandini's oldest daughter, Luisa, to Carter Tupper Remington. Luisa was barely fourteen years old, and fifteen years younger than Carter.

Carter Remington had eagerly sailed to California three years earlier to become a trading agent for a Philadelphia hide company. Hard work and insightful business decisions helped establish him as an unparalleled dealer in cowhides and beef tallow. Carter realized the potential rewards that resided in this most agreeable country, and he decided to make it his home. He joined the church, became a citizen of Mexico and wooed the young Luisa, a daughter of one of the most prominent men in the territory. In matters of the heart, age difference was of little concern. Don Pablo recognized that having Carter as a son-in-law would bring a needed degree of business expertise into the family. The match was quickly made and agreed to by all parties.

When Billy and Alonzo headed for the governor's palace, Hog Eye and Cisco rode toward a large two-story house that set at the edge of thousands of acres of lush green pasture land.

The second-story veranda offered a view of the Pacific Ocean and part of the community of Monterey. A large rather flat area covering several acres in front of the house had been prepared as a site for entertaining the wedding guests. A blend of violin and guitar music filled the air. "You ever see anything like this before?" Hog Eye asked.

"I always thought Don Carlos had a big house." Cisco was impressed. "I sure do like this country. It don't look like anybody stayed home today, does it?"

Cisco and Hog Eye joined a crowd that had gathered along both sides of a runway that extended one hundred to maybe one hundred and twenty yards across the flat. Starting at one end of the strip a horse and rider would race toward the other end. About midway down the path the rider would swing himself off to one side of his horse and reach down to the ground. The object was to grab the head of a rooster that was buried up to its neck in sand, and pull him loose from his confinement. Success was cheered and applauded. Failure brought forth laughter, and should the rider or his horse fall, pain and the possibility of serious injury.

"They like to bet on every rider," Hog Eye observed. He watched the next contestant pull himself back up in the saddle with a chicken in his hand. There was cheering, and the guests were busy collecting or paying off their wagers. "That old gentleman over there just took off his jacket and handed it to that lady. Musta lost it in the chicken jerk."

"These people would bet the buttons off their clothes." Cisco watched a *vaquero* collect a kiss from one of the señoritas. The crowd was beginning to separate and move away from the runway. "It looks like the game's over. They must of run out of either chickens or riders. Let's head over toward the music. It looks like they're about ready for some fancy footwork. Do you know how to dance?"

"I ain't heard anything yet I can't dance to." Hog Eye surveyed the area and watched the people begin to gather.

A space large enough to hold several hundred people had been marked off in a manner that offered some protection from the sun and a shield against the wind. Three sides of a grass-carpeted quadrant had been enclosed with a heavy white cotton fabric hanging from a makeshift pole framework. The grass was flattened, so Hog Eye concluded that this was not the first group to enter the enclosure and celebrate the recent nuptials.

Ladies were entering the courtyard and seating themselves around the perimeter of the cloth-walled ballroom. Back in one corner a group of five musicians continued to play their instruments. As usual, Hog Eye thought, the *caballero's* remained astride their steeds that were lively and brightly dressed for the occasion. They milled around in front of the open side, jockeying to get and keep the best position for viewing the females and festivities inside.

"I sure do like that music," Hog Eye commented. "It kinda stirs your blood, don't it?"

"I do believe I'm stirred more by what I see than what I'm hearing," Cisco answered. "There's some mighty fine-looking ladies in there just waiting to be twirled and shuffled. What do ya say we go over where we can get a better look at 'em?"

"I don't know," Hog Eye answered as he looked around. Guests were coming now from about every direction, and they all appeared to have dressed themselves as best as they could. "The way we're dressed we're gonna stick out like an elk wearing a corset. They're all in their finest duds and got their horses all spiffed up. Maria's seen that we ain't let go entirely on this trip, but I'll tell you it's been a while since this shirt was clean. My horse is not exactly in his parade posture, either. I'd hate to get off to a bad start in this country. Some of these people might be our new neighbors."

"Ah, come on," Cisco encouraged Hog Eye. "My papa used to always say that a good woman loves to smell horse sweat on a man."

"Well, if that's true," Hog Eye reined his horse toward the dance floor, "we're sure enough qualified to have ourselves some time. That is, if them's all good women in there. What'd he have to say about wearing a boot with a floppy sole?"

"That won't hurt a thing," Cisco answered. "It'll help you to keep time with the music."

The celebration inside was just beginning to start as Cisco and Hog Eye rode forward. The sound of guitars continued to fill the air. It did feel like fun times were coming. A dignified appearing older man that was addressed as *El Tecolero* was the master of ceremonies. In a most graceful manner he would approach each seated lady and then perform a few dance steps as he held out his hand to her. She would rise, take his hand, and they would move to the center of the *sala*. In time with the strumming guitars, the newly introduced lady would demonstrate a few delicate steps of her own before returning to her seat.

The introductions continued until all the ladies were called out. The men on their horses continued to shift positions. Cisco was right in the middle of all the jostling. Hog Eye stayed more off to one side. No one seemed the least upset that their dress and preparation was substandard. They had been recognized as new to the territory, welcomed and introduced to many of the men around them. These were by their very nature a gracious people, Hog Eye thought.

The dances varied. Some formed in lines, others in circles. *El Tecolero* was in charge and directed everything connected with the ball. Special verses were recited to enhanced some of the dance numbers, while others brought forth singing from the crowd. One dance, called the *fandango*, was performed by one man, and one woman on a small makeshift wood floor to the accompaniment of castanets. Hog Eye was mesmerized watching the man execute a series of graceful movements with heel tapping steps that moved him in circles around the almost stationary and yet alluring turns of the woman—all in cadence with the music.

A woman danced the bamba. Three handkerchiefs that had two of their opposite corners tied together were laid out on the floor like brightly colored circles. The unaccompanied female, with a tumbler of water balanced on her head, danced around the floor in rhythm with the music. Using her feet, along with incredible dexterity, she picked up and concealed all three handkerchiefs, and then continuing her smooth and elegant choreography returned the handkerchiefs to the floor. All without spilling the water. Having concluded her magic, she received uproarious applause as *El Tecolero* escorted her back to where her friends were gathered.

A tradition that grabbed Cisco's attention was one that they flourished upon the most graceful female dancers. As an acknowledgment of their talent, the men would place their *sombreros*, one on top of the other, upon her head until she could no longer dance and balance her collection. She then retired to her seat, and the hats would be reclaimed by their owners and redeemed with a gift of coins, each paying what he pleased and could afford.

"I got me one spotted." Cisco had found what he was looking for, so it was time to make his move. "Let's get to the dancing."

Cisco and Hog Eye had been watching the other horsemen dismount, remove their spurs and, with their *sombrero* in hand, walk inside and select a partner. After finishing the dance and returning the lady to her place, some stayed for future sashays while others retreated back to their horses.

"I believe I'll hold in reserve for a spell." Hog Eye had no reason for concern, but he wanted to be sure that his asking one of these Spanish ladies to dance wouldn't trigger a skirmish. "I might not be the dancer I thought I was. I'm gonna need just a little bit more time studying. It wouldn't do to embarrass one of these lovelies."

"It ain't that much different than back home," Cisco said as he swung down. "Here, hold my horse. I like the looks of that big ol' gal over there, and I plan to be ready the next time she sits down." Cisco slapped his hat against the lower part of his leg, and as miles of trail dust departed his garments, he entered the arena.

Cisco was only a few steps away from his target when a Spaniard flashed by him on a showy horse. He stopped in front of the girl that Cisco had picked out. He reached out with a bottle and poured a liquid on the ground at her feet. Cisco had watched many men come and leave the dancing area, but this was the first time he'd seen one ride his horse up to the lady of his choice. The rider had his horse prancing in front of the tall, pretty girl.

From the way the Spaniard acted, Cisco thought that somehow the man must be paying the girl a great honor, but looking around it was evident that there were more than a few annoyed by the rider's attempt to win her favor. *El Tecolero* for sure wasn't pleased, but it was hard to tell what the girl thought about the whole affair.

Cisco felt inside his hat and took a small hatpin that had belonged to his mother from under the hatband. He always carried the pin with him. It was the only thing he had that was hers. Cisco moved closer to the girl, along the left side of the horse. He carried his hat in his right hand, concealing the pin he had in the palm of his hand. He could tell that the liquid sprinkled on the ground was some type of wine. It had a pleasing aroma. Extending his left hand in a request for her to honor him for the next dance, he made a big sweeping motion with his hat, and then performed the very best bow that he could muster.

The crowd that was gathered in the vicinity seemed to approve Cisco's invitation. The horseman carelessly swung his horse to his left in an attempt to knock Cisco down, and probably would have caused the girl to be brushed backward out of her chair had Cisco not stepped between the girl and the horse. He reached out with his right hand to shield himself and the girl from the horse's chest. With what looked like a gentle touch of his hat, Cisco caught the horse in the shoulder with the sharp end of the old hat pin. Before the other men that were standing and watching the show could react to the danger they saw developing, the horse felt the pain and in one motion jumped sideways and whirled away from Cisco and the young lady.

Hog Eye couldn't see Cisco. He could still see the horse and rider, but a crowd had gathered around the far end that made it difficult to tell what was happening. He'd almost been knocked over when the rider spurred his horse through the opening. Everyone outside was trying to gain a better position to view the action that they knew was coming. It seemed to Hog Eye that the general feeling expressed near him was that the man's style was a bit wild and reckless, although it had been done before. In general the younger men were encouraging the change of protocol, while the older ones considered the move dangerous and beneath the dignity of better bred Spaniards.

El Tecolero had a hold of the horse's bridle. The rider was off his horse and moving toward the girl. Cisco was watching the advancing rider, now turned walker, as he approached. Trouble was on its way, but just what kind wasn't plain yet. There was no music to be heard. The crowd was watching the episode reveal itself. Without taking his eyes off the man, Cisco placed the pin back under the hatband and dropped the hat to the ground. He was prepared to defend himself. His heart was beating so fast he thought it might explode when he felt the touch of her hand on his arm.

"I don't know who you think you are," the man said as he stopped to face Cisco. "This will be my danc…" was all Cisco would hear. The men watching hadn't been able to react in time to prevent the horse from injuring the girl, but they stopped the rider in mid-sentence. The instant the girl laid her hand on Cisco's arm they encircled the aggressor, and he and his horse disappeared from sight. Before Cisco could fully realize that the danger had passed, music again fill the air, and the girl standing beside him with her hand still resting on his arm was ready to dance.

"What's all the commotion about?" Billy asked as he, Anita, Juan, Alonzo and Maria joined Hog Eye.

"That fellow rode his horse in the dance hall," Hog Eye answered. "I couldn't see much, but some didn't take it too good. Where's everybody been? We thought you'd be along before now."

"We had trouble findin' the governor," Billy answered. "Found him up at the big house. As soon as we told him that Don Carlos sent us, and Alonzo showed him the Mexican grant, we was welcomed and invited to join in on all the shenanigans."

"You could have pointed out that we needed to make ourselves a little more presentable," Maria suggested. "We couldn't match the way they're dressed, but we could have cleaned up some."

"I tried to make that very point," Billy answered. "They insisted that it was of no importance. Don Pablo said he wanted to meet everyone right away. The Bandini clan and Don Carlos must have hit it off, 'cause as soon as Alonzo explained who he was we got treated like family. Luisa had tears in her eyes when Alonzo told how his dad was killed. Carter Remington said he'd like to talk with me when things settle down some. They almost begged us to head on over to the dance."

"They'll have to meet the children later," Maria stated. "Lena stayed with them back at camp."

"Did ya find out where the ranch is located?" Hog Eye asked.

"East of here somewhere," Billy answered. "Governor Figueroa said he'd send out a couple of soldiers to show us the way. It sounds like Don Carlos has everything pretty much all lined out. Don Pablo even offered to lend us some cows to get started. It feels like it's too good to be true."

"Does it have a house on it?" Maria asked.

"By golly, I never thought to ask," Billy answered. "In fact, I didn't ask much about it at all. Guess I just figured we'd find out when we got there."

"Did anyone say how big a *rancho* we've got?" Juan wanted to know.

"Our grant says eleven leagues," Alonzo answered. "One for crop irrigation, four for dry land farming, and the other six leagues are grassland."

"Governor Figueroa did say that we don't have to pay any taxes for five years," Billy added, hoping that his introduction of the tax business would turn the thinking away from the size of the ranch. He had no idea how much ground it took to make a league.

"What'd you do with Cisco?" Anita asked. "He wouldn't miss this if he was back home."

"Take a look for yourself." Maria motioned toward the dancers. Cisco was in the process of placing his *sombrero* on the head of a girl that had captured the attention of many with her looks and demeanor. "Why would he stick that dirty old hat on that girl's head?" She barely got the words out before another man placed his hat on top of Cisco's.

313

"Pretty girl," Juan said. But after Anita poked him in the ribs, he followed up with, "Kinda tall, though."

Billy watched as the Don Pablo's family, with all their guests, arrived at the ball. These were obviously some of the most influential people in the territory. Hog Eye noticed that after they arrived there was no further talk about riding horses into the dance. The new Californian's attire made them stand out in the crowd, but as far as Maria could tell, their trail-worn condition didn't dampen their reception. They were all treated with respect and graciously welcomed by everyone, from the most powerful government official to the least of the Indian servants. Cisco kept expecting to encounter the invading rider, but he never saw him again. Billy and Maria were introduced to so many people that soon all the names became muddled, and they couldn't remember who was who.

"It was sure some show, wasn't it?" Billy and Maria prepared to settle down and get what sleep they could before the fast-approaching new day arrived. "That old Don Pablo is some stepper, ain't he? He can sure turn a fandango. Did you get the deal about breakin' them eggs on his head?"

"Billy, I swear," Maria said as she laughed. "Sometimes I think you miss half of what's going on. They wheren't whole eggs. They're eggshells filled with cologne. It's just a way that a woman can pay a compliment to a man and have a little fun in the process."

"I guess I never had enough of them female compliments to know one when I see it." Billy brushed his mustache with his thumb and first finger, then winked at Maria.

"I'll try and remember to break an egg or two over your head every now and then so you'll get the feel for it," Maria answered. "It wouldn't do to have Mattie grow up thinking her papa was neglected."

"It seemed to me like the trick was to sneak up on Don Pablo, knock off his *sombrero* with one hand, plant the egg on his head with the other, and then disappeared into the crowd before he could tell who did what," Billy said. "When that gold spangled juice started drippin' down on his jacket, he didn't look like he felt all that favored."

"That was his niece, and he laughed with everyone else when he found out who slipped up on him when he wasn't looking," Maria added.

"Don't think his horse cared much for it either," Billy said. "He sure shied away when Don Pablo tried to get on him."

"There's some men you can compliment and some you can't." Maria was on the blankets. "Then there's them that wouldn't know a compliment if it hit 'em on the head. It sounds like we're in for another big day tomorrow."

"I'll say," Billy agreed. "I never heard of a bull and a bear fightin' each other, but I guess that's what they got planned. I heard somethin' today that I wasn't sure how to react to. That ship's cap'n, Bradshaw I think his name is, asked the governor if it was true that Cap'n Walker's men had left California."

"You always said that he was coming to California." Maria sat back up. "Did you hear anything else?"

"Not much," Billy answered. "The governor told him that his latest information had the cap'n headin' east toward the Sierras. I never let on like I knew who they was talkin' about, and they never asked me nothin'. They might not even thought I heard the conversation. Don Pablo and Carter Remington were standing there too, and I was listening to Carter tell about the hide business when I heard Walker's name."

"Did it seem like they were glad to see him go?" Maria asked.

"Hard to tell," Billy answered. "Maybe I can find out more tomorrow.

Billy heard the *vaqueros* ride in. It was still dark, and Billy couldn't hear the conversation between the men clear enough to understand what was said, but it was apparent that Juan and Cisco had been awaiting their arrival. The two mounted their horses quickly, and they all rode off in the direction of the coming dawn.

"Where was them two headed?" Billy asked Hog Eye when he arrived at the cold campfire and started to stir the coals.

"Going on a bear hunt," Hog Eye answered. "That's what they told me. Said they'd meet us at the fight. You ever see a bear fight a bull before?"

"Not me." Billy watched Maria and Mattie stir beneath the blankets. "Didn't even know they had such things. How 'bout you?"

"Same way," Hog Eye answered. "Neither critter would be fun to run up against, but I'd say the bear would have the advantage."

"You think so?" Billy commented. "A mean old bull that's pretty much done as he pleased for years ain't likely to put up with any bear he runs up against. The young bulls come around and test them old bulls every year. They gotta stay lean and mean. All I ever seen a bear do is eat and get fat for winter."

"They ain't got no winter here." Hog Eye set the coffeepot on the fire. "These bears probably eat the year around. Seems like we can't agree on who's gonna win. Everyone around here likes to bet, so I 'spect that's why they fight 'em. Where's this here fight suppose to take place at anyhow?"

"Back that way somewhere." Billy pointed east into the hills. "We're ridin' over there this mornin'. Don Pablo said he'd send us a guide. We're gonna have a picnic when we get there."

It didn't take long to reach the corrals. Don Pablo's youngest son had been sent to show the newcomers the way to the arena. He was feeling especially proud and important to have been chosen for the assignment. The boy was practicing the art of Spanish graciousness and demonstrating his riding ability as he led the group away from the settlement and back to where a set of corrals had been erected on the Bandini *rancho*.

Billy noticed that all of the *ranchos* were named. This one was called *El Rancho de las Golondrinos*, "The Ranch of the Deserters." He thought there must be a story there, but decided not to ask until he knew more about the family. He tried to estimate the age difference between Alonzo and their young leader. They were probably about the same age. It was obvious that their Spanish guide had spent much of his time horseback. Maria watched as the young horseman drew admiring glances from the Suarez children. The interest was not one-sided.

Young Bandini was anxious to make the acquaintance of a group that was more his age, and from Mexico. It was a place he had studied about and one day hoped he could visit. The children were soon all huddled together, sharing experiences. The boy told why he'd been picked to guide the visitors. He had recently passed the test of *los silvestre coballos*. Using only a lasso, he had captured a wild horse, mounted him and ridden the horse until it was exhausted and could no longer buck or run. It was his rite of passage from boy to man. A dangerous undertaking, Maria thought. She wondered how many young boys died or received injuries that they carried for life after trying to prove their manhood. The young Suarez girls were attentive to the confident young man, and it reminded Maria of the first time she watched Billy ride into Santa Fe.

Off to one side was a corral that was different from the others. It wasn't exactly round, but it was constructed so it didn't have any square corners. The enclosure was built out of heavy timbers with sides higher than in the other pens. A large platform about five feet off the ground had been erected a couple of feet back from and along one side of the corral. The largest longhorn bull that Billy had ever seen looked out through the timbers.

The prisoner was not happy. In a flash he whirled to face any new

316

movement or sound that his senses detected. If a passing horseman or playing child was perceived as being too close he would paw at the ground with first one forefoot and then the other. Dust and clods were flung up over his back to mix with the saliva he tossed in the air as he swung his huge head. A warning bellow or snort would send a message to the intruder. If ignored, he would charge the corral fence that separated him from his intended victim. The fierce collision of animal and wood barrier would rattle the cage, serving up a notice to come no closer.

The picnic was to be held under the shade of a cluster of oak trees down by the stream. Music and the noise of people having fun filtered out to meet the new arrivals. As Billy rode closer he watched the crowd. He thought about how in this country a man that lacked a certain degree of expertise with horses was considered to be almost useless, and an individual without musical talent or the capacity to enjoy a celebration less than human.

"They sure enough know how to throw a picnic." Hog Eye, Anita, Lena and the Billy B. Alexander family rested under the shade of a tree. The Suarez children had already made new friends and were with some of the Bandini family down by the stream. The youngest girl kept running back and checking with Maria about the right and wrong of their activities.

"Looks like it's about nap time," Billy said.

"These people gotta sleep sometime," Maria answered. "They've been at this wedding fiesta business since before we got here, and they haven't shown any sign of breaking it off yet."

"They do like to play," Billy added. "I always heard life was easy in California, but you know this much partyin' can get to be like work. The Bandinis sure seem like a nice family. Don Pablo said that anytime we're ready to head on over to our place he'll send someone along to point the way. Part of their *rancho* must not be to far away from ours. He said if we find any of his cows on our place we was to keep 'em until we get our herd established."

"How do we know if they're his cows?" Maria asked.

"All livestock's got to be branded in this country," Billy answered. "If you notice, about everything around here is carryin' a brand 'cept our horses. Besides namin' our *rancho*, I guess we'll need to figure us out a brand."

"I hope you're right about the Bandini family being our neighbors," Maria said. "Doña Rosana seems like a special person. She offered to help us any way she can. I know she's busy taking care of her houseguests, but she said they'd be happy to care for the young children until we're settled in. Juan and

Cisco are making new friends, and the children all seem happy."

"Talking of Juan and Cisco," Hog Eye interrupted as he pointed to the east, "ain't that them with that bunch coming over the hill?"

Six riders were coming into sight. They surrounded a not very happy, large, adult male grizzly bear. He was dragging a stout piece of chain several feet long that was attached to one of his hind feet with a heavy leather strap. The other end of the chain was tied to a *reata* that was being handled by one of the *vaqueros*. Billy watched as the group moved toward the big corral.

It was an orchestrated game of bait and chase. One rider would move in close to the bear on a line directly between the bear and the designated corral. As soon as the bear made a charge or run at the rider, he would leap away and flee toward the corral, using all the speed his horse could gather in order to escape the claws of the furious beast. The rider controlling the rope would pull the bear up short if it looked like he was about to capture the bait. If the bear then turned on the rope handler and his horse, two or more *vaqueros* would have their *reatas* around the confused animal's fore feet, head, or all three quicker than Billy thought possible. Before the bear could tear away these new constraints, a fresh bait awaited his charge, and he moved the group closer to where the bull waited.

"There goes another bunch." Billy saw the riders leave the trees and head for the corral. Ladies were beginning to collect blankets to set on, and parasols to protect themselves from the late afternoon sun. They started moving toward the platform. The new group of riders, using a bait-here-and-run-there diversion, gradually entered the arena. Before the bull was able to inflict any injury upon man or horse, the *vaqueros* had their *reatas* on his head and all four legs. He was quickly down on the ground. When the other men arrived with the bear, the bull was being fitted with a heavy leather strap just above one of his front hooves.

"My Lord," Hog Eye said. "This ain't gonna be no little cock fight. This here's gonna be hellacious."

"I'm not sure this is good for the children to watch." Maria looked around to see where they were playing. The children were over with the Bandini family, and they were all headed for the corral.

The new California settlers followed them to the fight site. They watched as the women and children took their places on top the wooden framework along the side of the corral. The men were all on horses, and each one had his rope ready—a few even carried guns. The platform would be protected at all cost. Maria was helped up onto the scaffold. She had Mattie in her arms when the bear, which was now down and stretched out like the bull, was pulled into the arena. The loose end of the bear's leg chain was fastened to the strap above the bull's hoof. The men removed their ropes and left the corral.

The two great wild beasts were quickly on their feet and eyeing each other, separated and yet bound together by the chain. Each one now seemed unaware of anything moving around or making noise outside of the space defined by the length of the shackle that tied them together. At first they circled one another, each one showing his lack of fear and superiority over the other. The bear rose to his full height, balanced on his hind legs and roared. The bull pawed with his free hoof and tossed his head.

Both the men and women wagered on the outcome of the combat that they knew was coming. The bull made the first aggressive move. Head down, with his horns searching for the bear, he charged his antagonist. The bear, with what to Billy was unexpected agility and quickness in a flabby, lumbering body, stepped aside in time to avoid the bull's horns. He grasped the bull as he went by and plunged his teeth into the bull's neck, knocking him to the ground and sending both of them rolling in the dirt and dust. Instantly the bull was back up on his feet, throwing his attacker off to one side. One horn had been partially broken off when the two heavyweights slammed into the ground. The bull whirled to face the bear, but this time one of his horns hung down next to his ear, and blood covered the side of his face. There was a gash in his neck, and his tongue protruded from his open mouth as he gasped for air.

Now it's the bear's turn to attack, Hog Eye thought, but no attack came. Instead the bear stood back up and, with his mouth open to show his savage teeth, roared again. The bull sidestepped around the bear, looking for an opening. The bear turned with the bull, never taking his eyes off the brute.

Maria had to admit to herself that watching the battle was exciting. She had never been one that enjoyed fights, unlike some females she had known. Individuals physically punishing each other seemed pointless to her, yet in this instance, with all the people cheering on their choice to win the contest, she found herself drawn into the struggle. Maybe it was because she knew that in the wild that bull or bear would have not hesitated to attack her if they took the notion. It was similar to the feeling she had when Ojo came after her. It hadn't bothered her at all to see him killed.

The bull thought he saw an opening and pushed the skirmish. This time the bear caught him with his paw. His claws peeled down a three-cornered piece of hide starting just behind the bull's shoulder; however, he had not been able to avoid contact with his pursuer. The bull caught him in the ribs with his head and bounced him as far as the chain would allow him to travel. When the slack went out of the chain, it jerked the bull's front leg out from under him, and he went down. He was almost back up when the bear again clamped down on the bull's neck.

"I'd say about one more charge and your old bull ain't gonna have much left to take into battle against them young bulls next spring," Hog Eye said to Billy.

"If I was you I wouldn't get in no hurry to jump down and try to claim his hide just yet," Billy answered.

"At the rate he's going," Hog Eye chuckled, "I doubt he'll have much hide left to claim."

Hog eye had no more than finished his opinion before the bull threw the bear off to one side, pitched him forward and then caught him through the chest with his good horn, ripping open an ugly wound in the bear's side. His ribs were broken, and they poked out through the wound. A bloody froth bubbled out of the opening. Before the bear could roll out of the bull's reach, the longhorn was on top of him. Using his one horn as expertly as a man would use a pitchfork, the bull made a jab into the bear and tossed him up and over his back. When the bear hit the ground everyone knew that the fight was over. Everyone except the bull. He practiced another thrust and pitch with the bear. When the *vaqueros* started to enter the corral to turn him loose, he turned to fight them.

"Just by looking it was hard to tell that the bull was the winner," Cisco said as the group made camp for the night. Most of the guests had headed back for another night of dancing after the fight was over. Maria had gathered the young ones and headed for camp.

"It's a rough, deadly game," Maria said. "Doña Rosana said that the tradition of fighting bulls and bears was brought over from Spain. I'd just as soon they'd kept it there."

"That old bull looked pretty well whipped when they turned him out," Hog Eye added. He'd been sure that the bear would win, then things turned in a hurry. He knew Maria wasn't happy about the fight, but decided to risk entering the conversation about the conflict anyway. "Sewing his hide back down before they turned him loose helped his looks some."

"The bear actually looked better than the bull." Juan was going to get his opinion registered. "That is if you don't count breathing and being able to move around."

"I don't know if he'll make it or not," Billy added. "But I do know that old bull will be movin' real slow tomorrow, if he's movin' at all. If he makes it we sure won't have any trouble recognizin' him. He'll always be the one with a floppy horn and the scar on his shoulder."

No one had heard any mention of Walker or his men. Billy hadn't been able to find out anything about Joseph Walker, and he didn't feel comfortable just coming right out and asking about his old friend. If he was around they'd surely hear about it sooner or later. Swit was bound to be with the captain.

Everyone else was asleep, and Billy looked at how they were spread out around the camp. Little ones tucked in together. Alonzo, Cisco and Hog Eye bedded down under a tree. Lena and Anita were close to the dying fire, and Juan where he could react if Anita needed him. Maria and Mattie were nearby. In the morning they would head for their new home—the place that Don Carlos had provided. He knew that there was work and adventure, risk and challenges ahead. Probably some disappointments and tragedy were also part of their future, but he felt at home in this country and comfortable with these people around him. Billy B. reflected on how this whole thing had developed more by accident than planning. He'd always longed for family and a home. This was it.

Part Six:
Back to the Bear and Beyond

Chapter Thirty-two

"I'm not sure I can eat dog." Swit watched the dogs move from one campsite to another. Captain Walker and his men had returned from Monterey with additional horses, a small herd of cattle and a pack of dogs. "I'd just as soon left the dogs behind."

"You won't get rid of 'em now," Robert said. "Feed a dog once, and he'll follow you forever."

"All they get is the leftovers after we butcher a steer," Swit added. "That ain't much split up between thirty dogs."

"That, and all the trash we leave behind." Robert supported his earlier statement.

"Well now, I tell you what," Will helped himself to one more of Robert's biscuits, "Indians eat 'em all the time. They claim they're better than horse meat. Who knows, more likely than not we et dog when we was livin' with the Shoshoney."

"If you like 'em, you eat 'em." Henry had heard all he wanted to about eating dogs. "When the beefs give out, I believe I'll just stay with flour and beans until we get back to buffalo country."

"Yeah, and what'll you do when the flour and beans give out?" Will asked.

"That's just the point, lads." Woolly didn't intend to rule out any food source. "The captain knows, as we all do, that there's not sufficient victuals to see us back to the buffalo. Take me word for it, they're as palatable as horses."

"That ain't much of a recommendation," Henry answered. "The best thing you can do with a dead horse or dog is to just move on away from it."

"Maybe the captain plans to trade them dogs to the Indians for some of those big acorns," Swit offered. "Better yet, trade 'em to the diggers for a safe passage through their territory."

"If all you ever ate was worms and bugs," Robert added, "a dog now and then might be just the ticket."

With that statement the discussion about dog consumption ended. No one wanted to dwell too long on the possibility that before they reached buffalo country they would be starved down to the point of considering canine cuisine. It was now the first week in February, and everyone was gearing up for the coming trip.

Joe Walker knew he needed to get his men moving. While he was in Monterey trading for supplies, the men he left at camp had observed a group of Indians pushing a sizable herd of horses across an open plain. Two days later a group of Spaniards led by a brash young man stopped at the camp asking if anyone had noticed the horses. He claimed that Indians had stolen about three hundred head from the mission at San Juan.

After spending the night at Walker's camp, the Spaniards invited the men to help them retrieve their horses and punish the Indians. They would divide the number of animals they recovered equally. Joined by some of Walker's men, the Spaniards continued their pursuit of the horse thieves. Three days later they returned to camp.

"Leonard, Walker ain't here, but you're the clerk of this here outfit." Williams and Levin Mitchell had isolated Zenas Leonard as soon as they returned to camp. Bill Williams was doing the talking. "By God, you better get them damn black-eyed sons of bitches headed home before I hang some of their ears on my saddle. I'm doing my best to live up to Walker's rules."

"He's right." Mitchell was shaking his head. "I know if Captain Walker was here he'd agree. We're visitors in this country, but we just can't put up with that kind of treatment. It was bad enough back at the settlements when they took our horses."

Zenas Leonard had watched the men return. He noticed that the trappers had ridden in alone, not as part of the original group, and as far as he could tell they came back empty handed. "Where's all the horses you went after? Is that the problem, they won't give up half of the horse herd?"

"It ain't about horses, it's about Indians." Mitchell started to tell the story. "That pint-sized leader over there was gonna burn 'em alive. We stopped that, but they rode in anyhow and butchered a whole mess of 'em. Cut all their ears off for some reason. You know I ain't no Indian lover, but I draw the line at that kind of behavior."

"So you caught the thieves, and they wanted to fight it out. Is that what happened?" Zenas asked.

"Hell no," Williams answered. "We didn't catch shit. There wasn't but two or three old men in the whole bunch. They was women and children."

"What happened to the Indians that drove the horses by here several days ago?" Leonard wished that either Mitchell or Williams would just tell him what happened. It wasn't like either one of these men to be this concerned about Indians.

"Who knows," Williams continued, "probably back up in the mountains somewhere. That's just the point. We didn't find the thieves or most of the horses. The trail led us back into a forested area at the base of the mountains. It looked like they were camped back in the trees, but we couldn't see any of 'em. The kid decided that we should surround 'em and then just start shootin' into the brush. I kinda like to see what I'm shooting at."

"Our people backed off," said Levin Mitchell as he continued the story. "After the rest of 'em blasted away for awhile it was clear that there wasn't any fighters at the camp. Not one shot came out of the woods. The Spaniards finally emptied their guns, so we all rode in. The Indians driving the stolen horses had been there, left off a few of the nags for the people in the little village, and were gone. Three horses had already been butchered, and they was drying the meat."

"Where were their men folk?" Leonard was beginning to get the picture.

"I don't know," Williams answered. "There were a few old men there, but it was mostly women and their young'uns. They wasn't much better off than those diggers over on the Barren River, except they was peaceful."

"That's not all," Mitchell added. "The ones hiding in their huts were all herded over into a big wigwam. They locked 'em in, piled brush around the hut, and was about to set it on fire when we stepped in and turned 'em loose."

"My God," Zenas said.

"They went ahead and killed some of 'em anyway," Williams continued. When I saw them cut the ears off of a little girl, I damn near started killing me some Mexicans or Spaniards, or whatever the hell they are." Bill could see the leader walking toward them. "I gotta get gone, or just as sure as a fart stinks I'm gonna break my word to Walker. I'm headed up river apiece. I'll be back when I'm fit."

Zenas Leonard watched as Mitchell and Bill Williams, with his long, awkward stride, moved over to their horses, mounted up and rode off. Zenas had seen the young leader headed his way and thought how he had no idea how close he'd come to tasting death instead of delivering it. There was no doubt in Leonard's mind that the small number of trappers could have wiped out the vengeful Spaniards almost as easy as the Indians had been crushed. Just one move from the man headed up river and the young swaggering Indian fighter, along with his men, would be cold on the ground instead of returning in triumph. Leonard knew how cruel Bill Williams could be when he was filled with bile. The young man would never know that the only thing that stood between him and certain death was one man's word given to another. Zenas hoped that no unsuspecting man or animal crossed Crazy Bill's path in the next day or so.

Leonard found himself alone with the young Spaniard, trying to understand what the leader was telling him. As near as he could make out, the man was explaining that they had found the thieves but were unable to recover any of the horses. The soldier showed Leonard a bag full of ears that he intended to take back and display before the priests and alcaldes to prove that they had used every effort in an attempt to recapture the stolen animals. He apologized for not being able to stay at the camp longer. It was necessary that they return to the mission as soon as possible. Leonard agreed and walked away.

Captain Walker had been back from Monterey for several days when he announced that it was time to head back. Leonard opened his journal and wrote, "February 14, 1834, started for the Bear with fifty-two men, three-hundred and fifteen horses, forty-seven beefs and thirty dogs."

"I'll miss all six of 'em." Swit and Robert had been riding along together now for almost an hour without comment. "I can't say I knew 'em all that well, but we've been through a lot together. Did it surprise you when the Captain turned 'em loose?"

"Not much," Robert answered. He was riding along, thinking about their first trip over the mountain barrier that stood off in the distance. They were memories he'd just as soon forget.

"Will said that Captain Walker let 'em go 'cause they all had trades," Swit said. "You know, I watched George build a table for a lady over in Monterey. It was better than what most families around here have. She paid him ten silver coins. Did you know he was a cabinetmaker in his younger days?"

"I knew he's a good shot." Robert hadn't been surprised that George Nidever or the other five men had decided to stay in California. There was no mistaking the pleasantness of the country or the opportunities it presented.

"I guess they figure to give up trapping and make Californy their home." Swit liked the idea of staying in California, but not if it meant being on his own. He wasn't ready for that.

"I'd as soon have my home somewhere in the States." Robert thought that giving up the free life and living under the yoke of Mexico was too high a price to pay. Besides, he'd always gone where Henry went, and he didn't know a trade anyhow. Swit was right, though; they were six good men. Riding along with Swit was new to Robert. He mostly rode beside Henry, except when they were lined out in single file. Henry hated riding along in a strung out, one-behind-the-other formation. Every time it happened, Robert knew that before long Henry would ride up beside him and say the same thing he always did. "You know something, Robert, we look just like a bunch of piss ants goin' to a funeral."

They continued to travel upriver. On the evening of the second day they picked up two more men. Two Spaniards driving twenty-five head of horses arrived at their camp. They told how they had run off from serving in the army, and they asked if they could join up with Walker's bunch. Certain death awaited them back at the settlements. Increasing the number of horses in their herd, and the addition of two men obviously skilled in handling horses, was a good thing; however, Captain Walker explained that death could reach out for them on the trail ahead if they failed in their duties to this group of men. The following day Walker watched as the Spaniards quickly established control over the *remuda*.

The expedition continued its eastward movement until they reached the base of the mountains that had put an abiding print into the mind of every man. The Sierras run north-northwest to south-southeast for about four hundred miles. Captain Walker knew they were south of where they crossed before, and attempting to cross here didn't look any easier. He felt certain that the Indians knew the passes, and there were Indians living along the base of these majestic mountains. The problem was making contact with the natives. Most of the Indians scattered like quail and hid out whenever the strangers came into sight. When a village did welcome the travelers, it was hard to establish communication. An available source of meat was another problem. Most of the game animals that had once lived along the edge of the mountains had been hunted down and driven away.

The search for an up-and-over continued as the trappers moved southeast along the base of the mountain range. Joseph Walker could see that the mountain peaks were lower than the ones to the north, and they carried less snow. The grass was good on this side, but based on what they'd observed on their way to California, Walker felt certain that forage for the livestock along the eastern slope of the mountains would be scarce. Every step they took to the south, before they crossed the mountains, meant another step back north in their search for the trail they'd followed down from the Barren River. The next morning they arrived at a large Indian village.

"You ever seen any Indians like these before?" Swit asked Henry. It was evening, and the trappers had been invited to make their camp within the village. Swit had tried to get a count of how many huts the village contained, but every time he moved farther back into the trees some more huts would appear. It was hard to put a boundary around the settlement. Part of the colony was out for all to see, but it wasn't the whole picture.

"I'd have to say that all the Indians I've seen in California ain't been nothing like the ones I've known before," Henry answered. "There's quite a few Indians in this here bunch, though. How many would you say, Robert?"

"Seven to eight hundred," Robert quickly answered. Swit wondered how Robert was able to arrive at his count. He was probably right, though; Robert wasn't one to answer without conviction.

"One thing's for sure," Will said. "This bunch knows a little Spanish and the value of a good trade."

"They know about stealing too," Henry added. "Those gold candle sticks and all that other gold stuff come out of some mission. Did you get a good look at their horses? Most of 'em are carrying Spanish brands."

"I noticed the brands myself." Swit had been thinking the same as Henry. This tribe was in the habit of making raids on unsuspecting *ranchos*. He'd looked to see if he could find any with Mr. Gilroy's brand—he hadn't. "They've got some regular furniture in some of their huts. They might have stole that too."

"Maybe they traded for it," Will interjected. "It looks to me like they operate more like the church missions over on the coast. They got a melon patch and a vegetable garden. There's even a cornfield out on that flat. Ask Captain Walker what he thinks."

"How'd the palaver go today, Captain?" Woolly had been quietly watching Robert perform his magic with the Dutch oven, and hadn't cared to enter into the discussion about the habits of these particular Indians when Walker entered their camp.

"Good," Walker answered. "I hope I'm in time to savor some of Robert's biscuits."

"Just be a couple minutes, Captain," Robert informed their leader without looking up.

"I can already taste 'em." Walker walked over to where the other men were seated. He felt good about the parley he'd had with the chiefs. This was what he'd been seeking.

"I think we've found an easier place to cross the Sierra's. These Indians claim to know about a pass through the mountains just a few days from here. They're willing to send two guides with us to show the way. It'll cost us a horse, some tobacco and a bag full of beads, but we won't pay 'em until we get on the other side."

"Well now, I thought they looked like traders," Will said. "Henry and Swit has got 'em pegged for thieves."

"You're both right." Walker sensed that the camp discussion when he rode up must have been about this unusual tribe of Indians living in the shadow of these formidable mountains. "They call themselves Concoas. About ten years ago some of these Indians were living at the Santa Barbara Mission. They finally had their fill of promises and instead opted out for the free life. They stole everything they could carry, and all the horses they could find."

"I told you they was thieves," Henry interrupted. "I'm surprised the army didn't come after 'em."

"They said that the army did track 'em across the coastal mountain range and out onto the plain," Walker answered. "But it sounded like they gave up the chase early. The Indians continued moving northeast until they reached the mountains. Since their arrival they've invited any and all of their bronzed brothers to join up with 'em. The settlement has been growing ever since."

"From all the different brands on them horses I'd say they're still in the horse-stealing business." Henry thought there was more steal than trade in this tribe of Indians

"That they are," Walker agreed. "They're also in the trading business. They've put the skills they learned at the mission to good use and worked out a way to trade with the ships that sail up and down the coast. One of the chiefs acted like he knew, or at least had heard of, Captain Bradshaw. Maybe Bradshaw thought that we were Indians looking to trade when we waved him in to shore."

"What would they have to trade to Captain Bradshaw?" Swit wanted to know.

"Probably all the hides they can steal on their way over to the ocean." Henry got up and headed back to where his horse was grazing. "If they'll steal, they'll lie. Why do ya suppose Captain Walker ain't making the trade with 'em until we're on the other side?"

The Indian guides pointed the way, and Walker's expedition followed. As they started to climb, Swit thought how mountain crossings all seemed to begin by following up some stream or river that poured down out of the high country. He didn't feel as if he was a seasoned mountain man yet, but he wasn't a beginner either. He just couldn't shake the anxiety he felt. It was hard to imagine how this crossover would be any more dangerous or tougher than the one they had experienced getting into California. This time starvation shouldn't be a problem. They had cattle, extra horses and a pack of dogs following along behind.

The expedition worked its way up various descending creek basins, around isolated peaks and through mountain meadows. The crossover was not gradual like it had been at South Pass. You knew the minute you were over, and the unnamed streams, peaks and meadows were behind you. Some of the men started to call this route over the mountains Walker's Pass. Woolly even claimed that a wagon could make it over. Swit thought that was a little ambitious, but then he'd seen Woolly drive a wagon over places that to him had seemed impossible.

The Indian guides had gathered their bartered goods and were headed back to their village when Bill William's and his followers decided to leave Walker's group and head for the Gila River country. Swit was glad to see them leave. He'd noticed a change in William's bunch once they crossed the Sierras and felt released from Captain Walker's agreement with the California authorities. These men had lived within the controlling presence of Joseph Walker longer than any of them could have imagined was possible. They were ready to cut loose, and Swit could see it coming. The trip back would be no different than the trip out. Captain Walker would be in charge, and his position about how the Indians were to be treated was not about to change. Somewhere down the trail that was sure to mean trouble.

It was the first part of May, and Walker led his men north along the eastern side of the mountains. It wasn't as lush as the western side, but it had some water and a fair amount of grass for the livestock. When they reached a lake fed by a stream of sweet water flowing south along the base of the mountains, everyone believed that they could follow up this river and eventually find their way back.

"I figured we would have crossed our old trail by now," Swit said as the group continued north along the foothills of the mountain range. "We must have gone farther south than I thought."

"Well now, I'll tell you what." Woodrow was glad to be east of the mountains and headed north, but he missed that California plushness. "It's been two weeks since we crossed the mountains, and the only interestin' thing we've seen was that spring full of boiling water."

"That was something, wasn't it?" Henry had heard other trappers talk about hot springs, but he'd never seen one. "I'll bet ol' Robert could have baked his biscuits in there if he'd wanted to."

"Too sulphury," Robert stated.

"You're sure right about that; it did have an odor," Will agreed. "It was nice and warm on a clear, cool morning, though. You could see the steam risin' from miles away."

Every morning Henry and Robert, along with two or three other hunters, pushed out ahead of the main bunch in hope of finding game. Henry had returned to report that the river ahead was bending west up into the mountains. It seemed to Swit that they had been traveling west about as much as north, and he felt like they were moving farther away from the Bear River instead of closer.

Swit's mind was still trying to figure directions when the captain rode into their night camp. Joseph Walker was spreading the word. He had decided that they should swing their trail out into the desert. The Sierras were beginning to angle more to the west. He was convinced that they were only a short distance south of their old track. If they headed north and east they could eliminate the wasted westward movement. This would put them back on the Barren River at least a week sooner than they could reasonably expect if they continued to followed along the mountains.

It would not be an easy crossing. They could expect no firewood, almost no grass for the animals and water would be somewhere between hard and impossible to find. Swit listened as Captain Walker explained his decision, but he couldn't forget Billy telling how Jed Smith had led two groups of men out into this same stark wasteland and not all of them survived the crossing. Captain Walker was asking his men if they had any objection to following him out into the desert. Billy had also told Swit to listen carefully when the captain talked, then do just exactly what he said. Everyone else must have held that same value for Joseph Walker's judgment. No one was in favor of desert travel, but no one objected.

The departure started at daybreak, and after they left the mountains and foothills behind, all they could see ahead was a sandy and desiccated wasteland. Streams, both small and large flowing down out of the high country, spread out and disappear as the seemingly endless desert swallowed them up. They were soon moving along, wrapped in a cloud of hot dust. The wind provided a slight cooling effect, but it also whipped the sand into their eyes and made it a painful chore to just try and look around.

"I'll tell you what," Will said after they had stopped for the night. "The next time I have to take a dump you better come watch. I must of ate a mountain of sand today."

"It was tougher than I thought it would be," Swit agreed. "I figured it to be dry, but it never occurred to me that the horses and cattle would throw that much dirt in the air. It didn't seem to matter if I was riding flank or drag, you had to chew every breath."

"If you drink out of that puddle over there you'll chew your water too," Robert added. The Indians had probably dug out the water hole that Captain Walker had found. It was four to five feet deep and held a small amount of stagnant water. Enough to help a few men make their way, but not near what this size a group of men and animals needed.

"You're right about that," Henry said. "But at least it's wet. My hide musta sprung a leak. I'm drier than a popcorn fart. The captain always could find water faster than anybody I ever knew, but there sure ain't enough for all these critters."

As soon as the night's blackness started to lighten in the east, Captain Walker had the expedition moving. It was cooler, the animals were in need of water and Walker wanted to cover as much ground as possible. If they couldn't find a better supply of water today, they were in trouble.

The day turned out to be the same as the day before, except hotter. About mid-afternoon two dogs were the first animals to lie down and quit. The men continued to push forward, and considering the cruelty of the environment, made a respectable distance by day's end—there was no water.

Swit watched as Barrel and Muddle stomped and waved. They were for sure locked in heated debate. He wondered where they found the energy for their lively discussions at a time like this. He looked over the camp as the sun was dropping out of sight, and he knew that some of the animals lying down would not be getting up again. Most of the horses and cattle slowly ambled around in a bunch. One would move off to one side, and the others would think that maybe it had found some source of water and follow.

The dogs bothered Swit the most. They would walk in closer than usual and then just sit and stare at the men. A small, mouse-colored, scruffy little female mongrel caught Swit's eye. She seemed to be saying to him that he was her only hope. When no drinking water was forthcoming she slowly wandered off and uttered a pitiful howl. In a few minutes she was dead.

Scab was favoring his left hind leg. When Swit picked up the horse's foot to examine it, he was surprised at how the sand had ground away at the wall of the hoof. It had been worn down until he was walking on the sole of his foot. Even the slightest pressure applied to the frog would cause him to jerk back in pain.

"I got a horse with the same problem," Henry said as he and Woodrow walked over to where Swit was examining Scab. "Two more days in this sand and there won't be a horse that can move fast enough to scatter his own shit. We're damn sure in trouble. Robert just sits over there with those few scrawny twigs he gathered today. They wouldn't build a big enough fire to stink up a skillet."

"Woolly's cuttin' our supper off of that critter over there." Will was pointing toward a yearling that had found its final resting place. "I'd prefer a hot, juicy steak and biscuits, but raw meat's better than nothin'. There's some talk about our turnin' back."

"Most of it's coming from one of them Spaniards we picked up in California," Henry added. "Having him along is like losing two good men."

"What's Captain Walker say?" Swit wanted to know.

"He's for pushing on," Henry answered. "By his calculation we're more than halfway across. It's farther back to that puddle than on to the river."

"Now, you see, that's what I don't understand," Will added. "Why is it that everyone that's for headin' back thinks we should return to that little water hole back down the trail? I'd rather take my chances on Captain Walker findin' good water up ahead."

"I think the same. Are you for going on or going back?" Henry asked Woolly as he walked up carrying a very rare chunk of beefsteak.

"I go where Walker goes," Woolly Wilson answered. "But I'll tell ya now, I fear we're headed for grim and gruesome. There's more that thinks we should be backin' up than goin' on. Captain's having a meeting to decide which way we travel."

Joseph Walker believed that in times like this the will of the majority should prevail. He felt certain that he could find water tomorrow, and following back the way they had come was farther than trudging on through to the river. It was clear that a majority of the men favored returning. Unrestrained verbal fights about what action to take at the different campsites had been the exercise of the evening. Barrel and Muddle had ended their debate with Barrel standing with his hands on his hips and staring silently at Muddle. Muddle sat hunched down with his back to Barrel, every now and then turning his head to peer back at him from under his tattered old hat.

Before all the light faded from the sky, Captain Walker waved his men over to where he stood. In two sentences he expressed his opinion about their dilemma and gave his proposal. He would lead them to his best ability, no matter what direction the majority decided to travel. Heated debate started again, and Captain Walker asked for quiet. He told the men that the time for talk was over. It was time to decide.

Joe Walker couldn't sleep. After the vote was in he told the group that he intended to nap for awhile, and he recommended that they do the same. The march would begin long before daylight, and if they could get some rest they stood a better chance of reaching water. He wasn't really surprised by the outcome of the vote. He knew that more than half of the men wanted to head back to the last water they'd known. But he thought that when it came time to decide, a majority of the trappers would vote to follow his lead. Only two voted to return.

What bothered Walker now, and kept him from sleep, was his own decision. The facts were simple. This bunch was at a place where a wrong turn meant that some of these men wouldn't live to see the Bear River country, maybe none of 'em. Almost all the men were accustomed to risking their lives and were experienced at escaping death. They were hardened to the life but seldom foolish. He had handpicked each man for this expedition. No matter how they voted, when a majority of these men believed it was wrong to push on, only a self-aggrandizing oaf would close himself in his own beliefs. Walker was sure that there was water up ahead, but he knew there was more water and better chances of finding it closer to the mountains. If he traveled deeper into this desert and wasn't able to strike water, many of these men would die. He would be gambling with their lives, and he knew that was wrong.

It was midnight when Walker started preparing his men for travel. First they peeled the hide off a few of the dead cattle to cover the feet of what lame horses they could. He explained that he'd changed his mind about pushing on north, and they'd head toward the mountains while it was still cool.

"Well, I tell you one thing," Will said as he and Swit fitted a cow hide boot over Scab's left hind hoof. "That ol' moon is gonna be down before long, and we won't have light one until daylight. Stumblin' around in blackness can get you lost."

"Lads, don't tie her that high. It'll cut the circulation. Go down around the hoof wall where you can pull her up good and snug, " Woolly said as he reached down to help tie on the boot.

When morning arrived Walker continued to point the way, and the way was hard. Man and animal moved along as best as they could. Captain Walker took the lead, and his followers were pulled forward. As the day opened up and poured down its heat, the men and stock gradually spread out until some were as much as a mile apart.

The animals suffered more than the men. They were now into their third day without water, and some simply could not continue the drive. The dogs agonized the most. One would fall and die. Another would come over and lay down beside its fallen comrade. Before the dispersed assortment of men and animals could pass by, the second dog was dead. The sun now hung low in the western sky, and they still hadn't tasted water. Captain Walker stopped and began the business of pulling the expedition together. He knew they must continue to advance, but spread out like they were it would be easy for the men to lose direction and become permanently separated in the dark. Every effort was made to keep the livestock moving and prevent them from lying down. Once they stopped and went down—they stayed down.

They continued to move ahead. It was cooler, but Swit's mind had room for only one thought—thirst. He couldn't think of anything else. He watched a horse stagger and fall to the ground. Before death could claim the suffering animal, two men stopped, cut open the horse's jugular veins, and drank its blood. He decided that he'd try that if they didn't find water soon. The coolness of the night was helping. The stock was moving easier, and the pace had picked up. Swit noticed that the horses had moved ahead of everyone else and were angling off to the northwest. Captain Walker moved the expedition in behind them.

It was past midnight when Swit realized that water was only minutes away. Captain Walker was riding among the men, telling everyone to drink slowly and only small amounts at a time. Take a little, wait a while, then go back and get some more. He had the men drive the livestock away from the stream for the same reason.

When the new day broke Swit and the other men were still at work keeping the animals from foundering on water. He thought it was the most beautiful stream he had ever seen, but there was nothing for the livestock to eat. Only a few sprigs of grass lined the sandy banks. Animals and men had been able to rehydrate themselves but were weary and hungry. Moving upstream, the grass gradually became more plentiful, and a few scrubby little trees provided enough dried wood to make a fire. They finally stopped, ate and rested.

Captain Walker and Zenas Leonard walked around between the scattered groups of men stretched out on the grass, soaking in the stream, or just sitting alone with their own thoughts and enjoying a smoke. They rode out to take stock of the animals. In his journal Leonard wrote the results of their journey out into the desert of the Great Basin. "We lost sixty-four horses, ten cows and fifteen dogs. The men are all safe."

Chapter Thirty-three

"You know something, Joe," Captain Benjamin Bonneville was attempting to piece together his pants leg, "if Michael don't show up pretty soon I'm gonna fall right out of these britches."

"Two years in the wild have tested your garments, that's a fact," Joseph Walker agreed. He'd found the captain in a rather tattered state. Most of his men were out of the camp trying to take what pelts they could, even though it was too late to make much of a hunt. Bonneville was sharing his tent with a squaw, and more than one man had already ventured their opinion that the builder of Fort Nonsense was too generous in his purchases for female companionship. "I heard some talk about your hatmaking ability while you were visiting the Nez Perce Indians."

"It's odd the things that will pull you out of a tight squeeze." Ben was relaxed, and it was comfortable to once again talk with Joe Walker. He'd missed their early morning meetings. Most of the men they had fitted out for the trip to California had rode into his camp on July 12, 1834, just twelve days short of one year after he had watched them ride away. Since their return Joe Walker had supplied Captain Bonneville with pages of information, maps and answers about terrain, wild life, climate, people, government attitude and anything else he wanted to know about the territory they had traveled through. Now Walker was asking Bonneville about his activities during the last year.

"I'm sure you remember that old plaid cloak I've been caring around." Ben started his tale. "Well, last February we were working our way down the Snake River on our way to the Columbia when we found ourselves over in the

339

Imanha River valley. We hadn't eaten anything except a few roots for days, and the horses were all but finished when we stumbled upon a small village of Lower Nez Perce Indians."

"I've always heard that they're friendly to whites and raise some of the best horses around." Walker had not encountered any tribes of the Lower Nez Perce, but he looked forward to the experience.

Bonneville thought how Joe Walker always seemed interested in finding horses. "They were friendly and peaceful enough, but not too anxious to share any of their stored elk or salmon with us. We were offered a tuber soup of some kind, and treated to smoke the pipe, but no meat was served. You'll remember that the winter before last I spent some time with their brothers over on the Salmon. Anyhow, they'd heard of our expedition, and we were received with great respect but slim rations. I tried to trade for some meat, but they showed little interest in our trade goods."

"That is, until you got in the hat business?" Walker asked.

"The first time I removed my hat and exposed my bald head," Bonneville continued, "I was surprised at how the Indians reacted—especially the squaws. It was evident that they had never observed baldness in a man. At least not one caused by Mother Nature. They acted as if somehow I had achieved an immunity against the ever-present danger of being scalped in battle. It was like a badge of honor. I tore some strips of bright plaid cloth off of that old cape and covered my head with a rainbow-colored turban. My new headdress was soon the most coveted ornamental attire in camp. After creating all the colored headwear that the old garment would provide, and seeing that the new style found its way onto the heads of the right members of the tribe, we were soon feasting on elk hearts and dried salmon."

"It sounds like you were able to explore the Snake River country clear through to the Columbia," Walker said. "Was it what you expected?"

"Tougher than I expected," Bonneville answered. "Travel down along the Snake is impossible after you pass the mouth of the Powder River. The canyons are major. That's why we were west of the Snake and over along the Imanha. Then we moved to another tributary of the snake that the Indians call the Way-lee-way. The British call it the Grande Ronde River. Following down the Way-lee-way we rejoined the Snake River north of the canyon country, and followed it to the Columbia River.

"Did you stop at Fort Walla Walla?" Walker was sure Captain Bonneville would have visited the Hudson Bay Company's trading post. He wondered how the British had treated Bonneville.

"It was an easy day's ride south from where the Snake empties into the Columbia." Captain Bonneville had never known Joe Walker to ask questions about terrain or waterways. Apparently he hadn't traveled through this part of the west. "The trading post is located on the north bank of the Walla Walla River. At the fort I discovered that the word was out to all their trading partners to be friendly, but not to sell or trade any supplies to us. It explained why we were having trouble trading for any pelts or provisions from the Indians in the area."

"It doesn't sound like there'd be much chance of taking wagons along that route." While Walker listened to Captain Bonneville tell about the Snake and Columbia River territory, he remembered how Ben had planned to escort Cerré over to the Big Horn River after last year's rendezvous. Michael and his bunch were going to use bullboats to transport the companies first furs back to St. Louis. If Captain Bonneville and his men started out from the Big Horn, then they traveled a fair distance through some good trapping country to get as far west as the Columbia River. Bonneville was clearly more interested in mapping the territory between the Snake and the Columbia than gathering pelts for his fur company.

"You're right," Bonneville answered, "and besides that, the Snake goes another fifty miles to the north before making a big horseshoe bend and coming back south to join the Columbia. I need to find a cutoff that will miss the canyons and save traveling that far to the north. I'd like to try following up the Powder River and see if you couldn't get wagons along a northwesterly course between the Snake and the Columbia."

"It sounds like you're planning to stay out another year." Walker didn't think it was likely that any message from the States could have been delivered to Bonneville until Michael arrived; however, he'd always found the Army hard to predict. "Did you hear back on your letter to the Army?"

"No, not yet." Bonneville was apprehensive about what message Cerré might be bringing back from General Macomb. "I'm hoping they don't call me back. I gave Michael my final copy of the letter when we were camped along the Wind River. When he returns I expect to get an answer about my future here in the wilderness. Your trip into California and the excellent records you've kept have added greatly to the geographical success of this expedition, but I need to see if I can't find a better path to the Columbia. As far as our success as a fur company goes—well, it looks pretty sad. My men didn't take many beaver this past year, and I noticed you didn't bring back much from California."

"I'm sorry about that," Walker said. "We traded what furs we had for supplies before we left. We traveled by way of the Barren River on our return, but that's poor beaver country. If we're still in business this fall I'll take a brigade and head up into the Absaroka. The Yellowstone and Big Horn drainage has always been heavy with beaver. We'll pull some furs out of there for you."

"That's Crow territory," Ben said. "We tried to trap there last fall. The Indians kept us on edge, and we didn't get many beaver. The Crows will steal everything they can get their hands on. One of our brigades lost their horses, grub, traps, everything but their lives. Since we were in need of additional traps and supplies, I took three men and tried to find a way over the Wind River Mountains and back to our caches at Fort Bonneville. God, what magnificent country, but the mountains are formidable. I couldn't find any way across them."

"I told you about the trouble we had with the Paiute Indians going out," Walker continued. "They're a strange people. We had the same experience coming back. There were more of' em this time, and apparently they still weren't convinced that all we wanted was to travel upriver. I even tried to trade some dogs for safe passage, but they continued to threaten and squeeze down on us. No trade, no parley, no peace pipe. The men were in no mood to be pushed. I was afraid I might not be able to call 'em off once it got started. We killed fourteen in the first charge, and the Indians gave it up. Three of our men received minor wounds, but it could have been a lot worse. The men could have rode 'em down and slaughtered dozens more, or if they'd been willing to sacrifice enough men we would have been over run by the Paiutes."

"It would appear that they're destined to remain primitive. With the warlike attitude they demonstrated I don't doubt that the only reason they have survived this long is because they're grubbing out an existence in an area that few would care to live." Ben wondered if he would be allowed to survive out here another year. "If I can just get another year, maybe we can bear down on the trapping and trading and make up for our poor showing."

Ben knew that when he took the extra year on his furlough he put his Army career at risk, but now he was willing to go for two. He was betting a lot on Sam Houston's belief that the president and John Jacob Astor were the ones behind his being here. If that was true, and he could find a way for wagons to get to the Columbia and at the same time send back enough furs to satisfy his investors, he might save his commission in the Army.

Joseph Walker had already decided that he was staying. He would work with Captain Bonneville to help Ben achieve whatever he felt was necessary in order to label their expedition a success, but it didn't matter if the captain stayed or was called back; Joe Walker was staying. He already considered what they had accomplished to be more than ordinary. It was there to see if anyone cared to look. The trail for wagon travel out of the so-called civilized Eastern states, through the plains, over the Continental Divide and on to the Green River was blazed. Ben had explored and probed the territory between South Pass and the Columbia River. A reasonable path to California was now established, and two new ways to cross the Sierras had been found—one to follow, the other to stay clear of. It wouldn't be an easy trip, but the West was open.

Captain Bonneville in time would return to the States, and the story of their taking wagons over the Continental Divide and the routes they had traveled during their exploration would become public information. The silent partners in this excursion, whoever they might be, would see to that. To begin with, just a few would trickle this way, but Walker was sure it would soon turn into a flood. This free, wild country, along with its inhabitants, would soon undergo a change that Joe didn't like to think about. His family had moved toward the west and settled new territory for generations. Walker was at peace in this land, and he intended to stay and enjoy the life as long as possible. The trip to California had given him a zest to learn more about the area of the Great Basin. Life among the Shoshone Indians was engaging. He wanted to taste and see it all before it changed.

"Did it ever occur to ya," Henry was asking Robert as they stretched out under a tree in the early afternoon, "that just as soon as someone hears about a trail to get somewhere that they ain't been before, they'll start planning to head off down that path? If I've heard one, I've heard twenty tell me that they's fixin' to head for California."

"It'd be calmer if we'd say less," Robert answered.

Henry looked over at Robert. Now there's a man that had "saying less" perfected, Henry thought. He was right, though; it really didn't make much sense to tell all about this trail and that.

"I'll bet Swit goes," Robert announced.

"Goes where?"

"California."

"What makes you think so?" Henry hadn't heard anything about anyone going back to California. "Did he tell ya he was leaving?"

"Didn't have to," Robert answered. "He's taken with the *rancho* life."

"He should've just set tight then."

"That's not Swit's way." Robert admired Swit's straightforward manner. "He's not one to change directions in the middle of anything. He might not go until the captain goes again, but he'll go, and he'll stay too."

"If I ever do go back I'll stay off the top of that big ol' mountain in the winter time, and out of that desert all the time." Henry was watching his horse chomp his way back into traveling condition.

Swit, Will, Zenus Leonard and Woolly watched downriver. Through a little opening off to one side of a house-sized rock they could see Barrel and Muddle having one of their performances. Apparently Barrel held the upper hand. He was standing; arms folded in front of his sizable physique, watching Muddle. A broad grin spread across his face. Muddle was hopping from one foot to the other. He'd thrown his old tattered hat on the ground and was jumping up and down on it.

Will was sure that Muddle's up and down dance would soon bring forth a flourish of arm thrashing from Barrel. Barrel didn't change his posture, but even from this distance it was plain that Barrel's face had developed a reddish glow. Suddenly Muddle stopped, turned his back on Barrel, dropped his drawers and bent over, giving Barrel full view of his backside.

"Well now," Will commented, "I do believe ol' Muddle is gonna have the last word this time."

"Looks to me like he may have already used up most of his resources of expression," Leonard noted. "At this point I feel he has resorted to a more primitive means of communication."

"He's just putting a skunk move on him," Swit assured the group. "It's hard to argue with a skunk."

Woolly took a pull from his jug, then set it down where anyone could help themselves if they were so inclined, and started to chuckle. "She appears to be a bloody stand-off. I'm supposin' you'll be a writtin' all this down in your journal, Mr. Leonard." Neither Barrel nor Muddle had moved an inch. "You be sure now and state that once again Muddle has proved that a red face is always beaten by a white arse."

With that being said, Woolly jumped up, pulled down his pants and pointed his hairy rear toward the two combatants. Will was first to follow Woolly's lead, then Zenas, and finally even Swit joined in the barrage. Barrel took notice almost at once, dropped his arms to his side and slipped from sight as he rounded the rock. Muddle continued to fire away, seemingly not knowing that Barrel had moved from the target area, or that they were being blasted from afar. Muddle finally recognized that Barrel was missing. At about that same time he spotted the incoming bombardment. Muddle let out a whoop, straightened up, smiled and saluted. Barrel was peeking out from behind the rock, his face covered with another wide, toothless grin.

"Does anybody else think maybe we been had?" Swit asked, but no one answered.

Michael Cerré, with forty men and enough supplies to support another year in the wilderness, arrived in camp on the twentieth. After all the "welcome backs" and the "how have you beens" were exchanged, Captain Bonneville asked about Michael's meeting with General Macomb. Cerré reported that it wasn't much of a meeting. He had delivered the letter personally to General Macomb the morning of their arrival, and then returned in the evening to meet with the man. It seemed to Michael that the general was pleased with what the captain had written. He asked several questions about Captain Bonneville's travels through the territory, and if the captain was keeping a journal about his observations and experiences.

General Macomb never said anything about carrying a dispatch back to Captain Bonneville; however, Michael explained that he had to leave Washington and go on to New York to meet with their financial people. He never returned to Washington before heading back to the rendezvous. It was Cerré's belief that if he had been able to meet with General Macomb again, the general would have sent a letter back to Bonneville OK'ing his extended leave from the Army. Michael seemed certain that the general was satisfied with the expedition and that Captain Bonneville's staying for another year would not be a problem.

Captain Bonneville thought it was unusual that the general hadn't sent a reply. Ben was disturbed and happy at the same time. He didn't have any written indication of how his superior felt about his already having stayed an additional year, but then he hadn't been told to come home either. Captain Ben immediately began to prepare additional reports and another letter for General Macomb. Michael explained that he had taken a position with the American Fur Company and would not be able to deliver the documents directly to the general. However, he would take them as far as Council Bluffs and then forward them on to Washington. Michael's return with provisions, and his leaving the expedition, made it clear that this would be Bonneville's last year. He needed tactical information about wagon travel from the Snake to the Columbia River and beaver pelts.

By July thirtieth the Bonneville expedition was newly equipped and well rested. Michael Cerré took forty-five men and the few furs that had been collected during the past year and started for the settlements. Benjamin Bonneville left camp with fifty men and headed for the territory between the lower Snake River and its connection with the Columbia. Joseph Walker collected his men and set out to make a fall hunt in the streams that flow together to form the Yellowstone River. Bonneville and Walker agreed to meet where the Popo Agie Creek flowed into the Wind River in June of 1835. Swit, Will, Henry, Robert, Woolly and Zenas Leonard were part of Captain Walker's group.

Chapter Thirty-four

Zenas Leonard was looking out the window of his store in the new little community of Sibley, Missouri. His thoughts drifted back to the first time he passed through this part of the country. That was in 1831, and he was headed west to experience the adventurous life of a fur trapper. There wasn't a town here then, just the skimpy remains of Fort Osage, an old abandoned Army post that set on top a high bluff along the south side of the Missouri River. It was a well-known layover spot along the trail headed west.

On Lewis and Clark's historic probe into the new Louisiana Purchase, William Clark took note of the seventy-foot-high riverbank above a narrow strip of navigable water. The rest of the river flowing past this point contained rapids and boils that forced any river traffic to move to the calm waters along the south bank below the bluff. It had a natural rock ledge landing site, the water was deep and from the top of the bluff you could control the river travel. Clark noted it on his map and labeled it Fort Point. After his return and appointment as general in charge of Indian affairs for the Louisiana territory, Clark remembered the place along the river as an ideal spot for an Army post and trading house for the Indians. In 1808 the United States signed a treaty with the Osage Indians and designated a six-mile-square parcel of land along the river as a military reservation. It was called Fort Osage.

General Clark took charge of its construction and brought George Sibley west to be the Indian agent. By 1822 the government was abandoning their policy of attempting to restrict trade with the Indians to only government-approved traders. The river had made course changes, making the landing less desirable, and the Army had moved to new forts farther upriver. Fort Osage was closed. By the time Zenas Leonard arrived the Missouri River had altered its course once again, reestablishing the old Fort Osage landing site. In 1836, Archibald Gamble, who had married George Sibley's sister-in-law, bought property where the old fort had stood, laid out a town next to the landing site, and named it Sibley.

The town was developing as a supply point along the river and, along with the store that he owned, Leonard had purchased a steamboat to transport supplies and goods between Sibley and St. Louis. He knew that his one boat line would never make him a rich man, but it helped to provide for himself and his young family. It was a welcome addition to what had come to be called The Six-Mile Country.

"I don't guess a storekeeper would know doddlely damn about being bone-deep cold, seein' as how he's snuggled up to a ol' stove all day long." The sound jarred Leonard out of his daydream. He turned around and standing just inside the door was Will, Woolly, Henry and Robert.

"My God, how long has it been?" Zenas was shocked. First at seeing his old friends, and then by the worn look they presented. Woolly and Henry, more than the other two, showed the passage of time. Woolly's hair had turned white. Henry, who Leonard remembered as about average for height, was bent over and appeared to have shrunk at least four inches. It was only when he looked into their eyes that he saw the same men he had known.

"You four look the same as you did when we were chasing beaver and exploring California," Leonard lied.

"Don't we now," Henry answered as he started the rounds of handshakes and slaps on the back. "Ol' Robert over there has changed the most. He's just got too damn pretty. The buffalo gals won't leave him alone."

Henry was right, Zenas thought. Robert had matured into a real head turner. He moved with a confident, athletic grace, and just a glance in his direction would make anyone take a second look.

"Well now, I'll tell you what," Will thought how Leonard hadn't changed all that much, "the last time I seen you was in the summer of '35, when you and Captain Bonneville pulled out for the States. We stood there on the Popo Agie and watched you head off into the mornin' sun."

"Aye, Bonneville said he'd try and come back next year," Woolly added. "He never made it, though."

Leonard enjoyed seeing Woolly's furry face and gentle eyes. "Bonneville was busy trying to get back in the Army."

"We didn't know Captain Bonneville got kicked out of the Army," Robert said.

"He didn't either until we got back to civilization," Zenas continued. "Bonneville found out that he'd been released from the Army in May of '34."

"May," Will observed. "Cerré was headed back to the '34 rendezvous with news about the Captain's extension in May.

"When we made the settlements that August it seemed to me that the captain was more interested in getting to New York than rejoining the Army anyhow," Leonard continued. "There had been some reports out that Indians had killed the captain. But if the story that Michael Cerré told at the rendezvous was to be believed, General Macomb would have known that the captain was alive and requesting an extension just a few months before he was officially released. The story that Cerré told about the meeting between himself and General Macomb was either upside-down, or something else was at work. Either way, Bonneville didn't get his extension, and he was out.

"You'd a thought that if Captain Bonneville was worried about getting back in the Army," Henry said, "he'd of went straight to Washington. Maybe he didn't want back in the Army."

"That could be, or maybe he thought he didn't have much chance to get back his commission." Zenas had heard that Captain Bonneville headed straight to Astor's Hellgate Estate after finding out that he'd been out of the Army instead of on leave for the last two years. "It might be that he was trying to raise funds for another year's trapping. Washington Irving was visiting John Jacob Astor at Hellgate when the Captain arrived; maybe they wanted to hear all about his experiences first. Whatever transpired, Bonneville almost immediately left Hellgate and headed for Washington to turn all his journals and maps over to General Macomb. After that he spent most of his time trying to get back in the Army or writing his manuscript."

"Was Macomb riled when he found out Bonneville didn't come straight to him?" Will asked.

"I don't think so," Zenas answered. "I heard that the general wrote letters trying to help Bonneville get his commission back. Lewis Cass had replaced John Eaton, President Jackson's long-time buddy from Tennessee, as Secretary of War. Cass was from Michigan, and he didn't seem all that favorable to the captain's reinstatement."

"Sounds to me like Captain Bonneville was running in circles." Henry wondered if Zenas had been a storekeeper for very long. A lot of rumors probably went through a store in a day's time.

"Would the manuscript you mentioned be the same book that Washington Irving wrote about Bonneville?" Woolly asked.

"That's where it ended up," Leonard answered.

"You know, I read Bonneville's book back in '38," Woolly announced. Zenas noticed that Woolly's eyes had lost some of their compassion. "It took several pulls from me jug to wash it all down."

"Where in the hell did he come up with the story about our trip to California?" Henry wanted to know. "Called us a disgraceful expedition. You ever hear of such horse shit? It was the first time I was glad I couldn't read."

"Old Buffalo Man wouldn't let me read him one more word after I gave him Irving's account about our little jaunt into California." Woolly was smiling at Henry. "I never have understood why Irving felt it necessary to make it sound like Captain Walker was to blame for our lack of beaver pelts at the '34 rendezvous. He was more than a little loose with the truth when he said that Bonneville sent Captain Walker, along with most of us that went to California, back to St. Louis with Michael Cerré. Did you read Irving's book?"

"I read it," Leonard answered. "I'm guessing he felt like he had to make a hero out of Captain Bonneville, or maybe that's what Bonneville told him had happened in order to explain why his fur company went under. Either way, it was a lie. Wonder what he thought when my book came out?"

"Well now, don't that just about beat all?" Woodrow was setting in the chair next to the stove with his long legs stretched out. "I saw ya scribblin' in that journal all the time, but I never figured you was writtin' a book."

"I wasn't," Zenas answered. "That all happened when I got back to my people in Pennsylvania. I'd been gone almost five years, and most of 'em thought I was long-dead. There was a lot of talk and controversy about our country moving west, and everyone wanted to know what it was like out there. I just got tired of telling all about it, so I wrote a series of articles about my experiences, and the local newspaper printed them. Anyhow, a couple of years later they put it together in a book, and in 1839 I became an author."

"The hell you say." Henry was impressed. "Now that's a book I'd read, if'n I knew my letters."

"Me too," Robert concurred. "Guess I don't have to, though, since I was there."

"That's just what I mean," Henry said. "We was all there for the whole shitaree, but what about them that wasn't there? All they know is what Irving wrote. To them Captain Walker's gonna come out looking like boiled owl."

"Well now, I'll tell you what," Will said. "Zenas's book will set all that straight."

"There won't be near the number of pilgrims read my book as will read a book by Washington Irving," Leonard admitted.

"So did the captain get back in the Army?" Robert asked.

"Finally," Zenas answered. "He was headed back to the fur country when he heard about his reinstatement."

Leonard had been told that when Bonneville got back to Washington he began to write letters and visit with anyone he thought might help him regain his commission in the Army. At the same time he started to organize all his notes into a manuscript. Before the end of the year, Irving showed up at Bonneville's place and offered to help him with his literary effort. Bonneville turned him down, said that he wanted to do it himself. The next March he went to New York to have it published, but he couldn't find any takers. Washington Irving offered the captain one thousand dollars for his journals. Bonneville believed that his Army commission was history, so he sold his account of the expedition, gathered up his available resources and headed west.

"So the captain really was on his way back out?" Even though Bonneville didn't make it, Woolly was glad to hear that he was headed back like he said would.

"Bonneville was up somewhere on the Powder River when they got word to him that he was back on the roll call at Fort Gibson," Leonard answered. "President Jackson had sent a message to the Senate in January of '36 that he wanted Captain Bonneville's commission reinstated, and the appointment was approved."

"I wonder if Captain Walker has had the pleasure of reading Mr. Irving's book?" Henry had never heard Walker discuss anything about Bonneville.

"He wouldn't say much if he had," Robert said. "But that don't mean he ain't got an opinion."

"How is Captain Walker?" Zenas Leonard asked. "A lot of his people live around here. When I left Pennsylvania to come back to the Missouri frontier, they found out that I was with their 'Uncle Jo' when he went to California. They more or less took me into their fold and treated me like family. They even married me off to a Harrelson girl."

"You don't mean it?" Will said. "You're married. The next thing I know you'll be tellin' us you're a papa."

351

"That I am," Zenas stated. "Two little beauties, if I say so myself."

"Well, kiss a fat man's ass," Henry stated. "Did you know Captain Walker took himself a bride?"

"No, I hadn't heard." Leonard had missed listening to Henry express himself.

"Married the daughter of a Snake chief," Robert added.

"I didn't hear that she's a chief's daughter." Will wasn't sure that was right. "She's sure enough a looker, though."

"I'm glad to hear that Captain Walker's all right," Zenas said. "Whatever happened to Swit Boone?"

"The lad elected to stay on with Walker when we headed east," Woolly answered. "It's Robert's opinion that Swit's of a mind to go back to one of those *ranchos* in California."

"Walker's traveled the Great Basin country from rim to rim." Henry thought how Leonard's turn from trapper and clerk to storekeeper seemed to fit, and he was pleased that Zenas had set Washington Irving's story straight. "I'd say that Captain Walker knows more about that tract of wilderness than any other man alive, red or white."

Zenas Leonard could hardly wait to take this foursome home to meet his family and friends. His old California *compadres* would soon find out what it meant to be a member of Joseph Rutherford Walker's California expedition.

"I'll tell you what; let's shut this place down and start making the rounds," Zenas said. "I want to introduce you to the people here in Six-Mile Country."

Woolly straightened his old Scottish cap. Henry picked up his buffalo gun. Will looked up but showed no sign of giving up his chair. Robert headed for the door. He wondered what Six-Mile Country people would look like. They must be something pretty special.

Printed in the United States
47977LVS00003B/76-84